Smart

Hearts

IN THE City

*For Daniel
with great affection*

OTHER BOOKS BY

BARBARA PROBST SOLOMON

Horse Trading and Ecstasy

Short Flights

Arriving Where We Started

The Beat of Life

*and
admiration
Barbara*

Smart
Hearts
IN THE City

BARBARA PROBST SOLOMON

HARCOURT

BRACE

JOVANOVICH

New York   San Diego   London

WASTED DAYS AND WASTED NIGHTS by Freddy Fender & Wayne M. Duncan
Copyright © 1960, 1975 UNART MUSIC CORPORATION All rights of UNART
MUSIC CORPORATION Assigned to EMI CATALOGUE PARTNERSHIP All Rights
Controlled and Administered by EMI UNART CATALOG INC. International Copy-
right Secured. Made in USA. All Rights Reserved. WINCHESTER CATHEDRAL
by Geoff Stephens. Copyright © 1966 by Meteor Music Publishing Co. Ltd. Copy-
right Renewed. Administered by Southern Music Publishing Co. Inc. International
Copyright Secured. All Rights Reserved. Used by Permission. "Whiskey River" by
Johnny Bush Courtesy of Full Nelson Music, Inc. Administered by Longitude Music
Co. All Rights Reserved. Used by Permission. A portion of this novel appeared in a
slightly different form in *Partisan Review*, Winter 1986.

Library of Congress Cataloging-in-Publication Data
Solomon, Barbara Probst.
Smart hearts in the city/Barbara Probst Solomon.—1st ed.
p.   cm.
ISBN 0-15-183157-2
I. Title.
PS3569.O59S6   1992
813'.54—dc20   92-17762

Designed by Trina Stahl
Printed in the United States of America
First edition
A B C D E

To Daniel and Katharine Magliocco

and

Corlies Smith,

a great editor and friend

since the beginning

PART ONE

Liberty's

Fourth of July:

1986

CHAPTER

1

I HAVE BEEN IN THE AVANT-GARDE IN NEW *York—the avant-garde of losing money. A front-runner of the downwardly mobile. Precocious in tragedy—first on the block to reach widowhood.*

Katy Becker made funny quips in her head in rebellion against the instructions of Max Schecter, her lawyer. He wanted her to show up the following week at her pretrial deposition prepared to demonstrate how, as Lewis Eichorn's widow, she had been victimized by his older half brother, Beanie Eichorn. She was suing him for swiping, for his own expansion, what should have been Lewis's legacy. What Beanie Eichorn called the restructuring of Belle Hélène, his father's furniture business, had left Katy and her son, Matt, financially wiped out and delegitimized. *Materially nonexistent. Reconnoiter of the disenfranchised.* She gazed out of her bedroom window.

That crazy Fourth-of-July New York was sending up fancy firecrackers for the Statue of Liberty Centennial. A white light crackled. Manhattan was having the snappy dry spell that usually comes mid-August; you could feel the Jersey shoreline rising right into the city.

There is these days such a crowd, such a noisy clamor at the gates of victimhood, Katy mentally argued with Max; *why add me to this cacophony of Chicanos, gays, blacks, Jews, women, child victims, young-adult victims, over-thirty victims, the young old, the old young? Death and deformity have also made a big comeback. In lieu of having a tragic sense of life, we've become victims of life. Can't we build the case without turning me into such a nothing?*

She hated the notion that she'd been done in by Beanie, a sentimental, avaricious type, merely because he wanted his life drenched in money.

She remained at the window, now glancing down to the side street. A bookstore with a British façade and a French bistro with lots of white lace curtains had replaced the old shoemaker and tailor shops off East Ninety-third Street. Now, in the eighties, the city looked to her like a raunchy picaro disguised as a bridesmaid.

Since childhood Katy had identified with it, always checking its temperature with a blood relative's casual intimacy. *I am a girl*, she would say to herself at the age of eight as she walked to PS 6. *I live in the center of Manhattan. Manhattan is the center of New York. New York is the biggest city in the world. So I am a girl in the center of the universe. I am lucky.*

Her full name was Karen Tess Becker. In PS 6 Karen Tess was nicknamed K. T., soon slurred into *Katy*. She never felt the *Tess* had sounded right. When she was in high school her mother, Anita Becker, confessed to her that she had chosen it because of *Tess of the d'Urbervilles*—had Anita expected her only daughter to have a similar terrible fate? Was it an expression of her mother's solidarity with all womankind? Why had she given Katy's older brother, Jim, a sensible name? *James* was solid enough to weather changing styles, different eras.

Katy's cousin Snowball Ginzberg insisted that Anita was just being literary in thinking of *Tess of the d'Urbervilles*. "You attach too much importance to the naming of things; you are too afraid of signs of the darkness in life," Snowball had admonished her in one of their long morning telephone calls.

As far back as Katy could remember, Snowball had lived down the block from her. They had gone together through PS 6, Friends', and Barnard. Her first cousin once removed was Katy's closest woman friend. Because they had been together for the long haul and took an ample view of things, they had the luxury, in their meandering talks, of reordering their lives just a little. They could dip into a joint pot of memories and fish out whatever suited their mood, whatever they needed in order to get through a particular day.

In this subtle rearranging of experience the two women gave themselves the power to correct past mistakes. When they talked about men, it was not so much about those they lived with as about the ones who had evaporated from their lives at the wrong times. By criticizing and rehashing their ex-lovers' flaws in minute detail, the women got an extra strength. They verbally breathed life into the soured affairs for the extra time needed to avoid feeling the main thing had gone by in a *clack*.

Snowball took Max's side on the necessity of showing how Beanie had slaughtered Katy. Botched her future. "Don't take the legal scenario so literally. Besides," she insisted in the same phone call, "it happens to be true. The case has affected everything from your job choices to the way you raised Matt—even men. If you hadn't been so uptight about your being flat broke and Mike Braden's being rich, you would still be with him. Instead of this more-or-else stuff that goes on between you and Ethan."

Snowball had irritated her. Broken the rules—it should have been up to Katy to bring up the subject of Mike. It was still a sore point. She still thought about him all the time, but she'd been hoping that if she didn't mention him aloud he would vanish from her thoughts. "Ethan is not as nuts as Mike."

"But you really liked Mike."

"Ethan suits me fine. He's a good . . . transition."

"Transition to what?"

Katy hung up on her cousin; the conversation was going nowhere.

▼ ▼ ▼

Katy Becker knew Ethan Lemay from her time in Austin, Texas, during the sixties. Her husband, Lewis Eichorn, had been his philosophy professor. On a night like any other cool spring night in Austin, Lewis had been run over by a Saturday-night drunk driver. Katy had felt that getting killed was sad enough, but when Ethan came up north, he looked her up and reformulated her tragedy. He favored the rumor—because Lewis had been big in civil rights—that the car accident had been a put-up job by

6

redneck east Texans enraged because the university was integrating blacks.

She rather liked the *Lewis-buzz* he made when talking about her dead husband, even if she didn't agree with his theories. Ethan was a reminder of the time she, Lewis, and Matt had been a family. She helped him get the bargain apartment above her own and told him the hissing, groaning pipes were not ghosts, that the clatter was worst at six in the morning and eleven at night. He told her there was no money in philosophy, and unlike Lewis, he had no private income. He'd come to New York to become a sort of intellectual Texas country singer. Katy was startled at how quickly he started to make money at it. They began to sleep together after she broke up with Mike. Casually.

"Ethan," Katy would contradict him, "don't *embellish*—real life's no picnic. Just dead and leaving a widow plus a kid is enough. A bunch of local Mexicans didn't hold their liquor—you don't have to *add*." Katy had never imagined she would be a widow so early in life. She came to associate the event with the end of her youth, amazed that its debris never seemed to end. An awful word: *widow*. Heavy. Airless. Yet *window* was as nice-sounding as summer afternoon, the only difference the *n*.

But for Ethan, the days of his youth at the University of Texas were his days of glory. He always went back. His friends, too, remembered the sixties as grand. So he did what Austin asked of him. He was in San Antonio and Austin this week giving back-to-back concerts in both cities. Ethan claimed that the Floore Country Store over in the hill country in Helotes at the outskirts of San Antonio had given him his start. Families went there. And Mexican and Anglo cowboys. They liked progressive country and lots of Cotton-Eyed Joe.

Katy had told him, "Ethan, it will be murder, July in Texas."

"What makes you think Manhattan is cool?"

"It's my kind of heat, and the air-conditioning is good."

But when he left, Katy felt alone in the city. *Ethan in Austin, Matt in Houston!* She had forced herself not to play single-mother-of-an-only-son when Matt went off to college. There had been the reprieve when he was studying medicine at the Cornell medical center and parked in the apartment from time to time. She thought about her son: *Was it just some odd coincidence that he landed back in Texas? Which came first—was it his desire to be a flight surgeon in NASA's living-science program? Or was he drawn to it because the Johnson Space Center is located outside of Houston and he can get back to Austin from time to time?* She resisted her impulse to phone Matt—he'd figure out that she had no real plans for the Fourth of July weekend. Her inner voice urged her, *Let him go free, let him go free.*

The week before the Fourth, CBS had predicted thirteen million tourists would converge on New York for Liberty Weekend. *All the television anchors, male, female, black, white, mulatto, and Chinese, have great haircuts and clothes. When the weather hits over a hundred or* Challenger *dematerializes, they get this chatty, confiding grin while communicating disaster.* So when their tally of incoming tourists hit thirteen million, Katy braced for an invasion akin to *Aliens.* Methodically, well in advance, she dispatched her downtown errands. She heard disturbing landmark news—Altman's and Gimbels had announced their demises. The big department stores, like the thirties dream-palace art-deco movie theaters, were relics of the past. Midweek Katy hurried to pick up some towels as a token. Gault Millau had described her favorite household haunt as "tedious." Since when was Euro trash in a position to pass judgment on B. Altman's? Did they know it carried the best black silk bias-cut underwear in town? Did they *know* New York?

By early evening the sky had a funny dusty glow. The city was heading into a heat inversion. Restless, Katy listened to the television reports of the crowds gathering at the Battery. She felt out of it—the day before, she had even missed the tall ships sailing down the Hudson. *You are not alone. Thirteen million visitors have joined you in Manhattan. So join them.*

▼ ▼ ▼

The Upper East Side was dead. Katy walked past the Armory. Only its faded redbrick shell remained; weeds were growing in its inner spaces. *A shrewd developer must be finagling a permit to level the block.* Eighty-sixth Street, minus shoppers, looked sullen. A gang of kids wearing pale green Liberty-spiked rubber headdresses were coming up from the RKO Lexington. She went inside Golden's—the old Madison Deli reborn with a white interior—and sat down in the front booth. "Scrambled eggs, rye toast, and coffee."

The waiter yelled, "Two with whis-key."

"Isn't it easier to say *rye*? I mean, why call the toast *whiskey*?"

"Because that's the way it is. Whiskey."

"But *whis-key* has two syllables—*rye* only one."

"Lady, are you a schoolteacher?" With one hand he wiped his apron; with the other he balanced tin baskets

9

loaded with crusty rolls. His skin emanated odors of flour and warm fried chicken skin. He glanced out the window: "Madison looks like Hiroshima the morning after—the street's a tomb. My wife is with her cousins. Their place is near the Verrazano."

"The media said thirteen million are arriving—"

"Thirteen million? Never. My brother is in the hotel business. The chains are empty. But live and let live. If the media wants to lie a little, let them—it's a job like any other." He bent down, putting his face right next to Katy's. Then he threw his head back and laughed. "Thirteen million have come to New York. By air! By sea! By land! *To* New York, in a pig's eye—they haven't *come*—they have fled. Seven million New Yorkers have fled. The city is a ghost town." He kept on laughing, providing the chorus for his own joke.

Katy paid the bill and left. There was not one soul on Madison Avenue. Not one. It was nine-thirty. The world-class end-of-the-universe fireworks had begun. She saw flashes of light in the downtown sky. *Why not give it a try? Take the Volvo and head downtown.*

▼ ▼ ▼

She drove down Second Avenue. The city was motionless except for teenagers popping Roman candles. Then Katy saw it. So high in the sky that even in midtown she could see the lights fanning into red flowers. She continued south. The explosions were coming faster. She drove the Volvo straight toward the big Day-Glo sunburst, surprised that neither police nor crowds had stopped her. She was already below Little Italy. She had no trouble getting across Canal Street, despite media warnings that vehicles would be barred from going farther. She turned on Mercer, heading toward the white light.

▼ ▼ ▼

When Katy reached the Wall Street area she smelled, as she moved her arms to better navigate the car, her own salty odor: a mixture of heat, washcloth, and soap. The sweat came from fear. Next week she would be coming back down here for the deposition. *Max doesn't really think we have much of a chance.* The prospect of getting nothing more out of this than hefty legal bills that she would spend the rest of her life paying was too grim to contemplate.

Only in her mind did she feel capable of righting her situation. Having won back no tangible assets and with no good prospects in sight, she switched fantasies. She ruminated on the rightness of her cause.

Her favorite projection was a scene in which Beanie would capitulate in front of a cast of thousands. Her lawyers, as a sort of Greek chorus, would tell Matt about his brave mother. "A woman who under the worst of circumstances never signed a single document, kept every scrap of paper *and* envelopes, and had a perfect memory—what more could a son ask of a parent?"

Katy didn't see that her laudatory imaginary lawyer was asking his rhetorical question of the wrong generation—a son might wish for quite different attributes from his mother. It was Katy's dead father and his two brothers, those three natty New York lawyers who got their start in

Manhattan in the twenties, that she was answering, their instructions she imagined she was carrying out. The purity of her obsession was so intense—she was convinced she was defending her essence—that she was fighting like a child. She kept going not because of the justice of her claims, though they were just, but because she never noticed other considerations. She was impervious to the passage of time.

Round orange moons exploded behind the skyline of the Cotton Exchange and the World Trade Center. Katy's car was bathed in red-and-white light. That was when she saw Gabe Frolich. He was walking alone along Chambers Street, hands in the pockets of his Italian chino pants. The cuffs grazed the tops of his rose buckskin moccasins.

Katy saw him stalking Lower Manhattan, a ghostly Indian reclaiming Dutch territory, while simultaneously, in the moving camera inside her frontal lobe, she remembered a summer August night three years after the end of the Second World War when he briefly became her second lover.

Never in tune with literal logic, she, in her mind, believed that Gabe had psychically devirginated her. She saw deflowering not as the literal rupture of tissue, which had happened to her at fourteen with Bradford Culver, whom she had adored, but as a foreign assault on her inner moods. Losing her virginity signified the end of pure love. Katy confused it with her loss of absolute freedom.

Watching her old friend and lover of short duration walk toward her now on Chambers Street, the postwar August night she had spent with him arranged itself in her memory as the first time she had made love and felt nothing—the

Ur-moment when the gloomy limits of life had penetrated her consciousness. She had understood, then, those limits would be with her until the end of time. She had understood, also gloomily, that the numbers of men she might sleep with suddenly, perversely, had the possibility of being limitless. She had seen herself, as she had rocked in unison with Gabe, as newly lost, an infinite future stretching in front of her. She might end up being attached, ephemerally, to this man or that, but never again to *one* man, *the* man.

She reassured herself, after that first time with Gabe, that it would be good to accept the notion of life as making-do-with-half-a-loaf. But Katy had already felt a blaze of heat as sharp as the noon light through a rose pane of a cathedral stained-glass window. Not bothering to think fairly—the matter was too important to her to bother with *fair*—she had never forgiven Gabe for squelching a passion that was beyond his imagination.

The week after she had broken off with Brad, she and Gabe had gone to a Saturday-night dance at the White Waves Country Club off the Connecticut shore road near Southport. Both Katy's and Gabe's folks belonged. Katy's family rarely went to it. Indian Path, their place on the Sound, had its own tennis courts, so there was no need to go elsewhere. Also, it wasn't her parents', Anita and Jeremiah Becker's, "thing" to go to a club. Mostly German Jews belonged. Some anonymous Connecticut gentiles had joined White Waves for its docking rights. Gabe drove Katy to the dance in his father's Buick.

So many years ago, yet Katy could still smell the purply lipstick she had worn that night—its rancid odor of spoiled tomatoes rising in her nostrils as though she'd used it only yesterday. She had worn a white piqué halter dress cut low to show off her dark tan, the exact curves of her body. Gabe had cupped her hip tight, her legs and stomach squeezed against his fly.

"Why do you dress skintight?" he had whispered.

"For pleasures skin-deep," Katy had retorted.

Their dance steps aped the older couples'—stray post–World War II soldiers on leave, whom the club still patriotically invited to the dances free of charge. They brought with them girlfriends picked up in Stamford and Bridgeport. Katy followed Gabe's staccato rumba; he had learned its rhythms from his older sister. She bent her knees, swaying her cork-sandaled, red-thonged feet from side to side so her hips jutted out in time with the Latin American music.

"Braddy Culver's one lucky black boy that Bronx Science skipped him his junior year," Gabe said casually. "I hear Wisconsin took him. He made it in the midst of the GI deluge."

Katy hadn't thought of Brad as having a destiny as precise as Wisconsin. Once they split up he'd vanished from her mind. When she made love that night with Gabe in the backseat of his parents' prewar sedan, she was aware of Gabe's maleness—of his looking at her in a way that was different from Brad's. But there was no name for what she and Brad did. No beginning to it, even though Gabe marked the end of it. *I feel nothing*, she intoned to herself. Her idea of belonging to one man died in that green Buick. Ivy League rationality had been Gabe's ace in the hole. He was fond of quoting literary nuggets like "Men have died and worms have eaten them, but not of love."

Brad Culver was different. She had no memory of a time prior to his existence. Brad had always been part of her life. Her mother's cousins—the Ginzberg girls from Waylee, South Carolina—had brought his aunt Jessica with them from the South. The Becker family had dubbed the Ginzberg sisters "the newcomers" because they'd moved to the Upper East Side right after the First World War. They were southern Jewish women with a fine sense of *carpe diem*; during the war they had found themselves northern Jewish recruits to marry. Nat Finkle and Bert Wurlitzer had trained in boot camp outside Waylee.

Hewley Ginzberg was Snowball's mother. She had dropped Bert Wurlitzer's name after he left her, and she had never remarried. Anita Becker always said that had no war happened, and had the Ginzberg girls insisted on marrying Jewish in Waylee, they would have been old maids.

Since Anita considered New York help untrustworthy, she was delighted when Jessica suggested her cousin Tartan Culver as housekeeper. Tartan had arrived in the city with her son, Brad, in the heart of the Depression, when good jobs were scarce. There had never been a mention of his father.

Katy was convinced her recollection of events went back almost to her birth. In addition to remembering Brad's arrival in her home, she boasted of her memory of being wheeled in a navy blue carriage and lusting for a white fur blanket in an adjoining carriage. Hers had been of a stiff

15

gray broadcloth. Her mother admitted the existence of the broadcloth carriage cover but insisted Katy must have seen it only in a photograph.

Tartan also protested that Katy's memory of Brad being placed in her crib alongside her was false. Katy never understood why Tartan argued so hard with her; she knew Brad had been in her crib. They had played together from the very beginning. Katy remembered her older brother, Jim, staring sullenly, with that locked-out-of-things look he had, at her and Brad in the crib. To get her attention, Jim gave her a bag of jelly beans. Katy saw Brad in his worn flannel pajamas, his shoulder blades sticking up through them like scrawny chicken wings—he was so scared, the flannel was wet with the smell of his fright. Katy stared into his deep-set blue eyes, touched the fuzz of his hair, and fell in love with him right then. She stuffed his mouth with pink and purple jelly beans and patted his little shoulder blades, as though their smallness were the source of his pain and would respond to her touch. Seeing Brad squat in the crib in total, miserable muteness, Katy became aware of sadness. She kept touching him. She felt complete.

"Gabe!" Katy yelled, braking the white Volvo. When Gabe heard her voice, he stopped on a dime with a tennis player's grace. Katy noted with approval that his salt-and-pepper hair still had a thick peasant snap; his slanting, opaque gray eyes reminded her of a pasha's son with a Harvard degree. The Battery sky behind him flamed into orange, red, and violet.

"Gabe! Gabe!"

He looked surprised—like they were two culprits caught out in a shady deal. As though it were immoral, un-American to be found on Wall Street in the midst of the fire-cracker crowd.

Katy greeted him in their code language, filtered through many decades. The Wall Street skyline burned up one last time against the dusty sky. The cannons boomed a sharp military finale. Then it went dark; the fiesta of the century was over.

CHAPTER

2

SPARKS FROM CATHERINE WHEELS
fired wild into the air sputtered over Gabe's head. A
woman's voice wafted their way from a nearby thin alley.
Yo soy morena; yo soy ardiente. The music and the falling lights
made him look, Katy thought, oddly like an aging rock star
lost on Wall Street.

Gabe climbed into her car, amazed to find his old friend
so far downtown. On second thought, he was not so
amazed. *She's always had an overabundance of free time, a habit
of wandering in odd places for no apparent reason.* He glanced
sideways at her.

In middle age her black, deeply liquid eyes still had the
guileless, innocent look common to those who grew up
overly rich. She gave the impression of combining an orphan
lostness with the calm conviction that no matter where she
plunged or drifted, an army of invisible generals marched

behind her, ready as her true reference point. He liked thinking of her as unchanged; she had been so rich during their growing-up days.

He had caught a whiff of verbena when she opened the front door of the Volvo for him. It was the same Caswell-Massey lemony stuff she had used in their Columbia/Barnard time. *She stores her energy by never bothering to change her habits.* Once, in a fit of irritation, he had dubbed her a "domestic narcissist." *She detoured around the major events of her time. Never noticed even what might have applied to her. Now and then she landed in stuff that on anyone else would have looked trendy.* But he found the verbena smell comforting. Recently he had become nostalgic about the America of his youth. His second wife had just left him. He raised her name tentatively.

"Lee's in France with the kids."

"I hear Paris is hot."

"Heat always takes the French by surprise. There's no point," he added, though Katy had asked for no explanation for his Wall Street wanderings, "in my going to the loft party—the display is finished."

When they drove closer to the water they saw that small groups of people were straggling back from their lookout posts on the West Side Highway. They decided to head back uptown. The Plaza Hotel was tomb dead. "Amber and Friends on First must still be open," Gabe said.

Once Gabe and Katy had bumped into each other, they had taken it for granted that they would spend the rest of the evening together. Even if it meant sparring. Gabe fumbled for a way to explain Lee's abrupt flight that didn't make him sound too much in the wrong. Katy uncomfortably remembered that Gabe had been Beanie's shrink. It rankled.

▼ ▼ ▼

The restaurant was painted dark hunter green. The day's specials were scrawled in green Crayola on an art-nouveau mirror over the bar. *Frosted Ambers served with a side order of perecebes on a bed of shaved ice. Pork paillard with hot chirimoyas. Squid rings. Fresh pineapple in bourbon and brown sugar.* The perecebes and chirimoyas were flown in daily from Madrid.

They ordered two dry double Ambers minus the perecebes—Katy said the Spanish barnacles looked like dead fingernails—and watched the televised replay of the Statue of Liberty event.

Katy felt she was seeing a whole other show in an unknown city. Being downtown had proved disappointing. Now she felt less disoriented. The TV report had *finished* her Liberty Weekend. She fiddled with her drink, gearing up to raise the Beanie business.

"The anchorwoman on the VIP boat in the harbor is an idiot," Gabe exploded. "Interviewing Dr. Ruth as *the* exemplary immigrant! Is she the best Jewish immigrant Reagan could drum up for the Fourth? We are a people who produced Einstein—"

"Einstein's dead—Ruth has a big following."

"Why not Jonas Salk? We Jews are people of the arts, the humanities, the sciences."

"It has to be recent immigrants. You need to have come over because of the Holocaust. Like Elie Wiesel and Kissinger." Katy paused. "Since when have you put your money on the chosen? Is Lee, queen of fancy French tin junk, one of the anointed? I'll grant you she's good-look-ing—all that straw-colored hair and built like a boy—"

"Lee sells to Bendel's."

"So what's so wonderful about having a second wife the age of your daughter who flies to Paris merely to import tin jewelry? At her age we might have gone abroad to haggle, 'Wittgenstein yes, God maybe'—but never 'Tin yes, plastic no.' "

"Your country singer is hardly Pavarotti."

"You think Jewish women should live only with Jews? Jewish men don't."

"It's not his religion. He sings *country*."

"You think I've flopped? Since when is Lee's tin jewelry Matisse?" Katy speared a chunk of pineapple doused in bourbon. "You are coming on awfully stuffy, considering you took on my own brother-in-law as your patient."

"Beanie was minor in your life—he was only seeing me for short-term therapy. Anyway, I've split off from New York Psychoanalytic."

"That crook, minor? I thought Freud grooved on these lil' ol' minor details—who slept with whom, who stole from whom." Katy's voice shook, then she drew a deep breath and continued, grandiose, as if she were quoting from Tolstoy: "Who steals in a family happily forgets it immediately. Those unhappily stolen from remember it for-ever. Did you know that Karl Marx's uncle filched Marx's inheritance? And that with that money, he founded Phillips Radio in Europe? And there was Europe"—she finished, impressively waving her hand as though she were a Gallic orator—"Communism and electronics—just theft in the family."

Gabe couldn't help noticing how she *bloomed* when she talked about money. Her skin flushed, her breasts rose, and the tips of her nipples erected under her red silk chemise dress. *She savors it so, why didn't she make more of it? Go into it herself. Why did she fiddle with medieval history?*

Katy stopped her harangue to chew a piece of pineapple. Seemingly lost in thought, she listened to the late-night country jamboree that followed the VIP boats and Dr. Ruth.

> *Whiskey River take my mind*
> *Don't let her memory torture me*
> *Whiskey River don't run dry*
> *They're all I've got t' take care of me.*

Then she added in a low voice, "Betrayed by big business, Soho, Freud, and the left—and my childhood friend who swims in those waters, Gabriel Frolich."

"Come off it, Katy, that's mean."

"You don't think taking my crooked brother-in-law as your patient was somewhat odd? When you were my best friend? Did you tell Beanie we were childhood lovers?"

"Oh, Katy—that was so long ago. In our milieu there's always some crossover."

"Our milieu? I thought our milieu took sacred vows to Freud, transference, and strict professional ethics—that's why it cost us so much money. When I sign up for bargain-basement rates with EST, and everyone's nose is in my business, I want to be informed in advance."

"Well, I admit Beanie had some problems with you that I couldn't have figured on ahead of time. He had certain

22

loyalties to Lewis. Difficulty readjusting when you started seeing other men. Surely you won't deny Beanie had problems with you?"

"No. I won't deny it—he had problems with me because he was a crook."

"Every widow has a done-in syndrome. You should have been able to let go of the past by now."

"Since when have you been hobnobbing with my unconscious? Why are you always so not-on-my-side?"

"I am—but Beanie had tremendous burdens. So maybe having Lewis's widow flipping around was too much for him to take. Puritanical—but understandable."

"See what I mean about us thinking we were swimming with Freud, when we were really drifting into the muck of EST? I swear, only yoghurt made it intact from the sixties to the eighties. You *believed* Beanie's wacko details about me—I've never been able to trust a shrink completely since I found out about your voyeurism. Gabe, you cooked up a coward's threesome. Look, I know you are not kinky, I don't see you in bed with more than one at a time, and never gay stuff—but in an extraordinarily mealymouthed way, you ate your cake and had it too. You, me, and Beanie."

"You are perseverating."

"You're so cagey, Gabe. What you did could never be considered a breach of ethics. But I bet your letting Beanie slowly find out that you were my ex-lover—and me that you were his therapist—was a real thrill for you. Probably kept you from screwing a patient. *I* kept you sexually sane. I was your seventies and eighties antisocial coffee break."

"Katy!"

23

"Granted, the law can be pretty crummy, but it's no do-it-yourself subjective Freudian-EST swamp. There's a beginning, a middle, and an end to it. Sooner or later money changes hands—" She paused, thinking, *From mine to my lawyer's.*

"You're talking *fraud?*"

"You bet."

"You never were clear before."

"I always *intimated.* But for a long time there was no case—the words had not been said yet. How could I have been immediately clear? How could I have known I was right? How could I have known, in the beginning, that I wasn't the issue?"

All those years, had Beanie been blabbering the wrong script to him? "At the time I tried to be objective."

"You were my best friend and ex-lover—that was your role. If you hadn't been treating Beanie, I could have counted on you. My mind would have been clearer."

"Katy, I have to digest this. Look, things are not what they seem to be. I'm upset. Lee's left me for a crazy Brit. She's taken the kids with her. The four of them are in Saint-Paul-de-Vence. I'm scared out of my mind she'll take the kids to live in London."

"In England? For good?"

"She met this business freak on the Concorde. I don't know whether to think of him as Jewish or Brit—well, I guess Jewish-Brit. Before taking off to Saint-Paul-de-Vence, she brought him to our apartment to meet me. The guy is Cockney chic. Claims to be the leading seller of snow hoods and booties to the Sloane Ranger crowd. Said his 'shtik' is packaging his products in woodsy English boxes. He boasted about offering Church shoes a big deal to go in with him. Said that they insisted that their products had to keep the Church name. He told them he was a boy from the East End, and how would they feel if he called his line Synagogue Hoods? Lee laughed and laughed—really, Katy, I don't know where I am in any of this."

"Your kids forever in London?—Gabe, that's terrible!"

"Mike Braden was older than you ..." Gabe paused. "Did you love him—or was he merely a port in the storm?"

First Snowball, now Gabe! "Nobody is loved for themselves alone, Gabe—we all want a bit of gift wrap."

"Meaning rich?"

Katy stared at him. *He's one of the best friends you will ever have. But he's blinded. He can't see you. Hasn't a clue to where you've been.*

"I needed Mike." Nothing else came to mind. She was silent a long while. Then the words fell out. "There was my breakdown."

Gabe abruptly looked over her shoulder, to the TV news report. "Not a breakdown—just a heavy reaction to the car crash. You weren't alone after Lewis died. Katy, remember all the flicks we went to? You had a lot on your plate—losing Lewis, your mother, and Indian Path the same time. I tried talking to you about the place—Christ, it was my childhood too. Now I can mention it to you and you don't turn your head away. Oh God, I still remember those extraordinary English croquet games—your old man always arranging it so he won. The chicken barbecues, the light on the water, and those long, buggy July nights..." He paused; it was July and they were in Manhattan, nowhere near the Sound. "I never told you, but the week your family

25

lost Indian Path, I got drunk—I hadn't had a hangover that bad since I was a freshman in college. All I could think of was that novel *The Garden of the Finzi-Continis*—something special that I had been part of had come to an end."

Why was it so all right for him to moon about the grandness of her family's lost money but not okay for her to find warmth in Mike's? Or was Snowball right—had it been her own awkwardness about his being so rich? Why did her breakdown have to be denied?

Katy studied Gabe soberly. Then she burst into wild laughter. "I guess I was your first Finzi-Continis girl." She said it like it was a joke and not a joke. The country jamboree was over. In the second TV rerun of the evening, cornucopias of Day-Glo-colored firecrackers exploded again into the grand finale. Gabe and Katy knew what followed next—they had seen the American flag light up the sky over Wall Street earlier in the evening.

CHAPTER

THE MORNING OF THE DEPOSITION, Katy met Max Schecter and his litigation man, Tim Fenester, in the arcade of the midtown office building occupied by Schecter, Leary, and Fuccoli. Beanie's pricey crew of lawyers—Willard, Henry, Freund, and Mannheim—were on Broad Street. *A bad omen that her side had so quickly agreed that the conference should take place on Beanie's turf. Well, beggars can't be choosers.* She was on partial contingency. Max made it sound like welfare.

The three of them got in a cab. Katy hoped her team would give her last-minute coaching. They did not. *Did they believe they're so on top of the case there's nothing to discuss?*

Instead Fenester reminisced about his early legal-eagle days in New York in the sixties. His voice softened as if he were describing a religious experience.

"I marched with Plimpton, Schell, and Lindsay in the

27

lawyers' anti-Vietnam demonstration. Max, there may have been more dramatic marches to end the war, the kind with Mace and bitterness. But finally the Establishment bunch did do it. In their velvet-collared coats they walked with us in the rain from Saint Paul's Church to Foley Square. This—from guys who had worked all their lives within a hierarchy so stiff the summer sun in the Sahara wouldn't melt it. I still remember Schell standing there in the downpour saying it was time to question the legality of the Vietnam War. Time for the lawyers to take to the streets."

He paused to sigh. "Those days, I believed I could make law. I wanted to be out there like Harold Rothwax, doing the real thing. Not just in the same tired business of transferring money from one hand to another. Guys my age just out of Yale Law School were doing hefty pro bono at Paul Weiss. They had a biggie case against New York State."

"Tim," Max snapped, "Paul Weiss is a political firm. We never were."

Katy glanced at him. *Why is he suddenly so defensive?*

Then he recouped his equilibrium. "But we've always done our pro bono in the arts—we do our share for off-Broadway."

She studied him more carefully. He had bushy, wiry red hair, a rumpled sort of face, and a quick inner clock. His sentences would tumble out staccato, ahead of his thoughts. *Clear Type A.* He used old-fashioned Christmas-gift men's cologne. *A 1950s smell. Like his slang and viewpoint. Max is a Westchester type with a sociology in transito.* None of it quite meshed with his eighties Italian suit with side panels. Katy scrutinized them and the slight indentation at the waist of his flannel jacket. *He's in competition with Tim Fenester. Minds not being younger. Probably is having an affair.*

She leaned her head back in the taxi, attempting to put more space between herself and the two men. *Why at the last minute had she put on such a wrong, drab dress?*

She had spent the previous night trying on different getups for the occasion. Should she look impoverished? Or subtly flaunt her career status? What single outfit did she own that would show her as devoted mother, struggling but intelligent career woman, wronged widow, financial victim? Yet with sufficient power pizzazz to win on no cash and no clout an expensive, extensive court battle against an international real-estate combine? No piece of clothing hanging in her closet fit the bill.

Max turned to her. "I've drilled you for all conceivable scenarios. You are protected," he reminded her. "They might try to dredge up a dirty detail or two to knock your credibility. Strictly par for the course. Talk slow. Reply short. Keep your cool. Leave the rest to me."

Katy had never before been the subject of a deposition. *What* dirty detail? Her imagination flew to what she most wanted to hide—her humiliation over her powerlessness to deal with her mounting unpaid bills. Fear that Beanie's side might bring up her breakdown. Show her as nuts. As though she had raised Matt outside of the approved good-air-space bubble.

When she got anxious, the creases under her breasts sweated. In summer in the city it was a problem. Snowball, the one person to whom Katy confessed everything, including her bad smells, said to use cornstarch. She nervously splashed herself with a Lancôme perfume sample.

She was in the wrong line of work for the 1980s. In many ways she and Lewis had meshed. He in philosophy, she with a Ph.D. in medieval art. It had seemed pretty jazzy in the sixties. Their grand design had made okay sense. Her curator's job at the Schmidlapp's Medieval Art Collection would have looked just fine on a sixties resumé. There even had seemed something *good* about their combined interests. Now, squeezed in between Max Schecter and Tim Fenester, speeding a second time within a week to the financial district, the pursuits of Lewis and herself struck her as having been hopelessly arcane. *A bookish landmine swept away by a baby boom of swift junk-bond peddlers!*

Katy frequently bumped into the wives of brokers, arbitrage men, and investment bankers—some of those women were themselves downtown brokers—in the Food Emporium on Madison Avenue. The women had pale, pinched faces and stringy blond hair. In the summer they were in the Hamptons, Maine, or Europe. In the winter they wore brown mink coats to the floor and flat, pointy suede shoes. They wore no makeup, had anemic mouths and watery eyes. As they stuffed their supermarket carts with Pampers, pure-water Swiss-process decaf coffee beans, and arborio rice, they managed, oddly, to insinuate their possession of a vaguely antimaterialistic aesthetic. *Remarkable sleight-of-hand,* she thought. They exuded power, not style. *No-assed women make you feel like shit. Don't dwell on them.*

Her true sin, she felt, was continually having to stall about the fees she had agreed to pay. Willard, Henry, Freund, and Mannheim would nail her on her shabby economics. She mentally rehearsed her own defense. If she hadn't sued Beanie, just passively stood by while he and his conglomerate helped themselves to all Lewis's assets, she would have been a masochistic dope, a self-deprecating, negligent mother. So, she had stood tall and firm. And now, broke! Was it her fault that Lewis had been killed in the car accident? That they had planned their lives around two incomes—mostly his? That Matt needed to be educated? Why hadn't she been more nervy? Taken a flier on the stock market? Been brainy about the money drift of things?

She looked straight ahead. The driver had glued to his dashboard a pearl cross, a wooden hand to ward off evil spirits, and a photo of Madonna as a blond. *Had he, too, accumulated enough savvy to pick up a few stocks? Was she the only woman in town who hadn't played?* If Max lost the case she would have to forfeit her only collateral, her rambling apartment.

She closed her eyes. She loved the place. She had made it a home.

There was a bump; the driver stopped in front of a Broad Street office building. They had arrived.

▼   ▼   ▼

On the way up to the sixty-seventh floor Katy reminded herself that it had never been her idea to sue for *ten* million. In her calculations she had been cheated of *two*. But a million had been worth more when Lewis died, and Schecter disagreed. He had insisted on the ten. *How much money,* she wondered, confused, *does it seem fair for a woman to have in her own name? Money not earned, but inherited from a dead husband?* By *fair,* Katy meant to her friends, the kind of people who had been active in the anti-Vietnam War movement and still subscribed to the *New Yorker*.

31

She watched the easy way Tim Fenester seized territory. His body folded into an elegant, thin slouch as he exchanged quips with the opposition.

Fenester had been toe deep in counterculture. But he had made the transition—made partner in a prestigious law firm without skipping a beat. Women were more vulnerable to becoming prisoners of the style of an era than men. Take the movement. It shaped up women and freed them, she mused. *Freed them to cavort with the counterculture. But "Alice's Restaurant" was only a historic blip. Women don't weather well, changing trends in the mainstream of the world, good times or bad. Fifties gray-flannel-suit family life in the suburbs with tollhouse cookies, or Beatles flower children on hash. But the men stayed in the game—look at Tim Fenester. They could parlay a quick social change with grace. Because they never forget their survival is economic. Women dupe themselves into thinking they are having their flashy day, when what is wanted from them is merely women-as-theater for a new trend.*

She tried to brace herself for her ordeal by rising above it. *Think of money as an abstraction. As though you were Veblen or James Madison. Ah, Madison, how I could use you now. You would understand the property rights of a widow. You would know that equity is worth fighting for. And the equity is worth more than equity. You win back what's yours, you gain a psychological edge.* She wanted to leave her son, Matt, an unmurky past.

About money, her mood swings were extreme. When she fantasized winning the case she would slip into self-disgust at becoming a rich-woman-cum-"Dynasty." This was laced with a gloomy, more realistic scenario. Depressive panics at being creamed. The cumulative fatigue of years of money worry had reacted on her metabolism as if she had been undernourished and outside in freezing weather too

long. Katy experienced sudden energy drops. She shivered
easily.

▼ ▼ ▼

Katy had so rehearsed her self-defense against her flaws
that she was thrown off base when Carl Harris, the litigator
for the Broad Street firm, took her on a quite different tack,
a winding path of relaxed questioning. Even her taking the
oath had a mild, informal quality. It was done over coffee
in one of the firm's smaller conference rooms, which had
a spectacular view of the harbor that extended far beyond
the Statue of Liberty. The room had no paper, no books in
it. The chrome-and-leather chairs and taupe Belgian wool
carpeting—the senior partners eschewed using commer-
cial-quality (their reputation was that of a tough litigation
firm)—were a quiet contrast to the glass window, the city
below.

It amazed her how much time they took establishing her
early childhood. Katy enjoyed recalling it. Was this dilly-
dallying about nothing much their way of noting how she
responded to questioning?

"You grew up in Gohonk, Connecticut?"

"Summers . . . not during the school year."

"Where was that spent?"

"In Manhattan. We lived on Carnegie Hill." She added,
"Near where I live now." Max frowned. He had cautioned
her not to add things.

"With whom did you live in Manhattan?"

"When I was a child?" The question had surprised her.
Whom did they think she had lived with?

"Yes."

"My mother and father. And my brother, Jim."

"Did anyone else live in the apartment with you?"

"No—I have no other siblings."

"And the school?"

"I went to PS 6 through the eighth grade."

"And after that?"

"Friends'."

"Did you go to college?"

"I graduated from Barnard."

"Your husband, Lewis Eichorn, was a professor at Columbia University during the same period you were a student at Barnard?"

"Yes—" Out of the corner of her eye she saw Max lean forward again.

"Did you marry while still attending Barnard College?"

"No. It was after I had graduated."

"How long after?"

"The next week, I think."

"Yet wasn't faculty dating of students in the nineteen fifties considered a Columbia University infraction of rules?"

"Harris, you're far afield. I object to this question and instruct my client not to answer."

Katy shrugged. "He taught at Columbia, not Barnard. Lewis was a very stable person. He never broke rules."

"Would you describe your family home in Gohonk as a big place?"

"Yes."

"In addition to your family, did household help live there?"

"Yes."

"In your family's Manhattan apartment, did household help live in?"

Katy hesitated. "My family's arrangements over a long period of time were not always that precise." Tartan—Tartan. How to describe Tartan, who had nothing to do with the case? "We had a housekeeper, Mary Culver. Generally, she did not live in."

"Where did Mrs. Culver live?"

Katy saw that Fenester and Max were whispering to each other. *They look puzzled.* Would Harris next dig up whom she had skipped rope with in the fourth grade? This stuff was pointless. "On One Hundred and Fourteenth Street and First Avenue."

"So, Harlem?"

Why does he care? Why is he making a point that Tartan is black? "East Harlem."

"Did she have children?"

"A son—Bradford Culver."

"He also lived in East Harlem?"

"Some of the time—some of the time he lived with us. So that he could be in a better school district."

"So that when you stated that no one other than your immediate family lived in the apartment, you weren't counting in the help? Or was Mrs. Culver's son invisible to you?"

"I object." Fenester jumped in. "I find your remarks offensive to my client, and I want these irrelevant slurs attributing racist attitudes to Mrs. Eichorn stricken from the record."

Harris grunted a mild acceptance. "I certainly did not intend to accuse your client of racist attitudes. Far from it. What does Mr. Culver do now?"

"He is a landscape architect in Berkeley."

"Married?"

"With three children."

Then Harris went for the jugular. In a rapid ricochet that sounded more like edited remarks than questions, while reminding Katy that she was under oath, he swerved into her sexual past. His point was that she and Brad had had a sexual relationship before, during, and after her marriage to Lewis. "Isn't it true that Bradford Culver—then living in California—was the first person you notified of your husband's death? That immediately following the car accident you had him stay with you and your son, Matthew, in your house in Austin, Texas?"

Fenester kept objecting—he instructed her not to answer. But Harris continued his rat-tat-tat. He dropped Brad and brought up Mike. He began to sketch Katy as Michael Braden's mistress. *Braden* was a big, solid East Coast name. *Unbelievable. He sounds right out of a third-rate nineteenth-century French novel.* "Are we seriously meant to believe," Harris asked rhetorically, "that Mrs. Eichorn was the helpless underdog in a series of financial maneuvers—so helpless that years passed before she could afford legal counsel? This while she was solidly ensconced as the lover to a powerful and influential man? A man with unlimited access to one of the finest law firms in New York?"

Katy blinked. Disoriented. She had prepared a defense against allusions to her breakdown, her ability to care for Matt—her threadbare economics in a time of prosperity.

Instead Harris was accusing her of being rich. Of living inside the good-air-space bubble herself.

"Or did you choose not to use Mr. Braden's lawyers because while you were with him you were already contemplating leaving him for a younger man—one of your husband's former students, a would-be country singer—Ethan Lemay? You are, at present, living with Mr. Lemay?"

▼ ▼ ▼

A remarkable event then occurred in the Belgian-taupe-wool-carpeted conference room. A thing, a diaphanous black lace female presence, rose from one of the tugs navigating the Hudson and flew in through the thermal-controlled glass windowpane. Katy saw it. She knew the men did too.

It's Louise Brooks as Lulu, crossed with Marlene, plump and black-stockinged, singing "Falling in Love Again" in a Berlin twenties café. Marlene is grinning as she reduces her lovesick, besotted professor to crowing like a barnyard fowl as punishment for his lust.

The room suddenly smelled of musky sadism and powdered skin. The eternal female, disreputable fleshy odor swelled and snaked through the room, clothed in the fake sex-tease colors, pink and scarlet charmeuse over garter-held silky black hose. It, she, the thing, would not leave. Lulu/Blue Angel did not recognize the passing of time, did not know it was the 1980s and her blowsy, illicit day was done.

Harris accused Katy of a consistent pattern of taking lovers indiscriminately before, during, and after her marriage. Max instructed her to ignore the unfounded conjecture. Harris said he was talking fact, not conjecture.

So the black thing of stinky woman's white skin and sheen of black silk impertinently squatted above them. All in the room knew she was there, and Harris produced his trump.

He read a letter Lewis had sent Beanie shortly before the car crash, an odd, strangled lament of Katy's betrayal of him. Harris relished the crucial phrases. "She's never stopped sleeping with Brad—I know, I know. When I'm in the city next I want to meet with you about my idea of putting what Dad left me into a trust for Matt. In planning this I have taken into account the downside of my future. Katy and I will probably wind up part of the great American divorce statistic . . . Above all, I want things safe for Matt."

A second odd thing happened: The picture of Lewis that Katy carried in her head shattered. There was nothing left of his image. Faceless. Myriad shards. She would never again have a distinct visual memory of her dead husband. Before Harris had read the letter, she had taken for granted that she had been fighting for what Lewis had left them—her and Matt—she had been making no division within the family. She had endured the endlessness of it for the three of them. Lewis on her team, she on his. *Why had he done it? Why had he never confronted her with his fears? Why had he made her financially vulnerable to Beanie? Beanie, whom Lewis had spent the whole of their married life avoiding?* She felt empty. Unreal. She couldn't get Lewis back into her head. The snaky, white-skinned woman hovered nervily above her head. Stealing her energy.

"You yourself have indicated that your husband was a very stable man," Harris continued. "To use your own words, 'He never broke the rules.' So he must have seriously considered why he had decided on this course of action?"

Katy did not answer. She sucked in her breath. It was hard to fight for the assets of a dead man who didn't bless you.

Carl Harris and Tim Fenester left the conference room to make their phone calls to Judge Myrtle on separate floors. Willard, Henry, Freund, and Mannheim had a two-flight inner staircase that joined the spread of their offices.

Both litigators asked the judge for a ruling as to the parameters of what Katy need answer about her personal life. Fenester maintained that her private life was inadmissible evidence—the issue was fraud. White-collar crime. Harris insisted his questions were pertinent. He intended to present Lewis's divorce letter as evidence that Bernard Eichorn had merely been following his half brother's intent to set up a blind trust. His firm would prove that any discrepancy in the estate assets would equal the amount that had been set aside for Matt in trust. "So it would appear Mrs. Eichorn is fighting her own son."

Judge Myrtle was fatigued. The lawyers from both sides had called him just when he was ready to leave. His sister, Anna Myrtle, also a judge, and a terrible pest, was coming in from Philadelphia to have dinner with him. He disapproved of her. She wrote too many pop legal books, gave too many public talks. *Anna confuses the bench with social-service activity.* He would not mention this case to her. She could twist and turn the most straightforward trust accounting into a paradigm for minority rights. Even when there were no minorities present.

"Let your client answer now," he said tiredly to Fenester, "and I will rule on your motion to strike the testimony later. When I have had a chance to think about it."

Katy answered the questions. No to the one about Brad. Yes about Mike and Ethan.

On the way down in the elevator, Max said, "The letter isn't worth shit."

"But Lewis wrote it."

"He never acted on it. It has no legal meaning."

Katy was silent.

"Look, the stuff about your personal life was just an evasive crapshoot. Judge Myrtle will have to strike it out."

"Then?"

"As if it had never been said." He paused. "The main point is we found no blind trust."

CHAPTER ·

4

IN THE EARLY EVENING, AFTER HER
day in Broad Street, Katy, hands in the pockets of her blue
jeans, the back of her loose white shirt billowing in the July
wind, sat on a bench on the Carl Schurz Park boardwalk
overlooking the mayor's mansion and the East River. She
needed to mull things over.

*The point is, you never will know for sure what went on in
Lewis's mind. You can't haul him back for a repeat. Can't say to
him, "Look, I mourned and missed you. Even had a breakdown.
Sure, we had our quarrels. So after an entire marriage of yakking
to me about what a louse Beanie was—how he behaved as though
you should be punished because his own mother died of pneumonia—behind my back you sent him a jealous letter about stuff that
went on in my life before I knew you? Knowing Beanie never treated
you like you were his real brother you sent him a carte-blanche-to-
steal letter. You betrayed me!"*

She had thought she knew Lewis; now Beanie's lawyers had injected an uglier version of her marriage. Had Lewis written Beanie in a temporary fit of anger? Or had he been cheating on the marriage? Had he been involved with another woman? Why his sudden desire to alter his trust? Or was the letter a fake? Would Beanie have *dared* do that?

She paced the river walk—only the stray old people trapped in the Manhattan summer heat were watching the tugboats traveling north toward Harlem.

Or worse—had Lewis been afraid to tell her, after he had inherited his father's more solid assets, that he wanted to scuttle their simple joint wills—her stuff to him, his to her?

You can no longer conjure him up. You need to stare at his photographs to remember his face. The voice is gone too. You can't rage at dust.

Katy shielded her eyes from the sun. She felt so un-claimed. After the crash Matt needed a father. It had been handy for her to encourage him to remember a version of Lewis minus flaws. When she discussed the case with Schecter she had fantasized that winning it would benefit the three of them—her, a shadowy Lewis, and Matt. She and Schecter had gone over the facts so often that the bits and pieces of legal memory they worked on had become what she retained of her marriage. A blankness, an amnesia, protected her from remembering the lived-out day-to-day. When an old friend would pierce the fog and suddenly recall Lewis to her by reminding her of this or that forgotten incident, she would suck in her breath at the unexpected pain of his image, his voice.

You imagined your life would have a continuous flow, a connectedness. Well-built house rising from a firmly structured cellar. Instead you got unrelated, aborted chunks of time. Outmoded decades, outmoded styles. Childhood, marriage. The death. The breakdown. Would it have happened in another decade? During a different style of things?

They told you after his death to go out. See more people. The party was way over east, near York. Maybe fifteen couples. A small, cramped place. You knew none of the crowd. Except the man who'd brought you—and how quickly you forgot his name. You said you never drank much. So he brought you a weak gin-and-tonic. The room receded into a chiaroscuro landscape. You felt you were seeing tiny furniture from a sharp, distant perspective. You heard your voice recounting a strange, urgent story not at all in your conscious mind. How, when Jeremiah was a private in the trenches in World War I, he had known never to fall asleep while standing guard. Or he would have been shot. His enemy was the cold, the lack of sleep. You heard your voice announcing that you were a medievalist. And the room was so far away, the shapes so angular. The faces were of strangers. You knew you had to get away. You went to bed feeling a stranger had invaded your mind. Toward morning it hit. You saw a bloodied woman's head sticking up out of the sand. Dismembered limbs in violet and garish red—the red, the red. You have gone mad, you thought. Must not be alone with Matt. He will wake up and find his mother gone mad. You telephoned Snowball to come over, telephoned your internist. "Katy," he said, "I saw you last week. People do not go crazy overnight. You are sane. Just having a nightmare. Go back to sleep. Come to the office later in the day." So you called Bellevue. They had to understand. Had to recognize madness was real. Bellevue did. They kept you on the phone.

Asked you where you lived. Then told you to get dressed and taxi
over.

You ran out of the apartment building in your white lynx
coat that you had bought impulsively the year before Lewis was
killed. He had said it was too showy for an academic's wife.
You sat clutching it while waiting for the doctor to see the
line of people who had arrived ahead of you. A woman lamented in Spanish. "¿Donde está mi hijo? ¿Donde está
mi hijo?"

When it was your turn with the doctor, he unnerved you by
remarking that the woman was screaming because she was severely
disturbed. Was your empathizing with an obvious pyschotic a
sign you truly were nuts? Perceiving the sick as the normal
ones?

"Maybe she has lost her son," you suggested. "Maybe she needs
to find him?"

The doctor shook his head. What had he noticed about the
woman's behavior that so defined her as abnormal? Why did you
only sense her fear?

You had the feeling he was new on the job. He was nice. All the
other patients had been seen. He took some extra time. He talked
to you during the examination. Asked why you had thought of
coming to Bellevue; didn't you know anyone else in Manhattan? It
is not so easy to get into Bellevue. You could have called Gabe, but
you didn't want to explain to the doctor that Gabe was Beanie's
shrink, and you didn't need Beanie thinking you crazy, and Brad
was in Berkeley, and Anita was dead, and Jeremiah was semisenile.
"I called my cousin, she's with my son."

"Your pupils are dilated. Looks to me like one of your friends
spiked your drink with LSD. It can produce a delayed reaction.
Scary if you don't know it's coming."

He telephoned your doctor, gave him the diagnosis. Said, "She doesn't belong in Bellevue—once we start the red tape it will be hell to get her out." Promised to hold up your admission, provided a responsible couple took over.

Your doctor got on the phone to you. Furious. Nervous. "You never told me you were drugged."

"I didn't know."

"What kind of people do you know?"

"Bourgeois people. People like you and me."

He pretended not to know what you meant, but he took responsibility for your release. You called the Bradens. Before driving you up to their home—Hannah's Point, in southern Connecticut, a little south of Indian Path—Mike took you to the Empire Diner and you had a mammoth breakfast of pancakes and bacon and juice and lots of black coffee. You wrapped the lynx over you like a warm blanket. You were worried because Paula hadn't come with Mike to get you.

In your derailed period of death and craziness, men were drawn to you—every woman has her normal ration; this far exceeded it. When you went nuts and were full of deathy despair, you had your biggest allure for men. When you got back on even keel, you lost it. A magic attraction you don't understand—don't want to understand—got dumped. Of what use to know that when you're falling apart men like you more? A widow's dirty little secret. But Mike made no move toward you. You took note of that at the time. Bundled in your lynx, your eyes closed, you thought of Paula and Mike as the older couple. You felt awe. For Paula. For Mike. For their doing the right thing. They weren't part of your shaky world where strangers spiked your drinks with LSD and didn't tell you until weeks later. Three weeks later, anyway, you crashed. You had your minibreakdown. What caused it, really? The LSD, the car accident, no money, Beanie's playing hardball?

Katy no longer remembered. Though she did recall that the Bellevue doctor had been nice about forestalling her admission to the nut floor. At the time the gesture had seemed enormous.

CHAPTER

5

THE AIRLESS JULY HEAT IN KATY'S apartment oppressed her. She turned on the living room air conditioner, her thoughts gloomy. Beanie had come out ahead in the deposition. Katy surveyed the debris of her former life, a further sign of her decay. *The fall of the house of Katy Becker.* Her possessions—books, chipped furniture, old photos in dented frames, plus Matt's stuff that had traveled with them from Indian Path to Texas, then back again to Manhattan—struck her as forlorn remnants of heavy weather. Not that there was anything to dump.

She knew that whenever Matt flew into New York on a round-trip special he liked spending time alone in his old bedroom, fingering his abandoned things. So she had never asked him to throw out his junk, even after the Johnson Space Center had given him his own house. When they talked on the phone she avoided giving him bad news about the case. Instead she rummaged about for an upbeat legal tidbit to add to his enthusiastic descriptions about being chosen to be in on the medical end of the initial planning stages for a space station in low earth orbit.

Katy admitted to no one that her real reason for thinking she might defeat her more or less brother-in-law came from an oddly chatty confession he had made to her. Beanie had boasted that on hearing Jeremiah had been forced to sell Indian Path, he had driven his BMW down there to transplant some of Indian Path's double-lilac bushes to his place in Southampton.

In her reverie she saw him crouching in the night near the cluster of French lilacs, scooping a mound of useless dirt into a pail. *Weeds, Beanie—that's what you filched from Indian Path. You'd be incapable of knowing how to transplant a living bush.* She was convinced his needing to take for himself a symbolic piece of shrubbery from Indian Path, something that Jeremiah had created, was a sign of Beanie's weakness. And her strength. But viewed rationally, her notion was wacky. *Katy, old girl*, she scolded her wayward interior thoughts, *don't clutch at straws—not even lilac straws. If you're not careful you'll end up like one of those mildly balmy women in slanted, veiled hats and yellowed pearls who take tea in the afternoon and talk about their fine relatives from the good old days in Vienna.*

But the idea stuck in her head. She went upstairs to Ethan's apartment in order not to see the moth-eaten Indian Path sofa, the excess of her mother's old bric-a-brac. She and Ethan had never defined their relationship, but each felt free to use both places. She craved now the emptiness of his, its lack of a personal past.

Katy had helped him create its spare look. She had found

the thick green-and-beige-striped duck cover for his double bed, the white wicker rockers, and the cheap, oversized red Moroccan clay pot he kept on the floor near the window.

Banish the deposition from your mind. Instead listen to Ethan's pile of tapes.

Ethan had a lot of Freddy Fender. He had told Katy that early Fender was the best, that Fender's personal troubles later on softened his composition.

> *If he brings you hap-piness*
> *Then I wish you all the best*
> *But if he ever breaks your heart*
> *If the teardrops ever start*
> *I'll be there before the next teardrop falls.*

Because Ethan had a trick of embedding a secret phrase, a signifier, in his songs, she assumed Fender's music was also coded. Ethan claimed it was the incantatory words that counted: "The sacred stuff gives the work the elusive magic. First place your secret, then set your rhythms like ducks in a row, and the music will work. Seduce the public. Always."

> *"I'd like to dedicate this song to ma partnah,*
> *ma soul partnah, Mistuh Douglas Sa-on,*
> *Suh Douglas of the San Antonio Quartet*
> *. . . wherever you are, brothuh . . ."*

Ethan's own style, she mused, was not that different from Fender's. His breakthrough had come when he took "The Yellow Rose of Texas," originally meant to be a love

49

song about a mulatto girl, and made the miscegenation explicit. He had left his first stanza deliberately oblique:

Yellow rose budded on a June street tree—
The fruit of those crushed petals was me.
I'm standing by your side, little Joy Ride . . .

Then Katy stopped thinking about Ethan.

▼ ▼ ▼

Without her feeling the time slip by, it had become three in the morning. She took off her clothes, turned off the light, and lay naked, knees up, on the bed, watching the moving muslin catch dusts of light from the street lamp on the corner and smelling the dirt and fresh leaves drifting in from the park; the density of the black hair covering her genitals was surprising, almost as much as in puberty. She liked to look at the undulations of the unbleached muslin hanging loosely over brass window poles, the airy material picking up the early-morning breezes.

She peeled an orange and ate it. Quarter by quarter. Slowly. The oil of its skin added its smell to the dirt and fresh leaves. Katy lacked an imaginative sense of herself as victim. She was just beginning to grasp that the upshot of her legal effort might be that her one concrete asset would pass from her hands to her lawyers'. She had no training for the role of have-not. Seriously out of zeitgeist step, at inappropriate moments she had mumbled that she had had a happy childhood. In fighting her case, this put her at a serious disadvantage. She had no gut sense of being wronged, no childhood memory of lament.

50

Her distaste at perceiving herself done-in might even have slowed down her case. Winning and losing are subtle matters. On the other hand, Beanie's persistence in believing himself, always, as everyone's victim might in the end be his vulnerability.

Max said Beanie's deposition was such Swiss cheese he must never have confided in his own team. Never said, "Look, guys, get me out of this—okay, I stole—what is the cheapest this will cost me?" Never steered them right. His wanting his attorneys to see him as good, she prayed, would be his undoing. And her luck. Her slim trump.

She popped the last section of the fruit in her mouth. *What is the worst thing Beanie did to you? What is his worst flaw?*

Beanie's most inhuman act, the month after Lewis's death, when she had still been too destabilized to recognize his theft of his and Lewis's joint assets, had been—to draw her attention away from his own dealings—to insist she repay into Lewis's trust the money Lewis had lent himself to buy their house in Austin. Beanie and Lewis had both made those sorts of self-loans. It had been taken for granted that only on paper were they to be paid back.

At the time Beanie was shifting millions, he was hitting you for the fifty thousand you and Matt needed to live on. He tried to make you sell your home on the theory that it belonged to Lewis's trust, and that with Lewis dead neither you nor Matt had a right to it. Max said the reason Beanie had called in every loan, frozen the trust, was that he needed to squeeze you financially dry so that by the time you wised up to his thefts you wouldn't have the money to sue him.

Max doubted that Beanie disliked her personally. "He

was just covering his ass—anyway, his action wasn't actionable."

Beanie's second-lousiest trait was his picking Adam Klager as a silent partner. It infuriated Katy that in this bizarre way, money that should have gone to her and Matt had been diverted to the shittiest Mr. Fix-It in Manhattan. *Adam Klager, boy-wonder hangman-lawyer of the McCarthy era.* Now a balding, aging homosexual. *"Page Six" says he has AIDS. One of the few it would be hard to weep for.*

Max said, "Forget Klager—he's irrelevant. You can't sue your brother-in-law for being cozy with ex-Red baiters." *Why was Beanie's ratty life irrelevant, and her past not? How had Brad and Tartan become issues, and not Adam Klager?*

She stretched her legs flat against the cool sheet. *And your own worst flaw?* She condemned herself and Lewis for having been liberals who wanted to do good things and live off a private income without minding the store. That, as Katy saw it, had been their main sin. She worried enough about it to have mentioned it to Max. His response had been merely a shrug. "How you two lived your lives was your own business. Equity is equity, and theft of it is theft."

Even when Lewis had been alive Katy had raised the issue. "You want to be prince of civil rights, have the philosophical fineness of Wittgenstein, live like a crown prince in absentia, and not be bothered by the details of your father's business or mine. I think those are mixed ambitions." At the time she had felt like a heel for bringing up such mundane money stuff. Like she was the family materialist. Lewis had had a certain way of looking at her. So she hadn't insisted.

Your second-worst flaw? Not looking after your own assets that would have come through your father. Just because Lewis and Jim weren't interested in business, that didn't mean you couldn't have gone in. You could have worked with Jeremiah. You could have taken over everything involved with Indian Path. You might have actually liked the business end of things.

Her mistakes caused a deep pain in her heart.

Here she was in Ethan's apartment, a man with whom she was having the most temporary of affairs. With whom she had no real connection. Would this, and working at the Schmidlapp, become her final destiny?

Katy could not bear thinking she would lose the case, Beanie would have his way, and she would end here, stripped. Bone dry. The bleakness so overwhelmed her, she could not focus on details of the case that would have helped her cause. If Max and Judge Myrtle would have made a magical pact with her in which they assured her in advance an absolute win, she would have felt freer to recall the real damage Beanie had done to her.

She couldn't afford the luxury of such clarity. So, about much of the stuff that happened, she remained mute. In a purposeful daze. Content to equate his flaws with her own. Maximizing her own role in the shaping of her destiny.

The juice of the orange ran down her throat, her head flat on the pillow. Katy's planned ace in the hole, should she lose the case, would be her ability to make Beanie nonexistent. She would see herself as having gone from youth smack into an interesting adult life. The in-between part—Lewis, Beanie—would be erased.

Reclaim your identity—you were never the woman Beanie's

lawyers named. Flaws a million, but you were all the men you loved, and the times you loved them; you were the child; you were the mother of the child to whom you gave birth.

Her disaster insurance heavily depended on a triumphant childhood. She willed herself away from Ethan's white-walled apartment with its Moroccan pots on the floor. *Make real your ace in the hole—you, your crazy relatives. The lot.* She closed her eyes:

There were the colors you saw. Blue is the color of intelligent memory. Of his eyes. Of the blue door swinging open at the white beach house in Gohonk. Of the Mediterranean, of the cornflowers and bluebonnets growing wild in the Austin hill country, the blue of the East River in August, the colors of the old transatlantic French liners, of the Blue Mosque, of travel and the smell of Gauloises, and the Motherwell Gauloise, and "Blue Moon," and "Mood Indigo," and "The Blues in the Night," and "Sugar Blues," and not the blue of "Blue Velvet."

The white muslin wafted; Katy licked the oily peel of the eaten orange; some of its liquid had spilled on her throat, in her hair. *The unexpected blue of his eyes that she wanted always to remember, and for him to remember me. And the blue of grass, and of Delft, and the darkness of lapis, the sun hitting the Long Island Sound on the clear late-summer afternoons in the east when the water is so blue, so clear, and the cloudless skies, and the salt of the air, the mountain night, the sea slanting toward low stars, and Matisse's Collioure blue boats and conch-shaped beach. And the odd blue of his eyes against his olive skin . . . Did he love me? Or did that love exist only in her memory? Bleu marin or un vrai bleu. The smudged penned cards he had sent her from the world's wonder gardens, the world's disaster spots, even Wisconsin. For Katy. Never forget. We were us. Blue movies? Not really. A neon sign glowed hard blue in Soho: Bakelite Bijoux. Blue is the color of wetness, of the sailboat off Indian Path, the old-fashioned blue-bound school notebooks in France, the turquoise silver he brought her from the Indian reservation. The blue billiard chalk, the color of laundry blueing, she saw him; then, next to him, her father rubbing the square blue chalk—blue is the color of summer—on his pool stick in the basement of the white house at Indian Path. On the Sound. "Take aim." It was Jeremiah, not he, who always won. She remembered her father in the summer. Faded denims. The sun-sweat smell of his blue cotton shirts bought at Brooks. Blue is the color of intelligent memory—Had Brad loved her? Had Lewis? Mike? Had she been loved at all? And why did the question still matter?*

The muslin drapes blew in the hot wind, her skin was drenched in the odor of orange oil, the whiteness of the loft made her remember the clearness of blue on the summer day when she first loved him with all her sex. Afterward she had stared straight into his blue eyes.

California was three hours behind. Katy waited until late afternoon to telephone Brad at his office. She told him right off that Beanie's lawyers had come up with the crazy idea that the two of them had continued their affair during her marriage. She made her voice sound disarmingly direct so that he wouldn't feel his being named in her deposition was a big deal. She didn't want him to become anxious about Elise's inevitable jealousy.

Katy rode right past his silence on the other end of the wire—she knew he was thinking about Elise's wild imagination—and swung into the favor she needed of him. "Look, don't worry. It was just a Beanie diversionary tactic. But I thought it only fair—"

55

"That you should share this with me?" Brad sounded dry.

"—that I be up-front about it. Look, Brad, I do need your help. We know that most of Beanie's early money finagling had to involve his father's old Belle Hélène Harlem office buildings, but there is no way that Max's firm can figure their way through the workings of Harlem real estate. They won't even go up there. They don't know who is who on that scene. Please, Brad, help me."

"Why should I know who's who in Harlem? Katy, I'm a Californian."

"It's important—I'm losing the case." Katy paused, then invoked his mother. "Tartan says she knows people you could talk to for me if you came back to Manhattan. She says anyway you owe her a visit."

"If Tartan had her wits about her she'd be living with Elise and me in Berkeley."

"Tartan says Manhattan is her home—"

Tartan said said *SAID* . . . The pitch of their voices quickened, became higher, the words more indistinct. It sounded like crossfire from two squabbling children.

▼ ▼ ▼

After Brad hung up he sat alone a while in his office, gazing out at the San Francisco Bay. He turned over in his mind what to tell Elise. He knew he'd go east. He had his debt to the past. Though his view of it had never gone hand-in-glove with Katy's version.

CHAPTER

6

IN HIS BERKELEY OFFICE BRAD CULVER listened on the phone to his mother's harangue. She treated the art of oral communication with the same indifference she showed for her true name, Mary Culver. "You must come home," she commanded. "You owe it to the Beckers to help Katy."

"I am home."

"Don't talk drivel," she said, hanging up. Tartan never bothered with good-byes—she regarded her only son as permanently on tap.

She still doesn't comprehend that out west you are on the cutting edge of it. You dazzle them; you are a going-places black; there is no Tartan's boy.

In California he was at the center of where it was happening for a black. He was the most prominent landscape architect in the Bay Area, and Elise was always quoted for her pioneering work in child psychology. Some of their colleagues hated them for bending to the white establishment; others applauded their being terrific role models—either way, they *mattered*. In Berkeley he had felt free to create different versions of his past. Elise's black bourgeois Philadelphia family came in handy when chronicling how both of them had risen so fast in the professional class. On public occasions he found it simpler to claim her background as his own. On television it was important to be succinct.

In Berkeley rap sessions he intimated that he had risen out of the ashes of old Harlem, while his mother—the proverbial white-woman's maid—too old to move—had stayed on behind.

Other times he said he had had no Harlem childhood. He said that his mother and aunt had lived on an Italian block in east Harlem, that he had gone to a white public school and had the maid's room in the apartment of the white family for whom his mother worked. He pointed out that when he went east and wanted to look up his old crowd, there were only his classroom whites. He lacked validating black memories. Had no Harlem connection outside of his cousin Willie's place on Sugar Hill, and there he had been the poor relative. Referring to himself in the third person for effect, he would announce, "Bradford Culver came from nowhere."

Some nights, when the days were short and there was darkness even in California, Brad hesitated over this muffled version of how he had come to be. Something struck him as missing. He never lied to the rap groups. Everything he said, scrupulously, was so—but he was vaguely aware he always left Katy out. *She fits into no usable history.* He frowned. *Katy implicates you.*

Brad thought back to his trip to Texas after Lewis's car crash. *Beanie's lawyers were cracked if they thought they could rustle up some scandal about his being in Austin then. Although Elise would vehemently agree with Beanie that he had been the wrong person to send down there.*

Brad looked out of his office window, and he began to relive the details.

Immediately after the accident, Katy had instructed Snowball to ask Brad to fly down to Austin to help her with the funeral arrangements and the closing of the San Jaciente house. Brad always suspected she had given the errand to a third person to avoid colliding with Elise.

"Why my husband?" Elise had bitterly complained to Katy's cousin via long distance.

Brad was on the upstairs extension. He didn't add much to the conversation but let Snowball do the talking.

She defended Katy. "After a tragedy people turn toward the familiar—she and Brad grew up together. You can't fault her for not acting rationally right off the bat."

"Right off the bat? Since when has *rational* ever had to do with it—with Katy?" Elise exploded. "No—it's, What Lola wants, Lola gets. And Tartan backs her. Her love for Katy is *unholy.*"

Brad wasn't sure whether his wife had muttered *unholy* or *unwholesome*, but he knew Elise didn't go for Katy calling on him for this or that whenever it pleased her. Though the arguments Elise raised were practical, he knew she just didn't like the idea of him being alone with Katy.

"Logically, you and Gabe should fly down there," Elise

continued on the phone to Snowball. It irritated her that Snowball, Katy, and Gabe telephoned her husband at the drop of a hat. They always reminded Elise that the four of them had been pals since first grade. They made Elise feel like an interloper. "Why, your mother was a south-erner—you understand the way those people think. In Texas, Katy's an outsider. She reasons like a norther-ner—she has no true gauge of how the black thing works in Austin. Civil rights progress, my eye—she is making needless difficulties by having a black man residing in the same house as a newly widowed white woman and her son."

Brad kept silent. He remembered that Katy had written to him that though the integration situation in Austin was resolving itself more easily than in East Texas, now and again things still got dicey.

▼　▼　▼

The black business never did come up while he was in Austin. What jarred some of the local university families was Katy's behavior. They had wanted her to be sad. They had thought their role was to comfort her. She disappointed them by appearing too abrupt. Efficient.

Brad wasn't surprised. Even as a kid, Katy had a habit of waylaying sorrow by going into high gear. Still, until the car crash, Katy's main interest had been medieval history. Brad had been amazed that she plunged into business details with such directness.

She immediately telephoned the president of the univer-sity. Without waiting for him to finish his condolences, she told him that he had four days to decide on what tax evaluation the university would give her for Lewis's library and papers. If he met the figure she had in mind, she would leave them there. If not, she would ship everything to New York. Within the four days, he met her requirement.

In the midst of the funeral arrangements—complicated because there was to be an out-of-chapel service at the university before the coffin was shipped up north—Katy had made Brad drive her to a new shopping mall on the outskirts of Austin just to pick up a batch of Avery stickers. She obsessed about small things. She instructed the house-keeper to place the gummy circles on every movable object in the house, one color per room. Then Katy called the movers who had brought them down from New York to Austin. "Well," she said to the man who came to the house to give an estimate, "you brought us to Texas. Now you can help us leave."

Katy insisted that the faculty wives who came to visit her in the house off of San Jaciente Boulevard were merely a nuisance. She struck Brad as suffering from a sort of temporary amnesia—she didn't seem to remember that before Lewis's death these women had been her friends. When they offered to help her sort through her possessions, she refused.

"A family accumulates a lot of junk in no time," one of them insisted. "If you clear out the stuff now, your move will be much cheaper."

Instead of accepting their aid, Katy instructed the movers to ship everything to New York. "As long as it's not stinking in a pail. Just make sure you crate it by the color code, so I won't have a mess at the other end."

Brad reminded her that there was no other end. She and

61

Lewis had given up their New York apartment when he had accepted the philosophy chair in Austin. It might be months before Katy and Matt would be able to move out of Snowball's place into something of their own. "Take some stuff with you. Or you'll be poking through a bunch of crates in Morgan Manhattan each time you need to locate a pair of Matt's socks."

Matt avoided them, Brad noticed. The boy spent his days with his gang pitching ball.

Katy ignored Brad's suggestion. She gave the movers a two-weeks-hence arrival date with no interim storage planned. "I'll have my own place by then," she assured Brad.

She was so motored, so hyper, there was no helping her. She found a cheap apartment on the northern edges of Carnegie Hill the first week she was back in New York.

▼ ▼ ▼

During his Texas days and nights with Katy, Brad felt profoundly uncomfortable. Her habit of being aloof with strangers while impulsively giving her total trust to help, to people paid to work for her, reminded him unhappily of their childhood together.

In addition to having Tartan, Katy had always been surrounded by the help at Indian Path; there were Jeremiah's secretaries; Pat Mallard, who drove Jeremiah's long green Packard; and Keith, the office boy, who brought to the house an envelope of household cash whenever Katy's mother ran short. With the same abruptness she had approached the president of the university, Katy now matter-of-factly handed Eddie, her once-a-week yard man, fifteen hundred dollars to refurbish the San Jaciente house for rental to visiting professors. Eddie was as startled as Brad that Katy had converted him into her decorator on the spot. Later Brad recognized that Katy had had one of those loony ideas that worked.

Eddie took Katy and Brad down to Third Street, below the Driskill Hotel, near the old railroad station. Some years later, when the Austin sound became big, a row of night spots opened up on the street, but at the time of the car accident there were only a grain storage, a boot store, and the Goodwill. Katy strode through the thrift shop, making rapid choices. Eddie was adept at picking the good lamps, solid desks, and old bureaus needed for the empty house. He said he would come back for the lot with his pickup truck once Katy returned to New York.

▼ ▼ ▼

On the bumpy drive back to San Jaciente, Brad realized that Katy had so disarmed Eddie—her trusting him with her fifteen hundred dollars and asking for no receipts—that there was nothing he wouldn't do for her. He offered to bring his sisters to the house. They would sew up a pile of new curtains and slipcovers. "When the place looks good," Eddie observed, "you'll fetch higher rent." Katy nodded. The two of them behaved like co-conspirators. Within a day, Eddie and his family had the plans for the rehabilitation of the shabby white frame house under control. *Why*, Brad had wondered, *is she bothering to keep a run-down place in a town for which she's shown no enthusiasm?*

▼ ▼ ▼

Katy's final act was to drive with Brad to the German Smoke House on the road to San Antonio. Almost absentmindedly she ordered twenty-five pounds of smoked meat to be sent dry-iced to Snowball's. "Lewis likes Texas smoked meat," she said.

"Lewis?" Brad was worried she hadn't registered her husband's death. At moments she spoke of him as still alive, other times as though he had been dead for years.

Afterward, in the station wagon, she seemed more focused. She took Brad's hand. Her way of making a stab at recuperating a piece of their mutual past.

She said in a thin voice that it was odd that Lewis had been killed now. "We were still behaving as though our chief agenda was to alter in our own marriage the mistakes of our parents. Our correction of their flaws was what was meant to happen next—not death. Do you know what I mean, Brad?"

He grasped her hand, his silent acknowledgment that they had been passionate lovers at the beginning of their lives. He sensed that reviving their past had reassured Katy. Perhaps it was a reminder to her that she had existed, behaved freely, and, if he were to believe her version, indeed had almost wanted to die of love before she had met Lewis.

It was her stubbornness, her odd notion that there was only one of every quantity in life, that caused her outdated romantic conception of eternal love. He stared at the wild dark hairs tumbling in soft spikes off the base of her neck; her skin still smelled of childhood. Then he stifled his sharp desire of her with images of Lewis's unburied cadaver.

"You had no father, Brad. It's my worst failure that Matt will never have completely known his."

He looked at her. *Did she never wonder about Jeremiah and Tartan? Tartan claimed he was born in Waylee, South Carolina. Of an unknown father. But when he got his birth certificate for the University of Wisconsin, it read, "Harlem Hospital, 1931."*

Brad moved his body slightly away from Katy, removing his hand from hers. The Texas sun blazed into the Ford window. "Why your failure? It was fate."

"I didn't think I was on such bad terms with fate—I thought I could give it a helping hand."

As if to placate Brad—and win him back—she reclaimed his hand. "My therapist was never too hotsy-totsy about my ideas on fate." She sighed. "Tabor's nineteen-fifties memory room—that was more his style." She turned toward Brad. "Not that I handed his memory room the deep stuff. Not about you and me. *Capisc!?*"

Brad was silent.

"I suppose since you've become such a Bay Area honcho, you've told your black rap groups about me?"

"No."

She stared at him. "Do you mean it? Or are you just saying it to humor me because Lewis is dead?"

"No. I swear I never did."

She smiled at him as though making a joke. "You could pitch me as a Jewish woman . . . who was the child of two American parents." Her phrase struck her as funny, and she elaborated on it. "Every time has its dirty secrets. The nineteenth century hid sex, in the nineteen-fifties people lied to themselves about the place of money, and now our stinky little secret"—she took Brad's face in her hands, and, smelling of verbena, whispered in his ear, as if relaying to him some sultry bit of news—"is our American childhood." She paused, and added in a stronger voice, "We pretend it never took place. Like we're a bunch of stray ethnics."

Then she said abruptly, "Lewis's mutt ran away after the chapel service—I guess he didn't want to go up north with us."

▼ ▼ ▼

Their flight came into Newark just ahead of the blizzard. They had to change planes twice—at Dallas and Chicago. When Brad led Katy and Matt down the ramp and saw Snowball and Gabe standing at the gate, his heart sank. Katy and Matt had left New York as two-thirds of the family of an up-and-coming academic. Now, in their out-of-season bright pastels, they were returning home with him like a beaten-down gypsy family dressed for a summer block party. Matt, carrying a piñata, was wearing a Texas cowboy hat. Katy—she always had been a swift dresser—was wearing a yellow plaid muumuu beneath a dirty white cardigan.

Snowball had arranged in advance with Gabe that she would drive her cousins back to Manhattan while he stayed behind to make the arrangements for the direct transfer of the casket to the cemetery. "Tomorrow we'll go shopping," she said to Katy, "for winter stuff for Matt."

▼ ▼ ▼

Brad sat in the backseat next to Matt—he had given the boy his coat as a blanket. Matt had a loopy grin on his face; he still avoided looking at any of them directly.

Since Anita Becker's death, Jeremiah Becker had lived alone in a two-room suite in the Volney. The family said it was a blessing she had gone peacefully of a stroke without realizing the extent to which Jeremiah had lost everything. Indian Path had been sold—Katy had been vague to Brad about the details—to cover her father's business losses. When Jeremiah had finally lost, he had lost the whole show. Brad figured that he had held on to the reins too long and that his increasing dementia and weakened heart had contributed to his financial demise.

Jeremiah had raged about Katy's brother, Jim, bringing in unimaginative Harvard Business School types to stream-line his operation. Katy said to Brad she hadn't a clue who was right. Jim claimed to her that Jeremiah had been hopelessly locked into an outmoded shoot-from-the-hip solo way of doing things. After the big loss, Jim married a Dutch woman in Australia and started a sheep station in New South Wales. Jim always had been remote from the family. Katy often expressed to Brad her idea that it was something she had done wrong in her childhood that caused her brother's excessive irritation. Still, Jim tried to do what he felt was right. He had wired Katy to bring Matt to the sheep farm on the next school break.

Right or wrong, Brad thought, *Jeremiah was a man who created memories.* In its ripe time, Indian Path, with its great Olmsted trees, had had a dreamlike quality. Brad and Snowball had grown up there; the entire Ginzberg clan had spent the summer months with their cousin Anita in Gohonk. Brad had a reverie in which Jeremiah thanked him for saving Indian Path. He placed the speech as occurring while Jeremiah was presiding over one of his great seaweed bakes. His hazy fantasy stopped short at the idea of Katy. He did not dare imagine her as his half-sister.

The theories she liked to spin out for him were much more historic. She insisted to Brad that her father's will to flamboyant success had come from his being illegitimate. When her Austrian-born grandfather, while married to another woman, had made her grandmother pregnant with Jeremiah, her grandmother's family had given the couple money to go to New York. It was hoped that in a new country their legal disarray would pass unnoticed. "Most immigrants came to America," Katy liked to boast, "to better their lives. My father's folks came to expunge their sexual disgrace."

She maintained that seeing a classy Jewish tycoon lose it all in old age was threatening to his New York crowd. "Oh, he had been a model—in his time there were not many tycoons like him." Tartan, a Greek chorus to Katy's views, also assured Brad of that. "Our trouble," Katy further explained to Brad, "was that in the sixties and seventies Jews were supposed to be on the way up, they hadn't had enough time to find a gracious way of going down. We are not WASPs—our money isn't old enough to permit us to lose it and still hang on." She sighed. "We've developed no acceptable mode for failure."

▼ ▼ ▼

When they came out of the Lincoln Tunnel, snow was coming down thick in Manhattan. Snowball drove east through the Seventy-ninth Street transverse. Katy in-

structed her to stop in front of the Volney. Brad was afraid
to move—Matt had fallen asleep against his shoulder.

From the car window he watched Katy, Snowball's coat
thrown over her shoulders, walk into the hotel. She paused
in the entryway, as though remembering something. She
removed the dirty white sweater she had been wearing over
the muumuu and carefully rolled it into an inconspicuous
small ball. Then she pushed the snow out of her hair, put on
her cousin's coat properly, stood up straight, and marched
through the lobby to the elevator to tell her old man her
husband was dead.

PART TWO

A Family

Romance

CHAPTER

7

KATY WOKE UP THE NEXT MORNING in Ethan's studio loft mouthing an odd phrase—*Tears in the eyes of Tolstoy*. Why Tolstoy? When she went to sleep she had been thinking not about literature but about Indian Path and how Gabe misunderstood when he perceived her childhood as being identical to it. True, Indian Path had summed up Jeremiah and Anita's dreams and ambitions, and other people's dreams, too. So much so, she believed, that they began to confuse those dreams with Katy's real childhood. Summers there were more grand than winters in New York—Indian Path was stuffed with cousins, help, and the twenty Fresh Air Fund semi-orphans who arrived every July to live in the red barn under her mother's and aunt's joint supervision, but to Katy the place always remained part-time, good for weekends and summers. At heart she was a city child: she came from her parents' New York apartment.

Once awake, she reminded herself she was losing her lawsuit against Beanie. She lay back in bed, pulled the Wamsutta striped sheet over her face, and tried to recall her army of relatives: they were people who had nervily lived their overblown, chaotic, unsubtle lives in an energetic way that would have been unsuitable to modern American life—or fiction, for that matter—because they had an energy that made them not victims. She closed her eyes. Soon the whole bunch came clattering into her head. Even those uninvited marched in. They knew their history better than Katy did. And how they talked to her! She couldn't shut them up. Their voices reminded her how at home they had felt in America. They had always known where the good stuff was. They knew the right paths to walk in August, the spots where the salty sea breezes were strongest. How to build houses that were cool in summer before there was air-conditioning. They were what Manhattan had been about . . . She couldn't fail in court supported by such an earthy crew . . . One by one, the phantoms nudged her to get on with the show. They would lend her their strength . . .

▼   ▼   ▼

The apartment Katy had grown up in had been on Carnegie Hill, on the corner of Fifth Avenue and Ninety-fifth Street. Those blocks were her first life. As a young girl, she observed, from her bedroom window, the comings and goings of the pupils from the Lycée Français, which was across the street from the Beckers'. The school spawned small, pale, French-speaking, well-bred children in navy blue uniforms; Katy rapidly deduced France was a quieter, more solemn place than Manhattan. She preferred playing hopscotch in the gutter with a boy whose mother boasted of being a disciple of Isadora Duncan and whose father claimed to be a Polish nobleman, but all that was known for sure was that he smelled of horses and park and that he ran the local riding academy.

Katy walked the ten blocks to PS 6 four times a day—Anita and Tartan worshiped at the altar of fresh air—the icier, the better for soul and bowels; even in hurricane time Tartan didn't allow her to ride the bus. "Why have we been given raincoats and umbrellas and galoshes, if not to walk in the rain?" Tartan would ask. Twice down on Fifth, twice back on Madison. Every morning Katy would inspect her domain. The gold-domed Russian Orthodox church intrigued her. She imagined it filled with painted Easter eggs and maybe German spies hiding from Humphrey Bogart. The great robber-baron mansions still dominated Fifth Avenue during the Second World War; she wondered who inhabited them. Did Brenda Frazier—her photo was always in the newspapers—live in one? Katy would check the doors and boarded windows, but other than an occasional garbage collector emptying the steel pails left at the small side entrances, there was no sign of life.

Katy's sense of her world was geographical: Her border on the west was the park; on the east it was Lexington Avenue. On special occasions she and Jim went downtown, to Jeremiah's main office near Fortieth and Fifth. The elevator man, Pete, always said, "Here come Jeremiah's kids." Finally he told them the BIG SECRET: William Randolph Hearst had his hideaway love nest on the floor above Jeremiah's law office. "His mistress, the actress Marion Davies, lives there." Pete rolled his tongue over *mistress* like the word was a hot cruller to be savored. Katy immediately took note. There was more to this than had been said. She liked the word *mistress*; she fantasized that it could have something to do with her future.

At dinner that evening she asked her father point-blank what it meant to be a mistress. Jeremiah looked past Katy at the dining-room wall directly above where she was seated—he suddenly studied the painting hung there as though seeing it for the first time. He fielded her question with a non sequitur—did she understand the importance of his brother, her uncle, being one of the first Jewish constitutional-law professors in America? Jeremiah walked into his study and came back with the complete life of Justice John Marshall.

Katy scrutinized her mother's face. Anita was laughing; she clutched her long olive Chinese silk robe to keep it closed over her shaking bosom. Katy inhaled the sharp green perfume emanating from her waved dark brown hair, her breasts, her wrists. Anita had secrets; her startling good looks and intense round brown prune eyes dazzled her daughter, but her fluid moods puzzled Katy, thwarting her yearning for the definite, for some more explicit family geography.

Anita gave Katy's question about wanting to be a mistress that same dressy laugh she had given when recounting her own foray to the Yiddish theater. On the previous Monday night her mother had returned home very late. She came into Katy's room and bent over her bed to remove a flashlight and book from under the sheets. "Don't pretend to be asleep when you aren't. Use the lamp—you'll burn yourself putting that camp light under the blankets." She kissed Katy, then stood still a moment silhouetted in her bedroom doorway. Her bias-cut evening gown shimmered over her thighs and belly; her shoulders and back looked very naked to Katy.

"We went to the Yiddish theater and saw Molly Picon." Then she gave her special secret laugh. "We had the most wonderful food down there."

Katy had no idea why her mother was amused; her parents always went to the theater on Mondays and Anita always gave Katy the playbills. This was the only time she giggled about it. Because of the way her mother had slurred the name, Katy mistakenly thought that the actress must be called Molly Pecan. An actress named for a nut? That must be the joke. It did sound funny, so Katy laughed too. She assumed that the Yiddish theater must be on Broadway, near the movie palaces she and Jimmy went to with Jeremiah: the Roxy, the Capitol, the Paramount, and Radio City. Years later, when Katy, while at Barnard, discovered the Yiddish theater, she realized that her mother had been telling her about the Lower East Side that night.

▼ ▼ ▼

Katy stayed in Ethan's bed, mulling over what part of her past had been authentic—she tried to sort out what had actually happened to her, as opposed to what she had lazily come to assume it had been, mostly from reading Roth and Bellow novels. When she watched late-night old-movie reruns on Turner Network cable television, Myrna Loy and William Powell in the *Thin Man* series, and John Barrymore in *Counsellor at Law*, they seemed achingly familiar to her.

She saw her mother's look in Loy's crêpe suits, little fur pieces, and tilted pancake hats. Powell's crushed gray fedoras, jaunty New York patter, and clever remarks about F. D. R.—class and origins erased from his accentless speech—reminded her of her father.

Hollywood is assumed to be the dream and Bellow and Roth the American Jewish reality. For you it is the reverse. Hollywood contains the truth of your past. The exotic dream is those writers whose gusto, slangy language, and literary smarts turn you on. But those black-and-white Paramount, Metro, and Warner comedies contain the last recorded scraps of Anita and Jeremiah's real existence. Watching them on Turner cable is your final link to your childhood. So which is the chicken and which the egg? Had Anita and Jeremiah, breaking new ground in the modern mode, picked up their style from snazzy movies, or had the movies—and they had plenty of friends involved in New York theater—gotten their style and quick dialogue from stylish Manhattan Jews?

▼ ▼ ▼

As a child, Katy never needed Brad to alert her to Harlem; her mother had been born there. Go south from Carnegie Hill and you reach the world of downtown adventure and freedom—the big department stores, the world of Jeremiah's offices and power. But when Katy headed north she knew that she would immediately reach the Ninety-sixth Street border; there the Grand Central railway tracks abruptly surfaced; its trains zoomed past the magic and sadness of Harlem, the mysterious land of her mother's past. "O Harlem, Mama's Harlem," Anita would sigh, "heaven."

In 1917 Katy's maternal grandmother, Indy Jaches, died of a sudden heart attack that permanently surprised her three daughters and two sons. Before that crucial event their lives had been remarkably peaceful; they had lived calmly and eaten well near Madison and Ninety-ninth Street. Indy's death was the great tragedy, the initial cause of an easily evoked dark mood in Anita Becker. Indy's three daughters felt an abiding loss; their mother had been obliterated without warning. Just a cry and a grasp at her throat, and she had been taken from them; her daughters hadn't had a moment's time to run for a doctor. She had never lived to become a grandmother, so her children had never learned the habit of calling her any name but Momma. Katy secretly, in the privacy of her mind, called her dead grandmother "Grandma Indy." But when she needed to mention Indy Jaches's name to her mother and aunts, she always deferred to their loss and politely said "your mother."

Grown-ups fail to tell children the obvious. They don't hide merely the sexual secrets, the money secrets; things don't get told because no one remembers that children only know part of the scenario. Adults ignore the double energy their children use making forays into the future at the same time blasting scrim off stuff that has already become the past.

Though no Rand McNally map of the beating of hearts was handed to Katy before she came on the scene, by the time she was in PS 6 she realized that her family mystery was located in Harlem. Even before she explicitly recognized that her mother and aunts returned to it because it was their childhood home, she was aware that it contained some unattainable thing that attracted them. In the beginning all she knew was that her Aunts Jillian and Marcie came every Saturday to have lunch with her and her mother. After the women finished their coffee, licking crumbs off their lips from the thinly sliced lemon-orange cake, there was a pause in the dining room, a quiet that Katy associated with churches.

Then the three sisters, with her in tow, started their joyful pilgrimage uptown. The women abandoned the Becker Fifth Avenue apartment and headed straight for the markets beneath the Grand Central tracks on 116th Street and Park Avenue. They squealed and jabbered like happy homing pigeons. These were privileged moments—neither Jeremiah nor Jim was included. Katy felt a beam of light on her. It came from a heat the women emanated; they touched her and caressed her hair; she felt special, she felt loved.

Once their troop had crossed the Ninety-sixth Street border, her mother and aunts moaned with joy: "There's Swail's Fish Market!" That was their first stop. The women touched the gray marble pillars, commented that the white-tiled sawdust floors were the same as "when Momma bought"; the fish, they swore, smelled better and was fresher here than uptown. They laughed, sniffed, squeezed, and selected.

Her mother's and her aunts' trifold memories were always awakened by the familiar fish odors. The women talked excitedly about their youth—the marvel of the annual costume parties in Central Park, their May parties and June walks. Marcie explained to Katy how Jillian and she would get themselves up as geisha dolls; they wore Japanese kimonos, painted their faces white, and slanted their eyes with kohl. "By May you could buy bags of black cherries and eat them in the park."

When they were older, Marcie further elaborated to Katy, they went with their boyfriends on nighttime skating sprees at the rink near 110th Street. In late June, before the family moved to the country, they would buy slices of fresh watermelon and steamed Connecticut corn from the pushcarts; in the winter the vendors sold them roasted sweet potatoes that had been baked in the coal braziers in the bellies of their steel carts.

"My, the food was good then," her mother would sigh. Anita remarked that the best times were in the fall, just before the elections, when the politicians were stumping the streets. "The trees were at the height of their Indian summer color; the air had a crackle and it smelled of charred chestnuts." She described to Katy how she would strut with her school friends up Madison Avenue, heckling the politicians: "Tam-many, Tam-many, hocus pocus, kiss my to-cus!" On Saturdays Anita's father took her with him to the Alhambra. "I heard the actor ask, 'Who will be the next mayor of New York?' " Anita giggled each time she recounted the familiar story. "I thought he was asking *me* and I yelled out, 'Jerome!' " After World War I, bourgeois Harlem disappeared. And Grandmother Indy was dead. The family moved a few blocks south, to the Upper East Side.

▼ ▼ ▼

During World War II, amazing things could still be bought in the semienclosed stalls of the 116th Street market. The three sisters were nimble at picking out finds from the junk—French paste jewelry, the last loads of imported silks from Europe. Katy watched while they draped slithering bias-cut nightgowns against their bodies; the women smoothed the silk over their stomachs and thighs, swaying their hips slightly while deciding what looked good. Katy's mother giggled in the same semisecret way she had used when telling her about Molly Pecan and the Yiddish theater. Katy would study them silently, aware that they had forgotten her presence. She stood very still, content to sniff the aromas of winter wool and imported perfumes blended with the smells of brown paper and scaled fish from Swail's. After the women finished buying lingerie and bolts of cloth, they continued their triumphant march and went to the Puerto Rican stalls; there they loaded up on foodstuffs: exotic, pungent melons and dirt-covered vegetables. The stalls smelled of female silks, and butcher's meats, and spices, and slabs of cheese. Katy inhaled all of it and looked upward at the great glass-and-steel market dome. Paradise!

She liked listening to her aunts' and mother's chatter—the women spoke in short staccato cuts; without warning they jumped from fish to silks to Hitler: they were sisters. They gossiped cattily about other women they knew who did not come up to their measure. Katy figured out it was important not to look wrong; she immediately understood what was no good from the lowered inflection in her mother's voice. Wearing too many real jewels was a definite sin. The three sisters mocked women who did. "Can you imagine such vulgarity? Wearing big diamonds at lunch!"

Just before the war, Anita had made several trips to London and was up on the way women did things there; she was the most sophisticated of the trio. Her two younger sisters were attentive as she handed them stray bits of information relating to her international experience. "Don't think those British women know what to do with their jewelry—they jab their diamonds into their bosoms like safety pins," she would say authoritatively. "And I don't like their silver. Far too heavy—and their glassware—terrible. They are far behind American design. They've nothing like our department stores." Marcie and Jillian would listen as though receiving instructions from a high priestess: in matters of taste, Anita was the acknowledged front-runner in their crowd.

Marcie liked to explain to Katy that Anita had "struck out" by painting her living room a pale gray with a bright lemon ceiling before any woman on the Upper East Side had thought of doing such a thing. Anita then topped her revolutionary decorating feat by being the first hostess to use southwestern clay pottery for a Sunday brunch. Marcie described to Katy the sensation her mother had caused when she served food to her guests from brown glazed pots placed on a kitchen table covered with a simple black-and-white plaid tablecloth. Marcie was an apprentice to Elsie de Wolfe at Macy's Corner Shop—the first interior-decorating department in New York—so she listened carefully to what her older sister thought was right.

But the best stop was on the way home. On Ninety-ninth Street, on the east side of Park Avenue, just at the place where the railroad tracks rose into the sky, was the Polish woman's store. OLGA ZWEICKY'S ANTIQUES was crowded with broken bric-a-brac, brass chandeliers, and lamps with missing crystals; it was Olga's private flea market. Olga bought most of her stuff from the Hudson Valley estate sales; it was the end of the depression: no one was buying the candlesticks, the early-American chests, the big Chinese export pots, and the gold-leaf-framed Hudson Valley landscapes. Anita Becker was Olga's star customer. Since Katy never saw anyone else in Zweicky's, she assumed the place stayed open mainly for their visits. Her mother's compulsion to buy stuff there never abated; after the Becker apartment couldn't hold more candlesticks, Indian Path, with its thirty rooms, barn, and small cottages, soaked up the surplus. Katy guessed that Anita endowed the objects that she so carefully carried across the Harlem border with a sacred quality, but for a long time she didn't understand why.

On one of those special Saturday afternoons, Miss Olga turned to Katy. "I'll give you whatever you select; now let's see if you can pick as good as your Momma."

The four women—Olga, her aunts Marcie and Jillian, and her mother—watched her. Silence in the dusty shop. Miss Olga's fingers stank of the glue she used to mend broken chandeliers with parts of miscellaneous brass. How could you know what to choose? Where did you learn these things? Katy surveyed the bric-a-brac piled high. She was scared. She knew, because she had heard, that there was good stuff and bad, but she had no idea how to go about selecting. She saw a small, plain jar, of a blue as blue as the Long Island Sound on a summer day at Indian Path. Tentatively she reached out her hand. She looked at the women for a clue, but they said nothing. She grabbed it. The women immediately shrieked, "She's got it! She has the eye! The eye! The eye! Poppa's eye! Momma's taste!" They hugged and kissed her as though she had passed some ancient *rite de passage*, and in their joy they bought more stuff.

Jillian, Katy's younger aunt, then told her that her grandfather's "luck" in America had to do with his "eye." Saul Jaches came from a town on the old Polish–East German border, an hour south of Königsberg. When he arrived in New York in the late 1880s at age seventeen he had a small advantage: unlike many Polish Jews, he spoke German and was at ease in a German Jewish culture.

According to Jillian, what had separated him from most cloak-and-suiters and accounted for his quick success was his ability to draw, to design for himself. Legend had it that Saul had gotten his start by walking into elegant showings with a charcoal pencil and pad. He drew swiftly, stunningly, with deft, firm strokes; it was also said of him that all he needed to do in order to make a woman the best-fitting outfit in Manhattan was to wrap his arms around her waist. A cousin in the woolen business had bought a brownstone on Madison in the upper Nineties. Though Saul Jaches had to content himself with an apartment, he moved to the same block; soon he had his own factory and his own label.

▼ ▼ ▼

On Friday afternoons, after school was finished, Katy would go with her mother on more pedestrian trips to Harlem. Jeremiah's driver, Pat Mallard, would drive her and her mother across the Ninety-sixth Street border in her father's big green Packard. It was a convertible with white-walled tires and a long running board. Katy would beg Pete to open the top, but he always refused; he said that the hinges connecting the chassis to the stiff canvas roof were too complicated to fiddle with. In these more ordinary forays her mother would stop at Humel's grocery to provision; Humel's, like Olga Zweicky's, was on Park and Ninety-ninth Street, at the gateway to Harlem. Anita would buy fruits and vegetables in great quantity in order to prepare for the weekend, then Pat would drive them straight up to Connecticut, to Indian Path.

Some of Katy's school friends remarked it was odd that a family like hers shopped so much in Harlem—their mothers ordered underwear from Bergdorf's and Saks, and food from Gristede's. Katy had no answer. It wasn't until years later, after Matt was born, that she put all the pieces together. The brass candlesticks, yards of silk, and fish fillets wrapped in brown paper were her mother's desperate attempt to hold on to tangible pieces of her own mother's buried love, and Anita, Marcie, and Jillian had cast that hot beam of light on Katy those Harlem days because she was Indy's first female grandchild; Katy was love returned, the replacement for their dead mother. The three sisters were showing her off to the unseen presence of Grandmother Indy: they were taking her home.

NOBODY KNEW THE WHOLE TRUTH
about Indian Path any longer. Not Katy. Not Brad. Not
Jeremiah. Not Anita. Not even Tartan. Brad stayed late in
his Berkeley office, sifting through shards of the past in no
particular chronological order. Scenes from Indian Path
popped into his head; they were peculiarly blotchy—he
was no longer sure if what he remembered had actually
happened. It was odd, because he saw things as though they
had taken place on a stage, in a lush theater with a heavy
curtain; in the scene he and Katy were sitting to one side
of the stage, watching the grown-ups. He knew he had
mixed things up, because in the real Indian Path there had
been no stage. No audience.

*I don't want to go back to Manhattan. Don't want to. Time
Katy solved her own problems.* He felt dragged back to Harlem
by Tartan; she was forcing him to involve himself with

Katy's lawsuit like he was still a kid who had to be grateful to the Becker family. Why so grateful? For what reason? Brad's moody vision of the past had nothing to do with Katy's nostalgic notion or Tartan's misplaced sense of duty.

When Brad Culver thought about his mother, he sank into confusion: her strengths made him feel puny. Then too, he never knew whether it was her strength or her size. Everything about her was big: Her black eyes slanted slightly upward against high cheekbones; when she was in a temper they jutted out like round apples. When she stretched her arms she smelled of ammonia, flour, coffee grinds, and sweet gardenia perfume. She was so tall, broad shouldered, hipped, he never imagined her having been young. Throughout his childhood he begged her to use *Mary Culver,* her true name. Never knowing she was hurting, diminishing her only child, she insisted on sticking to *Tartan.* Brad had no interest in the past it evoked—the nickname the girl had received, walking the Waylee streets that were caked with hot red dust, plaid cotton wound around her head turban-style, held no charm for him. He never dared ask her who his father was; he cut her off from her Waylee stuff; he felt humiliated that she turbaned her head. She told him she did it to keep away the dirt while she cleaned. But Brad noticed that when Katy's mother did her closets twice a year with Tartan, Tartan's dark, waved hair was free.

It was Jeremiah Becker's idea to make his Fifth Avenue apartment Tartan's legal residence. Ninety-sixth Street was the border, the dividing line separating Carnegie Hill from Harlem, the end of the Carnegie Hill public-school district. PS 6 was the best public lower school in the city; its graduates, nearly all white, mostly went on to private high schools. Jeremiah convinced Tartan that she should keep her son in the district so that he would have his chance. Jeremiah knew the legal angles: he claimed Tartan could declare the Becker apartment her home. The two rooms off the kitchen were for her and Brad.

So Jessica Lawn, Tartan's cousin who worked for the Ginzbergs, kept the apartment she had with Tartan in her own name. She had no children needing to go to school in the white district. Jessica and Tartan shared Brad; they thought alike about him—the two women understood he was meant to do better; he was their future. They took him to visit their one male Harlem relative, Willie Lawn, a successful dental surgeon on Sugar Hill. He, too, thought Brad had promise. Willie admired his quickness, his light color; he told the women they were right, the boy could do well. It was understood that Jessica and Tartan couldn't locate on Sugar Hill; they would be out of place—there was real Harlem money up there. Willie Lawn found them a nice four-room apartment in Italian Harlem near First Avenue and 114th Street. "It's good that it's a little out-of-the-way," he informed his cousins. "Brad won't be growing up in the thick of Harlem. Keep him away from the element—mostly Italians live there. And I'll give you another idea—on Sundays take him to Holy Trinity in Yorkville."

Tartan and Jessica gave Brad everything: he lacked for nothing. But in the presence of his mother and aunt, he felt a stillness settle over him, a torpor—a sense of nonbeing; at times he was afraid to move his arms and legs near the women. He never laughed where they could hear, or raised his voice. He was sure they had a secret they never told him—he imagined that they wanted him *emptied* of an unimaginable sin so deep it could never be spoken. He thought there was a bad smell connected to that sin. At night he was wakened by his mother's guttural shouts; he crawled into her bed, she stirred in her nightmare, and he detected the bad smell on her. The night, his closeness to her, and her loud sounds frightened him. Daylight was different. A meeker time. They lowered their voices, even whispered, those big women, when they conversed with him. Tartan turned off the dining-room radio when she heard him listening to the blues; cheap music, she called it. Her continuous editing of life—"That's wrong for nice colored folks"—provided Brad with no clue as to how he was to walk toward that future, so big, so suffocating.

It didn't occur to Brad that he had claims on the present. He never mentioned to Tartan that he was the only boy in his class who brought no pals home. PS 6 was a small school then. During those sleepy tail-end-of-the-depression days, birthdays were simple; Brad was invited to enough of the afternoon parties. But how could he bring boys back to a place blocks out of the district? And who would have gone to Harlem?

He said nothing, and nobody—neither his mother nor the boys from PS 6—seemed to expect that he would return their hospitality. Nothing was ever asked, directly, of Brad. Before his tenth birthday he felt an unease—a dizziness. Days in advance of it he had continuous attacks of runny bowels he told no one about. During the school week Tartan and her son slept in the two maids' rooms off the Beckers' kitchen to keep Brad legal for PS 6. Brad inspected the social possibilities of his small "legal" bedroom, but on Friday afternoons, the day of school dates, the fishy, iodine odor of steaming shrimp stank it up. Also, he was never really sure that the room was his.

Tartan often remarked that her son was a boy who could have no complaints. At the Saturday surprise birthday lunch Anita Becker arranged for him in her Fifth Avenue apartment, Brad experienced his own meanness: he felt nothing but sadness as he pushed the creamed chicken and peas onto his fork. Instead of his schoolmates, the guests were his mother, Jessica Lawn, Mrs. Becker, and Katy. Jeremiah Becker had a brown leather jacket sent over from Davega's sports store. Mrs. Becker was a big believer in books; she gave him a child's edition of *The Iliad*. On her advice Tartan and Jessica had pooled their resources, and with Brad's future in mind, they had bought him *The Book of Knowledge*. "You are lucky," Tartan reminded him, while slicing the chocolate fudge birthday cake that was her specialty. Brad stuffed a piece thick with icing into his mouth; his stomach knotted; he was afraid he was going to throw up. He remembered the noise, the free way his friends raced from room to room in regular PS 6 birthday parties; Brad had no place to rest his fury, his inchoate rage, his abiding gratitude and dark, dizzying love.

Katy tapped his chicken-wing thin shoulders, reached down for his hand, opened his fist, and put her gift inside—her spy ring. "For Wild Bill from Calamity," she whispered. They had seen the Jean Arthur movie about Wild Bill Hickok and Calamity Jane; those were their code names for each other. He looked at her dark, round eyes, her wavy hair—at times she seemed a freckled miniature of Anita Becker. She was his jailer. His breath. Deliverance!

No one noticed—not Gabe, not Snowball, not the rest of the gang—that when they played with Brad it was through Katy: she was the negotiator. It seemed natural to them that Brad joined in when they visited Katy at the Becker apartment. And all of life's summers seemed to flow toward the Long Island Sound. It felt normal that Brad should also live at Indian Path.

Brad kept score. Which incidents seemed to go in his favor and which accrued to Katy's were of enormous interest to him. His chief obsession was those weekend times when Jeremiah Becker took over. True, Brad got to go along with Katy and Jim to special shows at the Capitol and the Paramount, and to the early dinners in Chinatown afterward. But he was excluded from Saturday-morning baseball pitching. Why? Oh God, why? Brad raged to himself from his Central Park vantage point, alone and hidden behind dense bushes at the edge of the playing field. Why did Jeremiah Becker never ask him to play baseball?

He watched Jeremiah pitching balls to Jim and even some to Katy, who was reluctant—she didn't know how to bat or run—she was just there as an extra. He would listen to Jeremiah call out to his son, "Oh boy, you hit a great one," and Brad wept.

"Jim hates me," Brad later insisted to Katy.

"His frowns don't mean anything—Jim's always sullen to me." Katy dismissed his complaint against her older brother as though she and Brad were one and the same. He said nothing, but Brad felt bitter because when it came to Jim Katy distanced herself from him: she always defended her brother.

When Brad realized that Jeremiah was taking Jim and Katy to games at Yankee Stadium, his solitary, despairing heart finally broke. His dream that he, not Jim, was the elected one crashed. The long, involved narrative he had worked out in his head in which he was the secret son of Jeremiah and Tartan (this would account for his light skin), that there was a hidden will Jeremiah would reveal to him on his deathbed designating him part heir (along with Katy and Jim) to Indian Path, couldn't survive the hard fact of his banishment from baseball practice.

Brad had had ample material for his hidden scenario. During the Connecticut summer dog days when Jeremiah went fishing with Brad on the Gohonk River—the Indian Path pier float was at the exact point where the Gohonk, running down from Danbury, emptied into the mouth of the Sound—Brad was the only one to sit in the rowboat while Jeremiah fished. Jeremiah taught him, not Jim, how to scale fish, how to deftly spear the juicy worms onto the double-hooked fly. He would take Brad in the car with him when he went to his favorite bait store in East Norwalk. Occasionally, in the car Jeremiah would sound like Brad's cousin, Willie Lawn. "You might think one day about set-tling in Connecticut. You are a bright boy—you might even consider going into business for yourself—there's a better element up here. There's more than one road to Rome, Brad." Without it being spelled out, Brad understood that "the element" Willie Lawn and Jeremiah Becker were re-ferring to had to do with Harlem and being Negro. But the words were never spoken, and he knew, instinctively, he wasn't meant to ask them to be clear. Jeremiah would drive back the long way, through the outskirts of East Norwalk, slowly passing country streets with good houses on them, so that Brad could clearly see that Negroes lived in them. But Brad hated those houses—they weren't good enough: they weren't Indian Path.

Jeremiah, a Fatima dangling between his nicotine-stained thumb and forefinger, wearing a crumpled white duck hat with a green plastic visor brim, a worn Viyella plaid sport shirt from Sulka's, and faded khaki pants, did the talking in the gray, salty-smelling boat. Brad was his listener. He felt superior to Katy because she had to come to him, and through his giving, editing, and withholding, she had to get the bits and pieces of her father's story. Though Brad realized Jeremiah had handed him something that Katy couldn't get directly, he had no more idea why Jeremiah wouldn't tell his youth to Katy and Jim than he knew why he had been excluded from baseball practice.

Katy would beg him, "Tell me, tell me what Daddy said." Brad always felt guilty for wanting to withhold a little bit for himself; he would end up giving her everything he had learned from sitting in the boat. Neither Brad nor Katy ever realized that the stories Brad relayed to her had very little to do with Jeremiah's real life.

▼ ▼ ▼

If Jeremiah thought directly about Brad, it was to cast him as a Negro version of the Jewish orphan he had come to believe—after acquiring Indian Path—that he had been. At the pinnacle of his financial success, Jeremiah had begun to enjoy looking back at his start—particularly while fishing—as though his rise had paralleled his favorite nine-teenth-century novel. Some days he saw himself as Oliver Twist; he liked passing on nuggets of Dickensian truths to Brad as cautionary tales. Other hot, dazy Connecticut summer rowboat afternoons, he liked quoting to Brad passages he knew by heart from Turgenev's *A Hunter's Sketches*; in a more melancholy mood he would recite Matthew Arnold. He felt he had overshielded Jim, who warred with him and took Deerfield and a future at Harvard for granted. One ninety-six-degree afternoon he recommended to Brad, as though he was Jeremiah's alter ego, and of no particular chronological age, *The History of the Venetian Republic*, and on another, equally sultry day, Keats's "When I Have Fears." Indian Path itself was a hymn to a nineteenth-century summer—both Jeremiah and Anita had been possessed of an eye good enough to reclaim the Olmsted grounds of the sprawling, sloping Connecticut estate with its brave trees grand enough to break your heart.

Though neither Brad nor Katy realized they were getting Jeremiah's truths at a slant, there were some phrases Katy immediately questioned. "He said," Brad recounted to her, after a Tolstoyan hour of fishing, " 'Would that I had the simple cares of a simple postman.' "

"He said *that*? Huh." By the way Katy stared at him and shook her head, Brad immediately understood he had brought her a wrong sentence.

▼　▼　▼

While Jeremiah had recast himself, the oldest Becker son, as a sort of Atlas who had uplifted the destiny of all his relatives, his middle brother—Katy's uncle Henry

Becker—the constitutional-law professor who hobnobbed with Brandeis and Frankfurter—had been working on another script. Henry liked a scenario in which the Beckers were descended from aristocrats; as communication at Indian Path was chaotic, there was no one to notice that Henry's family romance didn't jibe with Jeremiah's Jewish Horatio Alger story.

"Henry is a snob," Jeremiah would remark to Anita concerning his brother's pre–World War II transatlantic ship crossings for the purpose of connecting the American Beckers to a fancy Viennese tree of Beckers. Henry always traveled on the Cunard line and spent most of his free summer time in Oxford. "Henry thinks he is British," Jeremiah would occasionally say cryptically. What he left unsaid was that his middle brother was a homosexual and a shoe fetishist, and this, from time to time, had interfered with his ambition to become another Brandeis. The most Jeremiah said on the subject was that his brother had some odd habits and that it was just as well he had never married.

David Becker had neither the capacity to become a big industrialist like Jeremiah nor a distinguished legal scholar like Henry. The two older brothers had decided that the best thing to do with David was to send him to Dartmouth and gently ease him into a judgeship. That accomplished, David married a shy, remote young woman—a bookish *isolata* who stared dreamily out the window. David, wanting to be loved, found no love. He was the sweetest of the brothers; he clung to his mother and brought her cashmere sweaters and gladiolas until the day of her death.

"We are lawyers, not restaurateurs," the two older brothers complained to David after discovering he had opened a restaurant in midtown. David told them he needed a place to meet his friends. The Beckers were used to immediately living out whatever script crossed their minds; though they disapproved, they left David alone. In the family powwow at Indian Path so vaguely recalled by Brad, Dr. Grutman—the psychiatrist connected to Mayo Clinic—where Davy landed—told the two older Beckers that their big mistake was in not visiting Davy at his restaurant.

According to Grutman, Davy had bought his immense barn of a summer hotel in chagrin. He had set up a system in which the guests were given pails, ammonia, and cleaning mops so they could share in the cleaning of their bedrooms. After this quirk was discovered, he was put in the psychiatric ward of a local hospital; Jeremiah and Henry then immediately had him transferred to Mayo.

"Your brother is a loving man, and he craves being loved." Grutman detailed to Jeremiah and Henry how their habits—evening sessions in Jeremiah's New York living room spent arguing law before an imaginary Supreme Court, leaving out Davy as "not up to it"—hadn't helped. "Davy tells me you two never invited him in as a bridge partner. Is this true? Nor to your English croquet tournaments—you pay his bills, but that's not love." Grutman continued, "You are much too competitive a family. Davy tells me you call him 'son'—he is not your son but your brother."

"By twelve years. So why, Dr. Grutman, do you send me the bills for my brother's special sessions with you?" Jeremiah's tone was acerbic.

"You chose to give him extra care," Grutman went on

evenly. He paused and looked out the north windows at the rolling English lawns ending abruptly at the Sound seawall, which had been partially ripped up by bad hurricanes. "You don't consider this place a form of competition?" Grutman calculated one hundred and fifty acres, easy, of straight waterfront property.

"Why do you think your brother needed to buy the Ash Lake Hotel?"

Anita Becker saw her husband's face turn dark, blotchy red. Hearing Grutman—an outsider—involve his beloved Indian Path with his brother's bizarre hotel, using it as a symbol of poor Davy's madness, was more than he could bear. Meanwhile Henry, scowling, appeared ready to leave. Anita was aware Henry never had related to Indian Path—he was fond of his hotel suite on lower Fifth Avenue near Washington Square, and of his summers in Oxford—she understood his annoyance that Grutman was emphasizing Jeremiah's industrial achievements as the root of Davy's problems. Henry, she recognized, would have preferred Davy's downfall to have come from envy of his brilliance as a law professor. "Sit down, Henry," Anita commanded.

Henry admired his stylish, fey sister-in-law; she was the only relative who had influence over him. So he sat down.

"Why, Dr. Grutman," Anita continued softly (it was this speech Brad had etched in his mind, wrongly connecting it to Tartan, who had actually been in the city that weekend), "you have made a mistake. We are a simple family. My sisters suffered greatly in the depression. And they live at Indian Path. You do not understand—this is our home. Only our relatives and the children's friends come here.

How could this pretty place be the trouble? Look at this
worn old furniture. We are plain people. Our children go
to public school—"

Katy jabbed Brad in his ribs. "PS 6," she whispered.
"They are telling the doctor we go to PS 6."

Brad straightened his back against the wooden slats of
the swing. He was thrilled that news of their school had
entered into the adult conference taking place in the living
room, though he was confused as to the reason—what did
his school have to do with Katy's Uncle Davy going crazy?
"What does it mean?"

Katy knew odd things that could not be found in *The
Book of Knowledge*. Brad noticed that even Jim occasionally
asked her questions; sometimes her mother asked her
opinion.

"It means," Katy interpreted for him, "that there is
something important about our going to PS 6. It is the right
thing to do."

▼ ▼ ▼

Dr. Grutman reacted to Anita Becker's charm; he began to
see the estate through her eyes. Her silky black hair was
wound into a simple bun at the nape of her neck. In the
country she wore no makeup, no jewelry except her gold
wedding band. She was dressed in a pale green voile pleated
summer dress and olive leather sandals. She seemed to be
a sincere woman—Indian Path shrank to the size she had
suggested to him, he saw the scruffy bad spots in the main
sofa—then he looked again out the window and saw the
rolling acres of cleanly clipped lawn. It suddenly popped
out, though he hadn't meant to say it. Well, why not? They

were all Jews. "I guess I have always thought of this as Protestant territory."

Anita walked over to Jeremiah and firmly put her arm through his. "Dr. Grutman"—she laughed—"do you want us to be afraid of the mistaken ideas of some poor Yankee farmer? Jeremiah has never been afraid to go forward"—she paused to grasp his arm even more tightly, and she used the phrase the Ginzberg sisters had adopted for her good choices in Olga Zweicky's Antique Store—"we are front-runners. Why, other Jews should be grateful to us for settling in the good spots. Since when is it a sin to pick the best?"

Grutman surveyed the overly large double living rooms; there seemed to be too many doors with unclaimed, overly large dogs sniffing through them; Grutman couldn't locate in his mind who was a relative, who was the help, and to whom the scattershot collection of children belonged. These people were not graspable. Their modulated voices were neither New York nor not–New York. He had no verbal bridge by which to reach them. Jeremiah stood by his wife and grinned. He was a short man—no taller than Anita Becker. He had the same dark hair and eyes as she—they were one of those couples who had come to resemble each other. Grutman didn't continue the conversation. They were not people who would listen.

▼ ▼ ▼

The scene about Katy's Uncle Davy was mixed up in Brad's mind with seeing his mother on a scorching afternoon in a thin sleeveless dress at the end of the pier—some weekends she came to Indian Path to help out—embracing Jeremiah.

The weather was so clammy that when she raised her arms to his neck Brad saw the matted hair in her unshaved armpits, little black damp curls like black flowers or snails. Later it all became so blurry in his head he couldn't remember where he had been standing when he saw Jeremiah and Tartan touching and kissing, but he was sure he had seen it. Only he had to first recall the business about Uncle Davy and Katy saying PS 6 was important in order to have a vivid memory of it.

▼ ▼ ▼

Eventually Davy Becker stabilized and returned home. He bought no more failing hotels; instead, at Christmas he ordered two thousand engraved Christmas cards from Cartier's and sent them to all his friends. In the cards to the family—there were separate ones sent to Katy and Jim—he included a memo defending his business judgments, starting with his purchase of the midtown Maison Voltaire restaurant. Though it had seemed to be a financial bust at the time, he explained in his memo that had he been able to hold out, the site would have been perfect. "Jeremiah," he wrote to his brother, "my real-estate instincts were sound. The Four Seasons has now replaced my Voltaire."

After that, every Christmas he would send the family his estimate of the Four Seasons' annual net profit tucked between the Cartier Season's Greetings card and its tissue.

Anita Becker was not a woman to be easily sized up. Fluid, eluding category, she lived mostly in her head or through her eyes and sense of style. When she made occasional swift forays into reality, as with Dr. Grutman, she was formidable and took command. Jeremiah knew his wife dazzled strangers—he was proud of her for that—they gave each other plenty of sexual rope and silently went their separate ways with no talk about it. He found her aloofness and social indifference useful to him; more important, he admired them.

She had told Dr. Grutman the truth: Indian Path was only for family. When Jeremiah's Protestant business associates fished for a weekend invitation he would flash his secure, dark-eyed smile, and say, almost humbly, as though he were henpecked, "Anita won't permit business entertaining—one weekend a year she allows me my croquet tournament—will you come then?"

Though he never consciously formulated it, Jeremiah operated outside of class—in Anita he had the perfect wife: oblivious to social demands, she was invulnerable to society's roadblocks. Unlike his brother Henry, Jeremiah had no interest in drumming up fancy Austrian relatives; despite his mistaken tendency to rummage in Victorian novels to find models for his children's future, he himself was singularly of the twentieth century—everything about him and Anita was modernist and related to style. German Jews bored him; he went his own way. He lived alongside the gentile community in Connecticut but never attempted to be of it, though in Bar Harbor he started an advanced program for cancer research and in Fort Worth was guest of honor at a barbecue thrown for him by the oil crowd.

Jeremiah and Anita were friendly with some of the cosmopolitan Jews who lived in Sound towns near Indian Path. The woman director for the avant-garde Green Gazebo Theater frequently—without warning—dropped by for advice. Jeremiah didn't share Anita's fondness for abstract theater—he preferred Theater Guild Monday-night openings in Westport—and he didn't want the Green Gazebo crowd borrowing his Indian Path barn for their productions. But he gave them practical tips on how to set up their donor fund-raising for the Gazebo in the right way.

In his middle years, at the height of his powers, he began to obsess about his childhood, though at the time it had not seemed so, as having been lonely. The opposite was more likely: that Jeremiah had experienced his first sensations of disquieting isolation when he crossed the line between being successful and becoming extraordinarily rich.

Only in retrospect did Jeremiah's rise make him feel he had failed slightly. In the heart of the depression he had accomplished the unthinkable. He had owned no stocks and lost nothing in the crash. He walked in alone to meet with the Protestant bankers, and it was his optimism, his steadiness in a bad time, that helped convince them to stake him the huge sums necessary to take over a good piece of collapsed eastern seaboard Protestant industry: Jeremiah had seen the opportunity and had seized it.

He became a legend: a Jewish lawyer who had used Protestant money to buy out the WASPs. Jeremiah's corporate boards were Protestant; his lawyers remained Jewish. He liked smart inventors, and he had a gift for getting the cream of the crop before Du Pont could lay hands on them. New York and Connecticut Republicans came to Indian Path in the afternoons—Anita didn't want them staying on for dinner; she had no intention of meeting their wives—and Jeremiah advised them, but he remained to one side of politics. He understood Anita, how to please her. Despite her increasing reclusiveness, she had desires. She yearned to meet Toscanini; Jeremiah invited him to Indian Path.

▼ ▼ ▼

Katy tried to find the key to her mother's mood swings; she watched everything. She noticed an odd calm come over Indian Path a July afternoon the summer before Pearl Harbor. Anita, with a cardigan hung loosely over her shoulders, had been pacing the double living room; she walked rapidly to the east porch, then to the west. She walked outside, then silently went down to the breakwater. Her sisters, Marcie and Jillian, always hovering near her, followed behind. Katy stared at the straight backs of the three sisters waiting with their arms folded toward the sea. Why the stillness in the family? Was a relative ill? An electric storm coming in over the Sound?

Her mother raced up the lawn back to the house as soon as she saw Pat Mallard nose the green Packard through the front gate; her father and some of his men were in the backseat. Jeremiah emerged from the car holding on to the *Herald Tribune* and a Fatima; he had a deep grin the width of his face, and his dark eyes were light with triumph.

Well, Katy reasoned, nobody was dead.

Right on the east porch he told her mother. "We have the West Virginia coal mines—they signed."

Anita let out an uncharacteristic yell. "*Whoopee! Whoopee! We've got the mines!*" Right in front of everyone, she danced an uninhibited little jig, pulling Jeremiah into her impromptu dance. Suddenly there was noise and motion; Jeremiah kept laughing; Tartan brought out Scotch and ice for him and his men. Watching her parents' flamboyant gaiety, it occurred to Katy how young and good-looking they were. Even if they rarely took their trips together, she reasoned, there was something deep between them.

Katy collected "pieces" of things she observed and phrases she heard, and she kept them in her head, just as she kept her first pick—the blue vase from Olga Zweicky's antique store—in her colored-glass collection. The pieces didn't always fit. Anita told her that people were dying of starvation in parts of the country; it was why she voted American Labor Party, so that workers would have more. She even took Katy and Jim to see *The River*, a documentary about poverty in the South. How did her mother's unabashed, squealing delight over the adventure of the mines, Katy wondered, tally with her desire to help the workers? How could the Beckers own the coal mines and be on the side of the miners?

Katy had sorted out the family balance—her father and his brothers voted Republican; her mother's family voted Democrat. It evened out, the same way Jim's being a boy and her a girl made the Beckers a symmetrical family. She sensed that in Anita's holding out for the American Labor Party versus Jeremiah's holding out against Roosevelt, a sort of secret sexual ricochet was going on. Katy was curious about her parents' sex life; she felt some essential part of the family puzzle was missing.

She also collected pieces of her father's conversation with his men. She overheard him telling them that despite his being a lawyer he made a point of never negotiating for himself; he said this to them during their porch discussion about who would go to West Virginia to clear up the legal disputes with the local authorities concerning his purchase of the mines. "I'm not sending a New York Jewish lawyer into West Virginia to be slaughtered by *them*—I'm not an ass," she heard him argue. "We'll send down a Washington firm."

Katy liked the swiftness of his sentences when he talked to his men better than the lengthy Keats quotes Brad brought her back from his fishing hour with Jeremiah:

> *"When I have fears that I may cease to be*
> *Before my pen has glean'd my teeming brain,*
> *Before high pil'd books, in charactry,*
> *Hold like rich garners the full ripen'd grain . . ."*

Brad would sing out the entire sonnet, finishing with a flourish:

> *"Of the wide world I stand alone, and sink,*
> *Till Love and Fame to nothingness do sink."*

"Huh, he thinks love and fame are nothing?" Katy snapped her Black Jack gum against her front teeth. "So if it's nothing, why is it on his mind?"

▼ ▼ ▼

Jeremiah Becker had disliked Grutman when he had visited Indian Path to discuss Davy's treatment at the Mayo, but he continued to remember him. A few summers later, while he was playing cards on the west porch with his own doctor, he amazed Saul Koenig by asking him to set up a

106

consultation for himself with a psychiatrist. "The best, Saul."

Koenig's father had been a great doctor on the Lower East Side in the early days; Saul, a superb diagnostician, had lost his good hospital connections after an abortion scandal—he had tried to do a favor for a patient. It hadn't helped Koenig that he had never married, lived in bachelor quarters in the Hotel Delmonico, and was known for his variety of women and fondness for going to the races with writers like John O'Hara who had no connection to the world of established New York Jewish-backed hospitals he was meant to frequent. Before he lost his standing he had also done a favor for Anita Becker—she hadn't wanted a third child; Koenig had arranged for a curettage on medical grounds. Jeremiah was in his debt.

Jeremiah minced no words with Schumacher, the psychiatrist Koenig had picked for him. He walked hatless into his office, a Fatima between thumb and forefinger; he never raised his voice, he spoke rapidly, and he gave no notice of having taken in the physical details of the balding, big-shouldered, tweed-jacketed doctor.

Schumacher was too embarrassed—why did he feel so intimidated by a businessman?—to tell Becker that it was customary to sit down during the session.

"Let me give you the family history. My sister's son killed himself by swallowing pills in a Times Square hotel the night after he was informed of his admission to MIT. Eddie was valedictorian of his class. A bit overinvolved with his mother—a gloomy woman—but being first in class is nothing to kill yourself about. Now, Dr. Schumacher, I want to be straight with you. That's where it is with my sister. As for my brother Henry, until the war prevented it he spent his summers sleeping with British dons. He has a shoe fetish—he has a whole room of men's shoes. Henry is a brilliant scholar—I don't want to subtract in this thumbnail sketch from his distinction—but he always came back home with a British accent and their antiques. We are American, not British; do you see what I mean, Dr. Schumacher? I would say that Henry's fine mind is tainted with grandiosity—and that is why he has failed to become another Brandeis—also the fetishism. About Henry—you are following my drift?"

Schumacher nodded.

"I also detect in Henry more than a touch of sadism. I've argued with him about his perverse overly low grading of his students' papers—"

"I follow your shoe drift—but why are you supervising your brother's law courses? Dr. Koenig told me you are—"

"In industry? Well, yes." Jeremiah gave him no time to finish his sentence. "But Becker, Becker, and Becker, my law firm, remains. There is where I start the mornings. I don't supervise Henry. About the student papers, it's a little game we've always played—Henry argues one position, I the other. A type of tennis match." Jeremiah paused. "Henry has a tendency toward myth making; he's overly fond of Dostoyevski—"

"Is there something wrong with Dostoyevski?"

"Dr. Schumacher, in the end, it's always Tolstoy." Jeremiah made an impatient gesture with his hand.

"But I didn't come here to discuss literature.

Henry—because of his condition vis-à-vis the romantic aspects of his life—never has understood that I am a family man and I have family obligations. He never approved of my entry into industry. He had a dream—because in my early days I was particularly known for my briefs—our firm's rep was that we were lawyers' lawyers—that the two of us would always be together as two great legal minds. 'O Jeremiah,' he would say, 'those briefs! I was so proud of you. Not a lawyer in Manhattan can come near you in writing briefs—you made works of art! You hit high C! It was like perfectly pitched Mozart! Think what you could have been!' "

"But you didn't concur?"

"I'm not a purist. Just because you do a thing well doesn't mean you have to stay fixed at that level. Money's a reality, but in the end, the real money's in the imagination. In making things change—in moving forward." Jeremiah abruptly sat down and put his face amazingly close to Schumacher's. "Achieving something new that's necessary, that has a point to it, is better than a perfect brief."

Schumacher didn't interfere with Jeremiah's long pauses.

"Dr. Koenig told you about my younger brother's—Davy's—breakdown? Our early lives weren't completely easy. Our mother was a frail woman who didn't cope well, and our father was a black sheep. By the time I was twenty-two and back from France, I had paid all his debts—I sent the two boys through law school."

"Boys?"

"Henry and Davy. But there was nothing so remarkable, or unremarkable, about our family to have caused such a peculiar lack of stability in my brothers. We three went to De Witt Clinton High School. Davy always was excitable. When my troop train pulled out to embark for France, Davy jumped aboard. He was ten. I had to push him off. Now, Dr. Schumacher"—again Jeremiah leaned forward—"speaking man to man, you can well imagine, without my unnecessarily detailing it, there was nothing enviable about being a simple private in the trenches. Nor glory in being gassed. I was three years in a *château* hospital. As soon as I could—and I know, because I remember, some of my early letters home possessed a sadness—when I recovered I stressed the optimistic. The war was an eye-opener for me. I was the only Jewish man in our unit—very few of our men survived, and I owe my life to those Protestant boys. I sent home pictures of my buddies recuperating with me in the *château*, which was an extraordinarily fine-looking place, and I described the trips I was finally able to take to Paris, and I listed the objects I had bought to bring home. Limoges. I wrote to my brothers, 'Hold on, boys, and it will all be settled when I come back.' " Again Jeremiah paused. "I meant their futures. Davy misinterpreted the reality of war—he thought I had had something he did not."

"And did you settle their futures for them?"

"I went to work for a small Fifth Avenue Jewish firm—then a year later, I saw an opportunity for myself and my younger brothers—I took it over, though I kept on the men who had owned it, and I called it Becker, Becker, and Becker . . ." Jeremiah looked boyish; he had that uneven grin that gave him an odd air of both intimacy and remoteness. "I still believed then in tidy, simple solutions."

"How did you come to own the firm so fast?" Schumacher felt the cool wash of the Becker charm Koenig had described to him; Jeremiah was disarming—his ever-moving dark brown eyes combined a child's alertness with Manhattan savvy.

"Oh, I couldn't begin to remember how it happened. Luck. Then, you know, it was the twenties. But I'm not here to talk about my career. I've come to get your professional opinion as to whether this streak of instability that has cropped up in my brothers and sister could be inherited—will it affect my children?"

"Your son and daughter have you. And their mother."

"Then these things are not inherited? Madness in the family is just an old wives' tale?"

"What are your children like?"

"They have fine minds." Jeremiah hesitated. "The boy's a little oversensitive—I'm trying to instill self-confidence in him. Katy's more willful. I see Anita and me in them." Jeremiah stopped; he now took in the office furnishings. He did not mind the framed photograph of Freud, even though he would have felt greater confidence had Schumacher limited himself to hanging his framed medical degrees. Jeremiah felt dubious about the mental abilities of lawyers who kept framed phrases of Lincoln on their office walls.

"Anita is an extraordinary woman. My son and daughter are as physically good-looking as a boy and girl need be, but Anita was breathtaking. *Special*. I proposed to her an hour after we met on a blind date—it was on the corner of Fortieth and Fifth, and we were headed downtown. Anita does not have, thank God, my brother's streak of irrationality—occasionally her real-estate instincts have been amazingly shrewd. She was right about Sutton Place. She had an eye for its eventual worth. I should have taken it when it was easy to be done."

"You and your wife play Monopoly? You mean Park Place? Or Boardwalk?"

"*Manhattan*, Dr. Schumacher—not Monopoly. Anita knew I should have taken Sutton Place. But she has had real problems. Koenig might have told you he had to give her help with her moods. She had a depression after the birth of each child. Anita has had some unaccounted sadnesses . . ." Jeremiah stared beyond Schumacher to the wall of his Impressionist reproductions. "She recoils from intimacy."

Schumacher had been looking for a way to turn the direction of the discussion back to Jeremiah Becker; the man had requested a consultation but, so far, had discussed none of his own problems. "Then, the lack of physicality in your marriage must be difficult on you?"

Schumacher regretted his premature leap.

Jeremiah immediately shut him out, retreating into remoteness. "I have, Dr. Schumacher, never lacked for personal companionship. Men don't." Abruptly he stood up to go.

Schumacher understood that Becker was determining when the consultation should be over. Schumacher felt hesitant. He thought maybe he *should* interfere, make a suggestion—did Jeremiah Becker need his help? Schumacher had never treated an industrialist—sometimes the wife, but never the man. He wondered if Becker had a steady mistress, and if so—what sort of woman had he chosen?

Before Schumacher could think of what to say, Jeremiah wheeled around and voiced his only partially spoken preoccupations concerning his children. "Indian Path's a true family place. A fine place."

CHAPTER

9

CHRISTMAS WAS THE ONE TIME, WHEN Brad looked back on it, that he remembered feeling he had the edge on Katy. December two years after the war began particularly stood out in his mind.

Manhattan still had deep snowfalls then. Jeremiah came in late on the night of the twenty-fourth, carrying in his wet, cold hands big gift-wrapped boxes with dusts of snow on them. The thin red-and-green-striped shiny paper belonged to Saks Fifth Avenue; Brad knew from Tartan that it was a very expensive department store. In the Saks boxes were navy cardigans with mufflers and earmuffs for Brad and Jim, and a brooch for Tartan. Brad noticed that Katy's present, a girl's caramel-colored leather writing case with a matching key-locked diary, came from a different place—Jay Thorpe's—and he saw Jeremiah slip into Anita Becker's hand a tiny box, which she murmured she would open later. Jeremiah's big surprise for the family was a cumbersome fish tank with tissue-thin, glittering rose-and-amber fish.

"An oversized aquarium," Anita exploded. "More mess in the living room!" She and Tartan immediately moved it to an unused corner of the breakfast nook. Despite the plenitude of boxes in heavily embossed paper trimmed with gold-shot tinsel, there was a vague, undecided quality about Christmas at the Beckers'.

On the morning of the twenty-fifth, Anita Becker's father called to say that he would be dropping by; Anita and Tartan immediately moved the fat, overloaded Christmas tree into Brad's legal bedroom. The night of the twenty-fourth, Jeremiah, Jim, Katy, and Brad had decorated its piny boughs; the four of them had enthusiastically arranged the blinking lights, stalactite ornaments, hanging wooden Siberian winter scenes, and little Rhineland gingerbread people on the tree's prickly-needled branches. Tartan explained to him that the family didn't want to offend the religious customs of Katy's grandfather. In revenge for being forced to give up his room as a storage place for the huge tree, Brad lay on his bed and picked off all the marzipan and chocolate ornaments. He ate them slowly, one by one, and left none for Katy or Jim.

Later in the day, after Katy's grandfather had come and gone, Jeremiah went to his brother Davy's eggnog party—Davy had recently been discharged from the Mayo Clinic—and Jim went with him. Brad noticed that Anita Becker wasn't dressed for anything. She wore the same sweater and skirt as on ordinary days. Brad watched the way she moodily folded her legs beneath her in the double club chair by the living-room corner window; she seemed to want to spend the holiday listening to Bach on WQXR. Almost as an afterthought, Tartan asked her if Katy could join the Culvers at their cousin Willie Lawn's big Christmas dinner on Sugar Hill. Without looking up, Anita nodded an absentminded assent.

▼ ▼ ▼

"Run it off, Brad," Willie Lawn had said to him, after Brad had drunk a glass of eggnog. "Your face is pea green—get a touch of air."

Brad zipped up his Davega leather jacket and put on his showy new earmuffs; outside he raced past the block of townhouses toward Saint Nicholas Avenue. He thrust his head forward and down to dodge snowballs flying in his face—he was caught in a crossfire between two gangs—but he knew the icy poufs being pelted weren't meant to single him out: he didn't feel a loner. He felt good up here. Willie Lawn was chief dental surgeon for the rich colored people who lived on the hill. Jessica and Tartan had reminded him their cousin was a man to be proud of; they'd arrived for the dinner splendidly got up. His mother sported the same sort of small, round tilted felt hat and fur animal with blue glassy eyes, tail snapped into his mouth around her neck, that Anita Becker wore when she visited *her* relatives.

But no dinner at the Beckers' was ever as magnificent as Willie Lawn's feast after the mass at Saint Philip's Church. Coming in from the cold snap, with the winds blowing in from the Hudson, Brad relished the substance of his cousin's limestone house with its brownstone touches. He paused

116

at the first-floor landing to admire the dark stained-glass window, he liked running his hand along the polished heavy oak stair rail; the house exuded plentifulness.

And there, seated at the long, lace-covered table with its heavy cut-glass goblets and fancy china, was Katy, squashed between twelve of his relatives. Tartan had dolled her up in a heavy brown velvet jumper—only the yoke and sleeves of her pale blue blouse were visible beneath it. Tartan had no daughter; she had wanted to show off her charge to her fancy relatives. Determined to get the best result, she had brushed Katy's hair a full hour until it broke into waves of brown-black silk. Brad noted, and was amazed at, Katy's enthusiasm for his relatives' food; methodically she worked through the deviled eggs and multicolored fruit aspics, the wet turkey with thick giblet dressing, the creamed peas, and the whipped turnips. She then asked for slices of all the pies—mince, pumpkin, and deep-dish apple.

"Tartan laces the pumpkin with gin," Jessica said.

"Mary's a fine cook"—Willie never referred to his cousin as Tartan.

"Bourbon works better with pineapple," his wife, Sadie Lawn, added.

Brad was impressed with the gusto with which Katy had joined in the prayer before the meal: She treated it like school theater. When Willie finished, "And may the Lord protect us for the Duration, and return our boys safely home to us, and God bless this country, and God bless Roosevelt," Katy shrieked longer and louder than the rest—"Amen! Amen! Amen!"

Brad's secret desire was that Jeremiah Becker would recognize him, magically, as a member of his family; he

117

desperately wanted to be sent to Jim's prep school. On other days he had different dreams; he hoped Willie Lawn would reward his high grades by asking Brad to move in with his cousins on Sugar Hill. None of his daring projections, those years, materialized. Instead, his high grades earned him a place at Bronx Science, the public high school for smart boys.

Automatically—perhaps it had been understood from the beginning; had Brad been too dumb to understand it?—Gabe, like Jim, went on to Deerfield, while Katy and her cousin Snowball were sent on to Friends' Seminary downtown. Though at first Brad raged inwardly against going to Bronx Science, once in the enormous, all-male freshman class he felt free, like he had suddenly jumped over the moon: he was sprung. Free of Tartan and her mutterings—"black or white, their name is man"—free of the legal bedroom, of the Beckers' quixotic kindnesses. Overnight, in the Bronx, Brad became a man.

▼　▼　▼

When Katy would argue with Brad (in those days he still held on tightly to religion) that books, for her, took the place of God, she was speaking her truth—she saw religion as a summer vacation selection. She detailed for him her Julys away from Indian Path. One summer, in a Penobscot Bay French-speaking Quaker camp, she learned to ride horseback in French; the next, in a Massachusetts camp, she learned to pray to trees; the following year (at Snowball's mother's—Hewley's—suggestion), she and Snowball spent August in the Smokeys; both girls learned to ride Western style and on Sundays went to Baptist and holy roller meetings.

She confided to him that she felt her winters from the religious point of view were more Jewish; he didn't know quite what she meant. Not even after she described to him the Jewish spring festivals that she and Snowball went to near the Central Park Lake. While the older children in the small progressive reading group played Sephardic tunes on flutes, the younger ones, Roman wreaths crowning their hair, held hands and danced in a circle around an enormous wooden basket of figs, pomegranates, and apples. "Brad," she explained, "it's a modern way of being Jewish."

Katy made clear to him that she rather enjoyed reading her Scribner's children's Bible; it was also part of the modern way, meant to accommodate both Christian and Jewish children. She relished the lush, romantic illustrations of men and women in white lingerie munching purple grapes. The stories were pleasant—the villains were not bothersome; the main bad people were the Pharaoh's wicked butler and an angry, undefined mob who ganged up on Jesus; the book's plot line effortlessly passed from Old Testament to New in a muted, seamless way; a sort of ecumenical the-gang's-all-here approach. Not a book to quibble over details, this religion or that, it ended with a flourish: "I, Jesus, have sent my angel to testify to you for the churches. I am the Scion and Offspring of David, the bright, the Morning Star."

Later, thinking back on it, Brad concurred with Katy's idea that novels, not prayer, had been the unifying force nailing her to the real world of sin, damnation, and higher morality. She read voraciously, indiscriminately, then passed the books to him: *Forever Amber*, the Bobbsey Twins, the Jerry Todd adventures, *The Hobbit*. She claimed that she read to find out her own future and what had happened to the already dead. How could Brad forget those books? That time in their lives? Jointly, in the Ninety-sixth Street public library, smack on the border between Harlem and Carnegie Hill, they took their holy communion: their graduation from the upstairs children's room to the main floor was their *rite de passage* to the adult world. Whenever Brad recalled it, he remembered how Katy had pulled him toward the discovery of sex.

She began by showing him certain choice pages from a book she had found in the adult section; it had to do with dark, turgid sex. His penis became erect when she read him the sentences; his body rushed toward new sensations. Afterward—it was one of those nights that he slept in his own bedroom in his mother's Italian Harlem apartment—Brad recalled scenes from the passages Katy had thumbnailed; at first he conjured up only what she had read to him. He moved his wet, lambent fingers rhythmically in darkness; the fan whirred in warm breezes from Jefferson Park; he stared at the stiff cactus plant in the window, a cone of street light on its waxy spikes. He stuffed the sheet in his mouth so Tartan wouldn't hear his moan.

At breakfast his talk to his mother was sullen. Katy became the conduit through which titles of no interest to him other than their promise of gummy passages entered his life: *Antic Hay, Point Counter Point, Chad Hanna, Sons and Lovers, Dark Laughter, Saratoga Trunk, Kristin Lavransdatter, Anna*

Karenina, The Counterfeiters, A Portrait of Jennie, Chrome Yellow, Look Homeward, Angel, Brideshead Revisited, The Decameron.

Brad and Katy never noticed snobberies or slurs on Jews or Negroes in the books they devoured. They simply assumed the novels separated the world into two obviously distinct parts: children/grown-ups—not Jews/Christians or Negroes/whites. They were too greedily anxious to get to the dirty parts to think of criticizing the social behavior of the characters in the pages they rapidly thumbed.

Brad couldn't keep himself from moaning in the dark stairwell as Katy slowly read to him the "parts" in Zola's *Nana* describing the French courtesan's descent into nakedness on the floodlit stage of a Paris theater in front of a vast audience of men. The sex he anticipated had a futuristic awe to it; Katy had conjured a style of life in suspended, amorphous, shivering sin unrelated to Brad's explicit desiring of her. He would rub against her as he listened to Nana being despoiled, despoiled, and despoiled. Katy liked lingering over the moist details, details as moist and dark as Tartan's chocolate fudge.

Late at night, as Brad watched the whirring window fan from his small Harlem bed, Katy became the stripped Nana. He saw her naked, taller, and older, performing on the stage of Loews Seventy-second, the moving starlit ceiling and Moorish architecture a fitting frame to her luscious, imaginary Nana-like body. Her breasts became larger, her more ordinary dark brown hair turned long and russet red, exactly as it was on the cover of the Pocket Book wartime edition of *Nana*. Images from the book melded with real events. He recalled watching Tartan soap Katy's hair in the kitchen. Katy squealed at the last cold rinse: Brad caught sight of her parted legs; he saw her black pubis through her loose white cotton pants. He rhythmically masturbated himself, overwhelmed by his own smell on his fingers; then Katy's kicking legs and loose white pants faded into Nana, her transparent, gauzy stage costume was ripped off her by shadowy male hands. Now she stood alone on the stage of Loews Seventy-second, her arms stretched outward, her legs wide apart. The pubis was now black, now russet red, now black. Her breast tips were rouged round quarters, like on the Pocket Book cover. *Oh, ohhh*—he bit the sheet to keep Tartan from hearing: he shook—then it was over. The book's back jacket announced:

OF ALL LITERATURE'S GREAT COURTESANS . . . Salome—Sappho—Thais—the *one* glamorous figure at the head of the scarlet list is Emile Zola's magnificent creation, the immortal Nana! Rich men left their fortunes, their titles, their very honor at her feet—poor men left their love and even their lives. A whole world of shameless luxury surrounded her voluptuous person—she squandered fortunes, ruined lives with sublime contempt and abandon . . . No one who saw the matchless screen portrayal of Emile Zola by Mr. Paul Muni should miss reading this masterpiece . . . This Pocket BOOK edition is complete, unexpurgated, translated from the original French. Pocket Books Inc. KIND TO YOUR POCKET, KIND TO YOUR POCKET BOOK

Brad felt amazingly satisfied when Nana, deserted by her lovers, went down, down, down in the world. The idea that one could be amoral and go up, up, up in society had not yet occurred to him—it was Katy who, one day, said, "Well, why not up?"

The war was in full swing. Jeremiah was elated that his Perfect Wireless Time System had been taken up by the navy for use in their ships: "I knew it all along—the only completely accurate nonelectric time system in the universe!" He was in Washington advising the War Naval Board, getting his naval *E*'s for Excellence, and having photos taken of himself with generals taller than he. Anita was gone for patches of time to visit Jim in army boot camp. There was only one gardener, plus Gwindel—Tartan had contempt for him, he wasn't her kind of Negro, he wore a stocking cap over his grayed, Vaselined head and he cooked greasy, but he was the only houseman Anita could locate. Anita gave up competing with the war effort after a briefly hired temperamental Hungarian couple rammed the Becker station wagon into the police station in the center of town; they'd been on a drinking spree.

Indian Path took on a wild, overgrown look. Uncut, the double-lilac bushes bloomed into a purple-and-white forest; the roses proliferated—nobody any longer remembered why, before the war, so many gardeners had been necessary. With Jim gone, Anita trailing after him, and Jeremiah in Washington, it was unclear who, other than Gwindel and the dogs, still lived at Indian Path.

Anita's younger sisters, Marcie and Jillian, their men in the service, were there during the summer months to hold down the fort. They ran the Fresh Air Fund camp Anita had set up on the grounds, adding their own kids to the pack of twenty. Gwindel puttered in the Big House,

moving, as Tartan put it, the dust from one room to another; at night, in the Big House, he drew shut the heavy
blackout curtains obligatory for places directly on the
Sound. Katy and Brad were deployed as weekly food cour-
iers—there were no gas coupons with which to send Pat
in the green Packard up to Indian Path with the provisions
of sugar and meat Tartan wangled from her Harlem food
bunks. Saturday mornings, Katy and Brad boarded the
empty early train at 125th Street; they carried with them
Tartan's ice-packed bags of provisions and loaves of date
and nut bread she'd cooked for the campers.

Brad always remembered the year; it was the summer
the war ended. It started at seven o'clock on a Saturday
morning—he still saw the way Katy looked as he ran toward her with Tartan's packages smelling of cooked food.
She was waiting for him, standing still on the elevated tracks
of the Grand Central, with the unmistakable brave look in
her dark round eyes of a fourteen-year-old girl abruptly
and untragically left to her own devices. Her dark hair was
held back in a red chenille snood dotted with pom-poms;
in her starched white cotton blouse, navy skirt, and red-
and-white spike-heeled spectator pumps, she struck
Brad as being amazingly *sotto voce* patriotic. Almost military.

The train was nearly empty—two sailors were dozing in
the front row. Brad slept until New Rochelle. Then Katy
called out from the john for him to come and help her. She
sat with her ass resting on the sink, her legs splayed apart.
The brown leg makeup she held out to Brad to cover her
legs with gave off a powdery, greasy smell—something like

cheap lipstick; for the rest of his life Brad would never forget its odor. After he was done covering her legs from her ankles up to the top of her thighs with the stuff, he stuck the jar in his pants pocket. He never returned the Max Factor, but for as many years as it remained good, he sniffed at it.

"My, *Nana* sure was something!" Katy sighed. She stretched her legs out at Brad, wiggling and arching her foot to show off her nervy gold ankle bracelet. He heard the conductor call, "Mamaroneck! Mamaroneck!"

"Turn over," Brad whispered to her, taking the jar back out of his pocket. "The backs of your legs are white." She rolled around, pressing her stomach against the sink; the john smelled like asparagus piss. Trembling, Brad stroked the brown grease up her thighs; then he reached inside the loose white cotton pants until he felt the black pubis he had dreamed about, nights with his mother, in Harlem. Nana's legs. Russet pubis, the dark of Katy.

The train whizzed by the sullen shoe factories along the Boston Post Road, Chinese restaurants, Dobbs Hats, and sudden openings of beauty—pockets of the Sound revealed, with peaceful sailboats that looked like toys from the speeding window. She whirled back around, her red pom-pommed snood flying behind her moving face; he pressed against her; again he sent his hand like Columbus on an uncharted voyage, into her welcoming damp.

When the train stopped at Gohonk, they raced down the station stairs with their clumsy food packages. They found their bikes and cycled to the woods off the Gohonk River. In a small, deserted field of rough gold grass, Brad took her—*God, oh my God!* He fell against her, collapsed as a piece of worn cotton; he quickly covered with his too-aromatic hand her staring big black eyes looking straight into his face—*Let the war never end never end.* Then he added to his private sinful litany: *But no one be killed, just never end.*

CHAPTER

10

Unlike Brad, Katy never connected Tartan to Jeremiah. Less wary than he, her goals were more hazy; she had none of his imagination in placing the future's terrain as floating territory and emotions making up for past lacks. At PS 6, and later at Friends', she was an easy student: she thought of school as being like sex, being about pleasant things—there was something very *extracurricular* about Katy's pursuits; looking at medieval art in her Barnard days struck her as a pleasant task. She never thought of herself as a future heir to Indian Path—to have done so would have been to have imagined Anita and Jeremiah dead. Indian Path was simply *there*: her ongoing present.

Some time after Indian Path had been sold, and well after Lewis's and her mother's deaths, Katy, on impulse, drove up to Gohonk. She could have asked her cousin Snowball to go with her or have taken Matt, but she wanted to go back there alone. When she reached Gohonk, her heart dipped. Countrified shops had proliferated on the town's extended main street—Laura Ashley, Pierre Deux, Descamps, and a Waldenbooks. *Might as well be on Madison Avenue.* She drove without stopping, directly down the shore road to Indian Path.

The place had been cut up to make a cluster of expensive surburb-on-the-Sound houses. Katy avoided searching for the big house in this new set-up—did it still exist? If so, between what solar concoction and what rock-landscaped swimming pool was it hidden? She drove to the back of Indian Path, to its side entrance off the Sound inlet. The red barn—now puce, with big sheet-glass windows cut into its side—had been converted into a yacht club. Cute weatherbeaten country signs and a few wooden ducks decorated the lawn in front of it. Katy got out of the car, picked up one of the wooden ducks, stared at it, and dropped it back on the ground. She stood by the clubhouse for a moment, then fled.

▼ ▼ ▼

That summer when she and Brad first started making love together, there were no rustic objects added to the summer place recalling a past that had never been—no attempt made to countrify it—Indian Path just was. Katy remembered the way the second floor of the barn smelled of closed-in summer heat: oak furniture leftover from a previous time, and forgotten musty books, and rusted garden tools.

The big waterfront estates on the Gohonk shore road were boarded up for the duration of the war; only Indian

Path and an oversized gray nineteenth-century house inhabited by a widow of a pharmaceutical millionaire and her handicapped nephew were kept open. Drivers with enough gas to meander their cars down the shore road no longer had a deterrent to peeking at the estates: Indian Path's rusty iron gate, flanked by granite posts, was left haphazardly open; thick hedges on either side of its pebbled driveway hid overgrown blue, rust, and ivory hydrangea bushes. If the sightseers drove around the loop at the front of the main house, they got a full view of the lawn rolling down to the seawall. Frequently they felt cheated by what they saw—they had hoped to get a look at the sort of folks Fred Astaire and Ginger Rogers hobnobbed with on transatlantic crossings. Instead, Anita Becker's sisters, carrying picnic baskets of wax-paper-wrapped American cheese sandwiches and jugs of fruit juice, would be stolidly marching their Fresh Air Fund camp charges down to the pier for morning swim time.

"Lois-Jeff-Marty-Hallie-Steve-Sam-Hester-Willie-Jane-Rusty-Hector-Millie-Coreen-Dora-Ronnie-Pete-Freddy-Doris-Linda-Andy": Jillian and Marcie would chant the roll call on the way down to the rocky beach. Anita had instructed them to count noses in her absence. Especially near the water. Almost as an afterthought, the women added to their litany of names those of Marcie's twins, Henry and Agatha, and Jillian's only child, Laura. Anita's sisters had come of age a decade after she did, in the depression, and had had less economic luck: they had married and started their families late. Now both their husbands were in the service. Such biological bad timing had caused a premature weariness in them. Katy's aunts did all they

129

could do to survive the day and to get Gwindel to serve their charges and them something edible for dinner. In point of fact, nobody was running the estate.

Katy and Brad relished this unexpected gift of premature adulthood, and they enthusiastically attempted to fill the void. They would walk ceremoniously down the road to the red barn; along with Gwindel, they were the sole audience for the play that was being put on there by the Fresh Air kids under Jillian and Marcie's direction. Katy wore a dress the evening of the first production, and she draped a white sweater over her shoulders like she had seen her mother do when she went with Jeremiah to the Westport Playhouse opening nights; she also made Brad wear his best long pants.

The campers utilized the twelve horse stalls—unused since the turn of the century—as their makeshift stage. Marcie played a Lily Pons recording of *Lucia di Lammermoor* as a show starter (she never chose program music particularly appropriate to the theme of a play). Katy, Brad, and Gwindel rocked on the wicker sofa, waiting for the crêpe-paper curtain to rise on *The Cradle Will Rock*.

▼ ▼ ▼

After Katy and Brad started to sleep together, Katy took care, when she was in the city and around Tartan, to dress meekly. On an afternoon when she knew Tartan had a lot of work to do at the Becker apartment, Katy came in from the outside wearing a wide-brimmed natural straw hat with black-eyed Susans scattered over the brim. She smiled at Tartan and licked the chocolate sprinkles off a purply ice-cream cone she had bought downstairs at the corner Good

Humor van. Like a child enjoying innocent midsummer pleasures, carelessly, in a babyish way, she let the cream ooze down her dimity flowered print dress. "Here, Tartan—I bought a toasted almond one for you." Katy instinctively warded off the one person most alert to the terror of her and Brad having sex together—but her real ace in the hole was that she and Brad were needed to help run Indian Path. Tartan had no legitimate reason to demand that Brad stay behind in Manhattan.

Katy's specialty was making a more systematic bundle of the house bills than her mother; she would sit at Anita's desk, sort them out, and quickly forward them to her father's office for payment. During that wartime summer, under Katy's reign, all the family photographs were put into correctly catalogued leather albums; in the back of each album she neatly attached envelopes containing the matching negatives. Katy was great at discovering connections—when she found out that Carl Van Vechten's wife's niece had married a relative of Anita's, and that Willie Lawn's brother had been a Negro poet sponsored by Van Vechten at Knopf, she informed her mother of the coincidence of their joint heritage.

"Oh, my God," Anita sighed. "You'll end up as nutty as your uncle Henry—please, no genealogical wonders for this family. Look how he started, attaching us to those Viennese Beckers he dug up—your father says Henry paid good money to drum up those relatives—and for what? Where has Austria landed us? In Hitler's bed!"

Katy knew that Louie Berrotini, the nursery man, was Brad's exemplar. Every ten days or so he would drive up to Indian Path in his pickup truck and walk the grounds with them. He told them about Frederick Law Olmsted, who had landscaped Indian Path around the time he designed Central Park. Occasionally, when Louie had a big delivery of plantings and shrubs, he would drive Brad and Katy back with him to his Danbury nursery.

They had taken on, unasked, so much of the actual running of Indian Path that neither Marcie nor Jillian thought to keep tabs on them. The women kept the same schedule as their campers and went to bed early. When Katy was sure her aunts were asleep she would give Brad the all-clear sign, he would come to her room, and they would build a fire (Anita never would have permitted it) in her bedroom fireplace.

One night they lay together on her floor popping charred marshmallows into their mouths. Brad showed Katy sketches he had made, how the Indian Path grounds could be improved after the war was over—after he and Katy were grown up. Katy had never thought about the future, but his idea excited her, and she added a few of her own; they dreamed up extraordinary gardens. They also inspected the package of Trojans Brad had brought back from New York when he had brought up extra foodstuff Tartan had located in Harlem for Indian Path. They marveled over the rubbers—they stretched them, smelled them, and attempted to blow them up like balloons.

▼ ▼ ▼

Tartan, packing the food hampers for Brad to bring up by train, noted the changes in her son: he was a man; he was always at the Beckers'. It occurred to her that he might be fooling around with Katy, but the thought of it caused a pain inside her head so big that she couldn't breathe. She knew she had lost control of the situation. She had no power to tell Brad, at fourteen, not to go to Indian Path. So Tartan said nothing. She had no one to comment to. She hoped her mind had merely been wandering.

▼　▼　▼

There was a deserted boathouse just a short canoe trip up the Gohonk River (the Becker pier was at the junction where the Gohonk emptied into the Sound)—Brad had spotted it while swimming. He and Katy began to use the brown shack for making love. Katy liked lying almost flat on top of the wet leaves and rotting boards while Brad was inside her. The small space smelled pungently of wet wood; to her nostrils it had the acrid odor of overripe oranges. Katy reassured Brad that when they were in the boathouse they were invisible to the rest of the world.

The more they went there, the more varied their love-making became. They learned to touch each other in all their orifices; they took turns kissing fluttering eyelashes, licking tongues, bellies, vagina, and erect penis: their forays had a futuristic, rebellious quality. They were more ener-getic than erotic—with a simple touch, a stroke, a rubbing of open legs against one another, they both went hot. They didn't have to think along lines of arousing—they were always ready—the question was, Where? How long could two bold sexual adventurers, dependent on not being taken for near-adults by their relatives, sneak to the Gohonk shack without discovery?

▼　▼　▼

Taking a canoe trip up the Gohonk River seemed a great solution—Katy was convinced that their fucking would remain undetected if they were open and aboveboard about planning the river trip together.

"Why, Brad," she said, her voice dropping to soft Anita-like tones, "people never notice the nose in front of their face. You just must never confuse them with too much information. We must be cheerful and positive about our plans for the exploration of Gohonk River. We'll emphasize our being in the fresh air and the good we will be doing. We will familiarize Marcie and Jillian with the idea of our going, so by the time we take off, it will seem natural to them. Almost inevitable."

"What good?"

"Something for the war . . ."

"Connecticut's not Africa or Europe—there's no war effort along the Gohonk."

Katy persisted. "In addition to breathing such fine air and adding to our navigating skills, we need an errand of mercy. Blood to a hospital, aid to a dying man. Think, Wild Bill."

"The Helen Keller place is in Weston. We could put up stakes near it, Calamity, and hitchhike to her house."

"Wild Bill, you are a bull of a Bill! We'll write Helen Keller a note of admiration—thanking her for her inspiration and telling her she'll be our guiding inspiration throughout our lives. I'll read it aloud to Marcie and Jillian—I'll make them cry. After hearing my moving note to Helen Keller they won't dare think of what you and I might be doing in our sleeping bag. They'll only think of our generosity and how much trouble we have gone to to let that poor deaf, dumb, and blind woman know how she has helped humanity." Katy paused for emphasis.

"Brad, if you direct people's attention toward what they want to see and give them something generous to fix on, they won't underhandedly crawl back and stare at what gives them the willies. If my aunts thought you and I were doing *it*, it would wreck the whole rhythm of Indian Path. They'd need to call my mother back; it would ruin their summer, because they know she would blame them for being careless idiots; then they would have to worry about the campers—start separating the boys from the girls. They wouldn't know where to send me, or you." Katy relished the thought of disaster.

"You and I are needed here to run Indian Path. Jillian and Marcie are barely capable of taking care of my three cousins; they have all they can do to keep the campers swimming and making crêpe paper—now they're on to *Our Town*. Gwindel? He's blinder than Helen Keller—you know he ran the pickup truck backward yesterday and took off half the barn door—you had to fix the padlock."

"It didn't take me long."

"Do you think Gwindel could have fixed up his damage? All he knows to do is cook hamburgers with grease added in that doesn't belong in the patties. I bet he sneaks Crisco into the ground round. Huh, you call Gwindel a presence here? Why, we are doing Indian Path a favor keeping our sex life secret . . ." Katy sat up straight, picking off wet leaves from her naked breasts.

"How are we being wonderful to them by keeping hidden what has to be hidden?"

"We are responsible for making life easy for everyone.

And we should keep them thinking about the good we are doing. After Helen Keller, we go up the river with little letters of cheer for all sorts of people in need. Our real lives will remain invisible—we *are* invisible to them."

"You expect a blind woman to read your thank-you note?"

"Her triumph is so grand that such notes reach her—she has solved life, she has her ways. Her helpers will transpose it to Braille."

"Other than Helen Keller, how will we know who upstream needs a letter of cheer from a Friends' girl?"

Katy knew and ignored that Brad enjoyed deflating her private school. "We'll buy the Gohonk and Danbury newspapers . . . I'll explain to Jillian that the trip is connected to a social-service project my class needs to bring back in the fall."

"Bronx Science has no social service—we stick to the hard stuff—the nature of the real world." Brad rolled over to face Katy; she saw that mud was sticking to his back. "I've a better plan—we'll canoe up to the Danbury reservoir and ask Louie to pick us up there in his truck and drive us over to the Croton reservoir. I did a report for Sci about its being a hundred years since a team of men took the *Croton Maid* on a maiden voyage from the Croton reservoir through the aqueduct, straight into the Harlem River—"

"You're loony."

"Why? One of the kids at Bronx Sci who summers in Croton told me that he went down into the aqueduct manhole near the reservoir—it works; the stream still flows down into Manhattan."

"You mean we could actually land up in Manhattan?"

136

"Sure. This book I read said that the old Croton Aqueduct was one of the great architectural feats of the nineteenth century. That New York was at risk of perishing for lack of fresh water. The city had grown too quickly—the population was dying of cholera for lack of it. Fires were leveling Manhattan. Katy, do you really understand water? It's more important than heat, we're made of it, we die without it. Or doesn't Friends' consider water?"

"I thought New York's a city of bridges?"

"Oh, that comes later—that's the picturesque stuff, the Brooklyn, the George Washington. The bridges were needed as a communication solution after the waterways were perceived to be obstacles for reaching the city. But our real survival depended on getting the good water piped into the city. Maybe making the Brooklyn Bridge was poetry—but imagining the old Croton Aqueduct took more genius. The guys who constructed it were our Egyptian pharaohs building our native pyramids." Brad's voice trembled, he spoke with rare passion. "If New York hadn't been saved by the aqueduct and been able to grow so powerful—we might have lost the Civil War."

"So no Manhattan?"

"History's a real bitch."

▼ ▼ ▼

Katy and Brad planned their departure for the Croton Aqueduct for five in the morning. Brad had spent a week at the Forty-second Street library studying maps on its topography. By the time he returned to Indian Path he knew cold the terrain they were headed for.

A brave army of August campers led by Jillian and Marcie

marched along with them to the dock; they had come to
wave the explorers good-bye—the canoe trip was acknowledged in advance as Indian Path's great summer adventure;
no one noticed that the war was coming to an end.

A humid haze rising from the water where the mouth
of the Gohonk River joined the Sound gave the air a smoky
smell akin to that of burning rubber; the pines on the far
side of the Gohonk had the stately shapes of eternal, ethe-
real evergreens covered in gray snowdrifts. Katy's navy
wool sweater and wool socks smelled of wet, sea, and New
England summer.

Her instincts about her aunts were sound. While Brad
loaded the Sterno lamps, the cooking plate, and the extra
lengths of rope into the canoe, Marcie calmly handed them
a basket she had prepared containing extra rolls of toilet
paper, bags of marshmallows, and some country gentleman
corn that the campers had picked from the Indian Path
garden as their gift to Helen Keller. Neither Marcie nor
Jillian indicated any suspicion that Katy and Brad were
shoving off on a sexual adventure.

"It's as exciting as *Huck Finn*." Jillian sighed.

"Huck wasn't a girl," Katy corrected.

Brad looked alarmed.

"Twain lived in the nineteenth century . . . ," Jillian continued.

He needn't worry, Katy thought. Sexual references went
right past her aunts.

"I'm sure, dear"—Jillian kept on going, with what Katy
took for amazing vagueness—"that if Mark Twain were
living now, he would realize that there are . . . girls in the
summer."

Katy lowered herself into the canoe. Brad looked in the direction of Long Island and, in Katy's mind, rather ostentatiously remarked to her aunts, who merely smiled, that he saw no Japanese submarines on the coastline. Then they pushed off. Brad steered the canoe upstream in the direction of the Gohonk boathouse. The mist lifted, an edge of red-gold cut the sky, daylight sprayed the water, and the river surface fizzed.

Katy saw the campers standing at attention at the sea-wall, waving—the American flag, high up on the white pole, was catching the first breezes off the Sound. She heard them singing across the water, led by Jillian and Marcie:

> "From the halls of Montezuma
> To the shores of Tripoli
> We have fought our country's battles
> On the land and on the sea . . ."

Katy and Brad stopped in the boathouse to make love. Through its broken, spiderwebbed windows, Katy could still see Indian Path's fluttering flag and long pier as she stripped.

Brad balanced himself near the wall and pressed her buttocks against him, his sex deep inside her; he got her to fold her legs around him while in a sitting position. When her rhythm quickened, he twirled her around until they both came; he dropped to the floor, carrying her down with him. Adventurers staking new territory, they celebrated the start of their trip with their main voyage, their sex.

Brad rolled over on the rotting leaves. He showed Katy his package of Trojans and another of Ramses. "Do you think the brands are identical?" he asked. Katy lay on her back, laughing.

She stood up, naked; only her breasts, belly, and haunches had remained white. Breasts and braids bobbing, she danced in a circle around him.

"By the shore of *Gitche Gumee*, by the shining Big-Sea-Water, stood the wigwam of Nokomis, daughter of the Moon, Nokomis . . ."

Brad told her that with leaves crowning her forehead, her hair parted in the middle, and her braids ending in tight rubber bands, she looked like an Indian girl.

Then, still naked, they dove into the river behind the boathouse and made love one more time, underwater. Oh Brad, oh Hick, oh Kate, oh Calamity, o Christ, son of God—forgive me, o Morning Star, daughter of the Moon!

CHAPTER

11

KATY HAD ODD HABITS: ONCE AN IDEA seized her—such as camouflaging their sex spree with doing good for humanity—she felt compelled to carry out her fabrication. So, toward noon, after Brad secured the canoe on the riverbank under the bridge near Gohonk's Main Street, Katy left a little note at the town library:

> We are High School students who have come to appreciate the rewarding hours diligent reading can give. We are grateful to the Gohonk library for having showed us the way. In return for discovering the magic world of books, we offer you our volunteer services on Friday afternoons after we get back from our canoe trip.
>
> Sincerely and in appreciation,
> Karen Tess Becker and Bradford Culver
> (of Indian Path)

Then they ate hamburgers at the corner drugstore and walked over to Rosen's Sports Equipment Store to buy rope, lighter fluid, and the long-beamed flashlights Brad needed for the tunnel.

Flora Rosen's first impression was that two boys had walked into her place. Katy sauntered in, her hands, male-style, in her back pockets—she was wearing an oversized pullover and boys' jeans, and her hair was tucked inside a fishing cap. She quickly flashed a smile, and Flora Rosen recognized her as the Becker girl.

Flora was accustomed to seeing Katy and Brad come to Rosen's with Gwindel; they often helped him provision supplies for Indian Path. Each time they came in she would comment to her husband, Sheldon, "There's that Indian Path girl with that Portuguese boy who lives with them." Northeast of Gohonk was a Portuguese fishing village, and Flora Rosen had decided that all dusky, good-looking males native to Connecticut were of Portuguese stock. She prided herself on her social astuteness—she saw herself as the only challenger to the New England WASP fortress, and she allowed no new pieces of information leading to more complex conclusions to change her mind.

Being Jewish herself, Flora Rosen took particular pride in spotting Jews who had sneakily crossed over. "Takes one to know one," she would mutter to Sheldon. "I have a nose for my own." Hers was pinched; she had masses of short, waved, hennaed hair, and a thin but curved body. She fluttered her pencil-smudged hand knowingly in the air to back her verbal flow. In another setting—say, Paris—she could easily have passed for that sharp-eyed Frenchwoman

142

ringing up the cash register in the bistro Jean-Paul Bel-
mondo had just abandoned.

Her personal narrative, that she and Sheldon had done
this extraordinary thing in abandoning Brooklyn to settle
in Gohonk and, with no apologies to the locals, opened
Rosen's Sports Equipment Store—"Let them Yankees
plotz," she boasted to her city relatives, "Rosen's is what
we are calling it"—made her shaky on Connecticut's true
Jewish narrative.

By the 1940s there were a fair number of Jews living in
Gohonk and its surrounding towns, and rarely did they
bother to cross over. Many of them patronized Rosen's.
Since their presence didn't tally with what was going on in
Flora Rosen's head, she rarely recognized them as Jews, and
certainly not the Beckers. In her patchy fears vis-à-vis the
locals (on whom she believed she and Sheldon had forced
their store), the row of Gohonk waterfront estates, of which
Indian Path was the biggest, was the ultimate symbol of
those who, given the chance, would have raised the drawbridge against the Rosens' advance into Connecticut.

In the 1950s, when she read of Katy's marriage to Lewis
Eichorn in the *Gohonk Weekly Record* and the *New York Times*,
she realized with glee that her people had finally triumphed
against the goys—a *rabbi* had performed the ceremony at
Indian Path. When, after the wedding, Pat Mallard dropped
by the store for some fishing tackle for Jeremiah Becker,
she said to him that the Beckers sure must have been
put out: "I see the girl married a Jewish fellow. And
a rabbi officiating! I'll bet that didn't sit well at Indian
Path."

Pat repeated the remark to Katy; she drove into Gohonk at top speed, flew into the store, grabbed Flora Rosen's arm, and yelled, "Listen here, Mrs. Rosen. I am Jewish, my grandparents were, my parents are, my brother is—there was nothing strange about having a rabbi marry me and Lewis."

Flora Rosen adamantly refused to back down—even if it meant losing the big Becker account, she wasn't putting up with the temper tantrums of a high-strung rich kid given to weird actings-out. The girl was spoiled; she had the bad habit of horning in on what wasn't hers in the first place. "Listen, miss, you may have converted, and you may also have bats in the belfry. And there are some rabbis who aren't what I call rabbis, who will do anything for money. But Jewish you are not. Tell me, Miss Becker—what synagogue is your rabbi from?"

Katy's skin turned a deep, splotchy red. She pushed Flora Rosen backward; the woman's arms flailed wildly in the air. Flora lost her balance and crashed backward into a pyramid stacked with boxes of Keds sneakers; white and navy ones tumbled over her. She stared up, dazed, at Katy, who kept screaming as she picked up the boxes, "I am Jewish, I am Jewish—look here, you shut up with your mean remarks about phony rabbis—I am Jewish!"

Shoppers inspecting the nearby sale of inflatable rafts stopped, startled: it was unusual to hear a customer pick a fight, shriek that she was Jewish in the Gohonk main sports store. Flora Rosen staggered to her feet, glad she had stood her ground. To have relented, to have listened to Katy's version of her past, would have meant giving up her own story of how she and Sheldon had conquered stony WASP Gohonk.

Katy remained in a rage for an unusually long time. It had been she, not Lewis, who had demanded a rabbi in place of a judge—she felt that Flora Rosen had nullified her identity, wiped out her place in the world. "Is she God? Who gives her the right," she later asked Lewis, "to decide who is Jewish and who not? Do I pass judgment on her grandfather?"

Katy still clung to her inner scenario, the secret, roomy history of the world in which, starting with Adam and Eve, generations logically begat new generations, all strands neatly dovetailed, and there was a place marked for each life. She believed that novels were history's narrative; Cathy's and Heathcliff's respective descendants were not ghosts on a moor but the gentry class in England, dimly related to Greer Garson's Mrs. Miniver. America was more unruly. Only the South had a clear continuum: the twentieth-century Southern novels she read were about the descendants of their struggle, of that history.

The Jews were hopeless: a historical hodgepodge. Heine didn't lead to Proust; Proust clearly wasn't Danny Kaye's grandfather. A new crowd surfaced each generation. *We always end up a bunch of first-time beginners. The rise of Maimonides, the rise of the German Jews, the rise of David Levinsky—why are we always rising, rising, rising, like Christ on the cross, but never there? We're up at the top, then* bang! *Here comes the next generation, once more up from the streets, rising again. Why can't those who rose and rose, or rose and lost have descendants, like southerners? Like normal people?*

After they left Rosen's, they continued their plan to visit Helen Keller's home. They left the canoe secured under the Gohonk main bridge, took with them the bag of corn Katy's aunts had packed for her, and hitchhiked along the inland road. A friendly woman in a faded sweatshirt and shorts driving an old Ford station wagon stopped for them; she was going as far as Rockbrook, a woodsy colony of modernist summer homes near the Keller place.

She drove them directly into the colony, past the community tennis courts and swimming dam. She pointed in the direction of the redwood clubhouse, the American flag blowing in front of its entrance, and told them to drop in—iced tea, apples, and cookies were always laid out in the afternoon for the inhabitants of the colony. "Just say you are Hildy Stamen's guests for the day."

They thanked her and went inside the club. Katy examined a sign posted on the wall: CALLING—TO WINNER * CALLING ALL KIDS * SUNDAY-MORNING SCAVENGER HUNT * BIG PRIZE FOR THE WINNER. A group of women were gossiping in the corner; they folded their bodies against the deck chairs like country summer odalisques; one of them was painting her toenails red. At the other end of the room, two boys were in a Ping-Pong volley. Katy walked to a table that had big pitchers of tea and lemonade. She drank some tea and ate three Tollhouse cookies, then felt guilty because she knew about Rockbrook from her parents. She whispered to Brad, "This is a Communist colony."

"Are you sure?"

"Uh-huh—my parents know some of them from the

Monday-night Theater Guild openings—they were asked to a cocktail party at one of the homes here. I heard my father tell my mother he wouldn't be dragged out for a bunch of Communist idiots whose left hand didn't know what pocket their right one was in."

Brad scrutinized the adults in the room. At Bronx Sci, youth groups—offshoots of the Communist party—went in for heavy recruiting. He flushed, embarrassed, remembering a Negro classmate urging him to join, and himself being tempted by what he was offered: "Come to our big dances downtown with white girls—there are hot Jewish numbers dying to be fucked by us." Brad put distance between Katy and himself—he didn't want her magically intuiting his thoughts. His cousin Willie, his mother, and his aunt Jessica had drummed it into his head that a boy of his talent needed not to get tangled with Communists or Garveyites—it was clear in the family that he was meant for a fine, studious destiny.

Brad had assumed the Communists, like the Garveyites, to be a mostly Negro cause, but there were no Negroes in the clubhouse. He glanced at the seductive blond with the feather cut who was painting her toenails red—her knees were bent up to her stomach so she could more easily reach each toe. Her legs were tanned dark; she wore a tight white angora bolero over a draped white bathing suit; she was ravishing—all small curves. Brad had never seen Communists like these Rockbrook women: he had never imagined the existence of such people. He felt dislocated.

Brad yearned to bring an extraordinary achievement back to Sci in the fall. If his plan to canoe down the Croton Aqueduct succeeded and his hours spent in mathematical calculations of water tables produced the correct conclusions, then the aqueduct could be the Big Thing. He kept staring at the voluptuous woman in the white angora sweater; he wondered—would his feat be enough? Enough to get himself noticed?

Katy was also studying the clubhouse crowd; she had noticed that the surrounding summer houses were clustered close together. She frowned, wondering what it would be like to have neighbors in the summer. Would it be more fun? The Fresh Air Funders were, compared to her, babies. "To be frank," she had pointed out to her father, "if there were more equality in the world, there would be no need for us to think we are wonderful because we house semi-orphans in the summer—I've read such efforts are nothing more than fossilized nineteenth-century charity."

"Don't be frank," he answered, "be Karen Tess"; then he took *Major Barbara* down from the bookcase and handed it to her—there was no arguing with him about politics.

She, too, took in the blond woman in the angora sweater. Was Rockbrook the equality she wanted her father to go for? Better than Indian Path? In her heart she knew Indian Path was far more beautiful, beautiful in a way Rockbrook never could be; she felt confused, her mind dazed—she recognized that she loved Indian Path even minus neighbors, and she wasn't sure she was entitled to her feelings. She'd had enough—she wanted to leave. "Let's go," she said to Brad abruptly.

▼ ▼ ▼

Helen Keller's house was set back off the road, on higher land. A man came down to see what they wanted. "We are bringing Miss Keller a gift and a note from Indian Path," Katy said. He said nothing to them—they obviously weren't the only ones who had stopped by her home—but he took their offerings of corn and other late-summer crops from Anita's garden and promised to deliver them. "Miss Keller gets everything that is intended for her—but she gets angry if the intentions are wrong."

Katy got the feeling they had been too daring; maybe they shouldn't have brought Anita's crops to a personage as queenly as Helen Keller; maybe they had elicited her anger. She stood still. She shut her eyes and covered her ears. "It feels like I am in midnight—at the end of the world. Oh, Brad—what a punishment to be blind, to lose your senses—how much you'd need to trust!"

After they hitched back to Gohonk, they untied the canoe and pushed off. By nightfall they reached Lyons Plain.

Brad made a small fire by the riverbank. They cooked hot dogs over it and ate them on buns. Then he boiled water in a little pot over the Sterno stove; they put double the usual amount of Nestlé cocoa powder into their mugs. It was good, drinking it hot, alternating sips of it with the runny charcoaled marshmallows they roasted in the embers.

"Laying Plains," Brad joked, getting into their sleeping bag.

"Plain laying." Katy joked back. But when she lay on her back and looked up at the darkness of the night, she felt an almost religious awe: they were spending their first entire night together; as with adults, she mused, sleeping was meant to lead to breakfast in the morning.

▼ ▼ ▼

When they finally reached Waubeeka Lake, near Danbury, Louie Berrotini was as good as his word; he came from his nursery at the designated time to drive them to the old Croton reservoir. Louie's mop of gray hair was as thick, plush, and curly as the shrubs he grew—so much gray, hirsute health turned his hazel eyes slightly smoky. His stocky body was amazingly wiry—he moved so rapidly and with such grace that his loose overalls seemed to remain in place seconds after he had sprung into motion.

Katy insisted on stopping near Mill Plain to visit Ian Swenson, the farmer who had made her yellow wooden round birthday cake board. The cake was meant to go in the middle of the board, which had tiny holes drilled in the border for twenty-one candles. Anita had asked him to carve it because of the nice way he had of painting wood. Katy's board was decorated with clusters of forget-me-nots in between swags of green garlands.

"What's so important about it?" Brad asked—he was already seeing himself floating down the Croton water conduit; birthday rites seemed like small potatoes compared to their adventure.

"Well, I like it because it's mine—it's always been mine. Besides, it's unusual—the holes for the candles are dug into the wooden rim around the cake. Most people have to put their candles directly *on* the cake."

"What difference does it make?"

"Those things just do."

150

"You're too picky."

"I want to see Ian."

▼ ▼ ▼

He was in the shed behind his chicken coop and his truck farm; the tomatoes were lush and overripe. Katy liked watching his movements. Sand and shavings in his eyes, in his hair; a can of beer next to him—he turned his knife against the wood with a musician's grace: he was molding the neck of a ferocious swan. Stored in his workroom were red toy chests with Nordic decorations, children's stools, granny rockers, and parts of a dismantled carousel.

Katy leaned her head against a dappled stallion; each August he promised her he would finish the carousel by summer's end, and he never did.

"You've come back too early," Ian said. "After Labor Day I'll have a spare week to work on it."

"You say that every August—Brad and I are taking our canoe to the Croton reservoir."

"Croton? John Reed lived there."

"Who was he?"

Ian deftly smoothed down the swan's neck. "A Communist fellow from the First World War who traveled to Russia and wrote about it in a book."

"Did you know him? Do you know where his house was?"

Ian shook his head. "Oh no—he was famous. I never knew anyone like that." He and Louie talked business about the price of his crops, and he gave Brad and Katy wooden whistles before they left.

Louie drove them straight to the reservoir. It pleased

151

Katy, carrying in her mind the true history of the world, to come across this new patch of information on John Reed; she wondered if he were connected to the Communists in Rockbrook, and if so—how? Weaving an imaginary history in her mind, she tried this way and that to use the clues Ian had given her to tie up the mysteries. She liked figuring out stories about real people. Brad's geographical and mathematical understanding of waterways wearied her.

The stillness and pale light over the reservoir gave the surface of the water a glassine translucence. Louie parked his truck; he helped them lower the canoe and their provisions. When he saw they were okay he drove off.

They canoed over to the manhole Brad had been told about. To get to it, they had to push the canoe down the reservoir staircase; that night they camped at a discreet distance. They started early the following morning—even with the four big, powerful flashlights, Brad figured they would need the additional daylight coming through the ventilator shafts for the eight-hour trip. They hid their surplus gear in the nearby bushes. Brad's friend had warned him that the manhole was patrolled to keep kids from going down into the aqueduct, but in early-morning hours the guards were off duty.

He and Katy bundled up in heavy sweaters, long pants, and wool socks. Even in summer the canal was cold. Katy stuffed her braids inside her cap; they had to cover their heads because of the bats.

Brad popped the manhole cover. "Are you scared?" he asked her.

"No—a little."

"It's dark."

152

She nodded.

"But safe."

Brad slid into the hole first, then pulled Katy in after him.

They pulled the canoe down into the weir chamber. It was clammier than Katy had expected; she was startled by what sounded like a dog barking. "I hope there are no alligators . . ."

"Oh, come on—a frog, maybe." Brad flashed a light; the canal looked exactly as his friend had described it. He figured the width of the canal at about seven feet. The air chamber was almost five feet in height, the depth of the canal also about five feet. According to his readings, the conduit dropped about a foot per mile; it would be possible to float the thirty-three miles down to Manhattan.

"There are light ventilators every mile, and manholes every three," he reassured Katy. "Anytime you're tired, we'll climb out."

"No—you said Manhattan. I packed enough food."

They shoved off; Brad flashed a light against the hydraulic cement walls. "Sing," he said.

They hummed: "Oh, Susannah," "It Had to Be You," "It's a Long Way to Tipperary," "Paper Doll," "Bei Mir Bist du Schön," "Over There," "Ol' Man River," "The Chattanooga Choo-Choo," "Veni-Veni," "The White Cliffs of Dover," "The Ballad for Americans," "Swannee River," "Waltzing Matilda," "Down in the Valley," "Lili Marlene," "Alexander's Rag Time Band," "O Sole Mio," "A Tisket, a Tasket," and "Onward, Christian Soldiers." When they couldn't think of more songs, Katy recited "Annabel Lee" and "The Raven."

At a certain point, to check where they were, Brad pushed the canoe onto the stairs of one of the heavy concrete weir chambers they kept passing, popped the manhole, and stuck his head out. They took turns. Katy felt relieved to be breathing the air; it felt good to see the sky. They ate a cheese sandwich apiece and drank some hot cocoa she had put in the thermos.

They shoved the canoe back into the canal. Katy had no idea where the howling dogs were coming from—they ran along the edges and at times swam in the water—they scared her. She saw a huge shape rising ahead of them in the wet blackness. It made a horrible noise, like a deafening gargle. "Brad!" she screamed. "There's a weird thing moaning down here—we have to go back."

"You're imagining it. I don't hear anything but the dogs. Those are toads you see leaping in the water. How can anything be clear to you when you wear sunglasses in the dark?"

"It's a warning for us not to continue."

"Calamity—only the Headless Horseman lives down here."

Though she realized that Brad was only trying to distract her by reminding her that they were passing under Sleepy Hollow, his cuckoo story-telling spree reassured her.

". . . so Washington Irving was rebuilding his house, the Van Tassel place, at the precise moment John Bloomfield Jervis was constructing the Croton Aqueduct—Jervis had already finished the Erie." In Jervis's honor, Brad sang "Fifteen Miles on the Erie Canal."

They had hours to go, so he rambled on. "Nothing like

the Croton had ever been attempted in America. Jervis got his idea of taming the Croton River and channeling it into a gravity-fed system from the Assyrians and Romans—he himself came from Rome, upstate. He must have thought, When in Rome do as the Romans."

"Where'd you dig this up?"

"In the library. Washington Irving wanted to tell the real story of the Headless Horseman. So complicated, so awful, I can't even now reveal it to you, Calamity. But Irving chickened. He stuck on that phony ending about Ichabod Crane having been scared by a falling squashed pumpkin. Now, you know that if it had truly been that, he never would have bothered to write the story. Irving knew real things—he had traveled to Granada, he lived in the Alhambra built by Arab caliphs—why would he be taken with a pumpkin?"

"Beats me."

"I vowed to keep the secret, but the Headless Horseman spent about a quarter of a century hidden in what was to be the basement of Irving's house in Sunnyside. As I told you, Jervis was building the aqueduct the same year that Irving was fixing Sunnyside, and it was also when James Butler Hickok was born. Since I'm the reincarnated spirit of Wild Bill Hickok, these things have been passed down to me. The official story is that Jervis used four thousand immigrants at seventy-five cents a day to construct his modern marvel—or ancient marvel—depending on where you locate aqueducts in your mind. Even then it was no money. And dangerous work. The real poop is that most of the men who went deep down into the earth were from

Sing Sing. Everyone around here knows that they built the Sing Sing Kill. We should be passing under the aqueduct bridge, by my calculations—"

"We're going up in the air?"

"Don't worry—we're in the conduit. You can't fall down or up." Brad flashed his lights against the walls. "See those hard rocks? They mean we're passing through a tunnel carved in a hill. The convicts had to do the digging. There were deaths on Kill Bridge. Men fell off bad construction sites. In the winter of eighteen forty-one, during a raging high-water storm, a huge dam fell in. The aqueduct was glory for Jervis, survival for Manhattan, and hell for the workers. Twice during the making of it there were insurrections. The ringleaders were inmates from Sing Sing. Now, Washington Irving had persuaded Jervis to give him some of his Sing Sing men to use as his Sunnyside crew—Irving knew his guys were prison moonlighters. The leader of the gang—Dan O'Leary, an Irishman in Sing Sing for killing a cop during an Albany bank robbery—stole a white Arabian horse from one of the big Hudson Valley Dutch estates, and on a Sunday night, he galloped to warn his men at Sleepy Hollow that the state police were closing in on the striking inmates."

"You're making up the O'Leary stuff—you've never mentioned his name to me."

"I thought you wouldn't come down the aqueduct with me if I told you beforehand." Brad paused for a moment. "Now, where was I . . . Oh, Irving was fiddling in his attic, planning his swan pond, when he saw the incident from the window: he heard O'Leary warn the Sing Sing gang to scatter, hide in the forest, then try to make their way out west, where the police would lose track of them. Irving knew the state patrol was heading down from the north road."

"How did he know that?"

"From his attic he could see everything. He knew O'Leary had a good heart, worth saving, but on the other hand, Irving had a reputation, and if it got out that he had been using Jervis's crew of Sing Sing inmates to fix up Sunnyside, it would have made an awful stink . . . After all, he was supposed to be a fancy gentleman of letters. Some folks, even then, were on to him. They contended that he'd persuaded Jervis to route the conduit in a roundabout way, so that it entirely bypassed his property. Manhattan journalists, daily, were accusing the politicians of graft—Calamity, pour me some cocoa."

They drifted down the canal in silence while Brad drank and thought some more.

"Irving didn't have Jervis's excuse, that he was saving Manhattan. Sunnyside was just a gentleman's home being remodeled to contain added delights. So he didn't cry out in warning to O'Leary. The police saw Dan come galloping toward them, and bingo! They decapitated him with one gunshot. Irving felt sick when he saw O'Leary's head roll off, filled with squashed orangey brain that just rolled onto the ground—*plop!*" Brad paused reflectively. "Irving felt he was to blame for O'Leary's death. He never could write the truth because he had already foretold the event with Ichabod Crane. He was a decent, sensitive sort of writer, but he could never expiate himself from his failure to save Dan O'Leary. The evidence is clear as day."

"As mud. Brad . . . we're in night, and I'm getting tired."

"Come on, we're doing it, we're doing the big feat—the canoe is flowing southward just fine, and we're just fine inside it."

"It's so cold."

"Drink some more cocoa . . . Now we're getting to the best part. Irving saw the state troopers ride away after the shooting. He felt so bad he went downstairs and asked some of the Sing Sing men hidden in his house to go with him and give Dan O'Leary a proper burial. When they reached the spot in the wooded road where his body had fallen, there was no sign of a head, squashed or otherwise, or of the rest of him. The white Arabian steed had disappeared and never was found. In addition to feeling sick with guilt, now Irving was green with terror."

"What did he have to be scared about? He was safely on dry land, aboveground."

"Think about it, Calamity—just give or take a year exactly one century ago, when Jervis's men finished the aqueduct and his engineers took the trial run down to Manhattan in the *Croton Maid*, they saw Daniel O'Leary rise up from the canal between Sleepy Hollow and Sunnyside. It was a terrible sight. He rose on his white horse from the water, his hand on his head, moaning and moaning—Calamity, that terrible groaning you thought you heard was nothing but poor Daniel O'Leary cursing at Washington Irving. Irving was so distraught when he heard about it—the *Croton Maid* engineers thought O'Leary might have gotten trapped in the canal through the cellar passage he had been digging at Sunnyside—that his writings took strange, odd paths. He was a great friend of John Jacob Astor—they had gone trapping furs together. He got to know the West, and he met Wild Bill when Hick was fifteen, and he told him the whole story. Irving hoped that at some future time—one hundred years hence—the true version would be revealed. Wild Bill's spirit has passed it on to me."

"So if I'm Calamity, how come no furs or news got handed on to me? I was with you in the West, Hick, but I never met John Jacob Astor."

"When the *Croton Maid* pulled into Manhattan there were great fireworks displays in celebration, because the city had been saved. The engineers couldn't reveal that poor Daniel O'Leary's ghost was trapped in the canal near Sunnyside. Which is why Dan's calling out to us now: the hundred-year mark has passed—we're in the centennial. See—the news *is* being passed on to you."

Katy relaxed. "Hick, should we sing him 'When Irish Eyes Are Smiling'?"

"After waiting a century down here, do you think a sentimental ballad is sufficient?"

"We could throw him a sandwich." Katy trailed part of her tuna in the water. In the darkness there was a terrible noise—they both heard it—an animal, a head, a God-knows-what dove up and snapped it out of her fingers. Her thumb was bloody; she sucked it.

Too scared to talk, they paddled furiously forward.

At the next air ventilator, sunlight poured in; Brad recovered his aplomb. "It was a frog—don't throw food into the water. In here dogs' barking can sound like human groans."

"I'm not afraid of him," Katy said. To prove it, she sang "Danny Boy" at the top of her lungs, and she yelled into the darkness, "Don't be lonely, Daniel O'Leary, martyr of Manhattan—Hick and I will come back for you in fifty years' time!"

She knew there were bats flying overhead; Brad kept his flashlight turned off so as not to attract them. He told her that they were almost at the last manhole before Highgate Bridge.

The bad air and insufficient oxygen were making them dizzy; they took turns telling more tales to keep from falling asleep.

▼　▼　▼

The water level was changing; a strong light was coming through the ventilator shaft ahead of them. Brad checked his watch. According to his mathematical table, they were approaching the last weir chamber before the bridge: this was the manhole his friends had told him to watch for. "Katy, we've done it—it's Highgate!"

They pulled the canoe out of the water, onto the stone edge of the tunnel. It was hard work getting it up the steps of the weir chamber; two of their flashlights tumbled back into the canal. Brad popped the manhole; not hearing Katy behind him, he turned. She seemed in a trance, about to fall back into the water. "Hey, stay awake—give me your hand." He had difficulty reaching her in the dark; she kept slipping away from him. Finally he got a firm grip on her and managed to shove her to solid ground. Her body felt cold. As soon as she was outside she collapsed.

"Breathe, Katy—we're in New York."

She opened her eyes; she was lying on real grass. She

saw Highgate Bridge stretching across the Harlem River; its great arches made it look like a true Roman aqueduct. They had emerged from the tunnel at the edge of the cliff; the river was maybe a hundred feet down.

"Oh, my God—we're at the Harlem River! Wait till I tell the Sci gang—this is the real stuff."

It didn't matter now that it was hard work lowering the canoe down the side of the cliff; once Katy saw the daylight, she felt okay. She didn't complain about scraping her legs going down the rocks sideways.

It was late afternoon when they floated down the Harlem River. They had been in the tunnel eight hours, but it had felt like a year. Katy looked at the tugboats passing them; the cars whizzing by on the road hugging the river seemed diminutive; the row of small office buildings dotting the drive had a small-town feel. Katy noticed that a furniture truck paralleling their course bore an odd name—Belle Hélène. She giggled: furniture pêche melba!

She stretched her face up; the sun's rays were warming her skin. Brad had had the right idea. It felt great floating slowly downriver toward Manhattan.

Brad lifted up the canoe paddles and just let the boat drift; he reminded Katy that they weren't far from Willie Lawn's limestone house on Sugar Hill, and from Tartan's apartment.

He confessed to her that the trip had made him feel that he had gone beyond his mother, beyond the small bedroom overlooking Mount Jefferson Park. He couldn't grasp it all, but he was sure that the trip had changed his life. It was so good, so good . . .

By early evening they reached Carl Schurz Park, at the edge of the East River; the dimly lit city gave off an amber haze.

▼ ▼ ▼

Brad closed his eyes; he had done his feat: He imagined a battery of pressmen snapping their photo, their names written in white smoke above the skyscrapers. He heard ships' bells ringing from the fleet of ocean-going vessels chugging up the East River to honor them. "History happens in New York," he said with satisfaction.

"No," Katy answered. "I think when they call it history they mean it's happened in Europe."

Brad pictured a night of festivities and fireworks even grander than that which had greeted the *Croton Maid* one hundred years earlier. He hadn't a clue what they would do with the canoe, but compared to what they had just done, getting it back to Gohonk would be a cinch.

He looked out at the city skyline; the idea again crossed his mind that without the Croton Aqueduct New York would have been destroyed. And the Civil War lost.

Brad stood straight up in the boat and stretched his arms toward Manhattan, rising from the sea, shouting above the foghorns like in the movies: "We're coming on through with the *Croton Maid*—you would have lost the war without her!" Then he beat his chest like King Kong and called out, "Hurrah for the *Croton Maid*. Happy birthday! This beats Gettysburg!"

From the river neither of them could hear the real sounds of celebration going on in Times Square; they didn't know the war was over.

CHAPTER

12

THREE YEARS LATER, BRAD, SEVENTEEN, stripped to his waist, smoking a Chesterfield, looked out the window of the Touring Traveler Motel off the Post Road leading into South Norwalk. He wondered why a convoy of navy trucks from the New London base was heading south. Watching them whiz by took his mind off having to tell Katy about his scholarship to Wisconsin and all that he meant it to imply.

Say it now. When she gets her clothes on, tell her it has to be over. Explain it was kids' stuff. Convince her it could never be. Remind her you are Negro. Tell her you're quitting Harlem for good, Indian Path forever. You're not the local orphan—you're not her orphan, you're not Tartan's good boy, you're not her old man's black Oliver Twist. You are not the teacher's colored pet with mathematical promise. You are not Uncle Willie's nice-nephew-with-white-blood going to church every Sunday. You are Bradford

Culver, and you got your own scholarship to Wisconsin in the worst of all possible times—all those returning veterans already have their squatters' rights, and you got it—a full-time, all-time, bull's-eye scholarship. And thank you, Ma'am; no, I don't play football. You did it with your brain, Brad boy, and you are getting out, out from under all of them. What a fall it will be! In September you are taking a sleeper to Chicago, then, just like in the brochure they sent you, you're taking a second train up north to—oh my God—Madison, Wisconsin!

He smoked one cigarette after another, watching Katy. She pulled her panties up her tanned legs and snapped the ends of her bra together in back of her shoulders with a sporty flourish. The small roundnesses of her breasts unexpectedly struck a chord of guilt in him; her flesh seemed oddly unprotected—vulnerable—he felt a pang.

It occurred to him he would never see her naked again. Then he imagined himself inside his future—motoring across the Great Lakes, being a college man—his heart beat fast with the adventure of it. He waited until Katy buttoned her dress; always he would remember her in that pale, washed-out blue shirtwaist. "Katy," he blurted awkwardly—the speeches he had rehearsed had been longer, more elegant—"I don't love you. It's over—I'm going away. Don't ask me where."

Part of Brad had wanted it to end, to get on with meeting new people, sleeping with women who had never known him before his freshman year at Madison, Wisconsin; another, deeper side remained enmeshed with Katy. He had been able to daydream of a new existence in Wisconsin because he was sure Katy wouldn't let him go without a fight—he half banked on her strength to make him stay with her—the way he saw it, he was merely beginning to introduce the issue. To appease the terrible rattle of future desires and awful guilt inside him, Brad had conveniently endowed her with the strengths of her father, the magic staying power of Indian Path. Brad and Katy were so much flesh of the same flesh, past of the same past, that he had no distance with which to see her clearly.

He had struck Katy in her essence: she had no side, no guard against him. She heard only that he didn't want her—Brad didn't love her. The trimmings didn't matter; he had said the dread, unsayable *I-do-not-love-you.*

In Brad's experience people said things every day they didn't exactly mean; they fought; they used strong words. Sharp. A twist of the knife; the next day was the next day. It had escaped his notice that Katy had no recourse to such powerful sentiments—she didn't know how to volley in his style—she took him literally: he had overshot his mark.

Katy had no power to hold him; she took him at face value. It never occurred to her to assert her own position in the matter; and her new lack of desirability for Brad was not, she assumed, a negotiable item.

Brad had never meant her to go limp and silent; he panicked. He grabbed her shoulders and shook her: "Christ, Katy—say something, say something! No—don't. You left it to me—you are leaving the son-of-a-bitch part to me, and God damn you, God damn Tartan. Does my mother need to call herself by that crazy name?" he yelled at her. "Why did Willie and your family let her? Her name is Mary—Mary Culver, same as Jesus' momma. I forgot, *you* don't pray to Jesus—do you know what the smart nigger Leftie gang at Bronx Sci laughs about? You want to know how Harlem recruits for the Communist Youth? 'Come down to our parties in Manhattan and you can screw all those hot Jewish broads who want niggers.' That's *you* they are talking about—that's us!"

"What's *us* is that you don't love me—some moron at Bronx Sci is not us." Katy had found her voice; she was answering him.

So the silence was gone, and Brad was less scared.

"Listen—don't make me into the all-time shit. Okay, it's us—and I'm doing this for both of us. Next year you go where? Radcliffe? Bryn Mawr? Or will it be Bennington or Swarthmore? Where do I fit in? I'm your nigger Mickey Rooney, the boy next door? Okay—what are your future plans? Post Road motels from here to Boston?"

"You said you don't love me—"

Brad's breathing quickened; his anxiety became worse. He hadn't meant things to become so final so quickly—it was Katy who was doing that. She sounded like a broken blues record with that you-don't-love-me shit; he should have put it another way.

"Katy, okay—we were kids together. And that part will never change. Your old man . . ." He hesitated; his mouth parched at the wild thoughts exploding in his head; he didn't really dare think that Katy was his half-sister. ". . . was—was my only father. You are the closest to a daughter Tartan, born Mary Culver, got. We can't keep sleeping together—it goes against natural law."

"What natural law?"

Brad trembled with shame at the thought of being faced with Jeremiah Becker; Tartan's fury would know no limits—he literally felt her fists beating against his chest—in his mother's eyes his behavior would be unholy; she'd call him the devil. An animal. Why didn't Katy see they had put themselves outside the margin of normal society? His head was bursting: he heard Willie Lawn and Jessica and the whole lot of them cursing at him; Wisconsin would take away his scholarship. He was scared, so scared. "Have you the courage?" he asked her.

"We could have gotten married after college—we could have," she insisted.

"Are you nuts? Joan of Arc, of the nigger race? Queen Captain Courageous? Since when have you been so filled with rebellious iron?"

"Not that rebellious, Brad—but that privileged."

When Katy finally relocated her tongue, her sentences came out sounding older, oddly more sophisticated.

"We're not exactly living in the Deep South, so get off it. You think I wouldn't be invited to Monday openings at the Westport Playhouse because I'd had a light-skinned Negro boyfriend who is crackerjack at science and math and subjects like that? Huh! That would be the day—all that would happen if you and me went there together, and openly, as boyfriend and girlfriend, is that whoever is giving opening-night champagne parties by those kidney-shaped rock pools in New Canaan and Weston and Bethel would invite us to more of them. Those party people would say, 'Bingo, hurrah, and more champagne.'"

Katy paused to consider the picture; it flitted through her mind that her class at Friends' would be in awe of her, think her smashing if eventually she married Brad—she'd cause a sensation.

"So melodrama me no melodrama, and do me the favor

of not dragging Negro-and-white stuff into what is only our personal stuff—all that is happening is that you don't love me. If you did, the rest wouldn't matter. We could have made it—if you were clear about what you wanted, and wanted it badly enough, there'd be a way. Plenty of ways." Katy stopped, then added in a low voice, "You're a son of a bitch."

She threw her hairbrush into her straw shoulder bag, unlatched the door, and walked out. From the window, Brad watched her walking firmly—almost jauntily, he thought in terror—to the car lot near the drive-in movie. Her back was straight; she had amazingly broad shoulders for a girl. He stared after her as though committing his view of her to memory forever.

From the back, her bowlegs were more marked; as she walked, she scuffed each foot against the other shoe, making round, dusty moons on her anklebones because they jutted out—he had never seen another girl with those dusty moons. Katy reached up and ran her fingers through her wavy hair, the way she did before walking into the big house at Indian Path after they had made love together and she was revving up to see her folks, needing a lie, needing to look angelic. She got into the Indian Path station wagon; without looking back, she drove off.

A cloud of brown grit from her speeding Dodge covered the swinging painted orange sign, TOURING TRAVELER MOTEL. It was a small thing, he realized, but it was the first time in their lives she had left a place they had come to together without him—she wasn't fair: he was furious with her. Why hadn't she let him talk out the nigger-white business? Why did she never listen? She always pulled him away from what was deep in him, from what had to be talked out, to this brisk happy-ending stuff—the up-and-coming moral life as pronounced, received, and defined in Friends' Seminary: Go to Swarthmore, and the world will smile with you, Miss Buttercup!

His fears about what his mother and Jeremiah and Willie and Jessica would say receded; what remained was only confusion, a pounding in his head. He no longer remembered what he had told Katy to drive her so inexorably away. His heart beat so fast, so fast.

Don't panic. You can't die—it's all ahead of you. The big jumps in the future. Don't be scared. Say—Wisconsin Wisconsin Wisconsin. Chicago Madison Madison Chicago. Say—Wisconsin, make way for Bradford Culver; I'm coming on the train. Katy, don't leave. Christ, why did we have to talk about love?

Brad sat by himself in the dip in the bed Katy had just deserted. He pressed their pillow to his nostrils, inhaling the deep aftermath of their lovemaking, the smell of their flesh-fucked-of-their-flesh. Alone as he had never been, he laid his head down on the bed, pulled up his legs to his chest in a fetal position, and howled. Clutching one of her hairpins that had dropped on the pillow, he cradled his head in his hands; he shrieked like the wild animal he felt himself to be. He lay there and howled and howled; never again in his life did he make that cavernous sound, never again did he moan from that place deep within him.

Years later, when he and Katy tried to talk about it, she was married to Lewis Eichorn, he to Elise Bingham, and he reproached her for walking out on him. Katy insisted that it had happened the other way around—it occurred to neither that it had been mutual.

It was still the slow, sluggish August heat; Katy took the New Haven local back to the city. She stared out the window at the burned end-of-summer brown grass; the train whirred past the Post Road Dairy Queen; she saw Darien's main street, its newspaper building, and its movie theater—some summers she and Brad had biked down there just to walk around in a different town. When the conductor called out "Mamaroneck," she recalled their first wild time, with her reading *Nana* and the locked piss-smelling train john. Then her mind numbed; despite the intense heat, she felt cold. Without her having noticed anything was wrong, her body was shaking. She got out at the 125th Street station with the idea of taking a taxi home.

Weaving. She stumbled alongside the tracks in the direction of the exit stairwell. The moving train seemed joined to an almost naked, fat-armed woman sitting in the window of a railroad flat on a level with the station; she was fanning herself, leaning over a red geranium pot on her fire escape. STUMMEL'S KOSHER CHICKENS. RIVERA'S PALACIO DE MEUBLES. FATHER DIVINE. THE FIRST BAPTIST CHURCH OF THE HOLY APOS-TATE. FATHER DIVINE. DIVINE FATHER. GRANDMOTHER INDY. THE BLUE VASE. AS BLUE AS THE WATER AT INDIAN PATH. WHERE IS MY DIVINE FATHER. DIVINE BECAUSE HE IS DIVINE.

She believed she was seeing the market stalls at 116th Street, the pushcarts below. She heard Olga Zweicky's voice: "Can you pick as good as your Momma? If you do I'll give you one free." Only Olga was her dead Grandma Indy; Katy's aunts were taking her to Indy, to God, to the sky, it was so cold, she was drowning in water. Abruptly, with no warning sound, Katy fainted on the concrete track of the Grand Central.

When she came to, she was downstairs in the waiting room: one of the conductors had seen her fall, and he'd carried her down there. He had tried to make her comfortable on a dark brown bench near the ticket window. She looked up—all of Manhattan seemed to be leaning down over her, slopping cold water on her face.

A police officer—he had been cruising the neighborhood—wanted to take her to Saint Luke's; he insisted he had to leave her in someone's care. Katy knew the Fifth Avenue apartment would be empty, so she asked him to take her to Tartan's; it was only ten blocks from the station.

When Tartan saw the police officer helping Katy up her stoop steps—Katy looked like an Arab boy, with her wet towel wrapped turban style around her head—she screamed.

"It's the heat, ma'am," the officer said. "She suffered sunstroke at the train station."

The Italian woman whose relations ran Rao's saw it all. She came running with lemons, little black olives, and salt. She and Tartan put Katy to bed in Brad's room. "Let her suck the lemons—then eat the salt," the woman said. Tartan iced the back of Katy's neck, her wrists, her temples. The women waited until Katy's breathing was regular; after she fell asleep they went to the front room.

The Italian woman understood Tartan's fears. "She's not pregnant—it is a heatstroke. I can tell by the feel of her head, her skin—she hasn't got that look, if you know what I mean."

Tartan thanked her for the lemons; she believed her neighbor. When she was alone waiting for Katy to wake up, she thought, at least it wasn't the big nightmare—she wasn't carrying. Tartan knew she bore a terrible burden: she seemed to be the only adult who had noticed what had been going on between her son and her baby, her adored Karen Tess. She had no one to tell—not Willie, not even her cousin Jessica. She understood she had been keeping secret vigil for a long time over her private hell—there was nothing to do but stay with it and hope her burden would be over. She prayed Brad would get to Wisconsin and the two children would forget what had gone on between them; best if everything could be as though the bad thing never happened.

Oddly, when Katy came to—though she was lying on Brad's bed, looking through the same window and at the same stunted cactus plant he had done for nearly his whole life—Brad had flown entirely from her mind. She got up, washed her face, put on fresh dark red lipstick, and sprayed her arms, hair, and earlobes with a Prince Matchabelli pocket perfume atomizer she carried in her straw bag.

Tartan said nothing to her—she busied herself taking the spuds out of potatoes so that there would be no talk between them. Katy used her kitchen telephone to call Gabe Frolich. Tartan, who kept her eyes on the potatoes, noticed that Katy laughed a lot as she talked to him.

"Tartan, it's much cooler now. The winds are coming in off the East River. I feel fine—I have a date this evening with Gabe Frolich. After college he's going to medical school." She giggled. "If I get struck by the crazy heat again, I can be his first patient."

Tartan relaxed; she felt she'd been given a reprieve. After

172

she saw Katy into a taxi, she went back inside her apartment. She walked into her airless, dark bedroom and fell to her knees in front of a colored picture of Christ on the cross. *Dear God dear God oh my Lord my God let it be Gabe.*

Katy had never thought it would be Gabe—not for the long haul. She had hesitated in Tartan's kitchen. Call Snowball? The two of them could spend a delicious evening reclining on her cousin's organdy-canopied four-poster; Hewley Ginzberg Wurlitzer had lugged her simulated-antique South Carolina furniture with her to Manhattan at the end of the First World War. Not that the Ginzberg clan had arrived in the South in time for the Civil War, or even the Reconstruction, but Hewley had never given up on the idea of being southern. She always boasted about her brother marrying a South Carolina Cohn—the Cohns had buried their silver in their backyard in anticipation of Sherman's march. But the general bypassed Waylee, so the Cohns dug it up and kept it. Even though it was a reproduction, Katy envied her cousin her *Gone with the Wind* bed; it was a nice memento from Waylee.

Katy considered confiding her sadness to Snowball. She knew that, sandwiched between the sambas and rumbas they practiced together (Snowball had a bunch of them), they would end up spending the evening commiserating with each other, alternating despair with daring schemes about possible new men who might be coming down the pike. She decided against seeing her cousin: It would mean reliving Brad's rejection of her. Katy didn't want to think about that.

▼ ▼ ▼

Gabe was delighted to be picking Katy up at her folks' place at a time when her family was at Indian Path—only the two of them were in the apartment. Katy looked great. She was wearing a tight black cotton dress that went high at the neck and was cut deep in back, leaving her arms and part of her back bare. She was humming a number from the "Hit Parade" when she went to open the front door to let him in. Right away she padded barefoot to the pantry to get them ice and drinks. Gabe walked into the kitchen behind her; his specialty, he told her, was whiskey sours. Gabe made good ones, and Jeremiah's bar had the right fixings to put in them.

Katy opened the living-room arched windows to let some of the musty air out—the big front windows overlooking the park were protected from the heat by heavy green canvas awnings with thick white fringes; not many apartment houses still had those. Anita had fitted the deep club chairs and wide twin sofas in gray pinstriped summer duck—the plethora of starched slipcovers and pervasive smell of mothballs made the apartment seem extra quiet and empty.

They sat on the sofa. First they listened to Gabe's rebop records, then they fooled around a bit, getting sticky, and had to wash up before going out. Gabe didn't press Katy to continue their mild lovemaking—he had a nice, even feeling that sooner or later, but probably sooner, the two of them would bed down. It was glorious: the two of them alone in Manhattan on a fine August night, looking good and with no excessive cares bogging them down, the idea of college looming vaguely ahead. The whiskey sours made them the right degree of tight.

For a lark they took a taxi down to the tip of the island. "Wall Street is at its romantic best on a deserted weekend," Gabe said. "Why not take a quick jaunt on the Staten Island ferry?"

Coming back, they saw the Statue rise lushly green out of the night sea. Katy leaned against the rail of the ferry in her best Bette Davis *Now, Voyager* style; Gabe had placed his jacket over her shoulders—he could have been George Brent in the same movie.

The transatlantic steamers were making tourist runs to Europe again, but the ferry was as much of a steamer and the Narrows as much of a sea as either of them had known. Gabe insisted on making a great night of it. When they disembarked at Bowling Green they grabbed a second cab and went to the Blue Angel to hear Pearl Bailey.

Katy had a fresh whiskey sour. She leaned back against the small chair in the crowded room, playfully tapping her feet in time to the blues. She felt an enormous sense of relief; she felt free. She wore no bra, no panties under the tight cotton dress. Spiritually, too, she felt unburdened. Though it seemed a small thing, she and Brad had never gone anywhere that would have cost money. Katy knew he had to save what he earned, but it was awkward—he wouldn't have liked her offering to pay, and he had no extra, so they just did what was free. She looked around the nightclub. It was interesting, being in a place like this. Near the front door were newspaper clippings featuring Mademoiselle Claude Alphand, Imogene Coca, a Met diva she had never heard of—Natalie Bodanya—and an invitation to an opening for a handwriting analyst named Diana.

Amazingly, Brad, who had been the center of her

universe since she had reached in her crib to touch his thin chicken-wing shoulders in his bundled, small body of old flannel pajamas and had felt the grief in his stricken blue eyes, dropped out of her mind like he was yesterday's rained-on newspaper.

Over the years, when she thought back to that particular August day, she preferred dwelling on Brad's dumping her and her fainting at the 125th Street station. In the many versions she redid in her head, adjusting her memory to suit the changing condition of her life, she preferred to erase the great good time Gabe gave her that summer's end. Scenario-wise, it never fit.

▼ ▼ ▼

Jeremiah was pleased but unsurprised when Katy graduated Barnard with honors. The girl, he always said, had potential. But she seemed, he felt—though he couldn't put his finger on it—to have taken a step backward; she was not as focused as she had been as a child. Searching for a descriptive word for his daughter, as he watched her prepare at Indian Path for her winter wedding to Lewis Eichorn, a Columbia philosophy professor she had met in her last year at Barnard—he finally put his finger on it: his daughter had become astonishingly *inattentive*.

She was irritatingly vague about Lewis's family, and overly delighted with unimportant, temporary details; she boasted to Jeremiah about Lewis being older than Jim, old enough to have been in the war, like that was an essential accomplishment. Jeremiah conceded that you married the man, not his family, but, he argued with her, you should have the basic facts as to what the family habits were. Neither of his children struck him as *thorough*.

Still, the day after the wedding, as he stood at the mid-town Hudson pier used by the French Line, his arm around Anita—Jim and Tartan were also there—waving to Katy and Lewis, he had to admit that they made a fine couple. Katy waved back to him, leaning over the first-class railing. They were sailing for a month's tour of Europe; the ship was the *De Grasse*.

PART THREE

Stray Bright

People

CHAPTER

13

By THE TIME OF KATY'S NEXT MEETING
with her lawyer, Max Schecter, Indian summer had come
and gone, the high bloom of foliage was spent, and brown
leaves lay dry-curled on the ground. The days were shorter,
melancholic. No one had bothered to write much about the
Statue of Liberty's one-hundredth birthday, though it had
been big news in July. Katy sat in the Schecter, Leary, and
Fuccoli waiting room reading a snappy account in *New York*
magazine of a Catalan sculptor's plan to marry, dada style,
Liberty to Barcelona's statue of Christopher Columbus in
honor of the 1992 celebration of the discovery of America.
*Next the media will come up with an anniversary for Eve's eating
her apple.*

▼ ▼ ▼

"Scuttle the past," Max lectured Katy after she was comfortably seated in his office. "Bury the dead—stop questioning your relationship to Lewis. What was, was. Chuck your ambivalence. Take Hamlet—what killer lawyer would have wanted *him* as a client? Your problem is that you don't hate your brother-in-law enough. Beanie screwed you and your son, yet you waste your time and mine musing on Lewis's and your neurotic attitude to money. You make it sound as though Lewis's nineteen-sixties radical do-goodism caused his half brother to be a crook. I've news for you—no one *causes* a medium-rich man to embezzle on his way up to flashier stuff. Leave such psychological luxuries for the next stage. After we've won." He sighed. "If there is a next stage. Which now seems remote. Frankly, I don't see a smoking gun."

Max stood up and paced as he recapped their position: "We know that your father-in-law's primary corporation—the Belle Hélène furniture corporation, which was founded by his father—always made a lot of money. Almost until the time of Lewis's death. Then those corporations dwindled down to nothing. There are no cash reserves—yet you tell me that your father-in-law was an old-fashioned gent who kept his corporations loaded with excess financial backing and debt free. Beanie then liquidates as bankrupt Belle Hélène and all its satellite corporations, keeping only the worthless office buildings up in Harlem. At the same time Beanie suddenly becomes the chief partner in a booming new real-estate conglomerate, the Green Spruce Nine—"

"Max, you know Beanie seedbedded Green Spruce Nine by using his and Lewis's joint Belle Hélène inheritance as his private pot."

"Dear heart, knowing is not proving—where's our evidence? We've found zilch. His business adviser, Ronnie Munche, may be a creative type with numbers, but he's also been very clever. Smooth."

Schecter's rhetoric puts you in his employ instead of the reverse. Soon he'll start reminding you how suing Beanie was your idea, not his. How rotten he feels about having to take over your apartment as payment for a lost cause. Et cetera. Et cetera.

She saw Max take note of her misery—abruptly, he switched tactics.

"I see a small point of vulnerability. I did some checking up on Ronnie Munche—he has a blurry history. He's known as a Chicago guy who operates out of Delaware; he was involved in a major Maryland lawsuit concerning the misuse of funds of a philanthropic foundation. So far we've concentrated on the corporations, not on the Belle Hélène Foundation. But your father-in-law's will stipulates that the foundation's income must be used for the benefit of medical research and survivors of the holocaust. I'll bet dollars to doughnuts Beanie hasn't complied—he could find himself in real hot water over this. He can't disinherit you and Matt from the foundation. It's a trust—you have minority voting power. It's the only one of his corporations where you have an automatic right to demand the books."

Katy was on to Max's rhythms: at the end of their doom-and-gloom sessions, he would throw her a bone of hope.

"Maybe it's a fishing trip, but there's a chance that, via the foundation, we will gain a handle on Beanie's method of diverting assets out of existing corporations and converting them into capital for his Green Spruce Nine." Max leaned back into his leather chair, pausing for dramatic effect.

183

"Now, I want you to make your presence felt at the Belle Hélène Foundation. Reclaim your legitimate territory. Go to their functions. At the very least, we make Ronnie sweat. Always a good idea to make a clown with his hands in the cookie jar sweat. Loosens up the tongue. On the other hand, if all this delving leads to no—"

"Smoking gun?"

"—exactly—and is getting too pricy for you, Katy, you say the word. And we'll call a halt."

She wanted to kill him. *The bastard knew she couldn't climb down off the trolley car, even if she wanted to. That's exactly what Beanie and Ronnie were counting on—her being trapped in a financial vise and having to drop the case. Give in to such scum now? Midstream, with nothing to show for it?*

"No, Max. No."

▼ ▼ ▼

The next month, Katy received an invitation from the Belle Hélène Foundation—she was on their list, though she never went—to a special evening for the *American Rebel*, a non-profit magazine that managed, because of its articles on the causes of World War II, to be eligible for a Belle Hélène grant. The meeting was at Beanie's townhouse. *Perfect*; she'd get Snowball to come with her. *Max is right. Stand your ground—Beanie doesn't own the foundation.*

▼ ▼ ▼

The night of the party, Katy stayed late at the Schmidlapp. She was working on a new exhibit of Italian Renaissance drawings; she motioned her male assistant to raise the position of the Ferdinando Galli Bibiena.

" '*Architettura civile preparata sulle geometrie e ridotta alla prospettiva . . .*' " she read to him from the new Schmidlapp catalog. "Nice, isn't it?" She glanced at him.

His reedy, dark, few-years-out-of-college good looks remind you of Matt. But you can't telephone a grown son and carry on about missing him. Can't dump on him the load of being the only son of a widowed mother. With a daughter it would have been easier—you could have been more up-front. Felt freer to continue the closeness longer.

" 'Bibiena discovered the *veduta per angolo*,' " she continued in a monotone to her helper, as though her explanation were vital to his education. "It's a way of replacing traditional symmetrical perspective by lateral vision from a forty-five-degree angle."

She noticed he didn't respond. Again she thought of Matt. She didn't want him to know the case was going badly; he had told her his work was going well. And he had a girlfriend he liked.

Face it. You can't stand having him so far away. At heart, the eternal mother. But she was alert to his anxiety about her life—in their Houston–New York phone conversations he tried to mask his concern for her by asking offhand questions about what she was doing, sandwiched in between what new movies he had seen that were awful or good. So she always remembered to tell him what nice things she and Ethan had done together. Like Ethan was her perfect mate. And also what movies she had seen that were awful or good. *Maybe that's half the reason you remain with Ethan. So Matt won't think of you as alone.*

Her mind drifted back to her time with Mike Braden and to their affair. When it began Matt was still a scholarship student at prep school. *Funny what you remember. Why do Mike's remarks about Matt still stick in your mind?*

"Sweetie," he said, "do you talk to Matt about sex?"

"I can't do everything," you replied. "I lecture him on drugs."

"Sweetie, I have news for you." Mike kept on going with his unasked-for analysis of their mother-son situation. "He probably knows more about your sex life than you do."

"We just leave it oblique," you insisted.

That was when Mike began to take Matt to hockey games. *Matt didn't like it when you broke up.* Afterward he never mentioned Mike to Katy.

▼ ▼ ▼

She paused on the way up to her office to pinch a dead leaf from the bushy coleus planted in the giant Chinese export cachepot on the second-floor marble staircase landing. Once inside her private work space, she absentmindedly wiped the dust off her desktop with her sweater. *Stop housekeeping. Stop treating the Schmidlapp like it's your home—you're the curator here.*

She liked her work. She also liked telling her friends about the place's funny history:

The Schmidlapp believed they possessed the missing triptych of Hieronymus Bosch's *World Before the Deluge*. The Museum Boymans–Van Beuningen in Rotterdam, though not entirely convinced of its authenticity, wanted to enter in negotiations with them for it.

Herman Schmidlapp, the German Jewish clock heir, had acquired the triptych in Holland in the early 1920s. Bosch was of particular importance to him because of the artist's interest in the Hebrew religion and intense anticlericalism.

One of the scholars at the foundation suspected that Bosch was part Jewish on his maternal side and that the mysterious "M" signature embedded in his works referred, in German, to "*Mutter.*"

The other acquisitions had been a hodgepodge: a fair Sargent, Zuolaga's portraits of society women, and some Hudson Valley—the Schmidlapp collection of Rodin busts, the portrait of Loïe Fuller, and their Romanian room of court fans were another story.

Queen Marie of Romania had met Herman Schmidlapp after the First World War through his crony Sam Hill—Hill's father-in-law owned the Great Northern Railway. Marie introduced both men to Loïe Fuller, the American who had created a sensation at the Folies Bergères by dancing in the buff while twirling gauze scarfs over revolving colored gas lights; Rodin had adored her. Loïe and Marie persuaded Hill and Schmidlapp to open museums on the West Coast and in New York.

The foundation had taken Katy on to help in their plan for acquiring contemporaries of Bosch with a similar bent for Old Testament and alchemy; they felt a strong medieval concentration would give their small museum a distinct identity that would mesh well with the general drift of things in Manhattan. They also wanted to minimize the impact of the Romanian fan collection and Loïe's scarfs. Katy had been in charge of relocating them, along with Queen Marie donations, to the top floor.

▼ ▼ ▼

She'd promised to pick Snowball up in front of her lab. She took a taxi to the West Side. Going down Columbus, she saw odd signs lighting up the night. A small church was squeezed between Barnyard Sweet No-Cholesterol Chicken and Cubana Wong-Ton; the wacky orange neon message atop the church's roof—The Ten Commandments Are Not Ten Suggestions—struck Katy as more in line with the take-out menus of the food places adjoining it than with a specific religion.

▼ ▼ ▼

God, Snowball looks great! Standing in a rain-drenched trench coat on the night-traffic-busy wet downtown street, her tawny-haired cousin still impressed Katy as remarkable looking. When they were at Barnard and Gabe was at Columbia, Snowball had attracted men and women; in the 1950s, college campuses still produced beauties. Katy recalled how she would saunter up Broadway near Chock Full O' Nuts smelling of Ma Griffe. Snowball was a case of Galileo's law in reverse: magnetic energy rose from her sculpted ankles quicker than the speed of light, traveling up her colt's legs and long torso to her luminescent, honey-toned face; waist-length hair the color of straw framed her melancholic green eyes and straight Aryan nose.

Gabe swore to Katy that the Jewish male students were all mad for her cousin; they couldn't believe that this Viking daughter was one of their own. He said a classmate of his wanted to bring Snowball home to his parents just because he knew they'd be ecstatic if they thought their son was screwing a Jewish student who looked like Hitler's dream girl.

Snowball's most heroic achievement, her sacred element, was having no bodily blemishes. No other woman came near her. Certainly not Katy. She saw herself as too freckled, too lumpy in the wrong places, just one more tumultuous, dark-haired, irregular-featured female, one among many Barnard women students in the fifties.

She seems low. Katy held open the taxi door and kissed Snowball. She understood that her cousin regarded her great good looks as an alien event, of no great importance other than that they pleased Hewley, her mother, whose narcissism was rooted in an earlier era when physical female beauty was of primary importance. At Barnard Snowball had always insisted to Katy that her sole goal was to get a science fellowship for graduate school. She thought it would make up for the emptiness caused when her father had walked out on her mother. She wanted a career so as not to be caught short like Hewley had been.

But when Shawn split, leaving her alone with Agatha, she shattered in some permanent way. Katy put her arm around Snowball and embraced her again. Her cousin's sweetness, her blinking, orphaned vulnerability had a magnetic appeal that enmeshed Katy as tightly as, when they had been infants together in the same crib, Brad's thin Doctor Denton–flannel-covered chicken-wing shoulders had done. She recognized Snowball's meteoric rise as an exemplary woman molecular biologist—she had lucked out in the seventies' boom for women in her field—but her dazzling beauty hadn't protected her against loss.

▼ ▼ ▼

Katy stood with Snowball in the entryway of Beanie and Thonia's sleek, double-width townhouse. She fumbled with a pair of dark sunglasses: she wanted not to see the smug

189

richness of Beanie's life. *But who other than Andy Warhol would wear such glasses in the evening?* She put them back in her bag.

Until now she had managed not to witness Beanie's triumph. She had avoided dealing face-to-face with the concrete evidence of his place in the world, the power his money had got him. *While you and Matt were scraping the barrel, he was buying up art like there was no tomorrow. Easier to escape into Ethan's Austin sound, like Texas is your natural geography, than to remember there is another world in which you and Matt were meant to belong.*

"A businessman's art," Mike had been fond of remarking to Katy when she was with him at Hannah's Point, "always tells you when he made his boodle."

Or stole his boodle.

Beanie had three huge Schnabels and a vast Anselm Kiefer evoking Frederick II of Prussia, the Third Reich, and Richard Wagner. Beanie's wife, Thonia, the daughter of a German industrialist, owned her own gallery in Munich; she had gotten Beanie to buy the Kiefer. The paintings dominated the downstairs rooms—early-eighties Italian postmodern. (Beanie's father had possessed one small, discreet Sargent, hung in a large living room abundant in overstuffed peach silk sofas and Chinese silk screens.) Thonia—they were childless—was fond of remarking to her American women friends that American men never divorced their European wives.

Keep walking. Say hi to Lewis's friends. Did they think you'd vaporized, vanished from the scene like the proverbial ball of rolling dust? Did no one find it peculiar that your name and Matt's stopped appearing on Belle Hélène Foundation stuff? Did they think, with Lewis's death, that you had ceased to be?

190

Max is right. You can't run away from the clear knowledge of what Beanie's done and still win. You do know about money and power and foundations—you work for one. You jolly well know that no one would dare push Schmidlapp heirs around like they were yesterday's garbage. But it had been easier, that first year after Lewis's death, to slip into a fuguelike breakdown than to face the fact that her half brother-in-law was gobbling up her assets under the guise of helping her settle her joint interests with him. *You didn't want to believe helpful male family members no longer existed.*

When Beanie saw her, his eyes swiftly went to Ronnie Munche—Ronnie always seemed to manage to be at Beanie's side—and then back to Katy. "Well, hello there—"

"I thought I should participate more"—she paused, choosing her phrasing carefully—"in our family's philan-thropic projects."

Beanie looked very tweedy and at home in his lemon-and-black downstairs library. When he smiled, his sandy hair and fresh grin made him look like a kid. Only his eyes—they roamed in too many directions—were no good. "Well, welcome aboard."

She stood her ground. As one reclaiming her territory. Then she took stock. Coolly, as though her heart weren't beating like a trapped animal, she surveyed the scene.

One of Beanie's stars for the evening, wavy- and white-haired Henry Brody, was standing beneath the sockeroo Schnabel clutching the arm of his final mistress—Amanda Bollington Dunkel, a pal of Thonia's. Amanda was a lapsed British Catholic with a fondness for Graham Greene and American Jewish men. Katy had heard rumors about both

Henry and Amanda—stuff that had happened way before her time. Brody's main claims to fame had been pronouncing Stalin evil in advance of his old-time Greenwich Village Bohemian pals, and knowing Trotsky in Mexico City. In point of fact, he had been one of Trotsky's guards, and rather naive about letting visitors—including Trotsky's assassin—into the house. In order to show Brody that no one held Trotsky's death against him, one of his rich friends had helped him found the *American Rebel*. The review's lively, palmy days had been during World War II. About ten years ago, Amanda had seen in the moribund *American Rebel* and the fatigued Henry Brody her golden moment: *Carpe diem*. She ran off to Arizona with both. She started to promote Henry; through her friendship with Thonia she got Beanie to float the *American Rebel*.

Katy and Snowball walked past her. Snowball whispered, "Beanie couldn't have touched a New York museum wing for under thirty mill. Writers are the bargain-basement buy of the city. The good opportunities for philanthropy in the arts have already been snapped up."

"Really?"

"Rumor is that Saul Steinberg's wife picked up all of PEN for him for under two hundred thou a year."

"Where did you hear that?"

" 'Page Six.' "

The two cousins went farther into the room. Katy stopped. "Snowball—there's Gabe!"

So he still sees Beanie. Katy thought back to their Fourth of July conversation, how she had berated Gabe for being disloyal to her by treating Beanie. *So what's his function here? Hardly that of a therapist . . .*

He introduced them to an Argentinian woman, a Melanie Kleinian–turned–Lacanian who was explaining Gardel tangos to him.

"Ah, Katy"—he sighed, as if explaining his presence in the townhouse—"at least we are here for a good cause."

What good cause? Was the *American Rebel* a medical victim? Or a holocaust victim? Or any other type of victim? Was it new? Bohemian? A rebel? The crowd—bankers, lawyers, and some arbitrage men, all on its board—were "nice" Upper East Side. Their money was not so rawly fresh as the Boeskys', the Steinbergs'; they had just a little less of it, and their names were less often in the newspapers. Their morality consisted in *not* being named Boesky, in *not* being up for prison. In New York in the eighties this sufficed for honesty.

A gaggle of young critics were at the bar—they considered the heyday of the *American Rebel* a key part of their cultural history. *They have come here hoping to make connections. To meet an arrived critic, a real writer. Do they recognize that only the magazine's shell remains? What's the point in a little magazine that is not ahead of its own time? Who needs a laggardly avant-garde?*

The only thing the disparate group had in common, Katy thought, was that none of them, one way or the other, had been touched by the sixties. Beanie had been too busy making money, the critics were too young, Amanda had been keeping house on the Island, and Brody and his sullen cronies had spent the decade still pondering *Trotsky yes, Stalin no.* Was the absence of carnal knowledge of the civil rights movement and the goods and bads of the sixties enough of a tie to forge a tax-deductible cultural union?

The frail glue that bound them as a group was their total lack of firsthand knowledge about America.

But Beanie enjoys running the show. Paying for it to take place in his house, on his territory. Though he gets more kicks from his polo playing than owning art. Beanie really worked at the sport. Became a world champion—those press clips, and that type of fame was what mattered most to him. Being a first-rate polo player was his way of getting back at his father for marrying Lily. To Walter Eichorn, polo playing had been as alien as changing your religion.

She and Snowball walked out into the four-story greenhouse atrium.

A voice wafted past them: ". . . so Eichorn had to get his hotshot Barcelona architect to tear down four townhouses to get the Mediterranean look. They had a tremendous stroke of luck. They bulldozed just ahead of the landmark commission's decree."

The air smelled of cumin, saffron, and scorched lamb. Beanie's Moroccan *chouaye* chef, Snowball informed her (she was surprisingly more up on those details than Katy), had been stolen from the Mamounia in Marrakech, Churchill's favorite retreat. He was serving his specialty: *mechoui* of unborn lamb smuggled illegally into the States. He had turned it the entire day over low-burning coals.

The guests included two competing art dealers, one expert on nuclear deterrents, a Milano dress designer, one expert on biblical canon, a Channel Thirteen anchor, and two Russian dissidents. The evening's *American Rebel* discussion topic, led by Beanie and Amanda, was: The Mid-century American Jew: True Holocaust Victim.

An electronic device in the greenhouse flashed videos of outdoor scenes onto the back wall, behind the indoor

shrubbery. The pictures shifted from winter storms to summer gardens to the browns and rusts of Indian summer.
Katy watched Beanie, diaphanous disks of colored lights
flecking his head, silently mouthing his speech. He was
rehearsing.

Art, dreams, commerce had meant different things in
her parents' generation. Men like Jeremiah and Walter
Eichorn had been individualists in the creation of their
empires but conventional in their idea of charity. They gave
to their notion of the deserving poor. Their sons—types
like Beanie—were conventional in the expansion of their
inherited wealth—they made money off money—but solip-
sistic in their notion of philanthropy. "Tax deductible" had
replaced the old ideas of tithing; finally, absurdly, as with
Beanie and the *American Rebel*, the causes had become the
givers themselves.

So the Holocaust had become just one more equal-
opportunity gizmo; in America every victim for himself.

While Beanie was speaking, claiming a past suffering that
never had been his, Katy noticed a strange thing happen,
as bizarre as the Lulu who had floated above her head
during the pretrial deposition.

An old man with a long beard and a shawl and a good
face was chanting a solemn prayer. Wounds appeared on
his face and arms; he stretched his bloodied hands to protect
shadowy small figures helplessly floating behind him. Then
that mad bitch Lulu, with her sexy smell and rotten cackle,
went after him, nipping at his heels, laughing at his prayers.

"Scram, you old hen," Katy whispered, mortified that
the guests might take her for that impudent female squat.

So why should she care? The old man would never assign

his authentic history to Beanie. So there was just the problem of her own Lulu of a Lulu. Katy called out to her, *Go
after Beanie. He's nothing but a little boy from Andover furious
with his intellectual younger half brother and jealous of his rich
father, whose religion he went running from. Hear that? Tell that
to the moral old Jew. Tell him this isn't the scene he thinks it is,
tell him to scram—tell him how Beanie ran from guys like him,
but now that Beanie's a big shot, he wants everything—wants to be
them—the good, the maimed, the pure, and the Jewish dead. Their
past, his past. Moral old man, scram. You don't belong in this crowd.*

Amanda followed Beanie's talk with her own lugubrious
one. While she was speaking, Adam Klager walked in.

Katy saw by the way Beanie's skin mottled and from the
glances exchanged between him and Ronnie that Klager
was about as welcome at Beanie's *American Rebel* event as
Banquo's ghost.

She watched him standing in the doorway. Adam Klager
was a tall man whose domed bald head made him look even
taller; his face was now shrunken from the ravages of AIDS,
only his pale blue murderous eyes intact, as murderous as
when he had been a kid legal-eagle prosecutor helping Joe
McCarthy trap the Reds. Katy remembered Lewis telling
her how weird Klager was. Though a homosexual and a
Jew, he took special delight in setting up homo bait as legal
entrapment for Jewish Leftists in an era when no one
admitted to being gay. His father had been an old-time
New York judge, a Democratic political appointee. It was
rumored that when the judge had seen Adam going after
his own people he said, "My son pisses ice water." The
judge bequeathed his son all his assets, then died of a broken
heart. Katy had also heard that now that Klager *fils* was

196

dying of AIDS and in trouble with the IRS, few of his old gang claimed to know him. There were no columns written by his buddies about how they were helping him through his final agonies.

So here he was, walking on his own two feet through Beanie's door. *A regular party pooper.*

Amanda droned on.

"Snowball," Katy said to her cousin, "I'm going over to speak to Adam."

"*Adam Klager*—you can't."

"But I am."

The sudden notion that Beanie's silent partner, Klager, was on the outs with her brother-in-law and could have some interesting stuff to tell her was as tantalizing to her as a bottle of Perrier would be to a parched desert wanderer: Katy was a woman with nothing to lose. She went over to him; she was the only guest at Beanie's who greeted him. "I'm Katy Becker."

Klager's blue eyes stared through her, as though he were turning over a thought forming inside his head. "Ah . . . the sister-in-law." He smiled at her.

Does he take a childish delight in helping a widow of the Left? "We seem to be the two unwanted guests here . . . like we're both Banquo's ghost at a thane's banquet."

"Well," he said. "Well, well." He looked at her for a moment, then added, "Come see me in my office tomorrow."

Then abruptly, he left. When Snowball rejoined Katy she commented, as though it was an odd fact about Klager, "I heard he went to Horace Mann."

14

Ⅰᴛ ᴡᴀsɴ'ᴛ ᴜsᴜᴀʟ ꜰᴏʀ ᴀ ᴍᴀɴʜᴀᴛᴛᴀɴ law firm to be lodged in a townhouse in the east Sixties off Madison, but Adam Klager got a kick from knowing that when the New York establishment came knocking at his door for favors—since youth he had been the city's best arranger—they had to leave their names with the kid gay lawyers (black and white) downstairs and wait in his marbled lobby staring at classic Greek male nudes, as entwined as his art dealer could find them for him, knowing that on the next level, where he had his offices, there was a big orgy room where he had his rough trade. Everyone in town knew that.

▼ ▼ ▼

Katy, being female, was less thrown than the Wall Street crowd at the cluster of boyish gay lawyers in the reception room; the ornate decoration reminded her vaguely of her hairdresser's. She wasn't so up on the orgy stories; she was preoccupied with her own problems. Still, when she was led into Klager's office she was surprised to find him barefoot, in a knee-length Japanese kimono not quite tied shut. His bald head and the slipping robe made his nakedness even more randy.

"Call me Adam." He waved Katy to sit down in a chair opposite his desk and carelessly let his navy silk robe fall a little ajar: he took call after call, carefully repeating the name of the person on the other end of the phone while he orchestrated the conversation into a revealing scenario. Katy realized that he got a kick out of letting her recognize the liberal do-gooders of the city. He knew the men asking his help at the other end would have been mortified if they had known a third party was witness to their talk.

But, she admitted to herself, *he sounds like he's handing them good advice.* The walls of his office had no Greek work—they were jammed with political photos: Adam Klager, youthful founder of the Manhattan Junior Franklin Delano Roosevelt Club. Adam laughing with Bobby Kennedy. Adam in a box with Mayor O'Dwyer the afternoon the Yankees won the pennant. Adam with his high-school silver cup, first prize for the debating team. *He is a mutant: a cross between the smartest kid at Horace Mann and an old-time queen in drag.*

His milky blue eyes suddenly turned little-boy on her. After he hung up on the last of his callers—who, Katy had noted, were a syndicated newspaper columnist, a top dog in Federation, the senior partner of a takeover firm—he lamented to Katy how much finer his grasp of the law, how much fairer his billing practices than the white-shoe firms'. "I never charge by time; I'm accustomed to being paid for results."

Meanwhile, his father, in a framed photo, standing arm-in-arm with Governor Lehman, looked down upon them. Katy had been told that Klager never let Bobby Kennedy forget the McCarthy days; he kept his teeth in the Kennedy flesh, and they let him alone. Never went after him. No one did. Until he got AIDS. Then the IRS got him on a murky tax swindle. Maybe he was guilty of that, maybe not, but when he had no more power in his body, they had him disbarred.

He stood up and paced. "You're Jeremiah Becker's daughter, so you know . . . ," he said, acknowledging that they both were children of the same roots. "So you know New York. How it was—how things are."

She nodded.

He frowned. Remembering. As though every New York Jewish lawyer of his own and his father's generation were accounted for in his head. "I don't think the judge knew him."

"He was a sort of Connecticut Republican."

"Oh?"

"But he voted for Roosevelt in the national elections." She hesitated. "He did give money to the Rosenbergs—he thought that, legally, the case made no sense."

Klager's expression didn't change. "That was another crowd."

It occurred to her that, one way or another, her family had been connected to this city for over a hundred years.

Jews confused being Jewish with being, eternally, the freshly arrived immigrant. But other boatloads had docked since they came ashore—hello Hispanic, hello Korean. *Wipe from your eyes the Holocaust gold dust hiding your natural history. It blurs, it blurs. Forget your medieval church rubbings—it evades, it evades.*

She felt a tremendous yearning to know concrete stuff about what had happened in this city in the last hundred years; she wanted to yank back her true history, get to the nitty-gritty of what had gone on, street by street, store by store, cousin by cousin. Now it was too late—she had been looking in other directions while the real explanations could still have been directly passed on to her. Why had Jeremiah and her uncles been so careful to vote Republican locally and Democrat nationally? She'd never be able to piece together the whole of it, would never know what Tammany demons Jeremiah, as a young lawyer, had ducked from. Klager was right—Jeremiah had found another crowd. So here she was, his liberated daughter, back at the post-Tammany stand, taking a favor from Adam Klager. *Tell your old man that now you've become a post-modern? He would have slaughtered you.*

"Your brother-in-law is a man who mislays his friends . . ."

"I thought you might know something about the workings of the Belle Hélène Foundation?"

"You're barking up the wrong tree—I knew about other business. Beanie wanted me to arrange a sale to a Japanese conglomerate of a block of office buildings he personally owned in Harlem."

"On the East River? Those are the Belle Hélène original

201

office buildings from the time of the First World War. They belonged to my father-in-law—"

Klager shrugged. "When I knew Bernard, they were his. The prime asset of one of his Bermuda corporations."

"A *Bermuda* corporation? That's impossible—besides, the office buildings are worthless."

Klager looked at her. "Not if you count in the assets the office buildings own."

She sat there stunned. Trying to digest his meaning.

"I don't suppose your fancy law firm—I heard you're using Max Schecter"—he grinned—"give him my regards from the old days—would dirty themselves by actually going uptown and having a look at that office space. Bunch of paper pushers—they drown a client in paper and billable hours, but they've forgotten how to think."

Klager wrote down an address on a piece of legal paper. "Does this mean anything to you?"

"It's in the same neighborhood—but it's not Belle Hélène's address."

"It's a wheezy old trick, as old as the hills. Split a building in two."

"Did your Japanese connection buy the block?"

"Your luck. They were interested in Pittsburgh. The deal fell through." He wheeled around and pointed a blotchy, emaciated manicured finger at her. "The oral word of a dead man is worth chicken shit. I'll have the office type up a memo for you." He abruptly sank back into his leather chair, his watery eyes, color baby blue, staring beyond her, wondering who else in town he could take down with him.

She rose to go.

He drummed his buffed nails on his desk. "Details," he lectured her, as though performing for an unseen audience. "I've always prided myself on them." Then he motioned her to leave.

CHAPTER

15

MAX SCHECTER SHIFTED UNCOMFORT-
ably in his chair. He was trying to make Katy be more
reasonable: he needed the dying Adam Klager's help with
his client like he needed an audit from the IRS. "Judge
Myrtle has a rep for being squeaky clean. Myrtle might
bend in the direction of a widow and son being ripped
off by real-estate interests, but he'd walk away fast if
he felt said widow was involved with garbage like
Klager."

"You're deliberately getting it backward. I'm not involved with Adam—Beanie is," she argued. "Here I've
brought you a gem—Adam Klager's signed memo to
Beanie, explaining how he tried to unload Belle Hélène on
a Japanese conglomerate."

"Katy, if it was up to me, I'd carry your lawsuit for
nothing. But I have partners. And my partners have to eat.

Memo me no memo—you are way overdue on your next scheduled payment."

"When we began, you told me it would be contingency; midstream you changed it to partial contingency—but never mind, I will give you a check for fifteen thousand before the week is through, I swear. But then what? It was your idea that I check out the Belle Hélène Foundation—"

"True—"

"And when I do make a connection to Adam Klager, you brush me off like my ideas are crummy. Max, you keep switching gears on me—last July you yourself said there was something fishy about those office buildings. I even contacted a—a black friend to introduce me to real-estate people up there."

Her connecting with Adam Klager is bizarre. Not at all what Max had meant to happen.

"Adam says Beanie registered the Spoon Triangle office buildings under the name of a dummy corporation in Bermuda—can't we check this out?"

"You're naive—have you any notion of the costs of this sort of international sleuthing?" He paused, somewhat mollified by her promise to pay. He sensed she would come up with some of the money. "Okay, okay. Let's find out what we can at no further investment. Since you have some Harlem connections"—imperceptibly, even to himself, Schecter had slipped into the habit of treating her like she was Cagney, or maybe Lacey—"and our firm has none—see if they can find out whether Beanie listed the office buildings in his name with local real-estate people." He paused. "Not that it will make that much difference—the Harlem property is worthless. Katy, did it occur to you that Klager might have wanted to deflect you from looking at the foundation?"

"So what? So I'll waste a little time in Harlem."

Max hesitated. *Tell her you knew Klager way back when. It's no big deal.* Instead he nervously started to free-associate. His mind went this way and that, and he blurted out a non sequitur that he immediately regretted once it was out of his mouth: Max asked Katy whether during her Columbia days she had heard of a professor named Galindez.

"You mean in my time at Barnard?"

"Yes. Yes, that's it."

"The one who got murdered by Trujillo? My class put a wreath on his door . . ."

Say something. She looks bewildered. She'll think you're nuts. "It was an unusual case. Trujillo was a dictator and a rat, but the murder charges brought against him were trumped up. It's always interesting to lawyers to defend the bad guy."

She stared at him but didn't reply.

"Your entire class?"

"Before Galindez, we had no political murders at Columbia."

He noticed that she seemed to be waiting almost politely for him to direct his thinking to her case. He waited a little, then returned to Belle Hélène.

▼ ▼ ▼

Representing the widow of a civil rights activist had appealed to Max Schecter. In the sixties, when he had merged his solo practice with Leary and Fuccoli he had acquired a reputation for hiring gung-ho Yale Law School radicals.

"Pied Piper of the bearded ones," his associates had nicknamed him. After Katy left he paced the width of his office.

You don't need to dirty your hands now with scum like Adam Klager. He's sinking—he'll take you along for the ride. Max remembered running into Adam at a Bar Association event in the sixties; he heard in his head Adam's rasping voice jeering at him, "So, tell me, Max boy, about your days at Freund and Mannheim. So tell me—how come you think you're so different from me? Tell me about your boss, the liberal Judson Freund . . ."

And Adam will do Katy no good. Would be a bad move for her to come up before Judge Myrtle clutching a vague deathbed vendetta memo from Klager as main evidence.

Max mulled over it—he prided himself on being a good counselor. The obvious next step might strike some lawyers as getting a deposition from Klager. *Get him to talk while he's still alive.* On the other hand, anything to do with Adam could be a landmine. For Katy.

That night at the Bar Association Adam had answered his own question: "In the end, Maxie, the difference between us is that I'm loyal to my ideas and my pals and you're loyal to your parachute."

A deposition now would be pointless. But he would check out Adam's leads to Belle Hélène. If there were truth to what Adam had told Katy, there would always be time to call him.

Max looked out the window, let his mind go blank, then rang for his legal assistant to bring up from dead storage a file he had saved from his early days with Freund and Mannheim—after Judson Freund died, the firm had disbanded.

Early the next morning he sifted through the retrieved *New York Times* clippings:

March 13, 1956: A Columbia University professor, Jesus de Galindez, a Basque exile and professor of politics in the Spanish-speaking hegemony, has been reported as missing by the university. He was last seen by his students when he entered the Broadway subway station to go to his home on lower Fifth Avenue. Two weeks ago, Professor Galindez delivered a lecture at the university attacking General Rafael Trujillo, the acknowledged dictator of the Dominican Republic. . . . Galindez was known to have been planning to publish in book form his exposé of the Caribbean general under the title *The Era of Trujillo*. Intimates of the professor have indicated that Galindez, who had been a refugee in the Dominican Republic during World War II, feared for his life because of his firsthand knowledge of the excesses of the regime and his intent to make this information public.

March 1, 1957: Representative Porter says G. L. Murphy, the missing U.S. pilot employed by Dominican Airlines, was involved in last year's abduction of Galindez from New York City. Murphy had told of flying a "wealthy invalid" to the Dominican Republic from Ami-

tyville Airport the day Galindez disappeared. Porter holds the Dominican Republic responsible for Murphy's death, and demands a government probe into the Murphy/Galindez case and sanctions imposed on dictatorship. Porter has named F. D. Roosevelt, Jr., among a list of persons with business links to the regime.

March 17, 1957: Roosevelt, son, resigns as Dominican Republic counsel.

July 21, 1957: The Dominican Republic has hired S. S. Baron, the public-relations director for Tammany, to conduct a private probe proving Trujillo's innocence. S. S. Baron has acknowledged that he has hired the civil libertarian Judson Freund, a founding partner of the prestigious New York City law firm Freund and Mannheim, to conduct what he maintains will be a disinterested investigation. The Socialist leader Norman Thomas has objected, maintaining that "No private investigation paid for by the Dominican Republic can replace a U.S. government investigation." The office of Governor Averell Harriman has issued a statement by the governor objecting to Baron's

208

handling of publicity for both Tammany and the Dominican Republic.... The State Department has said it sees no precedent for such an act by a foreign country inside the United States.... The Justice Department demands that Judson Freund register as a foreign agent for the Dominican Republic.... The firm of Freund and Mannheim refuses the Justice Department's request: they maintain that their employer is S. S. Baron, not the Dominican Republic.... Tammany leader Carmine de Sapio retains silence on issue.

July 24, 1957: A spokesman for Tammany issued a statement today that S. S. Baron, the publicity director of Tammany, has been relieved of his duties....

July 25, 1957: Freund and Mannheim refuse to confirm reports that the firm's retainer from the Dominican Republic is in the neighborhood of one million dollars.

May 15, 1958: The liberal law firm of Freund and Mannheim has issued a report that there was no evidence to substantiate charges that Trujillo and his regime in the Dominican Republic had any involvement in the disappearance of Columbia professor Jesus de Galindez. Their findings indicate that Galindez, a secret Communist, was killed by rival left-wing agents....

August 31, 1962: The office of District Attorney Frank Hogan has declared Professor Jesus de Galindez legally dead. New York Assistant District Attorney Horman says he was abducted by the Dominican Republic in March 1956 and was slain by a Trujillo agent.

Max again thought back to that remote time, the hazy 1950s, when he was a bright-eyed junior associate fresh out of law school. Being close to Judson Freund and working on his report with him had seemed to him the closest he had come to a form of Manhattan magic.

He remembered the afternoon he, J. F., and Carmine de Sapio had quietly convened in one of the small conference rooms while, wordlessly, Adam Klager handed them paper after paper from his FBI sources. It had seemed clear to Max that Galindez had been killed because of the huge

amounts of money he had raised for the Basque govern-
ment-in-exile. Freund asserted that at least a million dollars
of those funds had disappeared with him at the time of his
death. Max recalled Freund leaning back in his chair: he
had said, "Even unpopular governments can be falsely accused, and, Carmine, that is why I have taken up this
cause . . ." Max had never doubted him. And he had seen
his own trajectory as harmonious with his generation's—in
his head he used the expression *we*. In the fifties "we
thought"; in the sixties "we evolved." It had never occurred
to him there had ever been a different drumbeat, other
modes of behavior.

"*Before Galindez, we had no political murders at Columbia.*"
Katy's words floated in his head. He thought about them
for a minute further. Then he rang for his legal assistant to
put the files back in dead storage.

CHAPTER

16

OWING MONEY GNAWED AT KATY. After work she stopped in at the Regency. They were playing a rerun of *A Man and a Woman*—she saw all movies about widows for clues as to how they managed to get by. Anouk Aimée was a svelte, gorgeous, windswept widow with a happy toddler daughter conveniently stashed away in boarding school, cheerful about seeing Mommy only on weekends. The movie was of no practical use. Perhaps the French were more orderly about life's mishaps.

Anouk's only pain seemed to come from letting Jean-Louis Trintignant make love to her in rain-drenched, windy Deauville to the beat of romantic music evoking memories of riding horseback with her dead husband through equally windswept marshes to background samba music. None of the widow films that Katy had seen had heroines who lay awake wondering how to pay tuition; they never seemed *ruffled* economically. Why were these women so much braver than she? Why didn't they need money?

Katy knew the plots by heart—the big moment always came when the romantic male lead got the widow in bed. Widow enjoys sex. Then remembers *him*. Then male lead reminds her, "He is dead—but we are alive." Widow says she can't go on enjoying herself. There is a struggle. The romantic lead wins; he carries the widow off to their brave new future. *End.*

When she left the theater it was night on upper Broadway. Nothing like that had happened between her and Mike. God, she missed him! Why had he never telephoned? Never attempted to undo their quarrels?

That night she crawled into bed and lay awake remembering the sums she owed. For the rest of her life she would recall those figures with exactitude. Fifteen thousand more a year. Katy believed if she had earned that amount extra, she could have gotten ahead of the game. Paid off Max Schecter. Been a sport. Been a lady.

She hated having to call Snowball for the money. But she did. Snowball acted as though the request were nothing. "Of course it's okay. Come over tonight."

▼ ▼ ▼

Snowball was distraught when Katy walked in. Katy guessed it had to do with her ex-husband, Shawn Wilson. *She has that dazed expression. The way she looked as a kid when she told you there was no more Snowball Wurlitzer, that her name would be Ginzberg, like her mother's.* "Shawn?"

"The divorce decree came through."

"And long overdue." Katy studied her cousin. *Her heart*

212

*has no narrative capacity. She can't distinguish between then and
now.*

Katy's own nature was less dark. She had taken the loss
of Indian Path, and Beanie's crookedness, and even Lewis's
death, as misdirected asteroids accidentally colliding with
her earthbound destiny, a destiny meant to be as solid as
Gibraltar. She suspected her inability to sink into profound
sadness was due to shallowness, some innate lack of spiritu-
ality.

"You're confusing your situation with your mother's—she had no career; it was different."

The two women sat in Snowball's kitchen. They never
tired of dissecting their emotional lives, rearranging the
pieces of what had gone wrong, what was due to the times
and what to them, how different their mothers' lives had
been. Anita Becker and Hewley Ginzberg had been first
cousins. Both their daughters tried to nail down their mothers' sexual histories—no detail was too small to be pursued.

"Hewley was only in her twenties when your father left,"
Katy continued.

"The hats in the photos made the women look older."

Katy knew the story by heart: Poor Hewley Ginzberg's
northern husband, Bert Wurlitzer, turned out to have been
a great mistake. He had no heart for the depression; during
the worst time of the thirties he lost his dental-supply
business. Hewley Ginzberg Wurlitzer brought Snowball
home from the Ninety-fifth Street playground one afternoon and found a scrawled note pinned to her bed: "Can't
bear it. If I stay I will jump and I know that will hurt you
and Snowball-girl. Love, Bert." The next month she got a
postcard from him from Shaker Heights, Cleveland.

213

A year later, Hewley heard Bert was living in bigamy with a Chicago woman of substance. She sued for divorce and changed Snowball's surname to Ginzberg. Gabe later told Katy that his father, a Park Avenue physician who treated the Ginzberg and Becker clan, had remarked that Wurlitzer's behavior was strange for a Jewish fellow raised in Larchmont.

"I feel awful for Agatha. I never wanted her to go through what I did."

"She's not. She's grown-up—you were a child. Besides," Katy added firmly, "this is just paperwork on a divorce you both agreed to. Shawn's not vanishing. Agatha sees him all the time."

Snowball was nervously stacking a too-neat pile of paper napkins in the wicker holder on the table. "After Dad remarried he sent me some letters from the Midwest. When they stopped I stood in a corner and held my breath." She sighed. "My dumb gesture improved nothing. No further mail came. So I invented a crazy fantasy. That he and Brad's father—Brad used to tell me when we were in PS 6 about his dad, who worked in the South—lived in a mysterious adult camp made up of males in bathing trunks dancing around a tree. A sort of male no-man's-land. Of not-thereness."

"Snowball—"

"No, Katy, listen. You know a lot, but not what it is to be ashamed of a parent . . ." She paused. Then briskly added, "I'll make us some tea. The Assam Irish is really good."

"Snowball—"

"No. I'm okay now. *Listen to me.* Bert suddenly reap-

214

peared with his third wife, Dolly, when I was at Barnard—she was a Mormon nurse. He took us to the West
End bar. Like he didn't notice it was sort of tacky to pick
a student restaurant for our great family reunion. He said
to Dolly, as though Mom and me were as funny as a Sid
Caesar show, 'Hewley and Snowball are stuck in the same
apartment where I left them. Can you beat that?' That's
just how he said it. 'Can you beat that?' His tip to the
waitress was so mingy I had to sneak back to the booth to
add an extra dollar. When he left he gave me a box made
of two kinds of wood with my initials and 'Salt Lake City'
burned into it. It was so awful—I wanted to show it to
you but I was *so ashamed for him*. I never saw him again."
She blew her nose into one of the paper napkins. "There's
something worse than being ashamed of yourself—being
ashamed of a parent."

"Snowball—"

"Say one of your nutty, upbeat things. If you give me
sympathy I'll kill you."

Katy thought what to do. She got up and searched the
bottom of her cousin's stove for the right pan. "I'll make
us scrambled eggs." She made Snowball watch each step,
turning her cooking into an elaborate ritual. "The eggs need
to be top quality. I prefer brown . . . from an old-fashioned
butcher." She rambled on, noticing Snowball had ceased
dabbing at her nose. "A copper bowl would be better. Then,
in a heavy skillet over a high heat . . ."

"Shouldn't eggs go on low?"

"All wrong. The pan has to be very heavy and blazing
hot. But just hot for as long as it takes to spit."

"Who spits? You're not spitting into our eggs?"

215

"I mean as long as it would take you to spit if you did spit. Then turn off the heat and whisk like crazy. Catch them while they're still runny, and serve them with a batch of plain buttered rye toast. Not the fancy Eli sourdough stuff."

Katy had never served eggs at a party—she had made up the story to divert Snowball from her blackness—but it struck her as not a bad plan. While they ate the eggs at the kitchen table, her ideas on eggs became more detailed. "Serve them with Scotch on the rocks, maybe a bowl of washed strawberries. It's really a very cheap brunch—nobody we know kills a bottle of Scotch. And wine doesn't go with eggs. Maybe a little caviar."

"Caviar, cheap? Beluga's out of sight." Snowball had pepped up.

"Good will do. The eggs and rye bread cost nothing. Caviar is the sort of thing men like to bring to a party."

"Did Lewis?"

"Bring caviar? Don't be silly. We were married."

"You are sounding very women's-mag."

"The wives of yesterday are the mistresses of tomorrow." Katy giggled. She glanced at her cousin. *She's forgetting her Shawn misery.* "If we make a Sunday ritual of it and stick to the eggs-and-caviar routine, soon the men will start bringing caviar unasked. It will make them feel in on special gaiety, a special lightness."

"What about cholesterol?"

"Forget cholesterol—you'll meet new people." Katy abruptly switched the subject to sex and their mothers to keep Snowball from sliding back into melancholy. "Hewley was only a kid—she had to have had something after your

216

father left? She couldn't have spent all those years just masturbating?"

"Do you think Anita had a lover?" Snowball questioned in return. "Why did your mother take so many sea trips?"

"They were so hazy about everything. They never used words like *menstruate* with us. It was always, 'Wipe yourself down there.' "

"How could they talk about concretes? They were such a mishmash of D. H. Lawrence and Victorian prudery . . ."

"Not that they were completely off in keeping sex hidden. I believe in each of us is this smelly, naked female taking a crap, and the energy of keeping her hidden is where the real sex comes from. Sex is the opposite of this airy group knowledge. This let-it-all-hang-out."

"Hewley confused sex and being Jewish. They both were sub rosa activities."

"True. Think about it. They *drenched* us in education—the best WASP schools, stuffing us with culture in a time when it wasn't usual to give the best of it to females—what a class chastity belt against our meeting lower-class Jewish males! Those extra megadoses of refinement were given to us in lieu of a defined future—there the WASP women were on firmer ground."

Snowball reached for a Belgian cookie from the stone crockery jar on her butcher-block pantry shelf. "How could our mothers know where we were meant to fit in? They themselves were so at sea. I mean—did you ever hear either of them use the word *goy*?"

"Snowball, they never said *anything*."

"Hewley and Anita went for *taste*—"

"Coded hysteria," Katy corrected firmly. "So we

217

wouldn't notice we were temporary poachers encircled by a moat with the drawbridge pulled up defending us against your average Jew, who thought goys were bad, and your average Christian, whose anti-Semitism hadn't been sophisticated out of him." She sighed. "You can't go naked into the world, armed only with taste. Not knowing basic stuff leaves you vulnerable. You need to know here's a bank, there's a grocery store, here's evil, here's prejudice. You have to have an inkling—even if you rebel against it and go in another direction—where you came from and where you're meant to fit in. Men are better at doing this."

"Katy, you're a sort of marginal mermaid swimming upstream against the current—at a time that women have scuttled the patriarchal, you want to discover its virtues."

"What's the point of attacking patriarchal men when there are none? Why bolt the stable door after the horses have galloped away?"

"Look, you sound lately like a hen rooted in the basics of life—but this born-again conservative dynastic bent you're espousing doesn't mesh with your real geography. You've always lacked a sense of direction in your choice of men—they bear no resemblance to your constructs."

Katy mulled over Snowball's criticism. "All that emphasis on being *classy* muffled my thinking on this," she said defensively. "If I had had some practice breathing down Lewis's neck, à la a Philip Roth woman, and *insisted* that he get the economics of our life in order, I'd have been home free with Beanie. Instead I was dazzled by Lewis's commitment to human rights, like it was either/or—fineness or practicality. Lame-duck"—she summed it up to her cousin—"we were leached-out, lame-duck Jews."

"You said you went to see Adam Klager—a jump like that hardly sounds super-raffinée."

"Lewis would have died a second death. Even Max had me over the coals on it. And Mike—can you imagine his ranting if he knew I'm talking to Adam?"

"You keep mentioning Mike Braden—now, there was a patriarchal man. Do you still miss him?"

Katy looked at her cousin. *Remember the August afternoon in Central Park, you and Snowball picnicking near the boathouse, when she told you Paula Braden was dead. The two of you wondering if it was all right for you to telephone Mike so soon after. It was all still in the future.*

"I miss being on his boat."

"That's missing *him*. You could call him."

Katy shook her head. They had quarreled about so many things. Even the dumb case. Mike had wanted her to use his lawyers. She thought of the insults, the humiliations, the sadomasochistic shit she took from Max because he didn't think so much of her suit. *With him it's, Now I'm with you, now I'm not. He was erratic.* She couldn't have stood getting into a similar hassle with Mike's lawyers. Having them in on Beanie's shit about a lover here, a lover there. Thinking her a deadbeat on her bills. Oh, Mike would have paid them. And ended up despising her. This way they parted angry—but clean.

She grasped both of Snowball's hands. "You do remember that day on the Lake in Central Park? The plans we made—"

Snowball kissed her forehead.

Katy didn't think she recalled it at all.

But her cousin said, "It was a nice afternoon."

219

CHAPTER

17

ON HER WAY TO WORK THE NEXT morning Katy walked through the park. The police department was readying the city for the Macy's parade. It promised to be bigger than ever; a new helium snowman had been added. Snowball's check was in her pocket for deposit, but Katy wasn't thinking about the case. Being in the park made her think of Mike; she remembered how it began:

Summer. She had taken Matt out west to see the Grand Canyon. Then put him on a Qantas flight to spend the rest of his school vacation on her brother Jim's sheep ranch near Melbourne. It had been a year and then some since Lewis's death, and Katy's feet had begun to hurt.

The day after her return she and Snowball had agreed to meet in the boathouse in Central Park; the small children who had not left the city had multicolored balloons—orange, thin blue, white—the muggy August weather made them pop quickly. The park smelled of dogs on the loose and of midsummer burned-out grass. The women took their charcoaled franks drowned in Gulden's mustard and cans of Tab out by the Lake. They sat in the grass; the crushed cotton skirt of Snowball's dress ballooned in the wind as she dropped to the ground.

The spot she and Snowball had picked was almost parallel to the Forty-second Street library; Katy recalled Brad telling her that it was the site of the original Croton reservoir. *The old Croton Aqueduct must have flowed beneath the park right near here.*

A French man and woman lying near them were examining a new Nikon; they were saying that the Forty-seventh Street photo was *une vraie découverte*. Womrath novels of her parents' generation had been peppered with French phrases, Katy had mused; *People don't do that anymore.*

Two black kids approached the French couple. Katy noticed the Frenchman was uneasy; the boys did seem surly. *Maybe he is wondering, should he behave better than the Americans, who lynch their blacks, or should he protect his Nikon.* "C'est beau, New York," he said to no one in particular. A policeman strolled by—he had been watching the interaction. The shorter of the two boys asked the Frenchman if the Nikon had an automatic lens. Or was it semi-. The Frenchman let him inspect the camera while the policeman watched; then the boy and his friend ambled off. A guitar group, dressed in retro-sixties—silk rags, torn jeans; and the men wore glittery earrings—were playing near the rowboat landing:

Winchester Cathedral, you're bringing me down.
You stood and you watched as my baby left town.

You could have done something but you just didn't try.
You didn't do nothing—you let him walk by.

"I get sad in Central Park in the summer," Katy said.

"We could walk over to the ballpark. Watch them practice."

"Walking in the bright light sometimes scares me."

"I brought you Dr. Fimmel's address—he's a fine podiatrist. He'll do wonders for your feet."

"The people in the park look so aimless—do you think next August we'll be drinking Tab together near the Lake? Tell me, Snowball—are we old?"

Snowball lay on her back on the lawn, brown matted leaves stuck to her blond braided hair and purple dress; she reminded Katy of the Bonnard *Woman in the Morning at Cannet.* She studied her cousin. *There is something oddly appealing*, she mused, *about the first deep nose-to-mouth twin line marks in the face of a woman with great bone structure.*

"Paula Braden died while you were away. The *Times* said suddenly—heart, I think. You ought to send Mike a note—they were so nice to you."

"Paula dead? Why didn't you call me?" Katy paused; she sensed Snowball's drift. "I have to digest this—you mean for me to go for him? With Paula barely cold? Like I was some Florida widow with a blue rinse? What a tacky notion."

"You complain men either have faces and souls like a hotel lobby or are freaked out on the counterculture," her cousin snapped. "He's not either. Why can't you drop him a line? Plenty of men called you after Lewis died, and you

222

were glad of it. Make up your mind—you can't be both the old bag lady of Central Park *and* a vestal virgin."

Dear Mike,

    I've just heard the news. Forgive me for not being in touch sooner; I was in the Grand Canyon with Matt until almost yesterday. I feel so sad for you—the two of you were such a couple. So close. I know how—

Dear Michael,

    My cousin Snowball has just told me about Paula. She was so vital, such an extraordinary friend, I can't believe this has happened—

Dear Mike,

    Not Paula. Life is too unfair. Paula was unique, truly unique, in her generosity, her élan; I keep thinking this can't have happened. Within such a short time, Lewis and Paula . . . I know how awful for you this time must be—

Impulsively Katy reached for the phone.

Why are you so uptight? Snowball is right. You were glad Lewis's friends offered themselves for borrowing—other women's husbands, loose cannons though they were—in the night. You've been through this. You know Mike's got to be horny. Sex follows death, like night follows day.

"Hjallo—"

Katy recognized the Germanic voice of Greta, their housekeeper. "This is Mrs. Eichorn, Paula's friend. Don't bother Mr. Braden; I'm sure he isn't up to receiving calls.

But do tell him that I called. I didn't hear the terrible news until yesterday—"

"He doesn't speak to anyone," Greta replied.

"I've been away on a trip." She heard Mike yelling who the fuck was making an idiot nuisance of themselves on the phone. "I understand."

"Wait, please."

There was a pause while Greta conveyed her message, her hand obviously over the receiver. Mike finally picked up. "Look, sweetie, I don't want your tears. I know you loved Paula. What are you doing in New York in August? Be here this evening in time for drinks. Maybe tomorrow we'll go for a sail—you can return to your steaming hellhole Sunday around five." His voice sounded strained as he boomed her orders to her.

"I—I have to see my cousin's podiatrist. Dr. Fimmel."

"Is your cousin having an operation? Bunions?"

"No—yes. I'll be there before dinner." Katy put down the receiver. Mike had moved fast.

▼ ▼ ▼

Dr. Fimmel's office was in the east Seventies, in a 1930s cement apartment building the color of pekoe tea, near Lexington.

Oh, my God—no wonder the address sounded familiar. It's Tabor's building—unbelievable—my old analyst from Barnard days, Dr. Tabor! Another one who bit the dust, another member of the dead club. Could Fimmel be using his same office?

Katy walked through the lobby. Unchanged. The same Aztec moderne.

"Looking for someone, miss?"

"Tabor—no, I mean Dr. Fimmel."

Fimmel's office turned out to be next to Tabor's old place. She hesitated, noting that the shiny new nameplate was for a Dr. Blatt. Another shrink? A second podiatrist? She rang Fimmel's bell.

▼ ▼ ▼

"Snowball spoke so highly of you."

"A lovely woman." He motioned to her to change, that he would be back in a few minutes. By "change" he meant her to remove her stockings and discreetly fold them into her shoes on the floor of the small cubicle, the way women did before a medical examination. But it was summer. Katy had come dressed for the country; she needed no privacy—she was bare legged. She could have slipped out of her huaraches with him right there.

She slid into the slightly reclining chair, her legs stretched out in front of her. *You smell of too much Diorissimo.* She had drenched, splashed her tanned skin, imagining herself later in the afternoon with Mike.

Fimmel sat on a chair in front of her; he grasped her right foot and elevated it slightly, inspecting the blisters and calluses, his eyes taking in her freshly painted nails and ignoring their vivid red color. She inhaled. The room had an iodine smell.

"Your shoes are too loose—your heels are flapping against the sole, causing the calluses." He cut, trimmed, and bathed her foot, as though it were detached from her body. He put down the right foot and started on the left;

Katy gazed at him. *Sturdy. Avuncular. But why are his nails so carefully manicured? Does his nurse buff them for him after the patients are gone?*

She moved her legs slightly, remembering she had worn her best beige silk bikini underpants. Inside her, because her gynecologist was old-fashioned about pills, was her diaphragm. She studied Fimmel's impassive face—in the lifting of right and left legs, in the overmoist body perfume on her skin, in the smell of the Ortho cream inside her—was anything revealed? And if it were? She was the mother of a grown son—why did she flush in embarrassment at the thought that Fimmel could leap into her imagination, her bodily orifices, and divine her preparations for Mike?

Katy glanced at the wall. On the other side of it, light-years away in time, was Tabor's former office. How many hours had she lain on Tabor's couch, keeping her voice neutral and her eyes focused on the ceiling, while Tabor, clever, always on the hunt, tried to guide her revelations back to Brad Culver. But the sentences, the confession remained unspoken. Brad was hers—she never relinquished Brad to him.

It was always the others she talked about, the love affairs at a slant—those, she freely granted to Tabor. She had tried to help Tabor help her dive past her smoke screen of the unconscious. Always helpful. Always willing to see the incestuous in her relation to Anita, Jeremiah, and Jim:

"Let us go darker. Deeper. More awful," she would urge her therapist. Generously, verbally, she had opened to Tabor the interior space of her rottenness. When the material she drummed up struck her as insufficiently abundant, she invented. But the secret wild times she and Brad had

had together, she hid—her perverse loyalty to some archaic notion of the privacy of the soul.

The odor of anxious anticipation of the country afternoon permeated the cubicle. Odd that in her five holy, three-times-a-week years with Tabor neither of them had thought to contemplate the effect of smells on her psychic darkness—her libido minus Brad Culver. Who was hers. Timelessly hers.

She hoped, lying on Fimmel's recliner, she hadn't gone fishy.

"Lanolin is still a good product. People underestimate the old standbys. Try a tube."

Fimmel turned to rinse his hands. He left her to dress, closing the door behind him, though he must have seen she only had to slide into her sandals.

Katy paid his receptionist. Outside in the lobby she stopped in front of Tabor's old door, which now belonged to a Dr. Blatt.

Abruptly she pounded on the door.

A dark-haired man much younger than herself answered. *He must be Dr. Blatt. A kid has taken over Tabor's space!*

He stood in his waiting room, puzzled at her unexpected intrusion. She saw Tabor's pale green walls and his two Rouault prints—*King* and *Queen*—had been replaced by taupe wallpaper and a Frank Stella museum poster.

He must have left a patient inside; he looks angry. Pretend you made a mistake. Say something, or he'll take you for a nut case. What could you tell him? That you and Tabor, two dopes, thought you had endless time. That the cream of your college years was dissipated here while you both plotted your entry into "real" life. You never imagined this classy event would include your returning

227

to his memory room with corns. In this place you and your therapist lassoed your future to nothing more weighty than the spinnings from your 1950s unconscious. Idiots! What gave you such magnificent faith in the curative powers of a memory room for a young woman with an unhappened past?

▼ ▼ ▼

Dr. Blatt stood his ground politely. He didn't want to be rude to someone his mother's age on a hot day. The woman finally said she had made a mistake, rung the wrong doorbell. He waited to close the door until he saw she was out of the building.

▼ ▼ ▼

Katy walked back out to her parked Ford. *Tabor's memory room exists now merely as a memory of itself remembering. The shards of insight gained in it are rusty. Outdated. Applicable only to that frozen piece of past time when you raced three afternoons a week from Barnard to grab the Broadway local to Seventy-ninth Street, then the crosstown to Lexington.*

The summer exodus out of the city had begun; Katy decided on the Hutchinson instead of the Bruckner. It was a pleasanter way to get to Hannah's Point. The cars on the West Side Highway moved slowly until they lost the New Jersey crowd at the George Washington. Katy rarely used her blue Austin station wagon; this was her first trip on the Cross County and Merritt since Indian Path had been sold.

She remembered how Mike Braden's name first came up in Tabor's memory room—Braden's Press had awarded her first prize for best undergraduate essay on history—Tabor had brushed aside as irrelevant her description of him and Paula. He saw them as minor actors with bit parts in Katy's life—to him, the significant detail was her getting a prize for her appreciation of Chartres.

How carefully she would place her Carpenter Library notebooks on the chair next to Tabor's couch. Each scrap of her daily existence, each dream had portent—if they got it right, her life would be saved. Immortality granted. Evasion equaled perdition. How come Tabor, the infallible Tabor, had overlooked Mike Braden?

Damn it, Tabor—come back! You should know things are out of hand. A kid shrink is squatting in your old place, I've had my feet pared in the adjoining office, and I am speeding up the highway to spend the weekend with Mike Braden, the man you unceremoniously dumped as unconnected to my psychic life. If you had considered him, you could have thrown me some pointers. Instead, our grand blueprint for my life has come out lopsided; it doesn't matter diddly-squat that once I wrote a paper of merit on Chartres; nothing is wrapped up yet. Tabor—you tricky bastard—you lied to me about the big wham—you never warned me you'd croak!

▼ ▼ ▼

When Katy neared Hannah's Point, her nose twitched at the salt breezes from the Sound. *Smells like Gohonk.*

She parked the Ford in the gravelly carport in back of the old mill house. In seconds Mike was at the side of the station wagon.

Mike came out the back door. "Sweetie—let me get your bag."

229

They stood looking at each other before going back inside.

He's sizing you up as a woman. Don't pretend you are not ready to sleep with him. You know all about opposite-sex condolence calls; you had plenty. Where death lurks, sex is not far behind.

He put her red Lark suitcase in the downstairs guest room. She had slept there many weekends when Paula had been alive.

"Yell if you are out of soap, toothpaste, or whatever. Greta swore to me she stocked it with enough towels for a princess."

He glanced almost indifferently at the twin beds.

"She made both up so you can have your pick—window or no window."

Katy sat on the bed a while before she unpacked. Mike had years on her; he was impressive. She enjoyed the details of his age—he'd kept his hair, thick, gray; his overly large head was set bull-like on a sturdy, outdoor body; his sun-worn, age-spotted hands dangled at his side.

The firm way he grasped a door handle, the pointy, intelligent flared nostrils, even his fisherman's khaki sleeves casually rolled up high on his arm vaguely reminded her of childhood; he appealed to her.

She walked to the window. If she squinted her eyes and focused only on the Sound, she could have been standing on the east porch at Indian Path. Katy let her thoughts drift until she looked at the time. She brushed her hair with her new Kent—she always bought something new and needless at the start of a possible sexual adventure; when she was younger she would change her diaphragm and douche bag with each new man—and went up to the library.

Mike was mixing Manhattans. Katy never drank them, but the idea of them evoked Count Basie, fedora hats, Humphrey Bogart.

"Sweetie, I've forgotten—what's your drinking habit?"

She didn't want to say she didn't have one—when she was alone, or with Matt, weeks went by without her pouring more than a Tab. "Vodka on the rocks—no—I want to try one of your Manhattans."

"I make good ones."

"With what?"

"Rye."

"Oh, rye."

She kept up with him; she had two.

"Sweetie, they have a kick." He kept standing on the far side of the room. Then he gave her the *Times* obit on Paula. It read oddly, not like a heart attack. Her eyes returned to the part about sudden-death-no-previous-illness; she looked up. Mike was gazing at her.

"Yup. Suicide. She killed herself. Or I did," he said, voice flat. "Every August for twelve years I remembered the anniversary of her train wreck; I tried to say the right words—her doctor said never to tell her that she was luckier than her husband and her kid, never to mention their graves—the bodies were so charred, who knew what pieces had been put in the two plastic bags they gave Paula."

"What more could you have done?"

"But this God-damned year I didn't. We sat in this library, just like you and me now. You remember Paula's laugh? How light it was. She spent the evening with a pile of maps, calmly planning our next trip. She went to bed early—said she was tired. Sweetie, at our age, separate bedrooms are a luxury, not a punishment. The next morning her best friend telephoned. Deirdre said, 'Mike, I'm a shit for forgetting yesterday was the day. Put Paula on.' *Jesus*, I thought—*Jesus, we all forgot.* When I went in—it was all over. So now you know the long and short of Mike Braden. Wife number one was gorgeous and had enough wit to divorce me. Wife number two was an alcoholic. Wife number three killed herself. A bargain I ain't."

Suicide terrified Katy. She had considered Paula a person who had conquered tragedy. A model—an exemplary woman she had wanted to emulate; Katy needed time to rearrange her feelings toward her.

But the emotion didn't complete itself inside her head: instead, almost instantly, Paula flew out of Katy's consciousness. She could no longer recall her dead friend's look, her voice, or that she had been the *doyenne* of Hannah's Point. Paula's presence in the house simply vanished.

"You did obeisance to her first marriage for *twelve years?*" Katy asked the question without noticing how abruptly she had shifted her allegiance from Paula to Mike.

"Sweetie, you still talk young—don't tell me about Paula's personal problems. I tried to save her—instead, I killed her. I'm warning you, Mike Braden is no one's savior now. Your Lewis died when he was still at the beginning of things; that's a tragedy—but at least he didn't swallow a bottle of pills."

"Mike—I've never told a soul. The night Lewis was killed in the car crash, we had a row. He accused me of dancing barefoot and bare breasted with students at a faculty football homecoming dance. And my only desire had been to become a medievalist. You remember my wonderful

232

paper on Chartres? The wild dancing was Lewis's fantasy of me—it had no reality. I screamed at him how I had been finishing my doctorate at Columbia when he had insisted on dragging me off to Austin. Here I was, making the best of a lousy situation—did he imagine my idea of fun was mamboing with a bunch of jocks on a crummy Texas dance floor?" She paused for effect.

"He was so mean to me that night, pointing out all my flaws, then driving off without me to a dinner where we both were due, I flew in a rage—I went out of control."

As she had in the old days with Tabor, Katy now relished giving Mike the lowdown on her bad behavior. "In my anger I flushed my gold wedding band down the kitchen sink drainpipe in a pint of Drano. When I realized I'd lost it I was beside myself. That's when the university police walked in the house with the news of Lewis's car crash." Katy stopped for breath.

"There I was with no wedding ring, knowing his last words had been curses in my ear, so when the local wives came to console me I didn't know to what I was entitled. Was I a widow? Or a worthless bitch? After the women left I crawled in the dirt near the cellar, not even bothering to think of scorpions or coral snakes—if a coral gets a piece of you, forget prayer—I dug deep in the cistern, but I never found the ring. When I came back to Manhattan, I went to Tiffany's and asked them to make me a new band. I gave them our initials and the style and the date. Of course I never told them my husband was dead. I just said it had got lost in transit. They told me I shouldn't worry; the store had calls every week to make duplicate wedding bands, wives frequently lose the originals."

"Nice try—but no cigar. Lewis didn't commit suicide. Husbands and wives always yell at each other; all men want their wives to have good tits and for other men to look at them—and they get mad when they do. Par for the course. What Paula did was *not* par for the course."

Mike stood at the opposite end of the room, his back erect, his speech almost formal as he outlined the plans for the evening. "I told Greta to make us a light supper—just some grilled salmon. Afterward, if you are in the mood, we can go for a late-night swim." He hesitated, then continued in a Boston monotone, his vowels broad and drawled out, "Paula and I always went in the buff, but suit your-self—there are lots of towels in the cabana house."

He was so formal with her, she couldn't be sure what he wanted. *But swimming in the buff? Maybe, standing at the opposite end of the room, this is his notion of a pass?*

Katy had only been with men her own age; she had come consciously prepared—sooner or later in the weekend they would end up together. His age both excited her—this was the first hair-down conversation she had ever had with Mike; suddenly, abruptly, they were together in another place in time—and blurred her imagining of his desires. She couldn't quite visualize that Paula and he—both of them had always struck her as beings of a higher realm—had the same juices as her crowd. She found him oddly moving: his need to be in control, his remoteness, his despair. Still keeping considerable distance from her, Mike finally said, "Katy, you can say yes, and you can say no—I am asking you to sleep with me tonight."

"Yes."

234

Mike stared at her more thoughtfully. "An elegant reply. No Why-Mr.-Braden-this-is-so-sudden?"

"No."

"Well, sweetie, so they wept and they fucked." He turned toward her. "How long did you wait?"

"Not very."

"I haven't been with a woman since Paula died. When you telephoned—I figure you've been there. The million calls from women—you must have got them from men?"

"There are differences."

"Tell me?"

"Lewis's friends *were* married; the women will want to marry you."

"Does that include you?"

"I never take advance oaths, one way or another."

He was silent. Katy felt Mike was studying her in a new way; then, abruptly, he walked out to the mill porch overlooking the harbor. Greta had already set the grilled fish out on the round white wrought-iron table and had plugged the mosquito zapper in to the patio-floor socket.

When Greta came to clear the table for the salad course, Katy noticed that she was a younger woman than she had remembered; or maybe it was that when Paula was alive she had worn a uniform. Her black pants struck Katy as awfully snug across the bottom.

"Is Greta German?—Her salad is first-rate."

"Danish—Paula never could handle household help; she grew up in the west."

▼ ▼ ▼

They were still sitting on the mill porch when the harbor went dark; the only lights were those of incoming sailboats, just the *zzzzst* of zapped mosquitoes invaded the salt air in the patio.

They went down to Mike's pool at the side of the seawall facing the Sound. Katy took her clothes off at its edge and dove in. Then Mike joined her. At first they swam naked but separate, their bodies in the dark never touching. Because he did not come near her, she felt his sadness, his sorrow, his being at the end of things instead of at the beginning. But when he pulled himself over the edge of the pool, she saw his solid, tannish buttocks, the wet on his skin catching shards of light from the passing boats; she appraised his body curiously.

How odd. To see him naked this way, knowing this is the body of the man to whom I will soon be making love.

When she climbed out of the pool, Mike covered her with a heavy white towel. Then he pulled her toward him, and while they lay on the grass, he rubbed her hair dry with a smaller towel, talking to her as much with his hands as with his voice. "Tell me what you want . . ."

"Another Manhattan." Her request, even to her own ears, struck her as oddly childish, not in her usual voice.

"Sweetie, you'll get sloshed—no one drinks Manhattans at midnight."

"I want it."

When he left her on the grass to get it for her, her excitement rose in the few minutes of his absence. In New York, she had imagined being at Hannah's Point; with the strength of her being younger than Mike, she would have consoled him—generously, sexually, she would have led him out of his sorrows. She had fantasized a scene in which she would have revealed to him that this was her return gift for the earlier kindnesses he and Paula had shown to her. Instead, starting with her knowledge of Paula's suicide, her sense of direction had come apart. It dawned on her that Mike, not she, was the one in control, shaping, fabricating her into a younger, more petulant woman than had arrived in the blue Ford hours earlier.

"It's nice, being by the water," she said, struggling to maintain her aplomb, when he returned.

"Child of nature," he christened her, ignoring her earlier reminders of the Barnard essay that had originally brought them together, and its intimations that she was on a chummy first-name basis with the Middle Ages and Chartres.

He kept talking to her, stroking her, admiring her movements, egging her on; *Oh my God, oh my God, he cried, oh I'm lucky, oh my God . . .*

Veering away from his scenario, she sought to reestablish her ground rules. "We have to sleep in the guest room where I am—I can't go to yours."

"Next weekend you'll come upstairs to my room? Sweetie, we can't spend our lives not using my double bed."

She wanted to make conditions, to erect barriers—suddenly she was afraid she was capable of giving all to Mike Braden, for no special reason. Amazingly, that first night by the side of the pool, Mike got it so they rocked in perfect rhythm. He kept asking her to tell him, tell him everything; and she forgot the marriage she had wanted to be so proud of, her dreams of sturdy matriarchy, dynasty building, even Matt; with not the slightest hesitation and with no advance interior warning, she relinquished what she had never given up to Tabor in his memory room, and what he had so wanted: her life with Brad Culver.

He kept urging her to tell more, touching her mouth while whispering to her—she kept talking because the version she gave excited him, until he pulled her along with him; together they looped over the edge, beyond where Katy'd been, beyond Mike Braden's unnameable loss.

▼ ▼ ▼

The next week, Katy awoke in Mike's bed to the peculiar sound of a woman singing in Danish. Through the window overlooking the front lawn she saw Greta poised naked on the pool springboard. She was wearing only a swimmer's cap and was dancing an exhibitionist jig. Her breasts bounced, then flattened when she paused to puff on a cigarette.

Katy woke Mike to look. He contemplated the scene by the pool and was quiet. He mumbled that he had seen trouble coming when he had asked Greta to drop off a box of Paula's clothes at the elementary school charity auction and she had started to wear them instead.

Katy saw to it that Greta was replaced by a Korean houseman.

That fall Mike and Katy rushed toward one another: until the weather turned bad they made love in his sailboat. In a Norwalk movie theater during a Saturday-night showing of *Klute*, Katy trembled as she sniffed Mike's breath next to her; she imagined him licking her later; and recalled the odor in his mouth when they were done and he rolled toward her in his sleep.

Mike relished the heat in her; he watched each new motion she thought up to please him. At midweek, when he was alone at Hannah's Point, he imagined the men she might be meeting at the Schmidlapp: he fantasized that they taught her the new moves. His mind went particularly wild when he temporarily slept with another woman.

Mike saw Katy was tempted by the illicit; he indulged her in her ancient, unfulfilled desire to be a mistress; they invented their own secrecy. He wanted her story; he would ask if she had slept with her brother. "Jim? You are crazy." He said he had slept with his older sister *and* brother. She never knew whether it was true or a turn-on. It didn't matter. Katy was hooked.

Instead of driving back to Hannah's Point from New Haven after the Harvard–Yale game, they spent the night at a Post Road motel pretending to be Humbert and Lolita. There were moments Katy was seized with an unaccountable sadness, a fright that Mike would vanish. At Hannah's Point she would wake in the middle of the night with the dread thought that he was dead or near death. She would pound his chest with her fists until he woke up, until his yells and curses convinced her he was alive. Other times, scared that Mike misread her as too sturdy, the polar opposite of suicidal Paula, and forgetting that he had gotten her out of Bellevue, Katy purposefully would blurt to him details of her breakdown, the LSD. She wanted Mike to see the true conditions of her life. But his hand would cover her mouth: what she had done before she arrived at Hannah's Point had no reality for him.

The winter's wild December blizzard was their perfect time. Mike warned Katy not to attempt Grand Central; the storm was too dense, the train would get stalled. From her living-room window, Katy saw the snow falling over the park at a blustery slant. Mike was alone in the country; Koo, his houseman, was off; she would have Mike to herself. Hannah's Point might be snowed in for days.

She gave the taxi driver double fare to drive her the old way, the quick way, through Harlem, to the 125th Street station. When she got off the New York–New Haven local, the road going down to the Sound was covered in deep snowdrifts. She located the owner of the last lone taxi parked at the station; he inched his car across the tricky narrow spit of road that joined Mike's semi-island to the mainland.

Mike thought her marvelous for getting through. He opened the back door as soon as he heard the honking of the car. She looked amazingly young, trudging in her blue parka and boots, with her bag, through the blurry drifts; moist patches of snow clung to her plaid muffler and her cheeks, wet twin apples; the sky over the water was muffled, white and low.

Mike's married neighbor watched them with a pang from her frosted window. Life had been good to her. Even so, it had been a long time since she had run confused and breathless in the snow to an assignation. She remembered that particular winter day long after she heard Katy and Mike had broken up.

CHAPTER

18

WHEN KATY WENT HOME FROM WORK
that day, her mind was still on Mike: *You could call. You could
even check out Adam Klager's tip with him. There's no law against
calling ex-lovers.* She punished herself with fantasies of another woman answering the phone. Sure voiced and casual.
The new Mrs. Michael Braden. After their breakup Katy had
avoiding getting news of Mike's new life. *So Mike will get on
the phone and say, "Oh, Katy—Katy Becker, my God, it's been
ages; you did hear I got married? And you? How we do lose track."*
In her reverie, Katy's was always the one nose pressed
against the window. She argued angrily to Mike's stray
sentences, which were still stuck in her head *You told him
you wished him well, but, m'dear, you wished him hell.*

▼ ▼ ▼

She walked into the kitchen. Ethan had nailed on her

241

pegboard the invitation to his gig for the Metro Retro Ethnicity do at the Sixty-seventh Street–Park Avenue armory. She studied it. *In his peculiarly energetic Texas way Ethan is beginning to make it in New York.* The benefit was for the

FRIENDS OF THE SOUTHWEST INDIAN MUSEUM

FRIENDS OF THE WHITE WHALE

KOREAN GAY RIGHTS GROUP

MOVEMENT FOR CATHOLIC WOMEN ORDAINED AS PRIESTS

FRIENDS OF ED KOCH

MAFIA VICTIMS OF THE MEDIA

CANARSIE LANDMARK ASSOCIATION

FRIENDS OF BELLA ABZUG

FRIENDS OF THE ENVIRONMENT AGAINST PERFUME

CHILDREN'S MULTILINGUAL STORY-TELLING ZOO GROUP

ASSOCIATION TO BAN FIFTH AVENUE PARADES

FRIENDS OF BEVERLY SILLS

LESBIAN GRANDMOTHERS' WORKING UNIT

JEWISH ORTHODOX WOMEN'S SUPPORT GROUP FOR THE PLO

JEWISH ORTHODOX WOMEN'S KABBALA READING GROUP

FRIENDS OF LITHUANIAN FREEDOM FIGHTERS

BLACK AFRICAN DOCUMENTARY FILM UNIT

MANHATTAN ASSOCIATION FOR THE COLUMBUS QUINCENTENNIAL

SPONSORS: CHRISTOPHER COLUMBUS–STATUE OF LIBERTY WEDDING; FRIENDS OF HISPANIC BALLET

UNDERWRITTEN BY GEORGIO ARMANI, TOSHIBA, IBERÍA AIRLINES, AND VICTOR'S RESTAURANT.

Katy recalled how Ethan had alighted on New York: for all her practical talk of caviar to Snowball, he had galloped onto the scene with no beluga, but with a guitar and a bottle of bourbon. He had ambled into her living room, tall, sandy haired, with a rusty tinge to his skin, disingenuous baby blue eyes, and fleshy, ruddy nostrils set in the downsides of a Bob Hope scoop nose. She noticed even then that he had an exact way of sizing up the usefulness of the people she had invited to dinner. There was a Philadelphia art curator, a midwestern university president, and an out-of-town art critic. The men had brought women who were not their wives to Katy's, and they were cool and angular and down dressed. At the time, Katy had thought the women had masked their sexuality with an extra dollop of grayness in the feeble hope that such overt carnal primness would earn them de facto wife status. It wasn't exactly an atmosphere that sizzled.

Ethan had spontaneously announced to her guests that he was going to do this hick Texas thing of singing a song he had just written. He sat down on her sofa, rested his guitar between his spread knees, and in a clear voice said that he was dedicating it to his lovely hostess because she was the widow of his dead professor, who had been so esteemed in the southern civil rights movement.

He wondered if Katy remembered how they had first met. It was in the sixties, when the dormitory-integration issue had inflamed the Austin campus. She was seated next to Lewis on the dais in the main auditorium. Ethan had noticed she was somewhat younger than her husband and not dressed quite right for a faculty wife—she wore blue jeans and had her hair tied up in a ponytail. "We don't eat northern shit down here," an East Texas student jeered at

243

Lewis's liberal jeremiad. "So, where are you from? Where did you go to school?"

Lewis's proudly confident response—"Harvard"—had scared Ethan; he hoped it wouldn't end with students pelting rotten tomatoes, or worse. In an effort to establish his allegiance to his professor, Ethan joined Katy and Lewis on the platform. He had heard Katy came from Connecticut; "I've a cousin in New Canaan, ma'am; I know how you must feel."

He remembered the wild look Katy had flashed at him—with the heat in her face, she'd looked like one of those steamy Gulf girls.

"The students are carrying on about Lewis because he went to *Harvard*? Huh," she mumbled, "this place is so backward, they don't even know enough to be anti-Semitic."

At the time Ethan hadn't had a clue what she was talking about. That was before he read up on New York sophisticates. After Lewis's death, during his condolence call, Katy had asked him if he would mind taking charge of Lewis's books; she wanted to make sure that they were properly catalogued in the university's twentieth-century library collection. Ethan was overjoyed to be of some use to his favorite professor's widow.

And now he was sitting in her New York living room! Ethan waited a bit, making sure he had the guests' attention. He kept stroking his guitar. He said that his style was a little Creole, a little country, a little Austin sound. Then he sang:

Ahh had mah book, ahh had mah guee-tah,
ahh rode the Greyhound from Corpus to Nu Ohleans;

244

Boy from Corpus, they cried, sing us your song.
Starry Gulf night, I bid yew adoo; hear what I say—
Adíos *my* corazón, adíos *my* corazón
Boy from Corpus, Momma wept, you done me no wrong.

Ah sang them uh tune from deep in ma travelin' heart,
Brown-eyed and to Prof. Lewis true.
Katy, star of my Manhattan chart,
Ah'm comin' up Naw-th for yew
Manhattan I do, Manhattan I do
for you my corazón, *for you my* corazón.

You laughed and kicked off your shoes when Ethan asked to dance with you. Next he twirled Snowball while you clapped to the two-step, and Snowball actually let go. She moved her body, claiming her beauty as part of her instead of going meekly and appeasing the world in face of so much physical luck.

Snowball had brought a fellow biologist, Eric Gatson. After the other guests left, the four of them tumbled into his Volvo; they went on a spree in the deserted city.

You insisted it wasn't dangerous; you got Eric to drive through Harlem—you showed Ethan where your Grandma Indy was born. "We northerners have our roots, too."

You said nothing when Eric drove past Tartan's place, but you pointed out Rao's. Harlem seemed a lunar landscape of bombed-out lots and blurry streetlights. Junkies were stumbling through shattered buildings near La Marquetta plastered with torn posters in Spanish of the Marlboro man. El hombre de Marlboro en terra incognita. *In no-man's land with tombstone shadows.*

Then Eric swung his car onto the FDR and headed toward the Brooklyn Bridge. *You revved Ethan up to watch for*

the curve in the highway when the lights from the Wall Street
district splutter over the East River like some gaudy Arabian dream
gone modern. Joy. Jouissance. The marvel of seeing the city
through the eyes of a first-timer—the four of you colluding
in the magic.

The Volvo roared across the upper level of the Brooklyn
Bridge; Eric and Snowball yelled to Ethan to turn his head
and look back. Night. "The skyline, the skyline!"

"Jesus Christ!"

You told him to watch for the streets named for fruits. "Cranberry. Pineapple. Really."

Ethan instinctively knew you would lead him to his future. Later
he described to you how he had devoured You Can't Go Home
Again *and* "Only the Dead Know Brooklyn." Thomas Wolfe's
portrait of himself as a young southern writer discovering
his identity, his talent, in 1940s Manhattan through the
ministrations of the lush, sexy Jewess Mrs. Jack, high priestess of the world of culture and old enough to be his mother,
had thrilled Ethan. *He confessed to you that he particularly liked*
the part when Mrs. Jack nurtured and seduced Wolfe by bringing
hampers of good food to his Brooklyn apartment. He said it long-
ingly. He sent you clues.

Ethan had kept tabs on his University of Texas class-
mates. Two had gone with Lyndon. One to the *Washington*
Post, three into Congress. *You watched him race to the railing's*
edge. He smelled the sea, saw the Statue of Liberty, the
small ships bobbing through the Narrows, the electric razz-
matazz of Wall Street's weightless lights suspended in the
sky. He threw back his head and moaned, "Thomas
Wolfe—Faulkner—Jesus Christ—I'm here!"

You didn't tell him his reference to Wolfe was hopelessly dated.

Face it. He turned you on. In an effort to please him, you and Snowball—her thin dress billowing and catching light from the reconstructed eighteenth-century lamppost—danced the length of the lookout. Converting one female molecular biologist and one female museum curator into magical Manhattan entertainers. You never told Ethan this was your first-time view of the Manhattan skyline from the Brooklyn side.

▼ ▼ ▼

Metro Retro Ethnicity involved a lot of walking. All five floors of the building were in use: simultaneous improvisations were taking place on ten different stages. The mobile audience was instructed to mingle with the actors, to interject their own plays; the actors frequently walked offstage to applaud the performing audience. *Tamara*, the detective play involving audience participation, had been a long-term money-maker; its producers hoped this spin-off of it would be another hit. Katy walked through its cavernous rooms searching for Ethan's band; the place, she thought, retained its musty turn-of-the-century cavalry stink.

▼ ▼ ▼

She found Ethan and *Texas in Manhattan* on the third floor. He and his band, the Helotes Six, were atop a floating barge covered with papier-mâché, beneath a poster of the American flag crossed with the Lone Star. Red, white, and blue strobe lights streaked the armory ceiling; the room's damp middle-of-winter horsy smell melded with the odors of authentic *tinga poblana* and *moronga taquitos*. Ethan sat on a platform in the barge, resting his guitar between his spread knees, and announced that he was going to do this hick

247

Texas thing of singing a song he had written when he first came to New York. A song that united the North with the South. Blacks with whites. It struck her as oddly déjà vu. She watched him give a sandy, randy smile as he pulled a miniskirted young woman on to the barge. "Ah need audience pa-tis-a-pashun. What's yuh name, honey? Ei-leyun? And yew ah at Hun-tah?" He held her tight and sang:

Mon petit amour, mi querida, *ma darlin' little one,*
There is a wound set deep in America's heart.
In all our whispered languages beneath our white sun
We were a country in bloody battle torn apart . . .
Mon petit amour, mi querida, *ma darlin' Ei-leyun*

Ethan's prefucking that student and he knows you're here. This is for your benefit. Instead of angry, she felt dazed. Head detached. No words coming out of her mouth. An old-womanish feel to her body; a bad smell coming from her skin.

▼　▼　▼

"Now all of us join in the chorus." Ethan pointed his finger to a middle-aged couple quarreling with each other at the *taquito* stand.

"This means you. Sing with me to mah de-ud friend and men-tuh, mah professor Lew-us Eichorn." He flashed a smile at Katy, asking her to collude with him in not seeing he had his hand on the Hunter student's ass.

We were fallen bluegrass soldiers—
Oh, mah darlin' Texas girl, how do I long
to tell you of those who marched with me,

ma petite wildflowah, to undo the wrong.
The dead make no sound
But remember, let it be, let it be!

Ethan's eating Lewis's memory, Lewis's history—a singing canni-bal. She managed to force into her head one sentence. *Drop him, he's no good for you.*

She waited for the next music break and went over to him. *It's hard for two people who've never quite come together to split—the essential furies are missing.*

Ignoring the Hunter student, Katy immediately went at him: "I think our seeing each other is contraindicated."

"Contraindicated? What kind of a cold word are you using for us?"

"I meant it."

"Now, honey—"

He's uncertain whether to protest or treat this as an equal opportunity.

Suddenly Ethan launched into a winding narration of what Katy had meant to him: her being this special New York woman like Thomas Wolfe's Mrs. Jack. While she and the Hunter student—his captive audience—listened, Ethan described their affair as happening like a melodious narra-tion: it had a beginning, a middle, and an end, with symbolic reverberations of North and South, small town and big city. Without answering, Katy turned and left. *A southern talent,* she thought. As she walked out she got a queer feeling that the out-of-town couple in the back of the room were talk-ing about her. *Your displaced Ethan paranoia.*

▼ ▼ ▼

Judge Ben Myrtle had brought his sister, Anna, to the Metro Retro benefit—they had nothing as elaborate as *Tamara* and the Armory in Philadelphia. But Anna was a pest. When she noticed the Children's Multilingual Story-Telling Zoo Group on the list of charities, she grumbled, "The only ethnic language spoken by children living near the Sixty-fifth Street zoo is French. Tell me, Ben, are they one of our culturally endangered American subgroups?" She wanted to eat Tex-Mex, so he took her to hear the Helotes Six.

When he heard Ethan Lemay sing lyrics dedicated to his dead professor, Lewis Eichorn, Ben Myrtle's eyes popped. "Annie—the country singer is the *lover* in the Eichorn case."

"Lover? What lover?" Anna was hard of hearing. Myrtle had to repeat himself twice. The audience shushed him. He shepherded his sister to the *moronga* stand in the back of the room.

"You told me you had ordered that puerile talk of lovers stricken out of the pretrial deposition—since when does one talk of two consenting unmarried adults as being *lovers?*" Anna had a special sharp way of pouncing on Ben. "But you didn't strike it out of your lazy head. Your legal habits are prehistoric—you're incapable of judging a woman's case."

"The law, Anna, is sex blind."

"Bullshit, Ben."

"Bernard Eichorn's chief counsel is on the board of the Explorers' Club. Now, Anna, this was a complex estate—they may have gone overboard in trying to protect the future assets of the Eichorn son . . . Look, Anna, the Eichorn woman is in the front row—you can feel that there is this sex thing going on between those two. Obviously she likes younger men. I can understand how the Eichorn family might have felt she would have dissipated the money . . ."

"Are you such a good investor?" she nagged at him. "Tell me about the mint you lost in blue chips, and look where I've landed with my art."

"Oh, Anna!"

Then Ethan pointed a finger directly at him:

> The dead make no sound
> But remember, let it be, let it be.

Lemay has you spotted. He thinks you are spying on him—no, no, that's crazy. The judge frantically remembered marching with blacks in the civil rights movement. Or was it a candle-light ceremony near the U.N. for victims of Hiroshima? His eyes frightened, his gut full of *moronga*, he bellowed, "Let it be, amen, let it be."

CHAPTER

1 9

THE NEXT MORNING KATY TOOK HER usual walk through the park to the Schmidlapp. She had no money, no man in her life (in her head she already had rehearsed what Ethan would be saying to her, what she to him), but her step was firm. Odd the way Adam Klager, of all people, had liberated her. *You have just had a tête-à-tête with a man who has done great evil, and you feel weirdly, marvelously revved up.*

Until Klager, the men in her life had been on the side of the angels. Or had said they were. *Their moral fineness put you in a mental straitjacket. Like you were walking through gray sludge.* It was sort of nice, listening to Adam's unabashed desire for revenge on Beanie. His lack of ambivalence exhilarated her. He had cleared away the debris and pointed her in the right direction. Given her a concrete task. She needed to find some record that Beanie had listed Belle Hélène as belonging to his offshore Bermuda corporation. Somewhere in Harlem, in a real-estate office or a city tax department, that information must exist. *Adam Klager isn't the type to send people on wild goose chases.*

▼ ▼ ▼

When Katy walked home from the Schmidlapp in the early evening, scenes from Harlem reawakened in her memory: drowsy thoughts of her mother floated in her mind; the pungent vegetable-and-meat smell of the 116th Street markets filled her nostrils. Why had Anita died so soon? Why had she deserted Katy? After Lewis's death, Katy had yearned to talk to her; she even bought a bottle of her mother's perfume—Diorissimo—and doused her pillow and sheets with it. When she smelled it, she saw herself, again, with her mother, in the middle of Olga Zweicky's antique shop; her aunts—Jillian and Marcie—and Miss Olga were with them, egging her to pick, to get it right. She heard once more the congratulatory lilt of their voices when she reached for the blue vase—"The eye," they cried, "she has the eye!" The women surrounded her, hugging her wool-coated chest, kissing her cheeks: they were bringing her home to their cheerful beginnings and diaphanous sadness, to her dead Grandma Jaches; she was free, she was a girl, she was love returned.

That night in her bedroom, she opened the trunk with all the files on the case and searched through the folders with the confidence of a woman who had been told early in life that she had the ability to see. Trembling, in almost an exalted state, she scanned them for clues. On one sheet was an ancient photo of the old office building owned by her father-in-law with a matter-of-fact description typed beneath it; accompanying it, on Belle Hélène stationery, was an explanatory letter to local commercial real-estate agents.

She stared at the sepia-tinted photograph of her father-in-law's factory, then back at the letterhead. *The street address in the rental space ad didn't tally with the numbers hammered in cement over the main entryway in the original picture!* Adam was on to something—Max Schecter should have sent an associate from his firm up to the Spoon River Triangle to *look at the buildings.* Her cheeks flushed, her skin hairs raised up, amazed, electric. *Don't call Schecter now—do it yourself.*

Since it was late, she paid a taxi double to drive her through Harlem. Near 125th Street, a vendor was selling plastic poinsettias and contraband Cardin neckties in front of the Iglesia Sagrado Milagro. Her cab went past vacated stores, walls of torn campaign posters. As they continued north, she heard, through the half-open window, the hiss of Puerto Rican Spanish: *Donde Esta Mi Hijo? Donde Esta Mi Hijo?* Carib talk wafted toward her on the smell of charred chicken skin and cumin. She jumped out of the taxi at Belle Hélène to inspect the building. The place was falling apart—the main entrance was boarded up, and a new small door with a different address had been installed at the far end of the building, next to Stoehmer's vacated kosher meat store.

Katy looked at the building; she would unravel its secrets. She breathed deeply, inhaling the fumes of the smoking gun Adam Klager had handed her.

▼ ▼ ▼

It was too late that night, so in the morning she called Tartan for help. Was Brad coming to New York, as promised, for his usual winter visit? Since their cousin Willie Lawn had died and his house on Sugar Hill was sold, Tartan and Jessica had got in the habit of celebrating Christmas in January, when Brad was free to come east. Katy needed him to find out if there were someone on the Lawn side of his family who could connect her to smart Harlem real-estate men; she needed to talk to a man on the inside.

In mid-December, Tartan located one of her cousin's nephews—he worked for Urban Renewal. He told her Brad should contact Arnold Clay, who knew everything that went on in uptown real estate.

▼ ▼ ▼

Brad flew in to New York the second week in January. The first night he had jet lag. He lay exhausted and suffocating on the old cot in his bedroom, lost in Harlem, knowing what he had to do, knowing his agenda was the right one. It was time to move Tartan and Jessica to his home in Berkeley. He and Elise had agreed—there was never going to be a right moment for this. He had to act on it now. Nothing here had changed but for the worse. Mount Jefferson Park had a rotting smell, even in winter.

Brad tried to do the right thing—he remembered a good piece of fur was important to the women; he gave his mother a mink collar, and Jessica a Persian lamb hat. They liked that bit of luxury better than the Kodak viewer and slide carousel he had also brought east for them—he had wanted to show them life in California before he introduced the subject of their move: he and Elise had made a large

255

modern studio apartment above the garage for the two women, overlooking the fine slope of his two acres.

"I'm tops, Mom—in demand as far north as Vancouver."

He had done the feat. Become the first black landscape architect to make a dent. Smack in the middle of North Berkeley. He even had Marin County customers. Elise insisted Tartan's natural vocation was producing guilt. She wasn't a rational woman, Elise would argue. Why would she hang on to Harlem?

▼ ▼ ▼

Tartan and Jessica took no notice that Christmas was past. They saw Brad's Kodachrome repeat of his family's bountiful California Christmas as an alien event taking place outside of time. Tartan ignored the fact that North Berkeley was where she was meant to be, that her son had wanted her to be part of the picture and inside the colored slides, not viewing them.

When she was satisfied that she had sufficient proof he was doing his work, she took off her apron and folded her hands in the lap of her heavy brown crêpe dress. She wore her pearl earrings and a gold clip on her matte silk bosom, real jewelry given to her by Brad on a previous Christmas.

▼ ▼ ▼

She's lost her wild look, Brad thought, noting in terror the small signs of her eventual death: *Her eyes are clouded, smaller—the savagery is gone. Except for the hair. It springs out high above her forehead, sharp as steel; the smell of Castile soap still emanates from her. Castile smells of the East. California has other odors.*

256

When Katy walked in, Tartan said, "The meal is hot. Keeping it sit won't improve the bird."

Brad had known she would be there; she always came. He studied her—saw the changes. Her effect was different.

She came wearing a kilt, a navy cashmere sweater, and shiny tan loafers; her brown hair hung flat and straight down her back, schoolgirl style. *She has developed that good country look some women outside New York go for. She is with some new man; even coming up here, she has dressed for him.*

Brad had been raised by females, with his nose enveloped in the mystery inside their skirts; he had women inside his head, he sensed things about them; but it was beyond his imagination to know that Katy was hyped up by her case, not by a love affair.

When he touched her arm in greeting, she did not respond: *She's in a passion; you don't matter to her.*

Brad had done the right thing; he had come back east to celebrate the holidays with his mother and Jessica. Now he wanted to lie on the floor—howl like a stuck pig in the midst of these three women.

He gave Katy a thick book with heavy color plates that had some of his work—*Gardens of the West*—her present to him was a bound volume of the Schmidlapp's permanent collection.

"Merry Christmas, Brad."

"Merry Christmas."

Tartan had her systems. First she said grace. She wanted Katy and Brad to sit immobilized at the round table while she and Jessica, gray-haired Rockettes moving in unison, rushed them platters of cut meat, giblet gravy, and

257

cranberry sauce. Jessica carried in to the dining alcove, her hand shaking, a cut-glass pitcher of iced pink fruit juice.

Brad opened his shirt; he began to relax. "Remember the green-and-red whipped-cream Jell-O layers?" he whispered to Katy; again they were co-conspirators, about to be overstuffed.

She giggled. "Where are the Jell-Os of yesteryear?"

"Braddy," Tartan interrupted, "don't eat the cashews; they hold water." She continued her annual ritual liturgy. "Katy, don't clear."

"It's nice exercise—"

"No. I have earned the right to peace at my own table."

Let her win—let her stay in Italian Harlem until she can't stand it anymore. He hated the dark room swollen with Anita Becker's leftover furniture and knickknacks—what Katy couldn't fit into the Schmidlapp she had brought here.

No boundaries. It's made nut cases of us all. No clear demarcations. The possessions of Anita Becker divvied up between the Schmidlapp and Tartan Culver's Harlem tenement flat. Nut cases, nut cases. Try them apples in a Berkeley consciousness-raising group.

Brad was strangling in Manhattan. He had betrayed Elise when he defended his mother's craziness in staying on in Harlem; he would betray Tartan and Jessica in forcing them to come to North Berkeley. Why shouldn't the women like California?—Brad Culver was *someone*; his mother would see that once she went there.

He knew he had outdistanced Katy, left her far behind. She leafed through *Gardens of the West*; she said the illustrations would make an interesting exhibit for the Schmidlapp. She had a way of fielding painful stuff between them by concentrating on aesthetics.

258

The too-bulky antiques from Indian Path, the darkness of his mother's cramped apartment dizzied him.

"So what if your mother yanked you out of Harlem; why is she staying there now?" Elise had cried. *"Just to humiliate us? To make us feel bad? Why doesn't she care about her grandchildren? Why should she want them to think their father came from bombed-out bimbo town?"*

Brad never had an answer for Elise. He knew his mother had meant the apartment in Italian Harlem to have been a temporary solution. She measured the start of time as the year she had come up north from Waylee with Hewley Ginzberg. She narrated the facts as though an invisible census taker were continuously at her side: she had the black story, she had the white story. Like two halves of a cantaloupe. The white part was Katy's line: her grandmother, Indy Jaches, was the mother of Anita, Marcie, and Jillian; they were Hewley Ginzberg's northern cousins, the part of the family that had originated in Jewish Harlem.

Tartan had left Waylee, South Carolina—so why now couldn't she leave a Harlem she had done everything in her power to remove him from? Why didn't she see her story as Waylee, South Carolina, straight on to North Berkeley, with a little dip in between? Why didn't she want to take credit for what he, her son, had become? Why didn't she know? Know? Know?

▼ ▼ ▼

But Tartan lived inside her systems. She kept keys to the apartments of Hewley, Snowball, and Katy; it never occurred to her to question her right to them. When she was in the mood she would drop in to check out their situations. She claimed there were territories she walked and territories that were not hers. Her world remained divided into blocks: "I am an East Coast person," she said, with no interest in whether the west was good or bad; it simply wasn't hers.

She did as she pleased. Snooped. Read Snowball's and Katy's mail over a hot cup of tea—she and Hewley called them "the goils." Locked up what she felt they were too dumb to lock up for themselves. Emptied the refrigerator. Called Gristede's. Charged up a storm and cooked food for them her way.

"Katy hires Jamaican day girls—their floors are gummy," she said to Brad, as if Carib lacks were a reason for her not going to North Berkeley.

"We don't drive," wheezed Jessica.

Tartan told Brad it was his duty to take charge of a meeting between Katy and the Harlem real-estate man Arnold Clay.

SEVERAL DAYS LATER BRAD PICKED UP
Katy in front of the Schmidlapp to meet Clay. Brad's Russian immigrant taxi driver, enraged at his own lack of English and New York knowhow, insisted that Park Avenue was merely another name for Central Park: *"Parks have trees,"* he argued.

"No," Katy said. *"Fifth Avenue has the park."* When she made him turn east on Madison, he retaliated in Slav invective.

Katy waved in the direction of the river. *"Wasser—Wasser,"* she tried, on the theory the USSR was nearer Germany than Manhattan.

The man calmed down: he turned to Katy, grinning: *"Du bist eine Yid?"*

"Si—ya, ya, da."

Lexington and Ninety-ninth Street bordered on the land

of moon craters; only the promised coming of an oil emir's new mosque relieved the bombed-out look of the neighborhood: an architect's vision of the mighty dome to be erected there, Allah and oil flow willing, covered the billboard of the empty corner lot. Scrawled beneath it was: BESSIE SMITH 1894–1937. JOYSTICK BOMBERS. SUPER DISCO. OUR BESSIE GIRL. OUR BESSIE. *Graffiti with flair.*

They curved around the FDR; discarded Christmas trees with red, pink, silver dangles and torn angels, yesterday's joy lay in the gutter in front of the Ponce de Leon restaurant on 119th Street. This time of year, Brad recalled, Manhattan had light as white as an August laundry day.

Clay was waiting for them in Jimmy's. Even in the darkness of the rectangular lounge Brad recognized his downtown/uptown style—Clay was obviously a man used to doing his business in both places. He had a neat executive short-hair trim, he wore no jewelry: a man on the clear upswing.

Brad walked to his corner banquette. "I'm Mary Culver's son, Brad."

"Ahah." He nodded. "I thought it was you folks."

Clay's clothes had a foreign touch—his charcoal wool suit and heavy-patterned wine silk tie looked Milanese. When he held out his hand, his buffed nails and natty, vulnerable Harlem optimism made Brad wince. Clay was a Manhattan black of a type Elise and he didn't think about in California.

"Your uncle Willie was the best dentist in the whole area . . . One of his sons tells me your mother is his first cousin? Any relative of the Lawn family is indeed a friend of mine."

He turned to Katy. "Jimmy's deviled roast rib bones, Mrs. Eichorn, are as close to paradise as you've a right."

▼ ▼ ▼

Katy sat down between the two men and inhaled Clay's expensive male aroma mingled with the smell of the deviled ribs, and she followed his lead about what was good to eat.

"Katy—call me Katy," she corrected him. "Business up here must be good."

"Katy, that's a fine name—yes, business is more than good. We are on the brink of great things. In the old days only the *Amsterdam News* took notice of our existence—now even the *New York Times* is reporting on Harlem real estate."

"Which is why I am here—Brad's cousin tells me you have your hands on the local real-estate explosion?" She paused to munch on the roast ribs, licked her fingers, then slipped in her special credentials:

"Brad may have told you I'm not alien to Harlem. Which is why I felt I could come here to see things for myself. Now, Brad's mother and Jessica didn't come to Harlem until the First World War—which was when my aunt Hewley moved to Manhattan because she had married a northern soldier, Bert Wurlitzer, from Larchmont, who lammed out. My maternal grandmother came from very near here. Madison and Ninety-ninth Street. So you see, I have legitimate claims on all sides to the area. I still remember coming to the indoor market stalls with my mother and my aunts Jillian and Marcie to buy good food—"

"Those girls probably came up here for hamhocks and greens. Maybe they went for pigs' feet and collards. Next time I'll take you to Sylvia's for some soul food."

"No—they just bought fresh-killed chickens and fish. But I do remember them saying that there was a time when the railroad tracks ran above Park Avenue."

"Do you mind my asking, what is that lovely scent you are wearing? I might buy some for my wife," Clay asked her.

"Ivoire. Balmain's Ivoire."

"Very pungent. So, your family are old-timers, like mine. You and I—I don't know about Brad—are indeed the root here."

"Count me out—I'm strictly Bay Area." Brad shifted in his chair uncomfortably.

If Elise were here, with Winicott and the Montessori method flowing through her ordered mind, she'd kill Katy for talking darky. She'd shriek at you: "Collards and pigs' feet! Balls! That's your mother's influence, shaming you, putting you back into sentimental shit garbage, drowning you in darky Harlem." Katy always takes what she needs—Harlem, Indian Path, her stories, your mother's stories—it all sits in her head; she'll never let go. She'll nag and flirt with Clay until he digs something up; Beanie was nuts to start up with her.

"Some in this town don't know we originals still exist," Clay continued. "Manhattan's not all show biz and foreign capital—it has its native stock—we do have our ways of recognizing each other."

"Which precisely is why I came to you—I need your help." Katy took a deep breath, then launched into her saga involving Beanie, Belle Hélène, and Adam Klager. "But I do want you to know, bad as Beanie is, he's never been a slum landlord."

"Katy, Clay knows you're talking about a string of office

264

buildings, not a tenement—you don't have to dot your liberal *i*'s."

Katy looked up at the revolving silver ceiling. "Am I liberal? Am I that? Am I to be chastised for wanting what's mine? Brad, I just want to make clear to Mr. Clay—"

"Arnold."

"To Arnold that *the* issue up here is not *our* issue up here. When Belle Hélène dipped, or moved elsewhere, Beanie rented the place to an international import firm—the Rasuds. Even so, it loses us money. I need the real poop on what is going on up here. Adam Klager, who's had dealings with Beanie, informed me that Beanie has listed Belle Hélène under two different addresses and as being part of his offshore Bermuda corporation. Now I need concrete proof of it."

"So Adam Klager is in on this? Not that shit's style to be involved with uptown—"

"He was a pal of Beanie's—they've had a business falling-out."

"Even if the bastard is dying of AIDS, Klager's nobody to have as an ex-pal." Clay let the foam of an imported beer slither down his throat. "I know of the Rasuds—they say they're Colombian coffee importers—spic monkey business. Riffraff we want to be rid of."

"If we clear our claim to Belle Hélène and the property can be turned around, I am thinking, why shouldn't my son have the benefit of it? Mr. Clay—Arnold—do you think it is too awful of me to make some money back on what is technically Harlem property?"

"Awful? It's wonderful. Whitey's coming back, whitey's coming back to Harlem."

"What about race relations?"

"Race relations?" Clay was shocked; he wiped the grease from his deviled-ribs hands onto a thick white napkin. "Baby, you and me are talking real estate."

He snapped on a jazzy pair of tinted-for-indoors eye-glasses. "With whitey coming back, Harlem will snap into motion"— he clicked his fingers—"like that. These days we have big plans up here. We have gold in these streets—Harlem gold."

He paused to chew the marrow in his rib bones. "It wouldn't hurt none," he added for Brad's benefit, "if some of our tony blacks moved back in. Helped rebuild the place. Put their money where their mouth is—but, oh no, *their* kids have to go to private schools in the suburbs."

Brad was furious: *Clay's putting you on. Doing flirty black-and-white stuff with Katy while turning you into the heavy—the shit-face black sellout who high-tailed it out of Harlem to snooty paradise in California. Like Elise says, they want to pull you back inside the rot, drown you in their stinking garbage.*

"All that stuff about Harlem being black Harlem is out-of-date Muslim crap from the seventies," Clay continued. "Nobody's buying them mess of turbans here these days. The smart guys know to make Harlem sizzle we need the whites back."

"What smart guys?" Brad shot back. "You are sounding off like you are on the payroll of downtown real estate."

"Listen, Culver, things got so bad up here, black kids didn't even know we invented jazz. Is Max Roach a down-town real-estate man? Max knows he has to bring jazz back to Harlem, get the kids to relearn their own traditions—get 'em off the dope that killed Harlem. Like vermin, drugs

266

eat away at a neighborhood until the building façades are rotted—the innards crumple, then they're rubble."

"In Austin, Texas, my son Matt's Mexican nurse told us if you live near the place where a great star has been shot down"—Katy breezed off on a different tack—"when you move into a new town, you bring magical powers with you—another longed-for star will rise close to the place where you settle. The day John F. Kennedy was shot, we were in Austin waiting for him to finish with Dallas—the university was in readiness, all decked out. So, my being here might bring you luck? Maybe Harlem jazz will be the new rising star?"

She's playing cutesy with him. Brad hated witnessing such junk; he cursed Tartan for her nagging insistence that he bring Katy to Clay.

"Uh-huh." Clay meditated. "I do see the correlation—Harlem, Max Roach, the new Cotton Club and Cab Calloway's housing development will be reborn on the ashes of King and Kennedy, and Harlem jazz will soar again—"

"Come off it," Brad interrupted. "All you've got here is shit."

"You've lost your real-estate eyes in California. You've seen the boarded-up streets? Look again. When a neighborhood suddenly becomes cat quiet—depopulated, buildings boarded up—watch out. That's the way it was in Houston—the big interests bought up the place on the q.t. Then, wham! Overnight, with most dummies still thinking downtown Houston was no-man's-land, the hot new financial skyscrapers just zoomed up. Culver, most of these blocks here have been spoken for. By the big interests. Some black. Some white—even foreign combines are moving in, the rich squinties have given us thumbs up. Soon Harlem real estate will split open, as ripe with sugar juice as a cantaloupe in mid-August."

"Bullshit—I heard those Harlem dreams when I was a kid."

"In five years' time we'll have the Apollo Theater back and the ground will be broken for the new Third World Trade Center on the street. *The* street. Even the Helmsley–Spear bunch is high on us—they know we are the only fat piece of Manhattan left. We've got access—it's a cinch to get here from midtown. No bridges, no tunnels—just up either highway, Amsterdam or Columbus. No shit—our Harlem Third World, with its helicopter pad, underground garages, and deluxe hotels, will be a bigger, better, and more expensive Third World than any of those two-bit Third Worlds the squinties have got. In strict no-crapping-around confidence—Cook's tour has their eye on us, they are projecting a tour of our night spots for their European clientele. I mean, Culver, Harlem night spots haven't been on a tourist map since before we were born."

"True, Cook's can drum up the European nostalgia trade wanting Josephine Baker reincarnated, but Third World types want the Waldorf—up here you guys talk pie-in-the-sky."

Clay was quiet. Almost as if it were an afterthought, a spur-of-the-moment plan, he offered to take them up to Belle Hélène; in his capacity as a real-estate broker he could get them inside the building—he had told the Rasuds that he would be showing the building to out-of-town buyers.

▼ ▼ ▼

They stood in front of it: its original turn-of-the-century carved-wood-door entrance was boarded up. Graffiti was smeared on the outside. FUCK MAMA ANGEL. UP YOURS ROXIE. STAR WARS IS A DAGO QUEEN. Clay rang the bell over which was a small sign: Rasud Brothers: International Coffee Distributors. A surly workman let them in.

Brad felt he had walked into the lobby of one of the old art deco movie palaces—the Roxy, maybe. In the far corner was an oversized elevator with wrought-iron open lattice-work doors and, next to it, a grand winding staircase with marble steps. Brad studied the tarnished gold plaques nailed to the green mosaic-tiled walls; he assumed the names on them to have been business concerns from the 1920s, when Harlem was still thought to be an upcoming new flashy part of the city. Now a collection of rubber tires, broken planks of wood, and rusty rubbish littered the abandoned lobby.

The man took them in the elevator up to the top floor, indicating they could start there and walk down.

Brad walked through a maze of deserted offices. He felt lost in this warren's nest of bygone businesses. *Had there really been a time real estate planners had thought Harlem could rival downtown?* He paused by a tiny window overlooking the Harlem River; he saw south to the cluster of bridges and islands where the river flowed into the East. *In another part of town, people would kill for the view.*

"Spoon Triangle," Clay pointed out, "was choice for industry in its time."

Brad picked his way through the dilapidated debris piled high in the middle of what once must have been a conference room. There were a set of conference chairs, an old

Philco radio, a gray mattress with its ticking spilling out, a broken set of Monopoly, two rubber trusses, some battered army lockers, a vinyl suitcase, sofas, and parchment-shaded lamps from the thirties. Racks of worn clothing stank of old-shoe smells and sweat. Whatever he touched was dusty. And no coffee beans.

"Between you and me," Clay said to him, "I wouldn't be surprised if half the stolen silver from Park Avenue had been recycled through this place on to Texas and South America."

"Mafia?" Katy came up behind them. "This is getting interesting—do you think Beanie has Mafia ties?"

"No way is the Mafia in this part of town," Clay said. "Crack, cocaine—I'd buy that."

"It's no good, Katy—even if the Rasuds are laundering stolen goods or into dope it's not Beanie's problem. He's just their landlord—not their confessor."

Katy walked determinedly into the next room.

Beanie watched her: *She's searching for things like an amateur sleuth. Like the Nancy Drew books she would read you aloud in recess in PS 6. Doesn't understand you don't find out about white-collar crime by wandering through your in-laws' defunct real estate.*

"Look—my father-in-law's office. I remember being here—I remember his desk."

Katy pulled open the drawers. But there were only a few dusty account books, an old bill from Mount Sinai for her mother-in-law's emergency appendectomy, and a torn photo of Walter and Lily, well bundled in British plaid blankets, comfortably ensconced on ship deck chairs. A framed clip from the *World-Telegram* hung on the wall above the desk; the family was standing on the deck of the *Île de*

France, Lily's face hidden by a cloche and a fur piece. Beanie, clutching his stepmother Lily's hand and scowling, was staring directly at the photographer. Lewis was climbing up the rail, one foot gaily suspended in midair. The news caption read:

Mr. and Mrs. Walter Eichorn of the Belle Hélène furniture empire return home from Switzerland. Mr. Eichorn commented that ominous dark clouds hang over Europe. He sees the future of the Continent as uncertain.

Lewis was another prince who abdicated—not for Wallis, but for Wisdom and Wittgenstein. Katy put back the stuff she had removed from the desk. *Don't play voyeur of the dead.*

She recalled that her father-in-law had claimed that his father—Elie Eichorn—had dreamed up the Belle Hélène name long before he had made the business. He liked telling how Elie, at nineteen, had left Europe in steerage. How he had stood crushed against the ship railing watching Europe recede, knowing he was leaving for good. His last sight of land was a huge portrait of a heart-smashing auburn-haired beauty on the dock side of a Bremerhaven building. On the bottom was the name Belle Hélène. He couldn't make out whether the face on the billboard was that of an actress or of an opera singer, or an advertisement for shampoo or ice cream.

Elie Eichorn's financial start came through caskets. By the turn of the century, his worth was solid enough to switch into furniture; his Belle Hélène Rose Bedroom suite and Belle Hélène Lilac Dining Room suite instantly made him rich. He had picked Spoon Triangle to erect a block of office buildings with showrooms because of its good access to the bridges; he had miscalculated Harlem's industrial potential. He had believed its real estate would go sky-high. The family, out of inertia, had kept the buildings. Katy's father-in-law, Elie's son Walter, liked to boast that it was said downtown that Elie Eichorn sure had shown Grand Rapids a new wrinkle or two: he had been among the first in his business to give his product a clever name.

Katy insisted, now that they were in the building, that she and Brad inspect various offices on each floor—Clay went downstairs ahead of them to chat the Rasuds up into giving more details about their arrangements with Beanie.

On each level there was more garbage. Brad couldn't abide watching Katy rummaging through it; he preferred gazing through the small dusty office windows and watching the boats coming down the Harlem River. He had no memory that he was standing not far from where they had emerged from the Croton Aqueduct the day the Second World War ended. Geography shifts things; standing inside a factory didn't orient him to remember drifting downriver in a canoe. It had been Katy, not he, who had seen the Belle Hélène truck from the river—either way, neither of them would have remembered the name of a passing vehicle from so long ago.

"Drop it, Katy—you're wasting your time on crap. You wouldn't give a shit about Belle Hélène if your folks hadn't lost Indian Path."

Now you've done it—mentioned the place, the bona fide loss. You meant to show up the Beckers—how sweet it was to imagine outdistancing Jeremiah. Running fast—was that a sin? To use every piece tossed your way to make something better? You wanted to surpass Katy, but not for her to fall down; that was it, that was your ticket—beating, winning, and still having all of them up there, strong, admiring what you became, noticing you. Damn, Katy Tess—jailer—torturer—lover—I never meant you to be picking over the garbage of your dead husband's crazy family like you were some thrown-away daughter of Harlem. Don't let go. You cave in, and I don't exist! "You're confusing one loss with another—it was Indian Path you wanted for Matt."

"Indian Path? Are you nuts? You think I'm some Manhattan Blanche Du Bois? I said good-bye to that when I was a kid. Jim knew it would end up being a white elephant."

"Jim?" Brad felt depressed. The resurgence of ancient pain. *She always excluded you from her talks with him.*

"Of course, Jim—it was as much his as mine. Brad, there are some marvels that belong to another century, and you have to soak the stuff up real deep at the moment you have still got it in front of you—you really have to see it—because it's nothing meant to continue. On my honeymoon I said, 'Lewis, I want to see the French towns, tuck them in my head, because in a decade, give or take, Europe will have another look.' I'm not enslaved to phony notions of the good taste of the past."

Tell her she was a blind girl. "How about your own past?"

"Indian Path," she persisted, "was lost, and on an off day, the memory of those Olmsted trees might be nostalgic, sad—particularly for you, Brad—but my son got cheated out of his part of Belle Hélène, out of a piece of his proper future, and only because Matt had the bad luck to have an early-dead father. I don't care how ugly this place strikes you, or how grubby the Rasuds are—if there is something I can dig out of this shit to uncheat us, I will do it."

"So it's fuck-off time—who the hell needs a landscape architect, that's it?"

"Brad, you did your feat; you don't understand I still have to complete mine. No, okay, you asked for it"—she lowered her voice—"I have to cover my losses. The men in my life have had such pretty careers. Including you."

"You're saying I was a shit to you?"

"Motive me no motive when I have real stuff that needs doing. To you Indian Path was an optimistic model of what one man could do solo in America. For Jim and me . . ." She hesitated. "It was what we couldn't live up to. Couldn't repeat."

She's saying you have no emotional claim on Jeremiah—only she and Jim had him. But if Tartan had never been entangled with Jeremiah, why did she always favor Katy? Why did she hug her secret?

With no more words in his head Brad pulled Katy, her skin smelling of Ivoire, toward him. *Tell her how you lay in her spare room in the San Jaciente house wanting to crawl like old times into her bed and hold her, she needed you, but by then you knew Indian Path and Jeremiah were as much yours as hers.*

He held on to her tight: *Tell her that in the Berkeley consciousness-raising sessions, you never gave up what went on between the two of you.* Tomorrow he would fly back to California and Katy would be off with a different Mike Braden or a new Ethan Lemay. He hated the idea of that unknown man, but knowing he must exist made it all right for Brad to reach for her now. *Too many chains to think things through clearly* . . . so he was silent; his hand trembled as he kept hugging her, kissing her neck hair, her eyes opening and closing until she reached for him, calling, Brad Brad Brad.

Say the words. Tell her you're taking Tartan and Jessica back with you. He pushed her away from him. "Clay's going to fix you up with Harry Struthers, the tax assessor for the district. He has the property listings." *Tell her.* Brad felt dizzy. Confused.

"I'm taking the women to California. Katy, it's time for them to go home. To my home."

Her face lost color. She went quiet, like the day in the Touring Traveler Motel off the Post Road near Norwalk. And had the eyes of a child. "You can't do that—you can't take them from their home and plunk them down in California like they were pieces of the Rasud storage dust."

"Don't hold on, Katy. Tartan is my mother—don't stand in my way; this is long overdue. You have to help me do it. Do you want to wake up and find that they've been knifed? Mugged? Murdered? Is this your love? Katy, are you that blind? Look around you—this is bombed-out bimbo war zone."

"Thanks to people like you—you never tried to build anything here."

"Katy, I've got their tickets. You can give their stuff to that charity—Harlem Restoration."

"My mother's furniture that she gave to Tartan and Tartan kept all these years? That's what you call 'the stuff'? You and your fucking future." Then she stopped talking. As though unsure whether to hit herself or him.

Brad stood there. Still. While she beat his chest and his face with her two fists— *She never touched you the time in*

275

Norwalk. Just turned around and walked off. So he didn't move. Even when he felt the bloody scratches on his cheek. Just kept looking out the sooty window at the river as though this weren't happening. Then he grabbed her shoulders. And pulled her down on the floor.

▼ ▼ ▼

Katy let him make love to her. He was talking. *Talking. Talking dirty.* Like he was making some crazy confession—how he had always known they were half brother and half sister. Now he had the facts. He mumbled about papers from Harlem hospital. All this at the same time he was coming inside her. *It's an eighties porno style he's picked up in California. Game playing. Mike would have been capable of similar if he'd thought it would turn you on.* She shifted his weight off her and with a Kleenex rubbed his come off her skirt, which he had pulled up to her panty line. She stood up and smoothed down her clothes.

▼ ▼ ▼

Brad was in anguish. *Don't let her walk out denying that you've a past together—a real history.* He tried to make her see its implications. Beanie had fucked her over, true. But she wasn't the only one who had lost stuff. Suppose Jeremiah had held on to Indian Path—what part of that inheritance would have been his? Should it all have gone to her and Jim? "All you ever gave away, Katy, was your mother's old furniture—you wouldn't even let me have part of the *memory* of Indian Path. Katy, I want you to understand that the sanest thing I ever did—for you and me both—was to walk

276

out on you in that Post Road motel. Don't you see it was for our good?"

Using snappy little gestures, Katy painted a fresh red mouth and whipped a comb through her hair. "Incest—how trendy." She giggled. "Why, Braddy—you've really gone hot-baths California eighties. You've even thought up a fucking eighties rationale for your shitty behavior on your way up the Wisconsin ladder." She rang for the freight elevator to come up for them. "Maybe *you* committed incest—but I never did." She took a small perfume flask out of her purse and sprayed her hair with Ivoire. "Don't go fancy on me. The point is, this isn't incest in the past but adultery in the present. Check it out with your wife, Elise."

Brad said nothing. Just stared at her.

"Don't give me your I-come-from-nowhere shit," she added.

"So, you tell me—where did I come from?"

Katy was silent.

Then the elevator came.

CHAPTER

21

KATY DIDN'T THINK ABOUT BRAD'S BI-zarre lovemaking until some weeks later, the day he took Tartan and Jessica back to California. She came over that morning to say good-bye.

The women wore their furs with their winter coats—Tartan the mink collar Brad had given her, Jessica the Persian lamb toque. Brad had bought them business class, but they were confused and insisted on carrying a lot of their own food with them. They had never been to California. Tartan said she felt more secure knowing they would be eating a meal she had cooked. She had been an ample, big-bosomed woman. Since she had surrendered her authority, her claim to walking through her own territory, her body had suddenly seemed powdery, weightless. She stared fixedly at Katy with a sort of childish, frightened, peaceful look. Like she couldn't fathom why her son had

278

turned her everyday existence into her past before her time was up.

Tartan insisted that Katy take all the stuff Anita Becker had bought at Olga Zweicky's antique store. She said that she had been keeping the antiques only until the time was right to hand them back. "The time is right. Matt should have them."

When the Sabra radio taxi came for them, Tartan, Jessica following, walked out of the apartment and did not look back. Brad was the last to leave. He gave his mother's door key to the Italian woman in the ground-floor apartment.

Katy stood on the front stoop and waved them good-bye. But Tartan refused to look up. There was no more Anita, no more Jeremiah; now there would be no more Tartan. Katy had promised Brad she would wait for the movers, so she walked aimlessly through the quiet apartment; for no particular reason she held on to the pair of Anita's brass candlesticks Tartan had thrust into her hands. *Banish the memory of you and Brad whispering about* Nana *in the kitchen. Forget how you both wore Jack Armstrong spy rings while you pretended to take command of the streets between Tartan's place and the Fifth Avenue apartment. You and Brad, spy king and spy queen of Manhattan Island.*

She mulled over Tartan's life: *In her entire New York time Tartan never lived in a real apartment house. Amazing how many 1950s movies take place in Manhattan brownstones with open windows, nice fire escapes, and cute gardens. Spencer Tracy and Katharine Hepburn in* The Desk Set, *Audrey Hepburn and George Peppard in* Breakfast at Tiffany's, *Marilyn Monroe and Tom Ewell in* The Seven-Year Itch, *and several with Judy Holliday. Even in films, now nobody leaves windows wide open to the street.*

As soon as she saw the movers were doing their job of crating the furniture for Berkeley, Katy left the premises. She wandered through the streets, the candlesticks still in her arms. She called Snowball from a phone booth and they planned to meet that night for dinner. Katy's Harlem days were over.

▼   ▼   ▼

She had expected Snowball to comfort her in her loss. Instead Snowball confessed a pain of her own; she started by reminding Katy how lonely she had been after Shawn had walked out. "You tried to help—but Katy, that blackness, that abyss is unknown to you. Every day I was in despair. So, so lonely." She grasped her cousin's hand; they were seated at a quiet back table in the Ginger Man. Her voice very low, she told Katy she had fallen in love with a woman colleague. They were moving in together. "I love you—I always will." She paused. "You never seemed to notice that after Shawn there was no other man."

Katy stared at her. "What about Agatha? Have you told her?"

"Yes—why are you making so much of it? Do you think what I'm doing is wrong? Why should my loving a woman be harder on my daughter than your living with this man or that was on Matt?"

"Oh no—I didn't mean it to sound that way."

The two women finished their Ceasar's salad in silence. Katy offered to drop her cousin off—Snowball lived in the

Seventies. Katy kissed her cousin good-night, then let the taxi go.

Maybe you shouldn't be walking home alone so late, so casually. Think more about the rapes, the muggings on the Upper East Side. She thought about Snowball being in love with a woman, and her mind flew back to their growing up, how casually she and Snowball had lain together on Hewley Ginzberg's reproduction of a southern four-poster while they obsessed about boys. *Rethink it.* Had Snowball wanted her in a way she hadn't comprehended? Had she suppressed her own desire for Snowball? Brad's weird remarks about incest floated into the edges of her mind. Did he really believe Jeremiah had fathered him? Until Snowball's revelation, she had dismissed his notion as wacky. Or had she been blind to the real truth? *Stop it, or you'll go crazy thinking the stuff that really went on was everything you didn't see.*

What would happen to her now? Would it still be her and Snowball? Or would this new woman always be joining them, and so they would go out as three? Or would Snowball drop her?

Katy remembered back to her junior year at Barnard. A Columbia history student had asked her to a party. When they arrived at the townhouse in the east Thirties, there were only men in the room. *And one other Barnard student, who you knew was a lesbian. You were wearing a sexy, tight black dress; you had meant to flirt with the men. Your date smiled at you and shrugged. And you realized everyone in that room was gay. There was dancing on the second floor. You heard the thumping and the music and you were terrified that someone would ask you to go up and have a look. Everyone was very polite to you. Sweet.*

And there was a fancy, tasteful spread on the buffet. Nothing bad occurred. But you felt unhinged. Like you should cut off your breasts, which you felt sticking out of your dress like two unwanted globes. You had gone there—it was a spring night—prepared to seduce and be seduced. And you felt stuck in that room as though your own sex were something grotesque and piggish. They were kind to you. But you clamped down on your sexuality. Went into the bathroom and washed off your perfume and makeup. That night you didn't try to seduce a single soul there. And you were at an age when you didn't know what to do with men if you couldn't come on to them. The Columbia student who had brought you disappeared upstairs. You never asked after him. You left the party by yourself. You hailed a taxi and the driver got mad because you threw up in the backseat. The next day you told Snowball about it.

Was Snowball aware even then that she preferred women? *You need to rethink your memory so that a more broadminded version of that evening gets lodged in your head.* After all, the whole world, maybe, was gay. She would rearrange in her head what she experienced in the townhouse until it reshaped itself into a modern memory: she would recall it as having been a casual, sweet good time. She hurried home in the darkness.

▼ ▼ ▼

The next morning she telephoned Gabe.

They met on their lunch break at the Jackson Hole on Madison Avenue. "Gabe, I'm confused—this just hasn't been the easiest time." She told him about Brad taking Tartan and Jessica to California and how Snowball had fallen in love with a woman in her office. "Now, don't tell me you've become a Trappist monk or are praying to some Indian Buddha, or I'll kill myself."

Gabe laughed. "No—just seeing the Argentinian Lacanian shrink who likes Gardel tangos. You met her with me at Beanie's house."

Katy sighed. "Brad's gone Californian. Snowball's in love; you've got this new woman. I don't see Ethan anymore; I'm the only odd one out!"

"It's just a revolving ball—none of it's permanent."

"Back in PS 6 I used to think that the four of us would end up as a team doing something noble together. Instead we've ended up with these splotchy *phases*."

"We've had some bad *incidents*."

"The incidents make it hard to think clearly. Gabe, the incidents just don't stop coming. When we were the four smartest kids in third grade rapid advance, I really believed that before we grew up the situation of growing old would have been remedied—a cure would have been discovered; we would have been the first generation never to die."

"You, too? That was my secret aim in becoming a doctor."

They were silent. They sat awhile facing each other in the booth.

Katy was pensive. "Instead we became a bunch of Columbia nuts hanging out in the Chock-Full-O'-Nuts on Broadway. You remember the summer after Brad finished in Madison—when the four of us were at Columbia? It was just after Galindez got murdered. We put a wreath on his door."

"Yeah."

283

"Max Schecter asked me if we had known him."

"Galindez? Now? How come?"

She shrugged. "Who can figure the workings of my lawyer's mind?" She stopped eating her hamburger. "All that education, and you wind up remembering doughnuts."

"The cinnamon were the best."

"The plain were better."

Gabe noted that her eyes were of such depth—the pupils disappeared into surrounding deep brown, giving an effect of round blackness—for a second he imagined he saw mirrored in them the checkered black-and-white doughnut shop on 116th Street. The four of them powwowing—Snowball, Brad, Katy, and himself. He looked at his watch. It was time for his next patient.

CHAPTER

22

BRAD - TARTAN - SNOWBALL - ETHAN, HER dead parents, Lewis—she felt abandoned by them all. But Katy's obsession to nail Beanie, making him give back to Matt what he had taken from her son made her a wilder, freer woman: She developed an outlaw's style of coping. She told no one how often she went to Harlem; she saw Arnold Clay to get more details on the Rasuds and to meet other uptown real-estate people he knew.

She felt she looked too vulnerable walking the territory alone in a raincoat, like she was a nice lady waiting to be mugged. Her innate instinct for confronting possible danger suited her loner's streak; she had always traveled light, never belonged to an organization or group—had she been a man, her behavior would have been considered eccentric; as she was a woman, it passed as one kind of conventionality. She fished out of a back closet the smelly, mothballed white speckled lynx fur jacket she had used for Lewis's formal academic dos and changed its nature. She strode through Harlem to her appointments wearing the lynx over a faded blue shirt, jeans, and high heels. Her hair was caught up in a navy bandanna and she kept a twenty-dollar bill in her pants back pocket. Only Matt wouldn't have been surprised at her getup. He understood that the rigid rules his mother imposed on him had little to do with the odd realm in which she floated; she seemed descended from another species. He knew she always had some sort of plan in mind. When Katy encouraged him to try for Harvard, and gave him offbeat pointers she thought would help him get in, he felt like he was being driven through its gates by a gypsy cab driver—he just had to make sure he scored high on the SATs or she'd have a shit fit.

▼ ▼ ▼

Harry Struthers, Clay's city tax man, finally dug up a fact for Katy. The three of them sat at a window table in the Terrace restaurant off Morningside Drive—the lunch crowd was Columbia University professors—studying a Spoon Triangle New York City tax map. Harry showed them there was no Belle Hélène corporation listed in the city books; a Chicago group, Flats, Inc., owned an empty lot behind Belle Hélène.

Katy thumbed through the street maps: for over half a century, the rectangular block facing the Harlem River had been penciled in as *Belle Hélène, Inc.*; the shift to the Flats in Chicago had occurred the year Lewis died. Katy remembered seeing something called Flats; it paid a tiny yearly dividend, and she had assumed it was a small-growth stock.

But it hadn't been in the regular portfolio; it had been listed as part of the Eichorn trust.

Her hands shook. *Beanie had never indicated during their real-estate negotiations that Belle Hélène, unlike the pieces she had sold him, had ever been part of the Eichorn trust.*

"The Chicago corporation that owns Flats, Inc.," Harry explained, "is listed as headed by Bernard Eichorn—and I've located one more interesting fact for you: One week after your husband's death Belle Hélène was split into two parts. A small piece was transferred to the Chicago Flats outfit, but the bulk of the block of offices became part of the Bermuda offshore corporation Adam Klager was involved in."

Katy blinked, stunned: she was bumping smack into the tip of the iceberg.

Beanie had been cool as a cucumber when he insisted she tighten up her belt, that public school would be bracing for Matt. When what he was really doing was trying to parlay her main asset to cover up his hand in the cookie jar!

Her feelings raced ahead of her; she knew she had it; she had to reach just a little further and she'd be over the other side of the mountain; she'd get the smoking gun. Instead of asking Harry for more details, she abruptly shut down her thinking capacity: she needed a moment to regain her equilibrium. In all the time she had fantasized about reaching this moment, it had never crossed her mind that being right would hurt. Cause pain in her gut. Part of her didn't want to comprehend how irrevocably it had changed hers and Beanie's destinies, that in a crucial decade, and at a crucial time in their lives, Beanie had had full use of her money and she had had none.

She gazed at the panorama below—on the west she could see across Morningside Park clear up the Hudson, on the east across to the Triborough and the East River. Harlem looked more like a real city from the sixteenth floor; the grimness of the streets was obliterated. What stood out was the surprising number of new buildings—she spotted shiny new centers of learning with Greek domes; and office buildings; and developments. Slowly, slowly, calming herself down, she asked Harry to tell her all he knew.

"The Flats corporation—they are big givers to the Fine Arts Institute—is part of a Chicago-backed international real-estate conglomerate. Some of its seed money came from Chicago banks, but it was your brother-in-law's funding of it that gave it a jump start. For obvious tax reasons it's not based in Chicago—"

"Where is it located?"

"By an odd coincidence, also in the Bahamas."

"You mean *everything* is in the Bahamas?"

"Adam Klager's firm was also involved in that negotiation."

Katy nearly passed out.

▼ ▼ ▼

Once home, she quickly telephoned Schecter. Now that she was so close to her goal, she began to lose her nerve; part of her yearned to backtrack to the comfortably more familiar position of defeat.

"Am I crazy, Max? Am I seeing spots before my eyes? Oases in the desert in place of sand? Am I having a delusion, or is that puny Flats stock that wouldn't give off enough income to buy three pairs of roller skates a sliced-off piece of what should be several square blocks of buildings?"

"Katy, I think we have our hands on the string. Chicago makes a kind of sense—Ronnie's a Chicago boy. This sounds like one of his bright schemes for funneling Belle Hélène's liquid assets into Beanie's new corporations. Look, we want to make sure Beanie can't claim that this Flats thing is a legitimate offshoot of his Green Spruce Nine. Are you sure you've seen Flats listed in the trust portfolio? I don't recall it."

"It was this tiny thing on an old trust accounting—one that we never used; you said it was badly prepared. It was right under the Merrill Lynch page—I thought it was a stray stock."

"You have all the old papers—can you find it? Katy, we need that trust listing."

She didn't answer. Just hung up the phone. *So Jeremiah was right. It was fraud.*

▼ ▼ ▼

She sat on her bed; she wished her father were alive. She would have liked to talk to him. She thought back to the time just after Lewis's death and right before Jeremiah's own; he had insisted that she take him to her meeting with Ronnie and Beanie about Lewis's assets.

He sat on a stiff chair in the lobby of the Volney, his eyes vacant until he saw her standing next to him. He had glaucoma in both eyes. She had remembered him as a whirlwind; it had killed her to see him so still. Helpless. An old man with an empty day to kill.

She walked with him up Madison. Midday, they caught the winter sun. She couldn't decide about his mind. Some days he forgot that Lewis and Anita were dead; at other times he couldn't remember Matt's name. He often gave

289

his grandson money he couldn't afford: Katy and Matt had an agreement—if Jeremiah went over the limit she had set, Matt would return the cash to her so she could put it back into her father's checking account. At certain moments Jeremiah's mind would leap free, and then his thinking became sharp. Katy's dilemma was that she couldn't count on it.

They went to Seventy-ninth Street, to Starks' on Madison. "They have good Maryland crab cakes; you like Maryland crabs, Daddy."

"Karen, why, this is a lovely place . . ."

He's using the chivalrous tone he puts on when he's disappointed. Why did you bring him here? It's the sort of medium place he loathes—he's looking at the ketchup bottle, the glitzy decor. You should have taken him to one of the Chinese places farther east. He'd have liked it better. More fun.

When she was a small child he had taken her to visit Horn and Hardart. He gave her a handful of nickels. She made sure to pick one of the sandwiches that demanded five of them.

"What makes the turnstiles revolve? Who fills the steel tubes with food?"

She pestered her father until he called the manager over and explained to him that his daughter needed to know how the revolving machines worked. The man took her backstage to the kitchen; he even let her put a wedge of chocolate cream pie in the turnstile. She watched the brass cubbyhole spin full circle, returning empty of pie.

"You are a lucky girl," the manager said. "You are one of the few children to have penetrated the secret of who fills the pie disks. You know our magical system."

Magic, she had thought as they sat waiting for the crab cakes. Jeremiah's magic—why hadn't she taken him to the Panda Garden?

Over lunch she mentioned Beanie's offer to do a buyout of the real estate she had inherited from Lewis's share of his father's estate. Katy didn't tell Jeremiah she had no choice; she didn't see how she could hold out and pay the IRS.

"Has Beanie offered to put up a bond if it's to be a long-term buyout? What provisions are there for default of payment? For inflation? We need to see the books on the real estate."

"Daddy, they've already done an outside appraisal."

"Any fool can appraise. I want the *books*. The corporation books."

Bonds. Real-estate books. Katy felt lost.

Jeremiah zeroed in. He spoke rapidly to her, using an entirely new vocabulary. Clipped. Precise. The vocabulary of money, deals, negotiations. The realities of a world in which he had been so powerful, so invulnerable he had never thought it necessary to hand on its nitty-gritty language to his only daughter; he wanted her to be highly stylized, like Anita, to do fine things at Friends' and Barnard. Half-aware of his mistake, at the last possible moment, his mind clear in patches, he attempted to pound into Katy the things she needed to know.

Katy watched her father carefully sip his black coffee. He ceased talking to her. He hadn't known how to put it any plainer.

▼ ▼ ▼

The morning of the meeting, when Katy picked up Jeremiah at the Volney, it was one of his good days. He smelled fresh—not that musty old-man odor. He had called in his old team that had been at the Biltmore; his barber and manicurist had him buffed, polished, and talcumed. *He looks real natty.* His gray flannel Sulka suit still held its shape, and he was wearing a fine royal blue tie flecked with tiny red jumping rectangles.

"You look sporty, Daddy."

Katy remembered how her father had gone hatless during the time in her childhood when men wore hats. Her grandfather Jaches had a nifty homburg. Jeremiah had laughed at the weather and gone free, his right hand always flicking a lit Fatima. The one mashed fedora he owned was pockmarked with cigarette holes. During the Second World War his men took up a penny collection and bought him a new fedora, daring him to wear it. He did for a while, then reverted to his mashed gray one. It was his luck.

"Very spiffy," she repeated for emphasis.

▼　▼　▼

Katy had given no advance notice that she was bringing her father to her meeting with Beanie.

"Oh, my God," her half brother-in-law muttered, his facial skin mottling. "Still Daddy's girl."

Let Beanie natter on about your Oedipals. Better to have an Oedipus complex with your father, who is a member of your own tribe, than to be chummy with a bunch of strangers who can't wait to sell you down the river.

Ronnie immediately veered into his routine. He presented Beanie's proposed buyout of Katy's real estate as magnanimous generosity, his desire to provide for his nephew by releasing cash to his sister-in-law.

Katy listened and studied the faces of the men. *Please, God, let it be one of Jeremiah's good days. Please, God.*

Ronnie had droned on, pointing out that though the payment on the buyout might appear small after he deducted his fee and the IRS claimed their share, with Katy's increased earning ability and Matt in public school, Lewis's family would do splendidly. "And they will be removed from a risky situation. We don't know—Beanie's ventures might fail."

"Why?" asked Jeremiah. "I don't see East Coast real estate in a bad place."

"Mr. Becker, Lewis left an in-debt estate."

"Why is the squeeze being put on Katy?"

"In-laws have their reasons," Ronnie continued sanctimoniously. "We hear her spending patterns are bad."

Jeremiah gazed at him. "Son, money is a reality, not a disease. If inheritance laws depended on the opinion of in-laws, there would be no inheritance in this country."

He turned to Beanie. "I noticed no disapproval of Karen Tess's spending pattern when you brought your family to Indian Path for extended visits—what's this nonsense?"

Her father then surprised her: he shifted her economic definition from that of a low-paid, dubiously in-debt medievalist to a portrait described in the colder language he had used in Starks' restaurant: he suddenly named her worth in dollars and cents.

He pointed out that when she and Lewis had married she had been a rich young woman with her own assets, her own income: what had happened to the Becker money that had been poured into that marriage? He mentioned the summers at the Indian Path cottage built for her and Lewis, Anita's furnishing of their home, her yearly income from the stocks he had given her. Things Katy had forgotten, things she never realized her father and mother had totted up: they never talked about money; they never came right out with it and told their children they were rich.

"Why," he demanded, "is my grandson being denied the flexibility of his own trust? Walter Eichorn didn't build an empire so that his semi-orphaned grandchild should be scrounging in order to accommodate"—he stared at Beanie—"strangers brought into the business."

"Belle Hélène needs new people—"

"The land beneath Belle Hélène's office buildings is worth more now than Belle Hélène," Jeremiah went on. "Real estate doesn't depend on new brains to go up in value. It just sits."

"My father made me sole trustee in the event that Lewis died. His will," Beanie snapped, "allows me to deal as I see fit; it absolves me of all my business transactions."

"You boast of being a sole trustee—? You're an idiot. New York State doesn't lean toward creating indigent widows and orphans. In a court battle Karen Tess would win against you hands down." Jeremiah turned to Beanie's lawyer. "You haven't told your client the court tosses out absolutions that come from the grave? Beanie, you have no power—the Supreme Court doesn't recognize your omnipotence."

Katy leaned forward. *Beanie has no omnipotent powers.* She was memorizing this new stuff like a child in grade school, phrase by phrase, to be stored for future use. Her father began to waver; his lips trembled slightly; his frame, now light as dust, fell back slightly; he receded from the tremendous effort of dredging up legal talk from his young days; he became an old man again.

Please don't fall back. Keep going. Then he picked up the thread—the thread of the trust, not of the real estate. He droned on until she began to understand Beanie's vulnerability as trustee.

Ronnie then took a new tack: he pointed out that Jeremiah should stop robbing Katy of her initiative. "These are stirring times for women—don't limit your daughter's right to a fresh start. Stop bringing up the past; the kind of money you are talking about is gone, and good riddance. Women are too smart for that now."

Jeremiah exploded. Katy was afraid he was headed for a heart attack. "You call depriving my daughter of her equity giving her a fresh start in life? You, a well-trained New York business consultant, have the nerve to insinuate that I am robbing my daughter of a chance to use her brains by preventing her assets from being stolen?"

"Mr. Becker, I am neutral in this negotiation—merely helping the Eichorn family settle this estate."

"What you call settling an estate I call fraud—I demand to see the books on Belle Hélène."

She sat there quietly, expecting more legal pearls to fall from her father's lips. Instead he changed his tactic: he stood up straight in the conference room overlooking the Hudson, raised his cane, and shook it at Beanie. He invoked another, more ancient law. He said Beanie knew it, and Beanie's father had lived by it, and every man in the conference room knew it: "You are your father's son, yet you steal from his flesh and blood? From those weaker than you?" He intoned, "He would revile you from his grave for shaming him."

He pounded the table with his free hand. "You built nothing on your own . . . You are his disgrace."

To Katy's amazement, Beanie turned pale as Jeremiah continued to wave his cane at him. It had never occurred to her that Beanie could be shamed. The two men stared at each other, then Beanie ran out of the conference room. Ronnie went after him; when Ronnie came back he said that Beanie was being sick in the men's room and the meeting was over.

On the taxi ride back uptown Jeremiah retreated into diffuse memories of Anita; his stare became blanker. "Did I do the right thing, Katy? Did I do what you wanted?"

"You were great, Dad."

She didn't dare tell him that despite Beanie's upchucking in the john she would have to accept the buyout plan—she had no cash. But what he had said about trusts and fraud and Beanie not being omnipotent stuck in her mind. Her lawyer had never indicated she had some options. Just the opposite—he was pressing her to sign off on the trust accounting. It occurred to Katy after the meeting that she might have something of a little value—her signature, her ability not to sign. She looked for a new lawyer and some-time after that found Max Schecter. She had been about to ask Jeremiah what he knew about him when the concierge at the Volney called to tell her that her father had died in his sleep.

▼ ▼ ▼

Though Max had sounded casual on the phone, Katy realized they desperately needed written proof that Flats, Inc.,
plus Klager's Bermuda offshore outfit, had originally been
part of Belle Hélène. The big trunk had always remained
on the floor in a corner of her bedroom: it housed years of
papers on *Eichorn* versus *Eichorn*. She knelt in front of it, no
color in her face, as though in prayer to an ancient deity.
She seemed to be reading Braille; her eyes were slightly
closed, and even without looking down, her fingers, darting
this way and that, knew what was there. By now her hands
knew by the size, her nostrils by the odor, what each piece
of paper meant. What if just the file they needed was
missing? Her fear of this was so deep her fingers momentar-
ily halted their nimble search. She reached down to the
floor of the trunk, then slightly to the left. She suddenly
felt the stiffness of an unusually fat maroon folder. Her
hands stopped searching and she lifted it out of the trunk.

When she located the mention of Flats, Inc.—she'd been
right; it was listed on the bottom of a Merrill Lynch page
as an additional stock—her excitement caused other visual
images to surface. A memory jarred in her mind: Ronnie
handing her the trust accounting right after she left Texas.
A large sum of money entered immediately after Lewis's
death jumped off the page. It flashed through her head and
at the same time she had experienced an odd physical
change. She had had a warning something was about to
happen, a sensation passing through her: an aura, a sense
of being hyperalert.

When she had first seen the accounting she had been
relieved that there was something to counteract what Ronnie had defined as Lewis's in-debt estate. Later she and Max

297

had always focused on what might have been removed from the trust, not what had been added to it. *Something she had no control of was transpiring.* She had no idea whether it was the time of year—or the anniversary of Lewis's death—but an amazingly sharp sense of his presence had come back to her. Like amnesia lifting. A figure popped into her mind; she remembered Lewis scrawling on a piece of paper the liquid assets they had left in their trust after making the down payment on the Austin house: *it was far less than the amount Ronnie had listed.*

▼ ▼ ▼

Katy turned animal. It didn't occur to her to be cool, or to call Max, or to think of what was right for the case. This was between her and Ronnie, and between Beanie and Lewis, and between her father and Beanie. She got Ronnie on the phone, and from untapped depths deep inside of her—she had heard descriptions of women being flooded with unnatural energy permitting them to lift trucks off their trapped children—she gave a guttural, animal cry; she yelled into the receiver without realizing what she was saying:

"*Ronnie, there was too much money in the trust at the time of Lewis's death. Max Schecter wants to know how it got into the trust and why.*"

It happened so swiftly, Ronnie was talking so rapidly, that Katy lost control of it. Some other voice was guiding her, shouting the questions. It had nothing to do with cleverness.

▼ ▼ ▼

In the back of his mind, Ronnie had always known there might come a time when the right question would be asked; it was why he had made Beanie put back into the trust a down payment on his borrowings from Belle Hélène: "It will show intent to pay."

Ronnie never discussed the matter with Beanie further, nor did he point out that no additional payments had been made. Nor did he tell Beanie what he would do if asked the crucial question.

"Tell the truth," Ronnie always advised newcomers in his consulting firm. "Never volunteer information concerning your clients, and never lie when questioned. Follow the Ronnie Munche rule and you'll never get into trouble."

"Lewis kept a record of what he had?" Ronnie blurted out nervously.

▼ ▼ ▼

Katy was sweating. Instinctively, she knew she had him, but it had happened too fast for her to know what she had done. *It felt like being given gas as a kid in the dentist's chair.* She kept going. "Records? A fine academic like Lewis? Of course he kept records."

Lewis, Lewis, why the hell didn't you? For a jealous man, you managed to tie me in knots to the male establishment.

In her wild adrenaline surge, Katy floated past Max Schecter, past Jeremiah, to listen to her own voice: she reached back into the grade-B movies of her youth, to Cagney, Edward G., Bogart. She was dancing, shooting the rapids.

"Listen, Ronnie," she snapped, "Max says if you don't get the files on Belle Hélène as of yesterday morning in his

299

office, he's going after you, not Beanie. He says either you talk fast or you'll be the first one he'll send up the river for trust fraud."

Never would Max Schecter have uttered those sentences. But Ronnie was so distraught, so impressed that Max, true to his rep, had leaped right to the heart of the matter, to the key question, that he didn't stop to think Katy's delivery had a nutty, obsessive tinge; in his unconscious, the Cagney style resonated as the *Ur*-truth of the land.

"You knew about the borrowing"—he hesitated—"not done by Beanie directly, of course."

"By whom?"

"Green Spruce Nine—frankly, we thought it a good investment."

"How much?"

"Well, Belle Hélène was just treading water; Walter Eichorn had an unhealthy habit of keeping his corporations too cash heavy—"

"How much?"

"Give or take—three million."

"In old millions? When a million was a million?"

"You might think of it that way."

"And the other corporations? They also invested in Green Spruce Nine? Where does Flats, Inc., figure in this?"

"Max knows about Flats?"

Katy could tell by his nervous breathing into the phone that he was shaken. *No way can he thread his imagination into figuring you had Harlem connections and Adam Klager's rage helping you. Confuse him some more. Dazzle him.* "And about Chicago. And the Bahamas."

"Tell Max to call me. He'll get everything."

She put down the receiver. Wandered aimless and bare-foot through the apartment. Gave Max Schecter an incoher-ent alert of what had taken place. Stuck three sugarless Chiclets into her mouth.

Then Beanie was on the phone to her; Ronnie had called him. "I can't get all my files to Max today—Katy, you people must be reasonable."

It was happening so fast, no one thinking through the swift phone calls, no one face-to-face, that Katy was having a hard time figuring out their positions had reversed. Out of nowhere, she had gained power. Her case was real.

She had never been the issue; she'd always been an irrele-vancy to the main action. *How can you see money become detoured in Harlem and zapped through to Chicago en route to the Bahamas? How do you see what is invisible? A crime has been committed, but how do you record the sound of a tree falling in a forest with no walkers in the forest? Who could have noticed?*

Katy sleepwalked into the kitchen, the heat rising in her cheeks like she had been face-whipped. She drank water. Went to the john. She sat on the toilet seat, pulled down her pants, her knees spread apart. She stared at the white tile wall opposite her, and she pissed a gallon.

She walked into the kitchen and picked up the phone. "Matt?" she said. "It's Mom."

CHAPTER

23

SOME SAY ADAM KLAGER'S BIGGEST coup, his finest manipulation of rumor, was the way he choreographed his own death to bring down his enemies; it happened the spring the big Wall Street junk-bond artists went to jail. The first reports that the cause of death had been AIDS were denied; within a week *U.S. News and World Report* confirmed it as fact. *Publishers Weekly* ran a story on the 1.5 million-dollar advance that an American publisher, in a joint package with a British publisher, had made Klager during the final months of his illness for his purportedly completed autobiography. Friends of Bernard Eichorn were shocked when *Newsday* published a list of prominent New Yorkers involved in illegal banking and real-estate speculations; Eichorn was considered to be a key figure in Klager's Gang of Ten.

The *New York Times* cautioned that conflicting publicity

releases given by the publishers—it was unclear who held European rights to the manuscript, the Americans or the British—raised doubts as to how much of the book actually was on paper at the time of Klager's death.

In an odd coincidence, the furor dovetailed with a *Washington Post* scoop: the foundation for the *American Rebel*—another Bernard Eichorn fiefdom—had been used as a foil for a southwestern group covertly selling American arms to Khomeini. According to the *Washington Post* exposé, Amanda Dunkel had used her position at the American Rebel Foundation as a trade-off for a political plum in the D.C. cultural hierarchy, the directorship of the National Art Council. The *Post* headline was blunt: "New York–Washington Culture Dunkelers Armed Khomeini." The *Daily News* came in with an investigative report linking the associate editor of the *American Rebel* to a homosexual scandal involving the dead Klager. The juiciest account was in the *New York Times*, which quoted lurid details from other papers plus an opinion sidebar from Madonna as an example of irresponsible journalism; they also came out on the editorial and op-ed pages as being against sexual harassment of homosexuals and prominent people in the press. It was pointed out in a Sunday magazine column that Amanda Dunkel had achieved a special kind of notoriety; few people's names become verbs in the English language: "The confusing of public patrimony with private enrichment has become known as 'dunkeling.' Some people say, 'Don't dunkel me.' Others prefer 'doing a dunkel.' Adverbial usage—'such a dunkeler'—is less popular." Amanda abruptly returned to England and married a divorced British peer involved with the breeding of racehorses.

303

Judge Anna Myrtle—she had just signed a contract for a book on unequal legal rights for women and minorities—read the accounts: her finest moment in forty years of argument with her younger brother. She relished every piece of press recrimination she could wave at Ben: Arms Espionage. McCarthy Red Baiter. IRS Crook. Adam Klager's Gang of Ten.

"And you let them harass this poor woman because she had a normal adult sex life? Ben, I warn you—it's only a matter of time before the press finds out you stonewalled on Eichorn's sister-in-law's case against him. You'd better move on this case—white-collar crime is about as popular as a skunk in heat. You've never shown much nose about the bench."

Max Schecter searched the Klager stories for a possible reference to the law firm of Judson Freund and his handling of the Galindez case. There was none: it went too far back in the history of the city. Nor did Katy's name come up in the increasingly sensationalist coverage. Max did nothing. He just waited.

▼ ▼ ▼

On a hot Friday night in late spring, Judge Myrtle was surprised to see Ronnie Munche walking through the non-smoking car of his Westchester commuter train. Munche immediately took the seat next to him—he said he was visiting friends of the judge's in Rye. He struck Myrtle as rather straightforward. He had a nice way of immediately joking that the only safe topic they had was the World Series. His only allusion to the case was that, sadly for those onlookers who cared for them, the Eichorns were a talented but neurotic family who had torn themselves apart over sibling rivalries that had exploded into symbolic money fights. He pointed out that he had turned his Eichorn files over to Mrs. Lewis Eichorn's attorneys some time ago and would be glad to be equally helpful to the judge.

The next week, when Beanie called Ronnie to protest that he had given Eichorn money to the *American Rebel* only to strengthen a New York cultural institution—he had known nothing of Amanda Dunkel's Washington machinations—he found Ronnie peculiarly cold. "Ronnie, you were the one who advised me to turn Klager down on that big loan he needed. You said, 'Drop him like a sleazy hot potato.' "

"I did—and kept you clean. This is just gossip-column talk. What can you do? Sue a dead man about a book that probably doesn't even exist?"

▼ ▼ ▼

When the Chicago, Bahama, bank, and real-estate scandal broke—it involved Beanie but not Ronnie—Carl Harris, Beanie's lawyer at Willard, Stern, Fuccoli, Henry, and Braunschweig, immediately called a meeting of the firm's senior partners. Harris saw the handwriting on the wall—the Wall Street scandals and worsening economy were producing a court hard-nosed on white-collar crime. Beanie would be indicted; with strenuous plea bargaining, an Illinois court would give him two years in prison with time off for good behavior. "Eichorn better come across as being as clean as Whistler's mother—a lawsuit with his brother's widow involving trusts is bad news. We've got to get rid of it."

305

Harris broke the news to Beanie that they wouldn't be able to keep him entirely out of jail; in order to do some effective plea bargaining, they needed to reduce his liability to his sister-in-law.

When Harris informed Judge Myrtle of Beanie's good intentions, the judge agreed that the time was right to talk settlement. In rethinking his calendar, Myrtle saw that he had an unexpected opening; he had his office contact Max Schecter. The two men had a private talk; they agreed on a basic formula for an ample redistribution of the Eichorn assets: Mrs. Eichorn and her son, Matthew, would come out splendidly. Myrtle emphasized to Schecter that such a handsome outcome for them depended on the parties working rapidly and quietly in unison and good faith. "This little family dispute shouldn't fuel more media dirt. Do you see my point?"

Max did. He also understood that for such a substantial share of Beanie's assets to be shifted to his clients, they had to be first in line as claimants. As he told Katy, they were stunningly positioned.

In the end, he had found her a disappointingly naive client. Balky. She wanted to go back to the beginning, confront Beanie, use her trunkful of research, and try in court the case that she had worked out in her head. She kept repeating that she had been a good wife and that in the deposition she had been made to appear bad. "Katy, just sentences—who remembers? You're getting better than a day in court—you're getting equity. You think the Surrogate's a narrative grab bag?"

Katy was sitting in his office opposite him while he talked. He remembered to smile at her: she was going to be his client for the long range—as would be Matt. "Let's work up a new will for you."

▼ ▼ ▼

When Mike Braden read that Katy's half brother-in-law was part of Klager's Gang of Ten, he recalled her complaints about the Eichorn trust. At the time, he had wanted her to use his lawyers to look into it and she had refused. He and Katy were alike in that they both had a soulful side to their natures, and they both believed deeply in the existence and rightness of tangible possessions.

Mike understood that if Beanie was a crook, and a Klager man, he must have hurt Katy in a way that was unforgivable. Mike had always loved her. Fantasized about them patching things up. Spending the next phase together. Matt was a grown man—there wouldn't be so much pull on her time. He wondered if she had married. In his mind he turned over a phrase: *Mike and Katy Braden.* He called her to find out what had happened to her case against Bernard Eichorn.

▼ ▼ ▼

When she began to visit him again that summer at Hannah's Point, she no longer got on the train the quick way, at 125th Street, but boarded at Grand Central. In the hot weather, midtown struck her as full of cranes and bad construction. *All the wrong things are done in New York. Disgusting things*, she mused. *Landmarks torn down. Carelessness.* But the city had a bizarre way of looking breathtaking when wrecked. Sitting in the train speeding through the tunnel under Park Avenue, she wondered, *What odd element makes its beauty burn so deep?*

307

CHAPTER

24

SEPTEMBER, COLD RAIN. KATY HAD taken a late-summer vacation from the Schmidlapp to sail across the Bay of Fundy with Mike. They flew up to Bangor on the morning plane with Chris Lawton, his one-man crew; they went straight to North East Harbor in an Avis. Mike intended to sail as soon as the Bermuda Forty was sea ready.

When they pulled up to the boat yard he handed her the grocery list. *It's his style to be in a hurry.* She glanced at it. He had marked beer for himself, grapefruit juice and Tab for her. "And get some hot chocolate for Chris—he's a lover of Swiss Miss and heavy metal."

She and Chris went to the supermarket near the boat yard while Mike went to the liquor store to buy Scotch; he didn't drink Manhattans on the yawl—Katy could never figure out why.

She didn't like the look of the women she saw on the docks. They walked the ramps in their Lily Pulitzer shifts with the aimlessness of casual, dumb money, their faces glazed with a false heartiness. Little-girl hairdos, and liver spots on their hands. *You are living on a Bermuda Forty—are you the same as they?* Katy watched while one of them loaded a carton of club soda onto the deck of an adjoining craft. She went to a phone booth on the pier and telephoned Max Schecter. He had asked her to check with him—he and Beanie's lawyer, Carl Harris, were coming down to the wire on the redistribution of the Eichorn assets. He was out of the office.

When Katy dreamed of winning, she had pictured either a courtroom triumph with a cast of thousands or a Dreiserian defeat; she'd never imagined half-baked justice would dribble her way while she leaned on one sneakered foot, putting quarters into a public phone in North East Harbor. She went for a walk in town. A needlepoint canvas in the window of an antique store caught her eye: WIN THE WAR: ROOSEVELT FOR PRESIDENT. She bought it and some yarn. Something to do on the trip.

▼   ▼   ▼

"Okay, you children of nature," Mike snapped when Chris brought the stuff back to the dock. "Provision her up."

Katy was constantly struck by Mike's physical presence: his neck was too short for his tall, heavy-shouldered body; it made his head seem unduly massive; the thickness of his gray hair gave him a bellicosely healthy look younger than his years. She saw him take in the speedy way Chris unloaded the groceries, Chris's agility in casting off the ropes.

He needs Chris for the anchor lifting; he can't do that anymore. He's furious at the easy way Chris takes off and earns money running boats down to Bermuda and the Keys. Feels humiliated at having to pay a stranger to help him with the yawl. Mike measured his age by his ability to sail.

"Our refugee from prep school thinks he's a sailor," he muttered when Chris was out of earshot. "Well, he ain't."

His affected Harvard version of Spencer Tracy rugged talk makes him sound sort of out-of-date Boston snobbish. His defenses against shyness. She half listened to his invective, the same way she let Chris's heavy metal tapes float past her consciousness.

"Katy, your hair gets in your way. After Paula cut off her mop she looked like a boy. If you'd trim it short, you'd be salty as a Chiclet."

Paula also killed herself. She lowered herself back down into the cabin. They were an hour out of harbor. She was intent on imposing her own will on the use of her galley space. What was stowed where was amazingly important to her. But the smallness of the cabin space imposed the repetition of ritualistic gestures; her own initiative seemed superfluous.

The two men were above deck; Katy remained below. She needed more of a sense of where they were going than Mike had communicated. A good sailor but a bad explainer. She had brought sailing books with her; one described the Bay of Fundy: *The Graveyard of the Atlantic.* She didn't know the rules of the sea.

When Mike came back down into the cabin she said flatly, "*May Day* originally came from *m'aidez.*"

"*M'aidez?*"

310

"As in French—we are going into French territory. I mean, the French and Spanish had something to do with the discovery of America. I mean, Columbus wasn't exactly a Harvard man . . ."

"I asked you to put the booze in the lazarette beneath the back bunk. Hard stuff in the head."

"Last week I saw a revival of *L'Atalante* at the Regency movie theater—"

"*L'Atalante?*"

"An old French movie about a barge. There is this girl; she marries the bargeman. He takes her away from her home; she doesn't understand that he needs to earn his living from his barge. So she runs away from him when they dock along a quay, in Paris. She's a country girl; she wants to see the shop windows and—"

"Sweetie, get your books off the bunk and stop babbling about some frog movie."

She straightened the cabin, then joined Mike and Chris on deck.

Mike was making plans. "We'll sail through the night—in three shifts we'll make it across in twelve hours."

"I've never night sailed," Katy said.

She saw Chris look at Mike like he had gone wacko. "I'll do your turn with you, Mrs. Eichorn." Then he went below.

▼ ▼ ▼

Mike steered while Chris sacked out on one of the bunks. Katy found a corner of the deck away from the wind. She wove red, white, and blue yarn through the *R* in *Roosevelt* and avoided noticing the fog and cold. Where she sat in the yawl, she noticed, was determined by Mike or the demands of the craft. She felt oddly passive—she made up for her lack of sailing knowledge by being energetic. Her needlepoint kept her from thinking about the graveyard of the Atlantic. She had also brought with her a tattered copy of Huizinga's *The Waning of the Middle Ages*, the new edition of *Swann's Way*, and *The Good Soldier*.

Mike looked at the Huizinga lying next to her. "Mind if I ask you a personal question?"

His sudden formalities of speech laced in between "Fuck the bastards" and "hot sex" boggled the mind. "Shoot."

"Are you bothered that I don't ask you more questions about your life away from Hannah's Point? Your work at the Schmidlapp . . . ?"

"She who writes esoteric essays on the Middle Ages when in Barnard," she answered fliply, "may find herself in age living aboard a yacht—"

"A yawl."

"—yawl." Thinking what her passions had been at Barnard, she felt suddenly old. A stranger to herself. Like some part of her future had been wrenched from her.

"Which brings me to the point of this—this Eichorn mess. Why didn't you use my lawyers when I offered them to you?"

"It just happened that way."

"Bullshit—you didn't have to go through this rigmarole. I offered you my lawyers long ago—you didn't use my connections because some part of you wanted a scenario in which I'm just as much of a money louse as Lewis's crazy brother. But, Katy, I'm *me*; I've got my faults but my name is Braden, not Eichorn."

So why did you have to impress your friends with who Lewis was, who my family was, when you knew I didn't have a pot to piss in? You wanted them to believe that a woman lots younger than you wanted you for you alone when it wasn't true.

"Maybe, Mike, I didn't want you to feel your lawyers, your money mattered to me as much as it did."

She saw him blink, then his eyes suddenly went very blue. "You're such a fucking liberal. Such a dumb child of the rich. Grow up—money matters to everyone."

"When we had our affair I didn't know I had a case—didn't know I was right. All I had was an intuition. If I had used your lawyers and couldn't have afforded to pay them—they would have convinced you I was a hysterical deadbeat. You would have paid them and had contempt for me."

"You think the only man worth trusting was a kid from Texas with whom you had no real involvement?"

Tell Mike the truth. In his presence you feel you are the most beautiful woman who ever walked the earth. Even lovelier than Snowball.

"You think I would have sided with a shit like Beanie who hung out with Adam Klager?"

She had meant to compliment him; instead the words tumbled out wrong: "Adam Klager helped me."

Mike looked stunned. Like he'd been hit.

"It's a long story."

"Well, well. I applaud what you've accomplished for yourself from afar."

Katy fumbled with her throwaway Cricket; it didn't light up—too much wind.

"Where's the Zippo I gave you?"

"I don't know—I lost it."

He grabbed the Cricket out of her hand and tossed it overboard.

Explain about Klager. Katy looked at the unlit cigarette in her hand, then at Mike. "Two smokers crossing the Bay of Fundy with one Zippo between them isn't terrific—I need your lighter."

He seemed taken aback by the extent of his own rage. Struggling to regain control of himself, as though she had never mentioned Klager. "When we dock in Canada, I'll buy you a gold-plated Zippo and take you to a frog restaurant."

"Will you stop saying 'frog' this and that? I may be a dumb child of the liberal rich, but you lie to yourself about who *you* are. We can never go to an opera, a ballet, a concert, because that's what your overeducated sister did, that's what your brother did, that's what the Bradens have always been known for—no, we have to play Clint Eastwood!"

"My idea of hell is spending time at shitty museum parties. Bunches of artist clowns crowding up Manhattan. Amateurs thinking that because they've won a grant or gotten a front-page *Times* review they can fix up a tiredly evil world . . ."

He looked back at the horizon. Seemed to dismiss her. She went back down into the cabin to check her gear; maybe she had packed a spare lighter.

The cabin floor was flooded. Chris, sprawled in the

smaller front bunk, was in a deep, late-adolescent sleep. "Mike—the cabin's filling with water!"

"No dumb games at sea."

Chris shook himself awake—he saw the water gushing in. "Mr. Braden, the sea-cocks are open!"

Then Mike saw it. He shouted to Chris that they needed to switch tacks. The two men rapidly turned the yawl to another tack, at the same time setting up the automatic bailer. Mike instructed Chris to rip up the floorboards to locate the leaking sea-cock.

The cabin was crowded and soaking; she went above deck. No other craft were in sight. Chris yelled her enough information, while pumping out the water, for her to realize that they were all right; the yawl wouldn't sink.

Katy had no real sense of what constituted danger at sea—would the Coast Guard arrive in time to save them? Her only gauge of what was happening was the degree of fear shown by Mike and Chris. *If you don't know the rules, you shouldn't play the game.* She saw Mike had located the bad sea-cock.

"Christ, one of the dock hands left off the cap. A five-year-old would have known better. Who the hell is the yard hiring?"

Chris stuffed the hole with rags. The bailer worked well; the flood had receded.

If we had switched tacks during the night and the leak had occurred then, we might have drowned. Delayed hysteria overwhelmed her; she was scared she'd do something dumb. *Like scream, "Let me off this boat."* She forced herself to breathe slowly.

Pretend you are twenty-one years old. You and Lewis are on your honeymoon aboard the De Grasse. *It's a rough night. You're dressing for the ship's ball, dressing for your future.* Katy thought back. *You'd be putting on makeup.*

She lowered herself back down into the cabin, past the men. In the head she concentrated on brushing her hair, putting on cologne; her hands still shook.

Put on your false eyelashes. Nobody can die at sea while gluing on lashes. Boats can't sink while you are wearing great eye makeup.

When she walked back into the cabin she seemed calm. Or somnambulant.

"We can make it to Canada, Mr. Braden. I've run sloops down to Bermuda stuffed with rags."

"Not this yawl," Mike snapped. "Head her back to Maine." He looked over the cabin; it smelled of salt, wetness, and soaked denim. The cloth had a peculiar odor now, horse stable. "Well, Katy, you did pretty good—you didn't yammer. Say—your eyes are glistening—what did you do to them?"

He has the illusion he likes natural-looking women. Never notices the ones he admires wear tons of gook, just skillfully applied. She didn't intend to admit she'd stuck on false lashes to keep from going crazy.

She took out the red clay roaster pot she had given Mike on their first boat trip together, when they went up the Inland Waterways. The roaster was shaped like a nesting chicken; it lived in the lazarette beneath Mike's bunk. Katy kept it carefully wrapped in a towel to avoid its being slammed about in rough seas. With rapid, automatic gestures she stuffed it with the two small chickens she had bought in North East Harbor, covering the birds with herbs and tarragon vinegar.

This pot is the one thing I've given Mike that is always aboard. The only object connected to me that ever remains on the yawl. My person, books, clothing are temporary visitors. Only the clay chicken stays. On a couple of their trips Mike had asked Matt to join them. Every now and then.

Chris was at the rudder now. The hatch was next to the galley; he watched Katy cook. "Mrs. Eichorn, wouldn't it be easier on you if you just opened a can?"

"No," Mike said. In the matter of fixing chickens, he and Katy were united. "Katy is making her special copulating birds. Before she came on board with her clay pot I never tried to roast fowl on the yawl. See?"

He held it up: "It's magic. Bastes through the chicken's eyes—beautiful, isn't it?"

"Chunky-chunk is quicker."

▼ ▼ ▼

None of the boat-yard men were available when they reached harbor in Maine; the hurricane was beginning—they were transferring their boats to a safer cove. Two dock hands finally showed up; they reached for the lines.

"Sea-cocks were open," Mike snapped. "And the compass is fucked up." Without waiting for their reply, he went rapidly up the pier in the direction of the yard office.

Chris waited for his return to inform Mike that he intended to jump ship. "I don't feel I'm getting the right vibes—I'm not in a mood to wait out a hurricane here in North East. But it was nice eating your food, Mrs. Eichorn."

Mike said nothing. Just watched Chris take his gear from the yawl and depart.

"Vibes," he muttered. "What have the right vibes to do with sailing? The old guy who ran this yard," he told Katy, "died last spring; the place has been bought by a hotel-chain conglomerate. I should have doublechecked the sea-cocks myself—my yawl, my fault."

▼ ▼ ▼

They waited out the bad weather in the motel next to the boat yard.

"Paula never could stand staying aboard during a hurricane," Mike explained to Katy, as though her predecessor still determined their choices.

They had a good view of the harbor—the winds were blowing up—but the room was dreary: oversized beds, birch-framed seascapes, a yawning television dominating the decor. Motels no longer intrigued Katy; she preferred sleeping in Mike's bed at Hannah's Point. Still, the antiseptic comforts of the Harbor View motel chain beat their other option: a Victorian New England roominghouse with mushy mattresses.

Mike sat on the bed's edge, holding a paper cup with Scotch over ice in it; he was tracking down his Hannah Point friends to find one willing to help them sail down from Maine to Connecticut. No one was free.

"Sweetie, they've got their lives, their nutty kids and mewling grandchildren coming in for the weekend. And I'm stuck here with three wild hurricanes coming up from the Gulf—why don't you leave, too?" he snapped, throwing her a new Zippo.

Must have bought it when he went to town for the newspapers. "Your pals haven't deserted you—they just can't fly up here at the drop of a hat."

"My, my—aren't we sweet reason. Katy, it's your turn at the telephone. Make your calls to Matt, your Snowball, plus all your other friends. And the Schmidlapp can't piss without you. But don't, dear heart, exaggerate your predicament. Make sure you communicate that you are sitting out this hurricane on dry land in the Harbor View Motel. I don't want to hear crap later about our being stranded in the middle of the Atlantic." He paused. "Why don't you follow Chris's example? Say the word and I'll put you on a plane at Bangor."

Mike will keep on sailing. But not in the same way again. No more brash solo flights. "You want me to help get her home?"

"Sweetie, yup."

"So help me. Explain how things work, okay? We did the Waterways, just the two of us."

"That was a lot easier. Remember the time when we started in Florida, the boat-yard man down there said, 'Where's your crew?' I pointed to you." Mike laughed. "He said, 'She's it? Well, good luck, sir.' "

He pulled her next to him. They sat side by side on her bed.

"I wanted you to have the chance to cross the Bay of Fundy with me. I planned it. I never meant for you to take your night turn at the wheel alone—if Chris hadn't meddled I would have explained it to you. Sure, you would have been a little scared; that's part of it—but you would have been safe. I would have been on deck. Night steering is like sex; you don't get it by watching—you have to have

319

had the experience. Katy, the *awe*. It was my best shot. The best I had to give you."

"We'll do it next summer."

"*Now* is when it should have happened. You would have had it, the adventure. For the rest of your life you would have remembered that you crossed the roughest sea at night with yourself at the wheel; you would have remembered Fundy, remembered me. You won't know how good a sailor I am, what I've taught you, until you sail in another man's boat. When it won't work."

He got up, abruptly switching on the Sports Channel; he was a Red Sox fan. He paced their room, absorbed in his thoughts.

Katy pulled off her damp sweater; she looked in her bag for something dry.

Mike kept on talking. "Katy, you screw good and you are not dumb about sex, and I screw good and I am not dumb about sex. But for all your brains you are dumb about the world and men."

He pushed her flat against the bed; he reached under her back, unsnapped her bra. "What gets a man about a woman is who has been there before. Who has used the territory and exactly how. If the guy was first-rate, that excites a man. Lewis was the polar opposite of Adam Klager—"

"How about me for me?"

"No one gets desired 'me for me.' There's always a kicker to it—if you'd figure that out, you'd stop beating up on yourself. And me. Honey, I may be rich, but I'm not a bastard."

"So why didn't you sleep with Lewis?"

Mike roared with laughter. "I switched to women for good when I was eighteen. There's nothing you can say about sex, because, sweetie, I've tried it all." His hands felt the bed beneath her. "Say, these are great work-benches."

"Come on, Mike. Beds."

"Workbenches. Okay, okay—beds. You win. Your pretty-pretty vocabulary. Let's make love." Soon they were going through the familiar gestures of what Katy liked, what Mike liked. It was the area in his life where he was most giving. His mouth, hands were tender in their explora-tions—it was his voice that was never intimate.

Explain to him about Klager. Level with him that Lewis left a can of worms. Gods of the Left leave no workable inheritances.

"You and me are on the yawl; Chris is still with us—I say, Katy, for Christ's sake, he's nineteen and horny . . ." Involuntarily Katy glanced at the motel bedroom door. "Katy, sweetie—he jumped ship. Stop worrying. He's half-way to Bermuda by now. I say, Katy, give it to him, the two of you, on the bunk. You plead, in your Friends' Semi-nary voice, 'No, Mike, I couldn't do that. I want to sleep with you.' But I insist. 'The kid needs it too. He wants to see you excite yourself—I want you to do it for me.' "

"Ohhh . . ."

He got out of her the reaction he wanted. He tumbled to one side of her, spent. He grinned. "They wept and they fucked. They fucked and they wept." *His need to evoke Paula, Lewis.* She watched his face in repose. He was soon asleep. Night. An American motel.

When Katy woke up it was early morning. She heard him making a clatter in the can. "Is that you, Mike?"

321

"Who the hell do you expect it to be? You know I piss through the night."

She dozed back to sleep.

▼　▼　▼

Later in the week they were able to sail the yawl out of the harbor. In spite of bad patches of fog, for reasons that had little to do with Mike or Katy life on the boat began to work. Their habits meshed—Katy remembered not to lose the Zippo. They were making eight-hour runs through the fog. When they pulled into a cove for the night Katy would take territorial possession of the boat. She scoured the pots and pans, pulled apart the kitchen stove.

"You can't bitch that this millionaire didn't keep you well supplied in Comet."

After supper they played checkers. *Feels like you are back in Camp Wigmachi. The counselor has posted a chart on the wall near your cot. Your weekly work schedule.*

They made it through to the Cape Canal in time to pull into a cove; the second hurricane had begun. Mike let down the first anchor, afraid it wouldn't hold. Katy could no longer see the harbor; the yawl was spinning too fast. She heard the putt-putt of the Coast Guard: *It's all right—they are near us.*

She lay down on her bunk, bit into a Granny Smith apple, and read an old *New Yorker*. She sensed Mike's confusion at seeing her so relaxed. *No anxious vibes are coming from you. He's behaving like he's lost something. Like the situation has gotten out of control because you are peacefully chewing an apple while the boat is whirling.*

322

Mike went up on deck, then came back down the hatch, his head soaked despite the blue woolen cap he'd been wearing. "Katy, the sails have gotten loose. Can you make it up on deck to batten them down? My back's gone out—any knot will do. If you can't, we'll wait for the Coast Guard."

He is angry at himself for having to ask you. She put on a slicker and went up. The rain was coming down in thick sheets. She crawled along one side of the deck, then did the same on the other. *Poor judgment, to be up alone on a slippery deck with winds at gale strength.* The yawl was circling too fast; her securing of the sails was haphazard. She went back down the hatch on her knees. Mike watched her strip and dry herself. He was clumsily rubbing Ben-Gay into his back shoulder muscles. "Let me," Katy said.

"Put on some dry pajamas first."

She did. Then took the Ben-Gay from him, getting it in deep between his shoulder blades.

"Aw—you're killing me."

"Lie flat." Katy knelt on the floor by his bunk; with all her strength, she kneaded his back. When she finished she put her face against the small of his neck. The ointment stank something awful.

"Start off with wild sex fantasies," she said to him, "you end up with Ben-Gay."

▼   ▼   ▼

Night. The yawl was still tossing. Katy had finished the *Ro* in *Roosevelt. Red, white, and blue—hurrah for the Fourth of July.*

"Hurricanes don't bother you much," Mike observed.

When it comes down to it, you have more of a claim than Mike on New England. You truly came from the sea. But women don't lay claim to the sea. Especially Jewish women.

"Why should I mind storms? I grew up along this coast." She thought of Brad and their canoe. *When Brad faces the Pacific, smells the water, does he remember our trip down the Croton Aqueduct? Or is he so sure of himself that none of that still exists for him?* "Before Gohonk, my family rented summer houses north of New London—Essex, Mystic, Old Saybrook. We faced Plum Island."

"I can't sail you by there. The island is off bounds—military property now."

"My Plum Island?"

"Must be—it's in the same vicinity. It's being used for germ-warfare experiments."

"We lived in a captain's house. It had a real widow's walk and secret passageways that connected through the closets. Jim and Brad would push me to go first while they beamed the flashlights—later they told me I wasn't smart enough to be afraid." She paused, recalling it.

"Most of the houses and boats in our strip were washed away in a hurricane—we were back in New York; school had already started. Except for Jim's sailboat. It was in the New London newspaper: 'Child's Sailboat Survives Destruction of New England Coast.' Jim said when he grew up he would come back to live in a white house of his own in Essex—"

Katy stopped embroidering her canvas seat cover; she *saw* the *Roosevelt* she had been weaving. *You can't remain a child measuring the world by Plum Island and sandbar flats. How did you manage to locate the very man who would sail you past it*

324

*and Gohonk? Okay, the entire human race yearns to go home, now
and then. But you went about it like a blind woman. You never
admitted the obvious. You've an adult son, and you still want to go
home. You want the grown-ups to stay uncomplicated, remain true-
blue.*

She blew her nose hard. "My father's family were Republicans—at the time it seemed awful. My mother at times
voted American Labor Party," she said, still wiping. "I still
remember when Roosevelt died, feeling so abandoned."
Her eyes filled with unexpected tears; Katy rarely cried.

Mike looked stricken.

*He associates tears with Paula; he envisions small sorrows turning
into monumental disaster. He thinks it's something he's done.*

Katy searched for a concrete emotion he could grasp. "I
miss Lewis."

"Was it my making you go on deck to tie down the
ropes during the hurricane? I never meant to scare
you—just wanted to teach you the right way to handle the
yawl. The only safe way to teach greenhorn sailors what
the sea is about is through small doses of fear."

*He knows you don't live for sailing, but you don't dare tell him
how much you mind that he sold Braden's Press. Maybe if he had
kept it going Paula wouldn't have killed herself.*

"Why did you sell the press? It was so—morally
sturdy—during the fifties. Why didn't you keep going?"

"Sweetie, you talk young."

"Your generation is so fucking proud of that big-time
investment you made in idealism; now you expect to be
rewarded as brilliant for speculating in despair? Huh—both
are luxury items. Marginal stuff." She swallowed hard a few
times, then told him the truth: "Winning the Braden first

prize for being brainy about medieval cities was a big deal at Barnard. *My* big deal. Look, I'm sorry about Klager. He was just there—he showed me a shortcut in the lawsuit."

"You had other options—going to Klager was perverse. Using Max Schecter was equally perverse—"

"Why?"

"He has a bad history—he was one of Judson Freund's boys—don't you know anything about the city?"

The yawl whirled and rocked. Mike lay down on his bunk, Katy on hers: the cabin table, both leaves down, between them.

"Forget it." Mike covered her mouth, not wanting to hear her explanations, her legal saga. "Let's do a cornball, Hershey-bar, movie-type fantasy. We're back in the nine-teen fifties. You walk into Braden's Press on Common-wealth Avenue, just the way you did then. A snooty, uppity kid. But there is no Paula, no Lewis, no Beanie. No New York Surrogate Court, no Chicago Federal Court, no Adam Klager."

"Do they come into the script at all?"

"No . . . and you turn me on."

"Are we Jewish?"

"God, Katy—I take you on the greatest sailing trip on the East Coast, we give each other terrific sex, and all you can ask in the middle of a pitching sea is—are we Jewish enough?"

"I want to know. Who is the Barnard girl in your fantasy? Am I white? Black? Jewish? Who am I?"

"I leave that part blank. Whatever comes up, comes up."

"You are like Jeremiah; you have that anti-Semitic streak despite the money you give Israel."

"I do not buy Mercedes cars—but loving the sea," he snapped, "has nothing to do with my escaping my Jewishness. As a kid in Marblehead I was wild for sailboats. Your generation is loony on roots—if you believe a Jew can't truly love the sea, then you're the racist."

"Okay, okay."

"Okay, you've won the essay prize, and you turn me on. The way you keep saying 'Yes, Mr. Braden,' with that look. That you-should-drop-dead-Mr.-Braden look. And I make a pass at you."

"Did I turn you on? Then? When I met you with Paula?"

"Remember, there is no Paula, no Eichorns, no lawsuits."

"So you make an actual grab for me. Right there in Braden's Press, with all those nice old ladies around? Why, Mr. Braden," Katy joined in the script, "I am shocked. Boston has failed me."

"Meanwhile the nice old ladies you have just mentioned are called away from Braden's Press. The mayor of Boston has died and the women are attending his funeral."

"While, back at Braden's Press, we are—"

"Copulating."

"Suddenly?"

"Almost as soon as you walk into my office. *Promptly.*"

"Then what?"

"We fall in love. And I take you for a sail out of Boston Harbor, on, say, a twenty-footer."

"Red sails in the sunset?"

"Something like that. Real grade-A cornball."

The yawl rocked faster; it spun in circles, out of control. Mike sprang up; in spite of his bad back he hurled himself up the hatch. "The dinghy's going under!" Katy put on her slicker, grabbed Mike's, and joined him on deck. The Coast Guard chugged near them. Mike called to them as they sided the yawl, "Hello there—we need your help here."

"It's pouring," Katy said. "Put on your slicker—you'll catch pneumonia."

▼ ▼ ▼

New London. They sailed by its bleak outline of summer cheapo houses; the New England coast looked end-of-summer sad. September fog; the July–August boats had pulled into their moorings weeks ago. They passed a few lonely lobster trawlers; they glided by them like pirate ghost ships. At the wheel Katy listened to the clanking of rusty buoys, the mewling of foghorns. After an eight-hour run by compass, she saw the slopes of Long Island. Dimly. The yawl had been pitching all day; finally, they had got the right wind.

Katy felt confident; her hands told her she had the boat under control. She was no longer fighting it, nor the Bermuda her: *It's working.* She didn't mind that Mike was below, charting out their course—in the beginning she had panicked when he disappeared into the head.

When he came back up, he stood there for a moment, checking her work. "Five degrees off. Not bad. Some people never get the feel of a compass. Still, steering isn't sailing. If you don't get sick in this sea, you never will. Some do, some don't." He paused. "You are making yourself positively useful." He raised the binoculars, searching the horizon for the next buoy. She saw him fumble; he put them

328

down and rubbed his eyes. "I'll take over the wheel—Katy, you try."

She took the binoculars from him. *Your eyes are a lot younger. You can't pretend you can't see the buoy; he needs to locate it. If you don't know the rules of the game, don't play.* So she pointed to it. She looked at Mike.

"You are doing fine," he said.

You thought it would be so simple. All you had to do was master his boat and win a lawsuit. You never thought through the crummy details . . . cataracts, arthritis. Terror struck her heart.

▼ ▼ ▼

The weather cleared. They pulled into a deserted cove on the Long Island side. They could make it back to Hannah's Point the next morning in a few easy hours. Another yawl came in alongside them. Katy had noticed her trailing their course: the only other pleasure boat she had spotted during the day's run to the Sound. She saw Mike wince at the name: the *Happy Jumping Jack.*

When he realizes the people are from Hannah's Point, he'll have a shit fit.

Her sea legs wobbled once she was on dry land. About a mile down the road she found a gas station; she telephoned Max Schecter from there.

According to Max, Judge Myrtle was giving them more than they had asked for: in addition to the transfer of a heavy portion of Beanie's assets to Matt, with Katy as life tenant to the income, she was to become director of the Belle Hélène Foundation for the next ten years; Matt would then succeed her. Myrtle wanted Max and Ronnie

Munche—whom, as Max put it, he perceived as neutral, ungossipy men of substance helping him right a family quarrel—to be the heart of the new board.

"Why suddenly so generous?"

"Katy, you can't sue Beanie now. He's coming up in front of a federal court in Chicago and he's going to get clobbered. A minimum of two years. You can't add to it. You're sailing with Mike Braden? Talk to him, send him my regards—I'm sure he'll see the point of what we're negotiating for you—"

He wants you to mention his name to Mike. Willy-nilly her status was being elevated due to circumstances totally unconnected to her. She hated being the vessel through which men made business contacts; when it happened she always pretended to the man using her that she hadn't noticed.

"You're in luck," Max continued. "You're benefiting from the current run of financial scandals and the explosion of minority rights—the women thing. Myrtle knows there's a new attitude in the city."

She hung up and walked the length of the sandy beach. She wanted to be alone for a while. Running the Belle Hélène Foundation would mean giving up her job at the Schmidlapp. *In the world of Max and Myrtle, your being a curator of a small medieval-art collection has no more reality than dust off a butterfly wing. No more existence than Lewis being a philosophy professor and civil rights activist. Rich kids' amateur flights away from the source. Belle Hélène is the source. Those who manage it can cheat you and exclude you from it, or uncheat you and give you your inheritance. But the world is Belle Hélène. You get more of it, or less of it.*

She sat on the beach, knees to her chin, lost in thought,

confused. *You never figured it would end in a draw. You and Matt get back your assets, but you get stuck with the same cast of ratty characters. Max and Ronnie have burrowed like moles into Myrtle's confidence. And where Ronnie goes, Beanie can't be far behind. Why can't injured parties negotiate directly with the judge? Why am I stuck with these* From Here to Eternity *leechy go-betweens?*

But Katy would never repeat Lewis's mistake. *If you don't know the rules of the game, don't play.* She would never have walked away from Belle Hélène and still have expected its income. Her mind drifted back to Adam Klager. He hadn't needed her help to bring down Beanie—*Why did he throw you a life preserver? He kept repeating that you were the widow of a radical professor. In his weird, lonely way, did he like helping the same sort of people he would have witch-hunted? Or only their widows? Or was this his way of F.U.-ing the Establishment? Showing them up as weak hypocrites who wouldn't help their own?*

Katy'd never fathom him. She got up and started back down the cove.

▼   ▼   ▼

Mike was friendlier to the *Happy Jumping Jack* couple than she had expected him to be; he had invited them for a drink. Katy moved rapidly around the cabin; she fixed herself up and put some egg tomatoes and celery sticks on a plate.

"With these sorts of people it will be easier to call you Mrs. Braden—Katy and Mike Braden—you don't mind?"

▼   ▼   ▼

They were a floppy couple. The woman appeared to be checking them out—she looked at the plate of celery, the ice bucket, and glasses, and she sighed. "Martin, I told you

331

she was going to turn out to be one of those super sailing women ... For me the last eight hours have been one steady upchuck."

"Katy never gets sick," Mike boasted.

Katy saw her situation reflected through the other woman's eyes: *The cabin is too antiseptic, polished down.* No stray objects, no leftover children's gunk. Like many pathologically shy men who have been in positions of some power, Mike was unaware his manner paralyzed visitors.

He makes them feel that they have been summoned as two drowned rats for a quick drink, then meant to leave.

Mike took the clay roaster out of the lazarette. "This is Katy's special chicken. The bird has sailed on Paula's—on our yawl from Barbados to Canada."

"Very decorative, Mr. Braden. A nice homey touch," the man muttered.

He's mad Mike put down his wife for vomiting too easily.

"Our shortwave is busted," the man continued. "Do you mind if we listen to the news? I keep hoping for a stock-market rally—I guess we all do. A big part of the financial problem is New York itself—"

Katy bristled when the city was attacked. "The fault was Wall Street—the greenmailers, the take-over artists, the crooks—"

"I know why you're saying that," Mike interrupted her, "darling. But the fault was the trade unions. They wrecked the city."

"Stop talking like it's a corpse." Katy abruptly went to the hatch sink and made herself a second drink. "No matter what—I'm staying with it."

"Do you provision at Mazzini's?" the woman asked Katy. "They have such good meat."

"I never ask my wife to stock the yawl," Mike answered for her, "or make breakfast. Or lift an anchor. Rules of sea. Good skippers take care of their first mates."

"A pleasure meeting you, Mr. Braden," the man interrupted stiffly.

The couple boarded their dinghy and motored back to the *Happy Jumping Jack*.

▼ ▼ ▼

Mike stood on deck watching them.

Katy joined him. "Max says I can't sue Beanie because he's coming up in front of Federal and he'll get two years on the Chicago indictment—"

"People like us—"

"—do not go in for primitive revenge." She finished his sentence for him.

"Exactly—the man's already had his life destroyed. It won't be good for Matt to think his mother is responsible for extending his father's half brother's time in jail. Or good for you."

She stared out at the Long Island shore. Why was it suddenly her fault Beanie was going to prison?

▼ ▼ ▼

All through the evening Mike kept watching the couple on the *Happy Jumping Jack*. "They ain't no sailors, no way. Hibachis! Seaweed clambakes on deck—stinkpot types. Every moron in this piss-poor world thinks he has a right to clutter up the sea with his dumb crud. Better to give it back to the sea lions, whales, fish, and birds. Now, swans, Katy, after they lose their mates, they never remate. Just keep paddling. But swans don't deserve much. Too dumb to build nests. They pull the same crap around each year, always putting it in the wrong place . . ."

Despite their wrong hibachis, the man and woman are having a good time; they are meshed as a couple.

His mood abruptly shifted. "Wouldn't have thought, umpteen years ago, that afternoon you, Lewis, Paula, and I sat having drinks on our lawn at Hannah's Point, that you and me would end up in the sack. Wasn't in the cards . . . I had a few thoughts. Sitting there. Watching you with Lewis. When a woman is looking subdued, refined, and there's no sex talk—just babble about politics and the control of nuclear energy—then you size up her man, gauge his sexuality, and you can guess at the things she's heard and done. That turns a man on; he gets curious. Not that I would have done anything. I truly loved Paula . . . But you and I, in our way . . . have been oddly enduring." Suddenly he stopped; his face turned fierce; he went up on deck. Away from her.

She pulled herself up the hatch.

He stood there, lonely, smoking a cigarette, facing the sea, not looking her way. "You brought the yawl back home, Katy. You stuck with it. A man has to be moved by something in this putrid world."

"You've never suffered from its meanness. 'Putrid world' is the vocabulary of aimlessly wandering flower children. Who do dumb things like fighting elements long since

334

tamed. Nature lovers, the lot of them, with murderous hearts. Mike, you were never *that*. Stop sounding off."

"I shouldn't have bitched at you about Klager—everyone in New York used him, one way or another. I've done a lot of things in my life, but I took a special pride in going after Klager and company in the fifties—that and sailing were *special*—. You were a kid, but there was something about you in that time that stood firm." He paused. "I lied about the sex part. That didn't come into my head until much later. I just found you . . . appealing."

She stood by the yawl rail remembering how wonderful, pure, Braden's Press had seemed to her then. *But you, Katy, never were that innocent. You lead people like Mike on. Even Lewis. Always telling them to go free. What you meant was a little free. So now suburban America, as well as the hippies, yippies, yuppies, and porno cable sex, is all hanging out. And now you want to put it back. Have again the dull, good old America of your childhood. But you are the grown-ups now: help him.*

"Suicides leave shitty voices behind—let Paula go."

He blinked. Was quiet. "Manhattan will be muggy. Stay on at Hannah's Point the weekend." He hesitated. "It's a little late in the day, but why not Katy and Mike Braden? We've one thing going for us—we like each other."

Katy looked at him; he'd voiced what both of them had understood for some time. Then she gazed at the sullen Long Island night; in the fog they must have sailed beyond Indian Path. She saw its ample lawns: Anita, Jeremiah, Tartan strolling beneath its hearty trees to the bulwark. Time had moved so slowly for her forebears, so sure of themselves, requiring such vast spaces. *Boom-boom*, their voices

335

sounded in her head, and she no longer judged them on how their lives ended, in darkness or light.

You will be going back to town as director of the family founda-tion. And with Mike. An unruffled woman of means. As though the outlaw years had never happened; nobody but you will remem-ber them. Will you really do better in the next ten years than Beanie?

Her impulse was to give gobs of money to women in need with children, women who had been humiliated, no explanations necessary, but she knew in the end she'd be too rational: such fuzzy thinking had bankrupted the city. She saw herself becoming someone different: informed by graphs, experts, and complexity.

▼ ▼ ▼

She wanted to give Mike something. Mark the moment. She had finished her Roosevelt needlepoint. "It can be a boat pillow." Then, like it was some private joke, she leaned against the yawl's rail, and in her thin voice out of childhood intoned into the salt air: "Oh, America you have gone and left me—Roosevelt, Roosevelt, I want you back!"

"Philanthropy's what the Braden name is about—I can give you a few pointers," Mike went on, not quite listening. "Your timing for a win is rotten. You couldn't have involved yourself in New York at a worse moment. The city is shit." When he saw her go somber and defensive about what she considered her territory, he switched to a more optimistic tack. "Cheer up—no decade is ever right. These are confus-ing days."

The next morning, when they sailed the final run, Mike returned to his thought: "Very confusing days . . ." He

336

stared at her. "Blame the millennium—figure, Katy . . . we are living before the next before."

He swung the yawl toward the Connecticut shore; in a few hours Katy spotted the outline of Hannah's Point: she saw that even in late September the sky had the clear look of a summer afternoon in the east.